PRAISE FOR BETH K. VOGT

"Vogts captivates us with the story of sisters, of family, in this third Thatcher Sisters novel. Themes of healing and hope prevail. I cheered for Johanna as she allowed love to heal her heart. This tale will leave you smiling and thinking of the characters long after you've read the last page."

RACHEL HAUCK, *NEW YORK TIMES* BESTSELLING AUTHOR

"Vogt delivers her best book yet with this tearjerker of a series finale. *The Best We've Been* handles difficult topics with grace and sensitivity while avoiding pat answers in its pervasive themes of hope and forgiveness. I can't recommend the Thatcher Sisters series enough!"

CARLA LAUREANO, RITA AWARD–WINNING AUTHOR OF *THE SOLID GROUNDS COFFEE COMPANY*

"Authentic and honest, *The Best We've Been* upends complicated relationship dynamics with a family as real as any I've found—the Thatcher sisters journey through the unexpected with depth and incredible heart in this third installment in the series. Beth K. Vogt is at the top of her game and this book is the treasure that proves it. It's a memorable addition to any favorites shelf!"

KRISTY CAMBRON, BESTSELLING AUTHOR OF THE LOST CASTLE SERIES AND *THE BUTTERFLY AND THE VIOLIN*

"Beth Vogt never fails to impress me with the depth and emotion of her stories and characters. In *The Best We've Been*, she tackles sensitive topics with grace and truth while weaving a compelling story of sisterhood and second chances. Don't miss this moving conclusion to her Thatcher Sisters series!"

"A fitting conclusion to our time with the Thatcher sisters. Again, Vogt handles sensitive topics such as infertility, betrayal, and faith with candor and grace. She reminds us that while we may not always like our sisters, we do love them with a depth that can surprise us, unnerve us, and often help heal us."

"Few things in life can simultaneously afflict and heal the heart like family, and Beth Vogt delivers all this and more in her heartrending, moving grand finale of her Thatcher Sisters saga. . . . Readers are sure to discover the power of forgiveness—between family and for the self—in Vogt's most insightful story yet."

"A deeply satisfying end to the Thatcher Sisters series, *The Best We've Been* takes readers on a thought-provoking journey with Beth Vogt's perfectly imperfect characters. Having read her other books, I truly wondered how Vogt would make oldest sister Johanna someone I could root for—and then she did it! Reading this story was a wonderful reminder that giving up control of our lives and trusting God to lead us will always have the best result, even if we cannot see that in the moment."

LINDSAY HARREL, AUTHOR OF *THE JOY OF FALLING*

"In the last of the Thatcher Sisters trilogy, the overarching theme of grace, forgiveness, and second chances brings us to the satisfying conclusion to this wonderful series. Vogt's talent for evoking emotion stands out, several scenes needing a tissue or two. A lovely exploration of real-life circumstances and complicated relationships."

CATHERINE WEST, CAROL AWARD–WINNING AUTHOR OF *WHERE HOPE BEGINS*

"*The Best We've Been* is a beautiful story of what happens when life doesn't go as planned and how it can pull us closer together. . . . It is a beautiful story of how family can come together when the lies are replaced with truth and when the choice is made to trust and find common ground. I loved every page, couldn't wait to return to the characters, and felt every emotion. A wonderful addition to Beth Vogt's books."

CARA PUTMAN, AWARD-WINNING, BESTSELLING AUTHOR OF *DELAYED JUSTICE* AND *SHADOWED BY GRACE*

"Beth Vogt has done a masterful job of wrapping up the Thatcher Sisters series with Johanna in *The Best We've Been*. Not only did I understand Johanna better, but I truly cared about her on a personal level. Very in-depth characterization. I didn't want it to end, and I'll continue to hope they find more sisters! I feel as if I've been adopted into the Thatcher family."

HANNAH ALEXANDER, AUTHOR OF THE SACRED TRUST SERIES

"With her latest book, *The Best We've Been*, Beth Vogt has cemented her status as a master storyteller. She tackles difficult subjects with realism and unexpected twists. Her characters linger in my memory just liked beloved friends. Written from a foundation of biblical truth, her books make my life better."

EDIE MELSON, DIRECTOR OF THE BLUE RIDGE MOUNTAINS CHRISTIAN WRITERS CONFERENCE

The Best We've Been

a Thatcher Sisters novel

BETH K. VOGT

Tyndale House Publishers
Carol Stream, Illinois

Visit Tyndale online at tyndale.com.

Visit Beth K. Vogt's website at bethvogt.com.

TYNDALE and Tyndale's quill logo are registered trademarks of Tyndale House Publishers.

The Best We've Been

Designed by Julie Chen

Edited by Sarah Mason Rische

Published in association with the literary agency of Books & Such Literary Management, 52 Mission Circle, Suite 122, PMB 170, Santa Rosa, CA 95409.

The Best We've Been is a work of fiction. Where real people, events, establishments, organizations, or locales appear, they are used fictitiously. All other elements of the novel are drawn from the author's imagination.

For information about special discounts for bulk purchases, please contact Tyndale House Publishers at csresponse@tyndale.com, or call 1-800-323-9400.

ISBN 978-1-4964-2733-5 (HC)
ISBN 978-1-4964-2734-2 (SC)

Printed in the United States of America

26	25	24	23	22	21	20
7	6	5	4	3	2	1

To Rachel Hauck and Susie May Warren,
my treasured mentors and friends:
Thank you for always reminding me that our journey along
the writing road is, first and foremost, a walk of faith.
Your unwavering trust in God strengthens my faith.

PROLOGUE

I was waiting. Again. She should be here by now. Where was she?

The auditorium was almost full, all the seats near the front taken. Everyone else's parents and grandparents clutched copies of the pale-blue programs, glancing through them to see the order of tonight's piano recital. All sorts of kids— some younger than me, some older—read books or played handheld video games or ran up and down the aisles. They probably wished they were anywhere but here on a Saturday afternoon.

I did, too.

I stood in the dim lighting backstage, pulling the maroon velvet curtain aside a bit more, trying to see if maybe, just maybe, Mom was sitting in one of the rows of padded wooden seats off to the side.

No.

I stepped back, letting the heavy curtain fall into place with a soft swish.

I couldn't do this. The air around me seemed stale, heavy with dust that danced beneath the stage lights.

I couldn't cross that stage. Couldn't sit on the padded bench positioned just so in front of the grand piano, its polished lid gleaming under the hot spotlights. Couldn't perform in front of all those strangers—everyone else's families and friends—when no one from my family cared enough to show up for me.

I shouldn't be surprised. I couldn't remember the last time Mom had come to a practice to listen to me play. Or even asked me what I was working on. Or stopped long enough to place a hand on my shoulder and say, *"That song is so pretty, Johanna."*

So many different people praised me for years. Strangers. Family. Teachers.

"You're so special."

"It's amazing—the way you play."

"Your talent will take you so far."

And I'd believed them.

But I didn't care what anybody else said. And tonight, I didn't want to play for myself or a bunch of people I didn't know.

How special was I really if I could be overlooked by Mom? Or worse, replaced?

I tugged at the high collar of my dress. The material bit at my neck and wrists, pinching at my waist. Of course there hadn't been time to go shopping for something new to wear for today's performance. There was never enough time for me anymore.

The sudden sting of tears burned my eyes, blurring my vision. I grasped the curtain again, the cloth soft beneath my fingertips. Maybe if I looked one more time—

"Come away from there, Johanna. It's almost time to start." The sound of Miss Felicia's voice caused me to stiffen.

I couldn't do this tonight.

I wouldn't do this.

No one could make me play . . . not if I didn't want to.

IF WAITING WOULD GET ME what I wanted, then fine, I'd wait.

I could get frustrated about wasting my time. About the fact I'd driven through lousy Colorado weather—snowy, icy roads—to get to this appointment on time. About being forced to do nothing but stare at a framed print of the historic Crystal Mill surrounded by aspens because someone else couldn't manage their schedule. Better an out-of-season glimpse of autumn than the detailed poster of the female internal anatomy hanging on the opposite wall.

I would focus on the certainty that by the time this appointment was over, I'd have a resolution to my problem.

Besides, there was always some waiting before or even

during a doctor's appointment. It was part of the routine. And more than one of the doctors at Mount Columbia Medical Center had told me that they hated to run behind schedule just as much as their patients did—if not more.

Of course, I didn't know this particular doctor. The only way to ensure my privacy was to see a medical practitioner away from my workplace. Maybe running late for my appointment was some sort of sign she wasn't a good physician. Habitually late. Lousy bedside manner. Questionable billing practices.

I shifted in my seat, all the more thankful I hadn't changed into the white paper gown I'd left folded on the exam table, instead of following the instructions of the efficient medical assistant.

As I debated the possible character qualities of the unseen physician, the exam room door opened and a woman entered, glancing at a chart—and then at me. "Johanna Thatcher? I'm Dr. Hayden Gray."

"Good morning." Dr. Gray might not be punctual, but I could be pleasant.

"I see here that you were originally Dr. Grammerson's patient." She set the chart on the small corner desk anchored to the wall beneath a set of cupboards, settling into the rolling cloth chair beside the desk.

"Yes, before she sold the practice to you. I didn't realize that until I tried to make an appointment. It's been a while."

"I noticed that." She leaned back, clasping her hands together in her lap. "You're not gowned. Do you have some questions before your exam?"

"I'm not here for an exam."

"You're not?"

"No. I came to see you because you took over this practice from my ob-gyn when she retired—"

"Right. And your records show it's been—" she glanced at my chart again—"four years since your last well-woman exam. It's noted in your chart under reason for visit as an annual exam."

"I realize I'm overdue for my regular exam—and I'm happy to do that, too." That was a slight exaggeration. No woman was *happy* about gynecological exams, and surely the woman sitting across from me, even as a physician, knew that. But I'd do what needed to be done, which was why I hadn't argued with the receptionist when she'd assumed that was my reason for calling.

Dr. Gray eased open the laptop resting on the desk. She had long, lean hands, her fingernails cut short, similar to how Beckett kept his nails trimmed.

This was no time to think of *him*.

Professional. Not too personal.

"I'm here to discuss an abortion."

Dr. Gray's hand stilled on the keyboard, her gaze returning to me. "Discuss?"

"Well, no. Not discuss. To schedule an abortion."

"Ah." She typed something into the computer. "How many weeks pregnant are you, Ms. Thatcher?"

"Fourteen weeks."

"You took an at-home pregnancy test?"

"Yes. I'm a pharmacist." This was a good time to connect

both as medical professionals and as women. "We both know those are 99 percent accurate."

"When was your last period?"

"November . . . November 23, to be exact. Although I do have irregular periods. And I spotted some in January, so at first, I thought I'd had a period. When I didn't have a period in February, I just thought it was stress. Work. My sister's wedding . . ." I let my voice trail off to avoid wandering too far into the personal zone again. I was talking to my medical provider, not a friend.

"Hmmmm." Again she tapped something into the computer, not looking at me.

I was losing control of this appointment. This was supposed to be simple. Easy. Come in and set up the needed procedure. No discussion. No *"Hmmmm"* from a physician who should be supportive. Dr. Gray was a woman, too, after all. I caught myself rubbing the back of my hand, pressing the fingers of one hand against the other, just like my father did.

I flexed my fingers. This was not complicated. I knew what I needed to do. Dr. Gray might be the doctor, but I was the patient and she was here to help me—by scheduling the procedure.

"I think it's best if we do a quick ultrasound to confirm your pregnancy, and then, if you're pregnant—"

"*If* I'm pregnant?" The word *if* did not apply to my situation. "What do you mean?"

"Well, while at-home pregnancy tests are almost 100 percent accurate, there can be false positives. And you did say you had some spotting in January. You might have miscarried."

"Miscarried?" I fisted my hands, sitting up straight. "I haven't had another period."

"You also said your periods are irregular. Even if you do go through with an abortion, you need to know how many weeks pregnant you are."

There was the word *if* again. "How long will an ultrasound take?"

"Not long at all. I have a portable machine. If time is a concern, you don't even need to change into a gown." She motioned toward the exam table and then stood. "I'll go and get the ultrasound machine. You can get comfortable."

I could get comfortable. *Right.* This was like having prepared to play one piece of piano music for a recital and, at the last minute, being handed a new selection and told, "You're performing this instead."

I smoothed out the long sheet of white paper covering the length of the exam table. Sat down. My feet dangled off the end, not touching the floor, as if I were a little girl.

But little girls didn't make doctor's appointments for wellwomen visits . . . or any other reason.

By the time Dr. Gray returned with an assistant wheeling in the ultrasound machine and then plugging it into the wall so that a low mechanical hum filled the room, I'd stopped my feet from swinging. Taken several deep breaths. Relaxed my shoulders. I'd get the ultrasound done and schedule my next appointment, which would also be my last appointment.

I pretended to listen while Dr. Gray and her assistant set things up. "Why don't you lie down here on the table? It takes a minute or two for the lights to come up. I need to enter some information—your name, the date of your last menstrual period."

The medical assistant helped me adjust my clothes, tucking a small towel inside the waistband of my pants, carefully lowering it until I seemed to be wearing hip huggers. "We'll be using some gel down near your bladder, so this should protect your clothes."

"Thank you."

Again, I wanted to protest. I knew I was pregnant. I knew why I was here. None of this mattered to me—not in the long run. But if this was all part of the doctor's routine, then I'd tolerate the inconvenient but necessary means to an end.

Within a few moments, Dr. Gray squirted a bluish gel onto my lower abdomen and then spread it around with the transducer handpiece.

I inhaled, tightening my core muscles—and then relaxed. "Not as cold as I expected."

"We try not to make it more uncomfortable than it needs to be." Dr. Gray's glance switched back and forth from the screen to my face. "The warmer helps."

"Right."

With a few circular swipes of the ultrasound instrument, white-and-black lines appeared on the monitor screen.

"Here's your bladder. It helps that it's somewhat full." Dr. Gray pointed lower on the screen. "Here's your uterus . . . and the uterus does have a sac in it. . . ."

She was quiet for a few seconds, her hand moving in a slow, deliberate search pattern.

"What do you see?" Maybe I wasn't pregnant. Maybe I had miscarried.

"I see the placenta, and it's near your cervix, so that's something we may have to watch."

The next moment, Dr. Gray pushed a button on the ultrasound monitor and a rhythmic swooshing sound filled the room.

"That's my heartbeat, right?"

"No, that's about twice as fast as your heartbeat. That's your baby's heartbeat." She pointed to a small white flicker. "See this? That's your baby's heart pumping."

Undeniable proof positive that yes, I was right. I was pregnant.

For once, I would have been fine with being wrong.

"Let me take some measurements to confirm dates." One of Dr. Gray's hands rested on the ultrasound machine keyboard, while her right hand twisted the handpiece on my lower abdomen. "There's the leg . . . and the baby's foot. . . . We can get a good image of the baby's face at this far along if you're interested—"

"No." I closed my eyes, turning my face away from the screen to stare at the aspens surrounding the old wooden mill perched on an outcrop above the Crystal River. "I'm not interested."

Dr. Gray's words, the vague black-and-white images she was determined to measure on the screen, were puzzle pieces slipping closer together so that the idea of my pregnancy was being framed into reality.

An unwanted reality.

Would the baby have my nose or Beckett's? Whose fingers? Whose eyes?

It didn't matter.

Couldn't matter.

"We're done here." Dr. Gray took a soft towel and wiped the gel off my skin, then switched off the machine, the silence in the room welcome. "We'll go store the machine, give you time to further clean up, and be back in just a moment, Ms. Thatcher. Then we'll finish up here."

"Fine."

At last I could get what I came for. I reclined on the exam table until they left the room, my stomach still lightly covered with gel, my fingers clutching the tissues the medical assistant had handed to me.

When Dr. Gray returned five minutes later, I was seated again, my feet on the ground.

"The dates on your ultrasound are consistent with your last menstrual period, which makes you fourteen weeks pregnant. That also means you'll start showing soon. Your due date is August 30."

Not that a due date mattered. "So when can I schedule the abortion?"

Dr. Gray swiveled to face me, hands clasped in her lap again. "I don't perform abortions."

I must have misheard her. "You don't . . ."

". . . perform abortions."

I blinked. Swallowed. "But that's the only reason I made this appointment."

"And as I said earlier, based on your phone call, my receptionist assumed you were coming in for a routine exam."

"I thought all obstetricians did—"

"No. Not all. Performing abortions is against my beliefs."

The conversation had taken a turn to the ridiculous. "Your . . . beliefs."

"Yes."

I resisted the urge to stand up. "This is my choice. You're a woman. You know about choice, right?"

"I understand that—and I respect your . . . choice." The woman sitting across from me offered a slight nod. "Not performing abortions is also my choice."

"You could have told me this sooner, Dr. Gray."

"Even if you decide to go through with the abortion, it's wise to do an ultrasound and determine dates."

"Fine. Then perhaps you could recommend another doctor who does perform abortions."

"I'm sorry, but I can't do that."

"What?" I gripped the edges of my chair. Our conversation was nothing but a series of roadblocks. "Why not?"

"I choose not to perform abortions because they could be harmful to mothers-to-be, like you, and they are most definitely harmful to unborn children. Why, then, would I help you get one?"

"This is absurd. I should report you to the medical board—if you are even licensed to practice medicine in the state of Colorado."

"I assure you that I am." A glint of steel darkened Dr. Gray's eyes. "I also assure you there's no state law prohibiting me from practicing in a way that supports my moral, ethical, and personal beliefs. My choices, as it were. And you are not prohibited from your choices, either."

"Except by you."

"Not prohibited. I'm just not the physician for you."

"Dr. Gray, you've done nothing but waste my time."

"I'm sorry you feel that way."

I stood, knocking the chair against the wall with a thud. This was some sort of lecture disguised as a doctor's appointment, complete with a black-and-white slide presentation.

I shook my head, dismissing the images of a tiny leg. A tiny foot. The rasp and whoosh of a heartbeat.

This morning was merely a detour—not a dead end.

Dropping by each other's homes wasn't something the Thatcher sisters did. Ever. Payton wasn't even sure Johanna was home. And if she was, Payton had no idea what Johanna would do when she opened her front door and saw her youngest sister. She couldn't remember the last time she'd been to Johanna's house by herself.

Payton could only hope Johanna was home and wouldn't leave her standing outside in the frigid March night air. Johanna was such a workaholic, it was possible she was still at the hospital.

And there was no way her sister could know the question Payton needed to ask her. The fear she battled . . .

She might as well knock and find out.

It took so long for Johanna to answer the door, Payton had given up, turning away to walk back to her car.

"Payton?" Johanna eased the door open, leaning against the doorjamb, head tilted to one side. Her feet were bare, and she wore leggings, a flowing black sweater, her platinum-blonde hair pulled back from her face in a halfhearted attempt at her usual sleek ponytail.

"Were you sleeping?"

"It's only seven thirty. No, I wasn't sleeping."

Payton took a step forward. Paused. "Do you mind if I come in?"

"What? Oh, sure. Come in." Johanna didn't back her welcome up with a smile. "So what are you doing here?"

Payton would ignore how abrupt that sounded. She hadn't expected a hug and an "I'm so glad to see you."

"I, um, wanted to check on you."

"Check on me? Why?"

"You seemed . . . off when we got together for the book club meeting on Saturday." Not that Johanna ever enjoyed the monthly get-togethers when the two of them met with their middle sister, Jillian, and did very little discussing of books. Her older sister came, drank her French press, and complained.

Typical Johanna.

Except she also hadn't been herself in January or February. She wasn't drinking her coffee. She wasn't eating much of anything at all—to the point that she'd gone from fashionably slender to gaunt.

She'd shut down. Withdrawn. It wasn't like Johanna not to voice her many opinions—even about a book she hadn't read.

Johanna trailed behind Payton into the living room. "I was fine then. I'm fine now."

That was a typical Johanna statement, designed to tell Payton that if anything was going on, it was none of her business.

She'd expected this. Trying to talk to Johanna over the phone—to get her to confirm or deny the dark suspicion Payton struggled to ignore—would have been more difficult. That's why she'd shown up in person, hoping Johanna would tell her straight to her face that nothing was wrong, instead of avoiding her.

Johanna collapsed on the couch. Pulled a blanket over her legs as she curled them underneath her. A bottle of water sat on the coffee table. *Water.* Not coffee. When—and why—had her sister become so fond of water?

Maybe she would drop the "Everything is fine" front if Payton kept pushing.

"Would you mind if I made some coffee for us? A jolt of caffeine would help me about now."

"I'm sorry. I don't have any fresh coffee beans in the house." Johanna's pale skin had turned even more white, and she seemed to have to force herself to even say the word *coffee.*

"What is going on with you, Johanna?" Payton launched the question, not sure she wanted to know. To have her fear confirmed.

"I haven't gotten to the store—"

"You didn't drink coffee at the book club the other day—"

Johanna gave a feeble laugh. "You know how I prefer my French press."

"Exactly. And you didn't bring your travel mug of your preferred coffee, either. Do you mean to tell me you've been out of beans for what? A week?"

"I'm busy, Payton." Johanna's words were a whisper of a protest.

"You've lost weight, too. I said the word *coffee* and thought you were going to throw up." Payton forced a short laugh. "If I didn't know better, I would think you were pregnant."

Johanna pulled the blanket up around her shoulders, fisting it against her chest.

Payton fought to breathe. Whatever Johanna was hiding, the family would get through it. They'd gotten through so much in the past months.

"I am."

She waited for Johanna to finish her sentence. Nothing. "You are . . . what?"

"I *am* pregnant."

"Oh, thank God!" Payton stepped forward, rounding the coffee table and kneeling in front of Johanna.

Johanna clutched the blanket closer, pulling away. "What did you just say?"

"I said, 'Thank God!'" Payton fought the urge to laugh. To cry. To hug her sister. "I've been so worried about you, Jo. I thought . . . I thought you had breast cancer like Jillian."

Johanna stared at her. No smile. Her eyes clouded. "Well, I'm not thanking anyone, least of all an imaginary god, that I'm pregnant. And I would appreciate it if you didn't either."

"I'm sorry." Payton reached for her sister's hand and ended up with a fistful of cotton material. "I'm just so relieved it's not something more serious like cancer."

"You don't think my being pregnant is serious?"

"Being pregnant isn't going to kill you."

"It certainly screws up my life."

"How far along are you? Are you dealing with morning sickness? I would imagine it will stop soon."

The ice in Johanna's blue eyes was worse than the lethargy that had been there moments before. This was the all-too-familiar big-sister glare that could turn Payton into an insignificant speck in mere seconds. The air around them seemed frosted. What was she thinking, imagining she could come here and force a relationship with Johanna? Get her to talk about what she was dealing with? That she could somehow help her?

"I'm not going through with this pregnancy, Payton."

Payton rocked on her heels, her back colliding with the coffee table, tipping over the bottle of water. Liquid spread across the surface.

"Payton! Look what you've done!"

"I'm sorry . . . I'm sorry." Payton grabbed a couple of napkins and sopped up the water, tossing them into a trash can positioned near the couch. This pregnancy must be harder on Johanna than she admitted. "Johanna, let's talk about this for a minute . . ."

"I have no intention of being a single mother just because I made a mistake with a man who couldn't be trusted."

"Fine." Payton scrambled for arguments. Options. "You don't want to keep the baby. What about adoption?"

"I'm also not giving up nine months of my life for some altruistic endeavor that benefits another couple who wants a baby. I don't care to have my life interrupted for that long."

"Johanna—"

"You can either support me or you can be quiet."

This . . . this was the kind of support her sister wanted from her.

"Is Jillian supporting you, too?" Payton moved to the far end of the couch.

"Jillian doesn't know."

"You're going to keep your pregnancy a secret from Jillian?" Payton clasped her hands together to stop herself from reaching out to Johanna. Her sister might slap her hands away. "If we've learned nothing else in the past months, haven't we learned secrets hurt our family?"

"She doesn't need to know." Johanna's words were edged with frost. "No one else needs to know."

Johanna wasn't the only one who could dig her heels in and stand her ground. "I'm not going to be part of this."

"You became part of this when you showed up here tonight and started asking questions."

"I thought you had *cancer*."

"Well, you were *wrong*. And this pregnancy is only a temporary issue. I don't want to have to hash this out with Jillian—or Mom and Dad. I don't welcome other people's opinions about what I should do or not do right now. And I didn't ask for yours, either."

"I was concerned about you." Payton gripped the side of the couch to stop from leaning forward, her voice trembling.

"Thank you for that, I guess. I'm fine. I'll handle this."

"I am not going to be a part of keeping this secret—"

"It's not your secret to tell, Payton."

With every word, Johanna twisted Payton's attempted act of compassion into something unwelcome. Invasive. Turned her into an accomplice. Johanna was forcing her to side against not just Jillian, but their parents, too.

Payton fought to regain her footing. "Are you going to tell Beckett?"

"No." Johanna's eyes darkened as she pulled even farther away. "Why should I tell him?"

"He's the baby's father."

"He's no longer a part of my life. I make my own decisions. I always have."

Payton shouldn't have been surprised by anything Johanna said or did, but this . . . this was deliberate, unrepentant deceit.

"Nothing to say?"

"What am I supposed to say, Johanna?"

"You wanted to know what was wrong. If I had cancer."

"I wasn't just on a fact-gathering mission. I wanted to help you—"

"You can help me by doing what I asked. Don't tell anyone. Everything else is up to me, and I'm dealing with it."

"You really think you'll be happier this way?"

"I'm always happier when things go my way, so yes."

"And you don't think Jillian—or Mom and Dad—will find out about this at some point? The baby is my niece or nephew. Mom and Dad's grandchild . . ."

"*Stop. It.*" Johanna jerked up from the couch, the blanket slipping from her shoulders. "Don't try to manipulate me by employing sentiment. You want to talk about Mom and Dad's grandchildren, get pregnant yourself."

Once again, Johanna was in charge, brushing past Payton as she paced to the front door, pulling it open. The wintry air filling the room was empty of her sister's signature Coco perfume.

Payton struggled for words. For a way to reach her sister. "Johanna, can't we—?"

"I'm sure no one will find out what we talked about, so long as you don't say anything." Johanna stepped back from the door, tilting her head toward the darkness outside. "Thank you for stopping by."

The impromptu visit, and their conversation, was over. There was no sense in arguing with Johanna. As far as her older sister was concerned, she'd won before the discussion even started.

2

THE DINING ROOM TABLE was a mess, but it was a mess with a purpose. Geoff's laptop sat near Jillian's, and several yellow legal pads were scattered around, along with an assortment of multicolored highlighters and pens. At the far end, the remnants of dinner waited to be cleaned up—slices of the two pizzas lingered in the boxes delivered a couple of hours ago and eaten while they worked. Mostly by Geoff, with a few bites slipped to their puppy, Winston, despite her protests.

"Your talk is coming together so well." Jillian leaned back in her chair. "How are you feeling about it?"

"To be honest, the closer we get to the conference, the less nervous I am." Geoff finished scrawling a note on one of the legal pads. "I expected to be anxious, but instead, I'm excited. Ready to do this. Of course, the opening slide should have both our names on it."

"What? No." Jillian shook her head, dodging the compliment. "I'm not the cybersecurity specialist. That's your area of expertise."

"But you helped me get the PowerPoint presentation together. Researched fonts and graphics . . . I would have just slapped some slides together, put some notes in a Word document, and called it good."

"We couldn't have settled for that. Not for such an excellent presentation."

"It's an excellent presentation *now*—thanks to you, Jill."

The clutter that had covered the top of the dining room table for weeks was worth it. Most of Geoff's spare time was spent preparing for the conference. Their date nights were sporadic, but he still walked Winston with her in the evenings. He didn't know she made meticulous notes on how to do a professional presentation. That she cross-filed everything in Word and Evernote and Dropbox so she didn't lose track of anything. She repeated the same routine whenever she was done working on the presentation for any length of time. He also didn't know she did some of her best research in the middle of the night when she couldn't sleep.

Post-chemo insomnia continued to have its benefits.

Geoff had always supported her during the months she faced breast cancer. Now she was determined to do the same thing for him, even if it meant she slept less and less. She could nap during the day—and she did. Winston stayed with her during the naps. Even now, their dog snuggled against her bare feet while she and Geoff worked.

They were a family of three.

For now.

"I was looking at the schedule of events again." Geoff draped his arm across her shoulder, a welcome moment of closeness. "Our hotel reservation is made. We can drive up Thursday afternoon and register for the conference after five o'clock. I'll be busy quite a bit Friday, Saturday, and Sunday."

"I understand."

"What are you going to do?"

"Relax. I might schedule a facial or massage. Read a book or two." She moved closer to Geoff, resting her head on his well-defined shoulder. Despite work and the conference prep, he still managed to get to the gym, going early in the morning, sometimes just a few hours after Jillian crawled into bed. "Gianna said she'd take care of Winston, so that's handled."

"I know you're going to be relaxing and reading, but you're welcome to sit in on my presentation if you want."

"Would you mind?" She tilted her head to look up at him, her cheek brushing against his scruffy jawline. "It wouldn't distract you if I was there?"

"You're always a distraction, but no, I'm certain I'll be focused on the talk Saturday morning."

"Very funny."

"I'm completely serious, Mrs. Hennessey." He pressed his lips against her forehead. "I've already requested a name tag that identifies you as my wife so you won't distract any of the other guys at the conference."

"Right. I'm 'Geoff Hennessey's wife.' Perfect." A laugh filled her throat, spilling over. "We're getting off topic. What else do we need to do for the presentation?"

Geoff leaned forward, disrupting their casual embrace, and shut first one laptop, then the other. Then he stood, pulling her with him and wrapping his arms around her. "I'm ready to be done for tonight. Ready for some distraction. What about you, Wife?"

His kiss was slow. Deliberate. His hands slid up her back, pulling her close, his touch gentle yet persuasive. In all the months since her cancer diagnosis, her surgery, her chemo and radiation, Geoff had never wavered in his desire for her.

Jillian leaned into her husband's embrace, savoring the warmth of his arms around her. The taste of his kiss. So much for work. But this . . . this was a good thing, too. She'd told Geoff she wanted more this year. More hope for herself. Hope for them. She'd even gone so far as to pick *hope* as her theme for the year, and Geoff had picked the word fun.

Well then.

She had to believe, had to keep hoping, their relationship was still good, despite the one topic they avoided. To not get tripped up by the future—by wanting him to change. Or by trying to figure out how to be content if he didn't.

Sometimes it was best to focus on now.

Jillian allowed herself to be drawn further into the persuasion of Geoff's kiss. To give all her attention to these moments. To give all of herself to her husband.

Two hours later, Geoff lay asleep in the bed next to her, his breathing even. And she was, once again, wide-awake. Jillian shoved the covers aside, stood, and pulled her robe from the foot of the bed. Slipped it on, belting it loosely around her waist. She shut the bedroom door with one last glance at Geoff, who'd rolled to his side, pulling the covers up around his shoulders. The steps leading downstairs creaked, but she'd wandered the house in the middle of the night enough times to know the noise never bothered Geoff or Winston. Even the dog slept through the nights when she didn't.

It took her a few moments to choose a mug, heat the water in the microwave, and add a tea bag, before she settled into a corner of the couch, where her still-new-to-her Bible and journal rested on the side table. If she was going to be awake, then she'd use the time for something other than watching a rerun on the cooking channel or a favorite movie or flipping through a magazine.

Jillian kept her Bible study simple by following a monthly Scripture-reading plan she'd found online. She wrote the daily verses in her journal, underlining anything that stood out to her. If she missed a day or two, she played catch-up.

This was her life now. She was no longer a career woman. She took things slow. Nothing too complicated. The days of the woman who multitasked and worked full-time were gone, thanks to lingering chemo brain. And she asked God every day to help her to accept who she was.

The crinkle of the pages in her Bible reminded her of how new her faith was. She'd owned the Bible for a few weeks, purchasing it at Payton's suggestion. Some days, her faith still seemed unfamiliar, but that didn't mean it was wrong. It was like breaking in a new pair of shoes until they didn't pinch.

Maybe some people wouldn't appreciate the analogy, would find it disrespectful of something as serious as faith, but God knew what she meant.

Jillian found today's passage—James 1:9-12.

Believers in humble circumstances ought to take pride in their high position. But the rich should take pride in their humiliation—since they will pass away like a wild flower. For the sun rises with scorching heat and withers the plant; its blossom falls and its beauty is destroyed. In the same way, the rich will fade away even while they go about their business.

Blessed is the one who perseveres under trial because, having stood the test, that person will receive the crown of life that the Lord has promised to those who love him.

She opened her journal and wrote out the verses. Then beneath that, she wrote a prayer:

I'm a believer, a new believer, but it counts, right, God?
I know something about trials. And I'm not
quitting. I didn't quit when I was diagnosed with
cancer—although I did quit on Geoff when I broke our
engagement. But he talked sense into me. And that all
worked out.

Now I'm persevering through wanting to adopt
when Geoff doesn't want children. We're at a stalemate.
But I'm not quitting on him. On our marriage.

I love him. He loves me.

Yes, I hope he changes his mind. You know that,
God. Geoff knows it, too.

I don't know anything about receiving a crown . . .
except it sounds like I only get it if I pass this test.

Okay. Fine.

But if You could make "passing the test" easier by
having Geoff decide he wants to adopt, that would be
great.

Jillian rested her pen on the page. Sometimes when she wrote her prayers, it was like she was a teenager again, writing in a diary. But her pastor had talked about journaling prayers, so she thought she would try it.

Words across the page . . . at times, awkward stuttering of her heart . . . and then there were times it was an exhale that allowed her heart to find rest.

She'd persevere through this, too.

Jillian took a sip of her tea, the liquid tepid. The air in the room cool against her skin.

Time to go back to bed, snuggle against the warmth of Geoff's body. Smile when he whispered, "Love you . . ."

If only sleep weren't still evading her, like some wraith taunting her with a silent "Catch me if you can." Two thirty in the morning, and once again, she was the only one awake in the house.

Maybe now was a good time to organize the chaos on the dining room table. Sort through the piles of paper, one piece at a time, and throw out the unneeded scraps. No need to rush. And it was better if she didn't.

3

This should not be that hard.

I'd made my decision. The best decision for me. Now all I needed to do was schedule my appointment. The right appointment this time.

But it was difficult to get out of bed, to shower, to get dressed, and to get to work on time—much less make a simple phone call.

The brief images I'd seen on the ultrasound replayed in my mind over and over. A tiny leg. A glimpse of a foot.

The echoes of Dr. Gray's voice accompanied the memories, no matter how I tried to override them with work details.

"There's the leg . . . and the baby's foot. . . . We can get a good image of the baby's face at this far along if you're interested—"

When I tried to fall asleep at night, it was as if the baby's heartbeat filled my bedroom like some sort of unwelcome background music.

What I was about to do—my choice—would silence that song forever.

I'd always believed in the freedom, the power, of choice. The rightness of choice. But I'd never connected choice to a life before. To a baby.

I slipped my hand beneath the opening of my white lab coat and rested my palm against my abdomen. Still separate but connected.

My choice would sever our bond forever.

Choice implied I had options. That I could choose something else.

What else could I do?

Go through with this pregnancy and give the baby up for adoption?

No. I'd live the rest of my life as the designated birth mom to my child with limited to no rights. I'd be straddling some invisible but explicit line between mother and stranger, having no real influence in my child's life.

I'd never lived like that, controlled by the actions of others . . . well, not in a long time.

I closed my eyes. Waited. Nothing. No movement beneath my hand. I didn't even know what sensation to expect.

It was ridiculous to sit here and wait for something to happen. I needed to decide about my future.

I had made my decision, but Dr. Gray seemed to forget about women standing together, supporting one another. Instead, her choice collided with mine.

Still avoiding the needed phone call, I removed the ultrasound photos from the top drawer of my desk. Blurry images of my son or daughter the receptionist had handed me four days ago as I checked out from my appointment with Dr. Gray, accompanied with a cheery *"Congratulations, Ms. Thatcher. Don't forget your baby's photos."*

"Johanna?"

Axton Miller's voice sounded behind me, causing me to slip the photos beneath a file on my desk as I turned to face him. "Yes?"

"I wanted to check on you. You didn't answer my texts, so we went ahead and held the meeting without you—"

"The meeting?"

"Our meeting with Dr. Lerner."

My stomach clenched. "I'm so sorry. I completely lost track of time."

"It's fine. We dealt with a few things and decided to reschedule. Things come up . . ." He paused as if waiting for my explanation.

I had none.

That wasn't true. But I wasn't going to confess to him why I'd missed the meeting. And all the evidence was hidden under the papers on my desk.

"I know this may be none of my business . . ."

Whenever anyone said that, what they said next was guaranteed to be an unwanted intrusion.

"I'm certain breaking off your engagement had to be hard."

Why on earth was Axton bringing that up?

"If you need to take some vacation time—"

"My missing our meeting has nothing to do with my ex-fiancé." And that was a lie. "I'm fine. I'm not upset about Beckett. I just forgot a meeting—"

"I can't help but notice you've lost weight, Johanna."

"It's what women do, Axton. We're either losing weight or gaining weight."

"Fine. I've learned not to argue with you. Just know that if you change your mind—" he raised his hands as if to fend off my response—"I said *if*, not when—then my offer still stands for you to take some time off."

"We have a lot to do." I should probably stand if I wanted to continue this conversation, but I couldn't seem to find the strength. I was tired all the time, but I'd deal with the reason for that soon enough.

". . . well aware of everything we have to do." I'd missed the first part of what Axton had said. "But I'm just as aware when my staff is pushing themselves."

"You're not pleased with my work."

He stepped back. "Not going there, Johanna. If you want to talk about something, let's talk. But I will not let you pick a fight with me."

My boss was mixing up the boundaries, blurring the lines between professional and personal. He knew I was fine with him being my boss—sort of—but I didn't want him to be my friend. I didn't have friends inside—or outside—the hospital. I could barely claim relationships with my sisters.

I stopped my hand as it moved toward my stomach again . . . as if I was protecting something . . . someone . . .

Not that Axton would interpret the gesture as anything significant.

Who was I trying to protect?

How many people would my decision hurt . . . whatever decision I made?

And why were my emotions all snarled up in protecting someone I'd never met or seen, except in an ultrasound?

I shut my office door after Axton left. Kept my back to my desk, trying to ignore the photos that seemed to have some magical pull that held me between "maybes," despite being hidden from view.

I pressed my lips together. Straightened my shoulders. Took my cell phone from the pocket of my lab coat. Found the number I'd noted a few days ago for a physician who performed abortions. Stabbed the numbers into the call screen.

The receptionist answered on the second ring, her voice a pleasant blend of professional and friendly.

Words clogged in my throat.

"How may I help you?"

Still no words.

"Hello?"

I disconnected the call, pressing my forehead against the office door. Closed my eyes, fighting to stay standing, but giving up.

For an absurd moment, I resisted the urge to call my mother. What would I say? I hadn't called my mother for help in years.

My fingers gripped the sides of my phone, and then I

faced away from the door, pressing my back against the hard wood as I allowed myself to slide to the floor. I drew my legs up against my body, leaning forward so my forehead rested on my knees.

I'd taken care of myself for years—through all sorts of crises, big and small. I'd handle things now, too.

"Maybe I could keep the baby." My words were a whisper, muffled against my knees. "*My* baby."

For the first time, I allowed myself to say out loud the thought I'd been evading.

Being a single mother had never been part of my dream.

Of course, I'd never dreamed of being passed over for a promotion.

Or Beckett cheating on me.

Or having to break off our engagement.

Or discovering I was pregnant.

But this was not the time to scroll through a life of disappointments.

I lifted my head. Straightened my shoulders, pressing them into the door behind me.

I could be a mom.

Because if I didn't have an abortion, no one else was going to raise my child.

Like everything else I did, I'd do it myself . . . and I'd have to live with this decision for the rest of my life.

⌒

"One advantage to getting married? People gave us some of the new board games we had listed on our wedding registry." Payton grinned as she moved her red game piece across the board and then flipped over another card in her pile. "Ta-da!"

"You're only saying that because you've won the last two games." Jillian checked the small stack of cards sitting in front of her again.

"Sorry, everyone." Zach shrugged. "I should have never taught her how to play Labyrinth."

"I'll take any advantage I can get when it comes to competing against you all."

"You haven't won yet, little sister." I selected a tile at the top of the game board, using it to slide another line of tiles across the board. Mimicking Payton's movements, I moved my blue game piece across the board to the desired location, then flipped over a playing card. "There you go."

"Nice. Nice." Payton nodded. "But that doesn't mean you're going to win this time."

Jillian spoke up again. "What's the plan, Geoff?"

"To not lose again."

"Great plan."

"I thought so. Now to execute it. But everyone else's strategy keeps messing with mine."

If Jillian's husband wanted to complain about other people's actions complicating his life, he could go right ahead. This was just a stupid board game. Nothing more. When it was all said and done, the pieces would end up in a nice box covered with the lid labeled *Labyrinth*, and everyone would walk away with their little victories—and no real difference in their lives.

A slight, almost-indiscernible flutter in my stomach interrupted my musings. Was that the baby? I was tired of all the waiting, the anticipating, the trying to guess what I was feeling. Trying to decide what I was doing.

Mom spoke up. "Your dad and I are thinking of making some changes to the house."

"Do you want me to buy some new chair cushions for the breakfast nook table?" I tried to keep track of the moves everyone else was making. "Maybe some curtains?"

"We were thinking about a more major project than that."

"New carpet?"

"We want to add a deck onto the back of the house."

"A new deck?"

"I've been talking to Zach about this." Dad nodded toward him across the table. "He's got a friend who builds decks, so we'll be setting up a time to talk."

"But why a deck after all this time?"

"I like to grill out and a deck would be a nice addition to the house. Improve its resale value. I'm not thinking of anything elaborate."

Jillian's focus had shifted to our parents. "Are you and Mom thinking of selling the house?"

"Not now, no. But maybe someday we'll decide to downsize."

I couldn't imagine my parents selling this house. "If you want to add value, then add a room to the house—"

"We're not interested in that big of a project."

"Not after watching me and Geoff and the kitchen renovation, right?" A smile colored Jillian's words.

"Well, there is that." Dad winked. "We may enclose the porch. We'll look at different options."

And now my parents were making decisions without me. That shouldn't be a problem. They were adults, just like I was. Just because Mom always had me pick out things like curtains and cushions didn't mean she needed my help or approval to add a deck. This was normal family life. Adults being adults.

The board game was forgotten. No one was making moves—except Mom and Dad, who were making decisions about my childhood home and no longer wanted my opinion.

But then again, I hadn't asked them for their opinion about their grandchild.

I stood. Backed away from the table. "Excuse me. I'm going to check on dinner."

"Now? We haven't finished the game." Jillian waved her hand across the board.

"Dad, take over for me."

"Johanna, your father and I are playing as a team."

"He can cover for me, Mom, and still be your partner."

On those words, I escaped to the kitchen. I gave a quick glance at the enchiladas in the oven, as well as the black bean soup in the Crock-Pot—Payton's contribution, to fit her vegan diet. Zach had carried the addition in, plugging the pot in so it would stay warm until we were ready to eat.

The mingled aromas of cheese and beans and spices turned my stomach. At least Mom hadn't started any coffee yet. Should I force myself to eat? Or just announce I wasn't feeling well while continuing to avoid Payton's stare, as I had been doing all day?

"Are you okay?"

Payton's voice caused me to spin around, my hands gripping the counter behind me. "What are you doing, practicing to be some sort of secret agent or ninja or something?"

"Really?"

"What am I supposed to think when you sneak up on me like that?"

"That I'm a ninja? That's a little far-fetched. Are you okay?"

"I'm fine."

She held up my glass of water. "You left this downstairs."

I wrapped both hands around the glass. "Oh. Thanks."

"So have you made your appointment?"

Payton was channeling me, getting straight to the point. "No."

"Why not?"

There was no easy way to explain that a small pile of black-and-white photos was tripping me up. That the echo of a heartbeat haunted me day and night, an uninvited internal serenade.

"Because I'm thinking . . . I'm thinking I might want to . . ."

"To what?"

"I might want to keep the baby."

Saying the words out loud should have eased the ever-present pressure in my chest. But it didn't. The heaviness shifted a little but still remained. Having an abortion was no longer an easy option, but keeping the baby made no sense. Considering being a single mother was irrational.

I pressed a fist against my sternum, my heart beating beneath it.

But there were two hearts beating inside me.

I wanted my life back, but there was no returning to who I was before I'd gotten pregnant.

And to go forward, I had to choose.

I faced away from Payton, not surprised when she came to stand beside me. "What changed your mind?"

"For weeks, this was just an inconvenience to deal with. To get past. Then you said something about this baby being Mom and Dad's grandchild. Being your niece or nephew. And the physician, who refused to do an abortion for me, did an ultrasound. I left the appointment with photos. I find myself wondering, *Grandson or granddaughter? Nephew or niece?*"

"Have you thought about adoption?"

"No. If I'm going through with this pregnancy, I'm keeping the baby."

"You're . . . pregnant?" Jillian's voice invaded the conversation between Payton and me.

I pressed my eyes closed. Refused to turn toward my other sister. To answer her question.

Payton had more courage than I did. She turned, taking a step away from me. "Jill—"

"I wasn't talking to you, Payton." Jillian spit the words out. "Are you pregnant, Jo?"

I faced Jillian, who stood several feet away. "Yes."

"When were you going to tell me? Payton already knows."

"I wasn't going to tell you. I . . . I haven't decided what I'm going to do . . ."

Jillian's eyebrows furrowed, her eyes narrowing. "You're going to make your decision about having a baby—and tell me later. Or maybe not tell me at all?"

"I don't know."

I tried to be honest, but it came off sounding so wrong. This was my life. My decision. And now I was facing both of my sisters, being forced to take part in a conversation I never wanted to have. To answer their questions. Would Mom walk in next? What little energy I had seeped out of my body, even as I forced myself to respond to Jillian. I hadn't started this discussion, but I would finish it.

"I wasn't planning on talking about my pregnancy today—especially not with Mom and Dad sitting right outside the door."

That was a slight exaggeration.

"The only reason Payton knows and you don't is because she thought something was wrong with me—that I was sick—"

"Surely you noticed how Jo has lost weight. How she hasn't been drinking coffee." Payton's laugh was sharp. Out of place. "I was scared. I thought . . . I thought maybe she had cancer like you did."

The color drained from Jillian's face.

"She showed up at my house asking me what was wrong." It wasn't Payton's responsibility to explain things. "Made a joke about thinking I was pregnant . . . and I told her I was. That's the only reason she knows and you don't."

Jillian's attention never wavered from me. "But you're keeping the baby. You had to tell us all sometime, Jo."

"I said I might want to keep the baby, Jill. *Maybe.*"

"And if you don't keep the baby, then what? Adoption?"

"No."

Jillian's eyes widened. "Jo . . ."

I held up one hand, shaking my head. "Don't judge me, Jillian. This is my decision. Not yours."

"But you can't . . . you can't . . ."

"I can make whatever choice I want. When you get pregnant, you can make your own choice."

"That's enough, Johanna." Payton stepped forward and wrapped her arms around Jillian, who shrank back against her.

I almost apologized—almost. But I couldn't. I hated hurting Jillian, but an apology would only prolong this conversation. Our relationships were shifting as if the floor were balanced on a beam that was weighted with our words. It wasn't my duty to keep everybody happy. I'd never worried about that.

At the end of the day, no one was there for me. No one hugged me. No one protected me.

"You two will have to excuse me. I don't think I'll stay for dinner—"

"Johanna, don't be this way." Payton still held on to Jillian.

"Be what way? Myself?" I shook my head. "I'm sorry if

you don't like how I act, Payton. This is who I am. Don't expect me to change at my age."

I didn't owe my sisters—or anyone else—an explanation of my behavior or my choices. We were all adults. Our choices were our own.

JILLIAN SHOULD HAVE BEEN used to this by now.

And she'd keep saying that to herself until it was true.

She was awake in the middle of the night. By herself. Not even Winston was willing to wake up and keep her company.

Shouldn't she be clinging to the assurance that God was with her? That God would help her? That He would never leave her or forsake her? It might help if she could remember the specific verses the pastor had rattled off yesterday at church. Or remember where she'd put her notes.

All of it was the truth, but the realness of it, the security of it, escaped her grasp.

She was alone. Again. And what was the use of faith if it didn't hold up when you needed it?

"Do you want to talk?"

Geoff's words broke the stillness, but Jillian remained facing forward on the couch, staring at the mantel in the living room, decorated with a tall metal letter *H* and a trio of frosted glass bottles.

There was nothing she could say that would change anything. Nothing.

"Jillian?" Soft footsteps sounded. "Did you hear me?"

"Yes."

He eased next to her on the couch, leaving space between them that seemed to throb with silence.

"What happened when you were in the kitchen with your sisters?"

Smart man, her husband. There was no saying, "Nothing happened," not after she'd insisted they go home right in the middle of a game of Labyrinth. After Johanna had exited the house without saying good-bye to anyone.

She'd given Geoff no explanation then. None when they got home.

No words.

She'd just retreated to their bedroom to curl up beneath the blankets and pray for sleep to stop the thoughts swirling in her head.

It was better to retreat. Better to withdraw than to even consider fighting battles she could never win. She couldn't stand up to both Johanna and Geoff. Couldn't ask for something she wanted and then hear no from the two people she loved the most.

Jillian wrapped her arms around her waist. She didn't move

away, but if she held herself, then maybe Geoff wouldn't hold her. Wouldn't expect her to lean on him.

"It's not like you to go silent on me like this."

Jillian stiffened. Geoff wanted an explanation? Fine.

"Johanna's pregnant."

The words left a bitter taste in her mouth, and she pressed the palm of her hand against her lips.

"Johanna . . . *Johanna's* pregnant?"

"That's what happened when I was in the kitchen with my sisters." Jillian still faced forward. "I found out that Johanna is pregnant. Only my sisters didn't tell me. Weren't going to tell me. I only found out because I overheard Johanna talking to Payton."

"Payton knew?"

"Yes."

"How——?"

"Don't ask me questions like how far along Johanna is or if Beckett knows. All I know is Johanna is pregnant." Jillian squeezed her eyes shut as if doing so would block out the scene from the kitchen. "Oh, and that she might have the baby. Or she might not."

"She said that?"

"Yes. Johanna said that. Do you think I'm making this up?" Her words were a brittle echo of the pain encasing her heart.

"I can understand why you're upset——"

"Really? You understand what it's like to find out that your sister—the sister you're supposed to be closest to—is keeping a secret from you? Not an 'Oh, I found something you're going to love for your birthday' kind of secret. *No.* My sister is pregnant. And she wasn't going to tell me."

"I'm sorry—"

"Don't. Don't say it. Payton had a secret about how our sister Pepper died. We survived that. But then you—the person I thought I could trust more than anyone else—you had secrets about your brothers, too. And now Johanna." She tried to swallow the acidic taste coating her throat. "I'm sick of family secrets. I hate them."

At least she was being honest. Geoff might not want to hear it, but she was going to say it. No longer choke back her emotions.

She was done with holding her peace—because the unspoken words burned like when she had mouth ulcers for a short time during her chemotherapy.

"Jill, you have to admit getting things out in the open is better."

"Now you say this? Do you even believe it?" She rushed past his reply. "And better for whom? You—because you feel better? Payton—because she told the truth? Johanna—because she can once again remind us that she's going to do what she wants? Everyone else is happy with this. But I'm not."

"I understand."

"No! No, you don't." Jillian rocked back and forth. "How can you know what it's like to find out my sister is pregnant—my sister!—and all I want is to have a baby?"

"You said Johanna may not keep the baby."

"That doesn't matter, Geoff." Explaining all of this was

making it harder. "At least she had a choice, which is something I don't have. You let me choose my engagement ring. What I wanted mattered then. But now . . . when it comes to whether we have children or not . . . what I want doesn't matter."

Geoff's jaw clenched, a sure sign he was shutting down.

God, help me say something—the right thing—so Geoff hears me.

"We could adopt the baby."

"What?"

"We could adopt Johanna's baby."

Geoff jumped to his feet, putting space between them. "Are you kidding me?"

"No. This is the perfect solution. Johanna doesn't want to be pregnant. She's not sure she wants to keep the baby. And we want the baby—"

"Not *we*, Jill. *You.* You want the baby." Geoff paced in a circle, coming to a stop in front of her. "Johanna being pregnant doesn't change anything we've talked about."

"Why can't it change things? Didn't you hear what I just said? Why won't you consider what I'm asking you? Let me talk to Johanna."

"No. We're not adopting your sister's baby. Do you realize how complicated that would be?"

"We'd figure it out, Geoff." Jillian remained seated on the couch, slowing her words, softening her tone. Maybe if she was calm, they could talk this out to a different outcome.

"No. This is a ridiculous idea. Just because Johanna is pregnant doesn't mean I'm suddenly going to agree with you about having children."

His words hit her as if she were standing along the shore and got taken down by an unexpected wave. Doused. Tried to scramble back to her feet against the pull of the tide, only to fall again.

No matter what she did, what she said . . . no matter how many times they discussed this, their family would remain the two of them—and Winston, of course. She'd be a dog mama. It wasn't that she didn't love Winston. She did. But loving her pup wasn't enough.

Maybe loving Geoff wasn't enough.

Jillian twisted her engagement ring and wedding band around on her finger.

Her *life* wasn't enough.

"It's the middle of the night. Not the time to be talking about this." Geoff's words signaled an end to their conversation.

"It's never the time." Jillian shook her head. "You never want to talk about it. You're never going to change your mind."

"Be reasonable. I've got to go to work in a few hours." Geoff stood in front of her. "Can we table this until the conference weekend?"

"Because you'll have spare time then?" Jillian's gaze centered on Geoff's bare feet planted wide apart. "You told me you're going to be busy. Or did you forget that?"

"I'll take an extra day off after the conference."

"Just go to bed." Jillian slumped back against the couch.

"Are you coming upstairs with me?"

"No. I'm not tired."

And that statement was a lie. She was exhausted—worn-out from going around and around with Geoff about this issue and never finding a resolution.

"You sure?" Geoff sounded concerned, almost willing to keep talking. Almost.

"I'm sure. Go on."

Geoff's footsteps fading into silence only served to remind her that she was alone.

This was her life now. This was the future. Her. Geoff. A dog.

And nothing else.

Her Bible lay unopened. That was fine, too. God wasn't listening to her prayers, so what good were they doing her? What Geoff wanted wasn't going to change. What she wanted wasn't going to change. How did they fix that?

The future seemed as dark and empty as the house in the middle of the night. They could fill it with things like a puppy and a renovated kitchen. She could throw in a feeble attempt at faith. But none of it dulled the ache for more inside of her.

5

PAYTON NEEDED to get out of the car. There were people waiting for her. For Zach. Well, sort of. They'd most likely start the meeting if she and Zach didn't show up tonight. But people were expecting them. After all, Zach had said they'd be there.

Of course, her husband hadn't bothered to tell her that he'd asked Paul and Sara Wagner about coming tonight until *after* he'd already told the older couple to expect them. That oversight had led to an interesting *discussion* several days ago. About how his wanting to go to a couples' Bible study didn't mean she wanted to go.

And now Zach sat next to her, the engine still running, drumming his thumbs against the steering wheel. Waiting.

Her husband and a lot of people she didn't know were waiting on her.

"Are you ready to go in?" Zach sounded as if he half expected her to say no.

"I'm not sure why I agreed to this." Payton gripped her seat belt that remained clipped against her body, even though Zach had parked the car outside the Wagners' house five minutes ago.

"It's just a couples' Bible study, Payton."

"I've never done any sort of Bible study before—on my own or as a couple."

"We're going to study the book of Galatians, not go skydiving."

"I didn't even know where the book of Galatians was."

"It's in the New Testament—"

"Thanks for that." She tucked the envelope she'd used as a bookmark more securely into her Bible. "I know that—*now*—but only because I looked at the table of contents on the drive over here."

"Relax, okay?" Zach twisted to face her. "Tonight's just about getting to know each other, getting our books, that sort of thing."

"Our books? I have my Bible. Why do I need another book?"

"There'll be some sort of study guide—some prep work for us to do each week before we come back."

"Zach!" Payton's attempt to face her husband was stopped by the shoulder strap of the seat belt.

"What?"

"You do remember I'm still taking college classes, right? I don't need any more homework."

"It's not homework. No one's grading us. And whatever it is, it won't be much—just enough questions to help us prep for the discussion each week. We can do it together. It'll be fun."

"Your idea of fun and my idea of fun aren't the same." Payton tried to lighten her tone. "Fun is going on a hike with Laz. Or watching an Avengers movie together."

She should stop talking. They'd already had one discussion about tonight, and she'd forced herself to swallow her protests, figuring this was all part of being married. Of being a believer.

While they'd sat in the car, two other couples had strolled up to the front door. Knocked. Been greeted with hugs, the faint sound of laughter drifting back toward the car.

As much as Payton wanted to go home, she didn't want to embarrass Zach, forcing him to explain why they were no-shows for tonight.

"My wife? Yeah, she didn't even know there was a book of Galatians. Kind of threw her for a loop, and I couldn't get her out of our car."

She could do this, especially since he'd said no one was grading her.

Payton released her seat belt, snugged her Bible under her arm, and opened the car door. "Let's go."

Zach remained seated, peering at her across the interior of the car. "What? Just like that, you're ready?"

"Sure. Sorry." She shivered in the night air. "I'm nervous about meeting new people. Just stick with me, okay?"

He was by her side in seconds, taking her hand, pretending to tip the brim of an invisible hat. "Happy to oblige, ma'am."

Her laugh eased some of the tension that had built inside her. "That's a lousy drawl, Zach."

"But I made you laugh, so it was worth it."

A petite woman with a stylish bob and warm brown eyes welcomed them, introducing herself as Sara. "Just add your coats to the pile on the bench and go on in to the family room."

Zach's friend and coworker Colin waved as he made his way over to them, his fiancée, Deanna, following close behind.

Zach greeted them. "I didn't realize you were in the community group, buddy."

"You mentioned you and Payton were coming, so I checked with Paul and he said they had room for one more couple. I convinced Deanna we should do it now that we're an officially engaged couple, with a wedding date and registry, too. It'll be fun."

Again with the "fun" assurance.

"I'm looking forward to it." Payton added the words *sort of* in her head. "I—I've never done a Bible study before."

"Really? Well, Sara and Paul are great." Deanna moved closer to Payton. "They've mentored so many couples in the church."

"Oh?"

"They've agreed to do our premarital counseling." Deanna slipped her arm through Colin's. "Did you and Zach do that before you got married?"

"No. We got married so quickly, we skipped that."

"Paul and Sara discuss things like finances and in-laws and children—just laying a good foundation, you know?"

"Sure."

"I mean, it's not a mandatory requirement—or like you and Zach are going to have problems because you didn't do premarital counseling. I'm sure you two will be fine."

How had she missed the memo on premarital counseling?

Sure, they'd met with Zach's pastor once when they'd decided to get married, but that wasn't the same thing. Apparently it also wasn't the "right" thing.

Paul interrupted the steady flow of conversation with a short, sharp whistle.

"Sorry, folks. I know everyone's having a great time chatting, but my wife wants me to call this evening to order. First, she wanted me to thank everyone who brought an appetizer or dessert—"

Wait . . . what? Everyone brought something to eat?

"—and now's the time to go get something to eat and drink. It's all laid out in the dining room. Then come back here and we'll get started. Five minutes, okay?"

"Why didn't you tell me we were supposed to bring something?" Payton kept her voice to a whisper so no one but Zach would hear.

"It's no big deal. We can do it next week."

"Were we supposed to do it this week?"

"Paul didn't mention it. Maybe? I'm sure there's plenty to eat."

"Zach!"

"Ask Sara, okay?"

As the couples regrouped, everyone sat guy-girl-guy-girl, choosing places on the couch, love seat, or the chairs and creating an informal semicircle. Several stacks of softcover books sat on the coffee table in front of the couch.

"Before we talk about the study, we thought we'd take some time to get to know one another better." Paul balanced a paper plate of appetizers on his knee. "Of course, some of us know each other pretty well, but we'll go around the room and hit the basics. Say how long you've been married—or for Deanna and Colin, tell us how long you've been dating and when your wedding is—what you do, and your favorite Bible character and why."

As everyone laughed and started chatting among themselves, Payton stilled, her lips frozen in a smile. Her favorite Bible character? These people assumed she could just pull up a mental list of people in the Bible and pick one. Could she say Jesus? Or maybe Mary? Paul? He was a disciple . . . or an apostle . . . something like that.

It was only the first night of the Bible study and they were having a pop quiz. And she was going to fail it. Or sound so lame because she couldn't come up with a better answer than Jesus.

Sweat dampened the armpits of her top. She might as well be warming up for a volleyball game. She needed to get through this evening—no walking off the court. Or walking out of the Bible study. She'd be brave.

Stupid and brave.

"I'm Sharon. Jordan and I have been married five years

and I'm a stay-at-home mom, but I do have my own online business, but y'all know about that. King David is my favorite Bible character." Sharon's outfit looked like she'd taken it right off a store mannequin, down to the coordinated purple jewelry and shoes. "He's a man after God's own heart, and yet he's not perfect. It challenges me that, even though I'm not perfect, I can be a woman after God's heart, too."

Everybody joined Zach in nodding in agreement.

"I'm Jordan, Sharon's husband. We've been married five years—" The stocky man seated next to Sharon spoke up.

"I already said that, Jordan."

"Oh, sorry." Jordan's face turned bright red. "I'm, um, in IT. My favorite character is Job because he taught me about persevering under trials and trusting God."

Others in the room mentioned Daniel. Deborah—some woman in the Old Testament who was a judge? Rahab. Did any of these people even read the New Testament? Or was there some unwritten, unspoken rule that mature Christians read the Old Testament?

Payton was so busy trying to keep track of everyone's favorite Bible character she had no idea of anyone's name—except for Sharon and her blushing husband, Jordan. And only because they'd gone first.

Meanwhile, Zach attacked the mound of food on his plate—mini wontons and chips and guacamole and hot wings—nodding his head and *mmm-hmmm*-ing as the other people in the room seemingly talked through an encyclopedic list of Bible characters.

None of them mentioned Mary. Or Paul. Or Jesus.

Could she just repeat what someone else said, or would that be cheating?

This was like all those times in math class when she'd tried to count ahead to see which problem she might have to work on the board if the teacher went row by row, student by student. It never failed that she calculated wrong, or the teacher changed direction, and she wasn't ready when it was her turn.

Everyone else was laughing. Agreeing with each other's comments. Getting along. Enjoying themselves.

And all of this was proving what she'd known all along: She didn't belong here.

By the time Zach introduced himself, Payton was tempted to whisper, "Excuse me" and go hide in the bathroom. But as if sensing her desire to flee, Zach took her hand, weaving their fingers together as he shared.

"My favorite Bible character is the Prodigal Son."

Payton knew this. Knew his story.

"I was a prodigal for years. I know this is a story of a forgiving father, but for me, I imagine myself as the son who sees his father waiting for him, watching for him, despite so many years . . ."

Oh, why hadn't she gone first? Payton knew this wasn't a competition. It shouldn't be. But how was she supposed to follow that?

"I'm Payton. And like Zach said, we're newlyweds." Had Zach said how long they'd been married? "I'm a college student, believe it or not, and I help coach a volleyball team."

People smiled and nodded. Surely someone else in the room played sports.

"My favorite Bible character . . . well, I know this probably sounds silly . . . but it's Jesus."

She waited for laughter. Nothing.

"I mean, that's what the Bible is all about, right? Jesus. It's His story. And I like when He tells stories . . ."

"Parables." Zach's comment was a half whisper.

"Right. The parables." She stopped again and Zach squeezed her hand.

Paul spoke up, thanking everyone for sharing and then starting to talk about the study guides.

At least the focus was off Payton.

She'd figure this out, one question, one answer at a time.

After all, that's how she'd found her way to God.

6

I WAS TIRED OF ALL the surprises in my life in the past few months. And now I'd ended up back in the same medical exam room as my first visit just over two weeks ago. Everything looked the same—except I'd managed to crack Dr. Gray's calm demeanor.

"Ms. Thatcher, may I be frank and say I didn't expect to see you again?" She hadn't bothered to look at my chart on her open laptop. She trained all her attention on me. "And most definitely not as a first-time OB visit."

"That would make two of us." I played with my keys. The cool metal of my house key, car key, work keys slipping through my fingers. "It would be stating the obvious to say I've changed my mind and decided to go through with this pregnancy. I'd like you to be my obstetrician."

Dr. Gray's fingers thrummed a quick staccato on her desktop. "I'm thankful to hear about your decision, but I'm surprised—shocked, really—that you want me as your physician."

"Dr. Gray, there's no denying we don't agree on certain issues. But I do appreciate how you treated me with respect during my first appointment, despite our differences."

"Respecting my patients, no matter what their beliefs, is important to me."

"And you didn't waver in what you believed. I also respect that."

She acknowledged my compliment with a quick nod. "Thank you."

"So you agree to take me on as a patient?"

"I would consider it a privilege."

A privilege? More like a chance to earn her fee. Or maybe I'd misjudged the woman and it was her chance to gloat behind my back, if not to my face, that she'd won. Not that I'd ever tell her how the ultrasound had influenced my decision. Not that she was asking.

I waited for a smirk, the slightest curl of her lips, to prove Dr. Gray wasn't the professional I thought she was.

Nothing. She remained respectful. The same attitude as last time I sat in this exam room.

It seemed I hadn't misjudged Hayden Gray.

"We did an ultrasound during your last visit, so we'll wait until you're twenty weeks to do another one." She paused to scan the information in my chart. "I'm comfortable with the estimate we have for your due date."

"August 30, right?"

"Yes. However, we are behind on some basic tests that need to be done during the first trimester."

"What tests are you talking about?"

"You'll be thirty-six when the baby is born. That used to be considered AMA—advanced maternal age—but nowadays, most doctors consider forty or older AMA."

"Thanks for that."

"I haven't met a woman yet who cares for the term. One patient of mine switched from another obstetrician after being called a 'geriatric mother,' along with being told she had to have certain genetic testing."

"I don't blame her."

"While you're at an increased risk for some genetic disorders, I'm not overly concerned. You do, however, need to decide what tests you want to take and what tests you want to opt out of."

"What tests are you recommending today?"

"We should do a Pap today to check for cervical cancer and sexually transmitted diseases."

"Of course."

"And then there is some routine bloodwork, what's referred to as a quad screen. A test called chorionic villus sampling, or CVS, which checks for genetic abnormalities, is usually done when a woman is ten to twelve weeks pregnant."

"I'm past that." And again, I was stating the obvious.

"Yes. However, amniocentesis, which is performed between sixteen to eighteen weeks, also tests for abnormalities like Down syndrome but carries a small risk for miscarriage.

While some national medical organizations recommend pregnant women over thirty-five have an amniocentesis, it is optional. Your risk of having a baby with Down syndrome is one in 224—less than .5 percent."

"You knew that statistic." I offered my first smile of the appointment at how she managed to put numbers to information so easily.

"I do this for a living."

I'd only ever dealt with these details as a pharmacist. Heard these words as lab requests and results. Never needed to concern myself with them on a personal level. And now I was processing all this information alone—no one to talk it through with, except for Dr. Gray, whom I'd met twice. How did I navigate this? I knew all the answers, but now the answers were more significant because they affected me.

Me and my baby.

"I guess I'm having a Pap today, then, and considering my other options." I forced a bit of bravado into my voice.

I didn't bother to ask if all her patients were fact gatherers like me. Just over two weeks ago, I'd been talking with her about terminating my pregnancy. Now I was discussing everything I needed to do because I'd chosen to have the baby. Facts were simpler to deal with than the realities of how my life was changing.

"All right. I'll let you get ready for the exam." She removed a gown from a drawer at the base of the exam table. "I'll go request a medical assistant."

Five minutes later, Dr. Gray returned, followed by a petite young woman with long box braids flowing down her back who had to be at least a decade younger than me—and all smiles.

"This is Kristin, my MA. You didn't have the opportunity to meet her last time. We work as a team. She's the one you'll contact with any initial questions or concerns. You can use the front desk number for routine concerns, of course, or contact me via the on-call line if there's an emergency. I'll make sure Kristin gives you that information before you leave today."

As Dr. Gray talked, Kristin set up a small kit with tubes and vials.

"I thought Kristin could draw your bloodwork first and then I'll do your exam. This is basic bloodwork, not the other screening tests we were discussing. How does that sound?"

It wasn't as if I had a choice. This appointment was all about getting down to the business of being pregnant.

Kristin chatted and smiled as she drew my blood. "Have you felt the baby move yet?"

"No. No, not yet."

"Most first-time moms don't feel the baby move until closer to eighteen or twenty weeks, so don't worry that you haven't. Once the baby moves, you'll know. And then the baby will be moving all the time."

I had considered how this baby was going to interrupt my life on a grand scale but hadn't stopped to think about the more intimate details, like feeling someone moving inside me all day long.

There would be all sorts of disruptions, big and small.

Dr. Gray finished the appointment. Efficient. Half an

hour later, I sat in my car with gauze taped on my arm where her MA had drawn blood, as well as a prescription for prenatal vitamins tucked in my purse.

I wouldn't be filling that through the pharmacy at Mount Columbia. I'd call a pharmacy near home and pick it up after work.

Work.

I needed to tell my boss that I was pregnant.

Needed to look over my maternity leave benefits.

And I'd also instruct Axton in no uncertain terms there would be no baby shower. The way he liked to celebrate employee birthdays, I needed to make that clear from the very beginning.

He was all about us being a good working team, but he never envisioned *us* being him, me, and baby makes three. How would he handle the news?

I started my car, cool air wafting across my skin as I waited for the engine to heat up. Plenty of women worked during their pregnancies, had a baby, and returned to work, maintaining their professionalism while raising a child—even multiple children. There was no reason I couldn't be one of them.

I could do this. I would do this—my way.

7

So far, Jillian's plan was working.

She'd called Payton earlier that morning and sent her sister on a wild-goose chase of errands on her way to the book club meeting, requesting she stop at the grocery store and pick up a specific brand of both orange juice and bagels. And then Jillian had texted Payton once she knew her sister was likely to be walking out of the store and asked for a particular brand of cream cheese for the bagels.

She'd even thrown out a last-minute prayer that there'd be a traffic jam on I-25. Not a bad one—just a harmless slowdown to detain Payton long enough to give Jillian the time she needed.

As she'd hoped, Johanna had arrived on time, declining

the offer of coffee but accepting water and following her to the kitchen while Jillian got them both something to drink.

"Johanna, I need to talk to you." Jillian handed her sister a cold bottle of water from the fridge.

"If you want me to apologize for not telling you that I was pregnant, fine. I'm sorry I didn't tell you."

Such were Johanna's apologies.

"I don't want an apology . . . Wait." Jillian forced herself not to think too far ahead. To ignore the way her skin flushed hot, then cold. "What do you mean, you *were* pregnant? You're not pregnant anymore?"

"No. I mean, yes, I'm still pregnant." Johanna skimmed her hand down the front of her loose-fitting top, revealing her slight tummy bulge. "What is wrong with you?"

"Nothing. I—I just misunderstood." Time was slipping by. She should have texted Payton and added something else to the list. Grapes, maybe. "Jo, we . . . I . . . Let us adopt the baby."

Johanna, who had started to take a sip of water, stared at her. "What are you talking about?"

"Let Geoff and me adopt the baby."

"You're telling me that Geoff changed his mind about having children?"

Jillian paused, a *yes* so close. But she would not lie to her sister. "Not yet."

"Ah." Johanna's smile was twisted, the single syllable weighted with so much meaning. "Jill, even if Geoff did change his mind at some point, why do you think I would let you adopt my baby?"

"I heard you tell Payton that you weren't sure if you were going to keep the baby . . . and we . . . I want the baby."

She was flubbing this. Didn't sound calm. Wasn't acting calm. She wasn't convincing Johanna of anything. How would she ever change Geoff's mind?

Jillian's fingers ached. She eased the pressure of her hands, releasing her grip. Took a step back, the kitchen counter pressing into her hips. Today, all she had to do was get Johanna to listen to her. To at least consider her request. Then everything else would fall into place.

Johanna gave a quick shake of her head. "I can't let you and Geoff have the baby."

"Why not?"

"Because I've decided to keep the baby."

She couldn't have heard her sister right. "You don't want to be a mother, Johanna."

The words hung in the air between them—an accusation.

"I admit this isn't how I planned on starting a family. I'd imagined being married first." Her sister cut off a laugh. "Old-fashioned, I know. But that didn't happen. And now I'm pregnant and no one else is going to raise my baby."

"Not even me, Jo?" Oh, how pathetic she sounded, begging Johanna for her baby.

"No, Jilly. Not even you. Especially not you." Johanna closed her eyes for just a moment, her shoulders shifting in a silent sigh. "Don't you see how complicated this would be? My son or daughter would call me 'Aunt Johanna' instead of 'Mom.' And one day we'd have to explain everything. We'd have another family secret."

Jillian's spine stiffened. "Oh. *Now* you're worried about secrets. How convenient."

"It's my right to raise my child."

Johanna's words were swift. Effective. Jillian had no rebuttal.

This conversation was a throwback to high school debate class. She'd always disliked how she needed to be ready with a comeback to the opposing side's argument. She'd been more of a researcher. The fact-checker, not the star at standing up to the opposition and fighting back.

Johanna fisted her hands as if readying herself for a combat. But Jillian had no right to fight with her.

"I'm here! I'm here!" Payton's voice sounded from the front room. "The traffic was awful from Castle Rock."

It seemed one of Jillian's prayers had been answered.

Payton swept into the kitchen, several cloth grocery bags swinging from her arms. "I got the orange juice like you asked for, Jill, and the bagels and cream cheese. I grabbed some fresh berries—" Her younger sister stopped. "What's going on?"

"Our sister wants to adopt my baby." Johanna flung the words between the three of them.

"That's impossible since you're—"

"It's impossible since I'm keeping my baby." Johanna blew out a breath. "I come in here and apologize for keeping all of this a secret—"

Jillian would not let Johanna twist this morning into her own story. "You did not come here this morning to apologize. You only apologized when you thought I was going to ask you to."

"I certainly never expected you to ask to adopt my baby."

"A few weeks ago, you didn't even want it." Jillian spoke the words through clenched teeth.

"I do now."

"If that's your decision, Johanna, of course Jillian and I will respect it." Payton stood between them, still holding the grocery bags. "Mom and Dad, too, when you tell them."

Jillian forced herself to nod in agreement.

Payton might as well have been her debate partner, standing up to concede the win to the other team. Not that there was any rebuttal to what their older sister had said.

Decision made.

Johanna had the one thing Jillian wanted—and she had it by accident.

"It's probably best if we change the subject. Redeem the rest of the morning." Payton gave a forced laugh as she began unloading the groceries. "Anybody else hungry? Want coffee? Um, sorry, Johanna. I know coffee's not sitting well with you right now."

"I've been trying tea . . ."

"Tea?" The word spurted from Jillian's mouth. "You never drank tea, even when Mom tried to give it to us when we were sick."

"Ginger tea seems to help ease the nausea some."

"Shouldn't the nausea be ending? How far along are you?" Payton opened the cupboard, causing Jillian to step aside.

"I'm out of the first trimester, but the nausea is lingering—"

"Really?" Jillian couldn't hold back the protest. "We're doing this?"

"Doing what?"

"We're going to start talking about Johanna's pregnancy like it's normal? No big deal?"

"My pregnancy is normal. At least that's what Dr. Gray says."

"Who is Dr. Gray?" Payton retrieved a trio of plates from a cupboard and then selected three glasses for the juice.

"She's my obstetrician, and according to her, so far everything looks good."

"Did she give you a due date?"

"Yes. The end of August—August 30."

Jillian was being ignored. Again. Did Johanna even remember what they had been talking about just ten minutes ago? Did either of her sisters consider how this conversation might hurt her? Realize she didn't want to hear this?

Payton's and Johanna's words blended together. Today was not going to be about books, but about babies.

Johanna's baby.

Jillian murmured a brief "Excuse me," escaping the kitchen and then exiting the house altogether, shutting the front door on the static of her sisters' conversation.

She needed a walk. A long walk.

Head down, hands stuffed in her jean pockets, she almost passed Gianna's house without hearing her neighbor calling her name from where she stood out in front.

"Jillian! What are you doing outside without a coat?"

"What?"

"Where's your coat?" Gianna tugged on the collar of her maroon jacket.

"I . . . I don't know . . ." Seconds later, she burst into tears.

"Jillian!" Gianna stepped forward and wrapped her arms around her. "What's wrong?"

"My sister is pregnant."

"O-kay." Gianna patted her back like a mother soothing a distraught child. "Is something wrong with the baby?"

"I wish . . . I wish I was the one who was pregnant. I wish . . . the baby was mine." Jillian pulled back just enough to rub her hand across her face, unable to look at her friend. "Aren't I horrible to say that?"

"No, you're not horrible!" Gianna's arms tightened around her for another moment. "Come on. Come with me."

"Where are we going?"

"To my house. Neil took Avery to his parents' for the morning. I was going shopping, but I feel like a cup of coffee instead."

"My sisters are at my house. They'll be looking for me."

"You weren't worried about that a minute ago. Have a cup of coffee. Calm down—or go ahead and cry if you want to. And then, when you're ready, go back home and face your sisters."

Jillian allowed Gianna to loop their arms together and lead her into her house. The walls were painted a warm blue, and like her own living room, there was a fireplace. But Gianna's mantel display consisted of an arched wooden mirror positioned against a taller wooden frame and what looked like antique milk containers. Even in Avery's absence, a few toys were strewn on the carpet.

Jillian sat on the couch while her neighbor made the coffee. Just sat. No thinking. No talking.

Gianna returned carrying a wooden tray, setting it on the low coffee table. She handed Jillian a mug of coffee and then motioned to the items on the tray. "Sugar—and all the other not-sugar options. Milk. Sorry, no cream. It's the best I can do. And if you like it black like my husband does, then just ignore all the folderol, as he calls it."

"Thanks." Fixing her coffee allowed her a few seconds longer to settle her emotions. "I'm sorry I interrupted your quiet morning and your chance to go shopping."

"I've been hoping we could have coffee. Spontaneous works best sometimes."

"If you call me falling apart on the sidewalk outside your house spontaneous, then sure."

"We all have our moments—and sometimes we can't avoid having them in public." Gianna raised her coffee mug. "Besides, it was just me."

"I—I couldn't stay in the house while Payton asked Johanna how far along she is . . ." Jillian brought the mug up to her lips but stopped herself from gulping the hot liquid. No sense in burning her mouth on top of everything else that had gone wrong this morning.

"I don't blame you. Knowing how much you want a baby, that had to be painful."

"I shouldn't be surprised. I usually get lost in the middle of the two of them." And that was a bit more honest than she'd planned on being with her neighbor.

"You're the middle sister, then? I'm the baby in the family. Always fighting to be heard above the roar of the crowd."

"Then you understand." Jillian cradled the mug in her

hands. "Our relationships have always been complicated, but I'd hoped things were improving. Maybe that was wishful thinking. And now *this*. I don't know if I can get excited about Johanna having a baby."

"You don't have to. I mean, why should you pretend to be okay?"

"But Johanna will get upset—"

"Is Johanna the only one who's allowed to get upset in your family?"

"It feels like it sometimes." Jillian didn't know if her statement surprised Gianna, but if her sisters were here, they'd be shocked. "Did I just say that out loud?"

"I'm not recording this conversation."

"Isn't my being upset like this selfish?"

"It's being *honest*." Gianna leaned forward, setting her coffee aside. "And sometimes we have to admit our feelings—even the less-than-nice-sounding ones—so we can work through them. You're not happy about Johanna's pregnancy. Why?"

"I told you why."

"Tell me again."

"Because I want to have a baby and I can't."

"There. You said it, and the world didn't fall apart. There was no huge cosmic gasp of disapproval. You're not an awful person, Jillian, or an awful sister, because you want the same thing your sister has."

"It doesn't do me any good to say it. It doesn't change anything."

"Okay, so nothing changes. What about just being honest?

Giving yourself room to breathe? Have you ever thought that you and Johanna can both be right?"

"Tell that to Johanna."

"I would, but I'm not having coffee with her." Gianna grinned, tossing her long hair back over her shoulder. "It's okay to want a baby and to struggle with your sister's pregnancy. It doesn't mean you don't love her."

"I don't like her very much right now."

"Fair enough. And that's also not the end of the world. You'll figure this out. It may not be today . . ."

"It won't be today." There was another bit of honesty spoken aloud.

"Fine. It won't be today. But that's okay. It's normal to be upset with your sisters sometimes."

"How did you get so wise in the way of sister relationships, Gianna?"

"Well, I have two older brothers—two very loud, opinionated older brothers. I had to learn how to hold my own with them. But my best friend all through high school had four sisters, so I got to watch that dynamic up close. I learned a lot."

"Did they get along?"

"No—at first, some of their fights used to scare me." Gianna laughed as she picked up her coffee again and relaxed in her chair. "But then I learned that you did not cross the Goldhahn sisters. If someone hurt one of the other sisters, those girls closed ranks and were a formidable force to face."

"Johanna, Payton, and I? We're just learning how to

trust one another. Johanna's pregnancy kind of knocked me off-kilter."

"I imagine it did the same thing for Johanna—not that I'm saying you have to worry about her right now. Take care of yourself."

Take care of herself.

Maybe it was time she stopped feeling guilty if she did that.

⁓

Jillian had come home from Gianna's to an empty house. No Payton. No Johanna. The groceries put away. A note on the kitchen counter.

Sorry we upset you. Call me. Please. Payton.

She wouldn't call Payton. Or Johanna—not that Johanna had left a note asking her to call.

She couldn't explain herself to either of her sisters, so there was no use trying.

And she hadn't wanted an apology from Johanna when she'd arrived for book club earlier this morning. She'd wanted something more. Something impossible.

Where was all the hope she'd talked about just a few weeks ago? Choosing a word to focus on for the year didn't make it so. How did she hold on to hope, ensure she had enough of it for what each day held, when nothing changed? When each day presented her with another no?

It was like the time her family had gone camping in

Rocky Mountain National Park and her dad tried to teach her to build a fire. He'd instructed her to stack the kindling and smaller to larger sticks just so. One careful step at a time. But when she tried to light the flame, she failed. Again and again, the tiny spark went out before it had a chance to catch hold and burn. In the end, she'd abandoned her attempts. She couldn't do it, no matter how hard she tried.

Exhaustion stayed with her like her shadow, although it never shifted, never altered with the time of day.

It was no surprise that here she was again, curled up on the couch with Winston cradled in her arms.

Awake and alone.

Jillian gathered Winston closer as if he could warm her, his furry body limp as he snoozed in her arms. His soft ears tickled her chin. At least one of them was resting.

Months ago, she'd traded positive thoughts scrawled on scraps of paper and stored in a glass jar, a gift from her best friend Harper, for faith. But maybe faith wasn't enough either.

At the sound of the back door opening, Winston stirred in her arms and sat up with a sharp bark, jumping off the couch and running through the house.

"Hey, good boy. How ya doing?" Geoff's laughter mixed with Winston's barks. "Jillian, you here?"

Of course she was here.

Winston's barks quieted as Geoff let him out to the back-yard, closing the door. His footsteps came closer. Stopped. "Jillian? Hey, I'm sorry. Were you sleeping?"

"No."

"Oh. You didn't say anything."

"I'm tired. That's all."

"Busy morning with book club?"

"We didn't have it."

Geoff came around the couch, kneeling in front of her. "But that's why I went to the coffee shop—to give you space. Did your sisters cancel or something?"

"No. Johanna got upset—"

"Again? Is she always going to complain about the book you're reading?"

She rolled from her side onto her back. Pulled herself to an upright position. "No. I got upset and walked out."

"Okay." He pulled off his ball cap and ran a hand through his hair. "Now I'm confused."

"Johanna and Payton were talking about Johanna's pregnancy, and I didn't want to hear it. It's too hard to listen to."

"Johanna made a decision about what she's going to do?"

"Yes. She's keeping the baby." Jillian forced herself to say the words. Maybe the more often she said them, the less the truth would hurt. "But no matter what decision Johanna had made, I would have been upset, Geoff."

And here she was again, explaining herself to Geoff. Communication déjà vu. Why was it so difficult for him to understand?

At her words, Geoff stiffened. Stayed where he was. No move to comfort her. No words of understanding.

They were, once again, moving to their appropriate and oh-so-familiar positions—away from one another.

Geoff shifted his glasses back into place. "Why are you letting this bother you, Jill? This isn't your problem."

"How can you say that?"

"Because it's the truth. I understand you were hurt Johanna didn't tell you first—"

"This is not about being first! I'm not sure she was going to tell me *at all*, especially if she hadn't decided to keep the baby."

"But she did decide to have the baby. And it was Johanna's decision to make."

"Everybody gets to make their own decision but me."

"What?" Geoff's brows furrowed, disappearing behind the frame of his glasses.

"I said, everybody gets to decide what they want to do but me." Jillian enunciated each word.

"I don't understand."

"Johanna gets pregnant. She decides to keep the baby. To raise it herself. That's her decision. But it hurts me to think about it." She weighed her words before speaking them. "You . . . you've decided you don't want children. And that hurts me even more. Because I do. *I do.*"

"We agreed—"

"We agreed on nothing." Her voice rose, overriding his objection. "I tried to be okay with your decision to make you happy, but I'm not okay. I'm not happy."

This conversation was nothing but a replay of words, but she couldn't stop herself. "You have no idea how often I think about having a child. How often I think that if I say this or that, maybe I can change your mind."

Geoff muttered something under his breath, refusing to look at her.

No change. Her words never budged his no—not even over to a maybe.

"I can't do this, Jill. Not now. You know the conference is less than a week away. We agreed to talk after that."

"What I know is nothing will change. Don't offer me some kind of false hope by saying we'll talk."

"It's not false hope. We will talk."

"Why should we talk about having children if there's no chance you'll listen to me? No chance you'll even consider what I'm saying? How I'm feeling?"

Geoff eased to his feet, standing over her. "What is this?"

"What do you mean?"

"Answer the question. What is this? Because what you're saying . . . it almost feels like a threat."

"A threat?"

"Are you saying the only hope I can give you is that I'll change? That I have to agree to children—or else? Nothing else is good enough?"

If she told Geoff that he was wrong, that her hope could survive on less than that, she'd douse what little bit still flickered in her heart. She might as well fill a bucket with water and raise it over her head, turn it over, and empty the contents until she was soaked through.

Jillian twisted her rings around her finger.

She couldn't let Geoff extinguish her hope.

She'd do it herself.

"Yes. Yes, Geoff, that's what I'm saying. Knowing you won't change . . . it steals my hope for my future. For our future."

Geoff turned. Strode away. Faced her from across the room. "What does that mean?"

Her resolve to face the issue head-on faltered, the distance between them tangible. "I'm too tired to talk about this anymore."

Geoff's shoulders slumped. "Jill, you know I love you—"

"Yes." She closed her eyes for a moment and then forced herself to reconnect with her husband. To remember that he did love her. She couldn't forget that. "Let's just not talk about this right now, okay?"

"If that's what you want."

Now Geoff was telling her that she could have what she wanted?

No emotion flared at his words. Anger . . . indignation . . . nothing. Maybe all of that had been snuffed out too, along with hope.

Geoff took Winston's leash from the table in the foyer. "I'm going to take Winston for a walk."

"Good idea."

"Do you want to go with me?"

"No . . . I'm tired. You go ahead."

Geoff accepted her answer without argument. Once the house was still again, Jillian started to pull the blanket off the back of the couch. Stopped. It was a false sense of comfort, wrapping herself inside its folds.

At times like these, she missed Harper the most.

What had Harper said the last time they talked?

"When are you coming for a visit?" Harper's question came at the end of their hour-long phone call.

"Oh, I wish I could!" Just the thought of visiting her best friend warmed Jillian, as if she and Harper were sharing a hug.

"What's stopping you? Buy a plane ticket and come see me."

"But you're working . . ."

"When I'm working, you can relax. Walk on the beach. When I'm off, we can have some good, old-fashioned Girls' Nights."

Harper made the idea of a trip to North Carolina sound simple.

And maybe it was.

That's what she needed—a good, old-fashioned Girls' Night with Harper.

8

I WASN'T GOING to enjoy tonight. But being here was necessary—and I would survive. Besides, I was standing outside Axton Miller's front door, so it made no sense to go home without talking to him. This was the perfect opportunity to tell my boss about my pregnancy. Away from work, away from other employees. I'd have to deal with everyone else at the hospital soon enough.

Tonight I'd face Axton. And his wife.

I remained standing outside his home in Monument, on the north side of Monument Hill. With the hospital also located on I-25 heading toward Denver, he didn't have to worry about driving that troublesome part of the highway into work when it snowed. No matter what the forecast said.

A press of the doorbell sounded musical notes, and the wooden door swung open moments later, revealing Axton's wife, her petite stature accentuated by my height.

"Johanna! I'm so glad you're here. And right on time, too." She stepped back, ushering me into the expansive black- and white-tiled foyer. "I've wanted to have you and your fiancé over for dinner for weeks now."

I froze under the glare of an Italian chandelier as the woman's eyes widened and her voice trailed off.

"It's just me tonight." I forced my lips to form a smile.

"I'm so sorry. Of course, Axton mentioned you're no longer engaged—and there I go saying the wrong thing the minute you arrive. You're going to wish you hadn't come tonight."

I'd been wishing that before Axton's wife mentioned Beckett, but I wasn't going to say it out loud.

"You're not responsible to keep up with everything going on in my life." If the woman only knew what her husband was going to tell her after I went home. "I'm sure you're busy enough as it is."

"Oh yes." Relief tinged her high-pitched laughter. "Sawyer and Shaw, our twin boys, graduate from high school in May. I'm planning their party—it's a group celebration with several of their friends. And there are all sorts of year-end activities."

Somehow, I'd forgotten the Millers had twin boys.

"Will your sons be joining us for dinner?"

"Axton and I gave them the option to eat with us or take their dinner down to the family room. They've both got homework. Papers due."

I'd stepped into some perfect family backdrop. Perfect house that looked as if a designer had coordinated the paint and flooring and lights, even the artwork on the walls. A successful husband who probably adored his petite, talkative wife and forgave her every verbal faux pas. Perfect family with two parents and two boys—twins, no less. And I knew how people loved twins.

I pulled my hand away from where it rested on my abdomen as if shielding it from all the too-good-to-be-true surrounding me. This wouldn't be my child's life, but we'd still have a good one.

"Axton's in the kitchen. I put him in charge of the salad." She led me through the living and dining rooms and into a massive kitchen that anchored the back of the house—all gleaming white marble counters and white cabinets with glass doors. And there was my boss, slicing yellow peppers and tossing them into a wooden salad bowl heaped with mixed greens and tomatoes.

"Welcome, Johanna." Axton greeted me with his now-familiar smile that produced crinkles at the corners of his eyes.

"Hello, Axton. Thank you for having me over for dinner."

"Poor Johanna. We finally manage to get her here, and what do I do but mention—"

"Don't worry about it, um—" I racked my brain, trying to remember Axton's wife's name—"Dorothy. It's forgotten."

"Call me Dot. Everyone does—well, except for Axton. He calls me Dottie. Always has."

"I started off doing it to annoy her. Trying to get her to

notice me." With a grin, Axton tossed a slice of pepper into his mouth.

"What, did you two meet each other in grade school?"

Dot's laugh was a high trill that scaled my spinal column and reverberated in my ears. "No. We met in college. We were both freshman and I had no intention of getting attached to anyone."

"But I changed your mind, didn't I?"

"Took you a while." Axton's wife's grin was flirtatious.

"True. Two years."

"Two years?" I guess Axton didn't get everything he wanted when he wanted it. "You ignored this guy for two years?"

"I couldn't really ignore him, what with him calling me Dottie and showing up in my classes all the time. I started thinking he somehow figured out my schedule."

"I had my ways." Axton winked.

"What convinced you to go out on a date with him?"

"I felt sorry for him." Another trill of laughter that rang in my ears like a too-long peal of a doorbell.

"A pity date?"

"Not exactly. He'd gone on a ski trip during Christmas and he broke his ankle. Poor guy was miserable in his cast and crutches. I took him cookies and we stayed up late talking and the next thing I knew, we were going to the movies that Friday night."

"Smooth, Miller, breaking your ankle to get her to go out with you."

"Breaking my ankle was an accident, but I was not above using it to my advantage. I admit it."

"He was waiting for me at the altar, leaning on those crutches."

"Did you two get married that quickly?"

"No, we got married a year later. But he kept the crutches and I came walking down the aisle to see him balancing on them. He handed them off to his best man before we said our vows. We still have them somewhere." The oven timer dinged, and Dot opened the door, releasing the rich aroma of cheese, tomatoes, and meat. "I hope you like lasagna."

"It smells delicious."

Setting the lasagna on the counter, Dot pulled off the oven mitts. "I'm going to let that rest while I run downstairs to the spare fridge and grab some extra salad dressings. I like a variety of choices. You two keep talking."

The Millers were keeping the perfect-family persona up, right down to a meet-cute story, complete with the perfect blend of romance and humor. And soon I'd have to confess my own anything-but-perfect family scenario.

Axton watched his wife as she left the kitchen, his eyes warm with affection. How had they managed to keep their love alive for so many years? Not my business—and knowing that wouldn't change anything for me.

"Axton, I was wondering if we could take a few minutes to talk this evening."

He seemed to hesitate. "Of course, Johanna. But I'll warn you, I try not to talk about business on weekends if at all possible—unless it's an emergency."

A pharmaceutical emergency. Right.

"This is a bit of business and personal combined."

"Is everything okay?"

Now it was my turn to pause as Dot's voice floated into the room just ahead of her. "We'll let you boys know when dinner is ready."

"Why don't we talk after dinner?"

"After dinner it is."

Dot swept into the kitchen, carrying a trio of salad dressings, and took over, talking the entire time she arranged the food on the expansive island in the center of the kitchen. Lasagna, salad, fresh rolls, tall glass pitchers of water and tea. Her topics pinballed back and forth from her favorite flavor of tea—Mango Tango—to her lasagna recipe—a longtime family favorite—to how she always liked to use two dressings on her salad because one was boring.

"Johanna—" Axton spoke up when his wife paused for a moment to search in a drawer for a serving utensil—"would you like a glass of wine? I have a nice merlot."

"No, thank you."

"Axton, what are you doing, offering Johanna wine? She's probably not drinking while she's pregnant."

Dot's unexpected statement was worse than her high-pitched laughter, causing me to freeze where I stood, bracing my legs against the island. At first, she didn't even realize what she'd said. What she'd done. She trilled another laugh, plopping a square of steaming lasagna onto a plate and offering it to me. Only when I didn't accept it did she notice the silence stretching between Axton and me.

Surely every step of this pregnancy wasn't going to be difficult.

"Is everything all right?" Dot's gaze flickered back and forth between me and her husband.

"I didn't know . . ." Axton spoke first.

"I hadn't had a chance . . . This is what I wanted to talk to you about."

Pounding footsteps interrupted my fumbling attempts to explain, and two lanky teenage boys burst into the kitchen, all arms and legs, their brown hair sticking out beneath baseball caps that were positioned backward on their heads.

"Hey, Mom, is dinner ready yet? We're gonna eat downstairs." One boy took a plate, spinning it on a fingertip like a basketball as he positioned himself near me.

"Yeah, I've got a decent rough draft of my paper, so this a good time for a break." The other brother, so similar in height and coloring, but not as identical as Payton and Pepper had been, took a plate too, jostling for a position.

"Shaw. Sawyer. Settle down and say hello to our guest, Dr. Thatcher." Axton motioned with a salad tong.

"Johanna is fine."

Quick handshakes accompanied mumbled *hello*s. Then the boys filled their plates and disappeared back downstairs, with promises to return for seconds.

Dot set her plate on the counter, any hint of her usual humor gone from her eyes. "Johanna, I'm so sorry. I thought Axton knew you were pregnant and had forgotten to tell me. You know how men are."

I certainly did.

"No, he didn't. I was planning on talking with him

tonight." I tore a piece of my roll apart. "I haven't announced it to anyone yet. My parents don't even know."

"Well, you're not showing that much, but you do have a certain look about you—and then there was the way you rested your hand on your tummy earlier. It's such a maternal reflex."

I didn't realize I had any maternal instincts. Or reflexes. Hormones must cause all sorts of changes in a woman.

"And Dot has an uncanny ability to spot pregnant women." Axton piled lasagna onto his plate, the action returning a sense of normalcy to the evening. "She sometimes knows when a friend is pregnant before they do."

Too bad I hadn't known about Dot's superpower before I'd accepted their dinner invitation.

Dot might as well have slipped up and revealed an upcoming surprise party or someone's special Christmas gift. Couldn't unhear what she'd said. Couldn't stuff the proverbial pregnant cat back in the bag.

The aroma of the lasagna teased me, undermining my desire to run. To end the evening prematurely.

"As awkward as it is right at this moment, I, for one, don't want to miss out on dinner. I haven't enjoyed food much the past few months, but things are starting to calm down." I dusted off my fingers, my roll a shredded heap on my plate. "I probably need another roll."

"Absolutely."

"And salad, please. But no wine."

My attempt at a joke received a short burst of Dot's laughter and a grateful smile from Axton.

When we were seated at the dining room table, Axton

resumed the conversation. "So. Your pregnancy. No sense in waiting until after dinner to talk about it."

"Are you sure?"

"I don't mind." Dot sipped her wine, probably trying to tamp down her curiosity—and failing.

Talking now meant I could go home sooner. "It's unexpected, that goes without saying, but I'm planning on working during the pregnancy and after the baby's born, too, of course."

"You'll want to take maternity leave."

"I haven't looked into the hospital policy yet."

"Easy enough to find out."

"Johanna, let me throw you a baby shower!" Dot seemed ready to jump up from her seat to go find paper and pen—maybe her iPad—to start sketching out details.

"What?"

"A baby shower. It'll be so much fun. And of course, you probably need everything. A car seat, high chair, crib . . ."

I'd wanted to discuss my pregnancy in a nice, businesslike manner with Axton. And I'd thought I would have to fend him off when it came to a baby shower.

I didn't want to think about a shower. About everything I didn't have, starting with a husband. I didn't even own a single piece of maternity clothing yet. But one day I'd have to abandon leggings and loose tops and admit my body was changing to accommodate a baby.

A baby.

I choked down a bite of lasagna. Dot Miller was ruining this meal for me.

"Honey, this is not the time to talk about a baby shower for Johanna. You know what? Let's table all discussion of her pregnancy for the rest of the evening. She and I can talk about it more at work tomorrow." Axton returned his attention to me. "Is that okay with you?"

"Fine. Perfect. Thank you."

For the first time since I'd met Axton Miller the day he'd shown up at Mount Columbia hospital and stolen my promotion from me, I found myself liking the man. No reservations. If anyone could handle his wife, he could.

Then Dot offered Axton a small, conspiratorial smile. This was the woman who'd fended off his advances for two years. *Two years.* I could only hope I could get Axton to listen to reason tomorrow—and not to his wife.

9

TWO SUITCASES SIDE BY SIDE on their bed. His. Hers. And Winston curled up between them, his chin resting on the edge of Geoff's mostly packed suitcase. Everything was compartmentalized in the travel packing cubes he preferred. Jillian had bought him new ones for his last birthday, and now his suitcase looked ready to handle a multicountry trip, not a mere weekend away in Denver.

Meanwhile, her suitcase contained only a few items. Her pajamas, which were a comfortable pair of pink leggings and a white top with a scoop neckline. Jeans and a soft cashmere sweater, along with a pair of wedge ankle boots. One outfit and something to sleep in. Certainly not enough for their upcoming weekend in Denver—the one she was less and less excited about, not that she'd admitted that to Geoff.

"Do I need something fancy?" Jillian stood in front of the closet, sliding hangers back and forth so that they clicked against one another.

"Fancy?"

"Is there any sort of formal dinner or banquet at the conference?"

"I don't think so."

"That's no help, Geoff." She faced away from her closet. "Did you look at the schedule?"

"I know when I'm speaking. What workshops I'm attending."

"Are you bringing a suit?" Jillian kept her voice neutral, low.

"Should I?"

"I don't know. I've barely packed my suitcase." She sat on the end of the bed and tossed him his phone from the side table. "Pull the conference up on your phone."

"Why?"

"So we can look at the schedule of events. Wait . . . did you buy tickets for a banquet?"

"I don't think so. We'll know when we get my registration packet tomorrow. Why don't you pack something, just in case?"

Geoff sounded like her—unable to remember whether he'd done something or not. "Geoff. Pull up the conference schedule. Please."

She'd lost any desire to go to the conference, and now Geoff's laissez-faire attitude confused her, making it seem as if he didn't care if she went with him. He was sending her mixed messages.

All she wanted to do was shove the suitcases aside and curl up in a ball on the bed. But it wasn't because of the effects of chemo and radiation. She was tired of fending off the circumstances of her life. Tired of being okay when things weren't okay.

"I'm going to stay home this weekend."

Geoff blew out a breath. "What? We've planned this getaway for weeks."

"I—I've been thinking about this since Saturday, and I think it's best if you go without me." Despite the suddenness of her statement, it was the right thing to do. "It's ten thirty at night and I have too much packing left. I'm tired. I'll stay home."

"You can pack tomorrow morning."

"I don't want to go."

"Fine. Don't go." Geoff shoved Winston away, causing him to jump off the bed, and slammed his suitcase shut. "I don't understand you anymore, Jill."

"What? I decided not to go to the conference—"

"Is this payback?"

"Payback for what?"

"Because I won't agree to have children."

"This is a decision, Geoff. It's as simple as that. I'm tired. And yes, I'm always tired, but maybe I shouldn't have planned on going to the conference in the first place. It's a business conference." Jillian stood, stepping away from the bed. "I'm not pouting because of your decision not to have children or because Johanna said no when I asked to adopt her baby—"

"When you what?"

Jillian stopped. What had she said?

"Answer me, Jillian." Geoff faced her, as if blocking her exit from the room. "Did you really ask Johanna if you could adopt her baby?"

Geoff's question, his tone, scattered her thoughts. She tried to pick them up like papers that had been torn from her hands by a strong wind and were blowing away faster than she could reach them.

Winston perked up from where he lay on the floor, a barometer of the tension in the room.

She wasn't going to lie.

"Yes. Saturday morning . . . when Payton and Johanna and I met for book club . . . I asked Johanna to let us adopt her baby."

Geoff removed his glasses, rubbing his eyes with the back of his hand. "Why?"

"Why? Because she was thinking of having an abortion . . . and I thought we could convince her not to do it."

"Don't say 'we.' I had nothing to do with it."

"It doesn't matter. She said no."

"It matters, Jillian. What were you doing asking your sister if we could adopt her baby when we don't agree on this?"

"What you mean is we can only agree if I do what you say." Jillian's voice rose to match Geoff's. "And don't you dare accuse me of not telling you something, Geoff Hennessey! You married me without even mentioning that you had a younger brother who died or an older brother who ran away from home. And you also didn't mention you had no intention of having children. You're no better than your mother."

Her accusation sparked the air between them.

"This is not about me—"

"Your mother refuses to talk about Kyler or Brian. You learned oh so well from her, didn't you? What else haven't you told me?"

Jillian flung the question at him . . . and then all the fight left her. She couldn't think. Couldn't react. It was as if she stopped in the middle of the street and dropped what few papers she'd managed to retrieve . . . and the wind swept the rest away.

Winston wandered back and forth between them, whining.

She couldn't do this. Not tonight. Not tomorrow. Not anymore.

Jillian backed away, hands held up, palms out. "I'm sorry . . . please. No more yelling. You're right. I shouldn't have asked Johanna. She was as upset as you are."

And it hadn't made any difference anyway, not that he remembered.

But that also wasn't the point.

She stopped moving when her back pressed against the wall. "Geoff, please. Go to the conference alone. The weekend we planned . . . it's not going to happen now."

"If that's what you want."

He needed to stop saying those words.

"It is." Jillian found the strength to close her suitcase, pull it from the bed, drag it over to the closet. "I'll deal with this later."

"I'll head up to Denver early tomorrow, then."

"Fine. I'll talk to Gianna and let her know she doesn't have to watch Winston."

"I'll finish packing my toiletries."

"I'll let Winston out one last time for the night."

Jillian led Winnie downstairs, the subdued puppy sticking close beside her until he slipped through the doggy door. The replay of her apology cut through her thoughts like the waving of a white flag. Giving up. But it was better than arguing. Than yelling.

She'd had no other choice.

This was a little earlier in the day than she'd planned on dropping off Winston with Gianna, but her plans had changed. She hoped Gianna would be flexible . . . and not just for today.

Her neighbor opened her front door, her hair loose around her shoulders. "Jillian . . . hi."

"Hi." This was no time to be distracted by—or envious of—Gianna's long hair. Jillian had decided months ago to accept her post-chemo short hair. To enjoy it. Gianna had probably worn hers the same way since high school, attracting a lot of attention then and now. Jillian gripped Winston tighter so he couldn't squirm out of her arms. "I apologize for being earlier than we'd talked about."

"That's no problem. I'm home today."

Avery slipped around her mother's legs. "Hi."

"Good morning, sweetheart." As always, the presence of the little girl caused Jillian's heart to ache.

Avery pointed at Winston. "Puppy?"

"Yes, this is Winston, my puppy." Jillian knelt down, while Gianna reminded her daughter to be gentle. "You ready for this?"

"It'll be fun." Gianna sat beside Avery, guiding her tiny hand as she stroked Winston's head. "Who knows? Maybe by the time you get back, I'll convince Neil that we should get a dog, too."

"Um, I needed to talk to you about that."

"Okay. But the list of instructions you gave me the last time we talked is pretty thorough."

"It's about when we're getting back."

Gianna offered her a grin. "Did you and Geoff decide to stay another night? That's not a problem."

"I'm not going to Denver."

The glint of humor disappeared from Gianna's brown eyes. "I'm confused."

"I mean . . . I am going to Denver . . . to the airport. I need to leave in thirty minutes if I'm going to catch my flight."

"Let me put Winston in the backyard and you can tell me what's going on while I get Avery a snack—only if you want to, of course. Even if you don't, I'm still fine with watching your dog for however long you need me to."

It was odd to put Winnie in Gianna's backyard, even though he seemed content to explore the new area, sniffing the ground. This entire morning was odd. And if Jillian went through with her decision—with this day—then her future for she didn't know how long was going to be even more peculiar.

Jillian stood at Gianna's kitchen sink, the window giving a clear view of the back of her own house. She'd made her bed this morning. Picked up Geoff's damp towel from the floor and hung it on the rod in the bathroom as she'd packed her toiletries after buying her too-expensive, last-minute plane ticket. Left him a note on the kitchen counter. Too few words. But at least there would be some kind of explanation waiting for him when he got home from the conference. The only way she'd go through with her plan was if she didn't answer any phone calls or texts. Her note sat next to the note he'd left for her, scribbled on a piece of paper torn from one of the legal pads they'd used to plan his presentation: *I'm sorry about last night. I'll miss you this weekend. Love, Geoff.*

She could go back. Remove her note from where it sat on the still-new kitchen counters. Tear it up.

Geoff would never know what she had planned to do.

But then there would be the credit card charge to explain later.

And they needed this.

She needed this time away.

"What's going on?" Gianna had settled Avery at a child-size table in the breakfast nook with a cup of juice and a string cheese.

"Geoff's still going to the conference. I mean, of course he's going to the conference. He's speaking at the conference." Jillian paused to catch her breath.

"But you're not going."

"I'm going to visit my friend Harper in North Carolina—the Outer Banks."

"That sounds like fun."

"I hope she thinks so, too, when I show up."

"What?"

"She doesn't know I'm coming . . . and Geoff doesn't know I'm going out there, either."

"Jillian . . ."

For the first time, Jillian realized she was pulling Gianna into her marital mess. "I need you to not tell Geoff where I am."

Her neighbor stared at her, eyebrows furrowed. "I—I can't lie."

"I'm not asking you to lie. Just don't tell him—"

"Unless he asks."

Jillian gave a swift nod. "Geoff and I . . . we need some time apart."

"You're separating?"

Were they?

"No. A separation requires lawyers and drawing up papers and negotiations. I'm taking a break."

"What about counseling?"

Counseling would require that they talk, and that wasn't happening.

"I guess it's something to consider when I get back. Right now, I need to get away. Geoff and I can't seem to talk to each other without arguing."

"All the more reason to stay."

"I have a plane ticket. I'm going. Geoff will be back Sunday afternoon. If you can take care of Winston like we planned, I'd appreciate it."

"Sure."

"Geoff may need some help while I'm gone. I don't know. Winnie has a dog door, so that helps during the day."

"I'll ask Geoff if he needs help—for however long you're gone."

"Thank you. And now . . . I need to go." She accepted Gianna's hug.

She was leaving without saying good-bye to Winston. But then, she was leaving without saying good-bye to Geoff.

Winston was fine. Geoff would be fine.

And she would be fine, too. Once she got some space.

⁓

Thursday bled into early morning Friday. Jillian had driven to Denver, not realizing until she saw the signs directing her to either short-term or long-term parking at the airport that she'd be leaving her car in the long-term parking lot for who knew how long.

She'd survived the delay out of Denver, thankful she had a direct flight to Norfolk. The delay also gave her time to rent a car to drive from Norfolk to North Carolina, something she'd forgotten to do when she'd booked her flight. She'd ignored Geoff's texts, exhaling once she could put her phone on do not disturb as the flight prepared to take off.

And now, hours and hours later, here she stood outside Harper's condo—technically Harper's mom's beach condo. The salty scent of the ocean enveloped her as she waited for her best friend to open the door so she could finally say, "I'm here."

"Who is it?" Harper's question was muffled behind the door.

"Harper? It's me, Jillian."

"Jillian?" Even as she asked the question, the porch light switched on.

"Yes—"

The door swung open. Harper's clothes were disheveled, with her T-shirt slipping off one shoulder, a messy bun on top of her head, and mascara smeared under her eyes. But then Jillian needed to scrub the remnants of makeup off her face and change into clean clothes. "Jill! What . . . ? How . . . ? You're here?"

She gave a laugh that had a bit of hysterical relief in it. "Yeah . . . surprise."

The next second, she was wrapped in her best friend's arms, crying her eyes out.

Harper's hug . . . it wasn't like coming home. Home was back in Colorado. Her best friend's hug was like slipping into her most comfortable pair of jeans. She fit with Harper. She never felt wrong.

And Harper hadn't changed. She still hugged Jillian with every last ounce of her strength. Like she wasn't going to let her go—ever. Which was fine with Jillian. Because when Harper let her go, she just might collapse.

Too soon, her friend's hold on her loosened and she took a step back. "Come on. Get inside." Harper looked around as she pulled her in.

"It's just me."

"I thought so." And that's all she said as she took Jillian's suitcase, setting it on the floor before giving her another brief hug. "I can't believe you're here."

"I should have called or texted or something."

"How did you get here?"

"I flew into Norfolk and then rented a car."

"You must be exhausted. Are you hungry? What can I get you?"

"Water would be great." Jillian remained standing just inside the door. "So this is your mom's condo."

"Yep. Typical beach decor. Wicker furniture. Paintings of the beach—as if you don't see enough of it just off the balcony. And lucky for you, it has two bedrooms—and there are clean sheets on the bed."

"I wouldn't notice if there weren't any sheets at all on the bed." For once, Jillian thought she'd actually sleep when she crawled into bed—for a few hours, at least. "I should probably explain why I showed up on your doorstep like this in the middle of the night."

"Tell me that Geoff knows you're here."

Her friend knew her too well.

"He doesn't. He's at a business conference in Denver for the weekend. He thinks I'm home with Winston."

"Jilly . . ."

This was where she explained everything to her best friend. Where it all made sense, so that Harper understood. Where Jillian understood her impulsive decision to fly more than a thousand miles to show up on Harper's doorstep in the middle of the night.

Even though she needed to, Jillian couldn't explain the "why" of it all now.

"You deserve to know what's going on, Harper."

"Yes. Eventually. But you look ready to fall asleep standing up. And I'm not completely awake, not to mention I have to be at work in a few hours."

"I didn't even think about that. I'm so sorry. I shouldn't have—"

"Jill. Stop. You're here. I'm glad you're here, although I'm sorry for whatever upset you so badly you . . . well, ran away from home." She picked up Jillian's suitcase, took her hand, and led her to a bedroom down the short hallway off the living room. "Let's both try to get some sleep and we'll talk tomorrow—today—once I get home from work."

"Sounds perfect."

Reality and exhaustion collided, destroying any ability to explain. To do anything but follow Harper's instructions. Bedroom here. Bathroom there. Sleep as long as she wanted. Food in the fridge. Spare condo key in a seashell-shaped dish on the table. Take a walk on the beach when she woke up if she wanted to.

Harper's words were blending together like one long, run-on sentence.

Before Harper could leave her in the guest bedroom, Jillian leaned in for one more hug—and didn't want to let go. "Thank you."

"It's going to be okay, Jill."

"You don't know that."

"No matter what happens, you'll be okay. That I do know." Harper released her. "Nothing's going to change tonight. You're here. You're safe. Now try to get some rest."

10

I WANTED TO BE HOME.

Alone.

Heels kicked off by my front door. Lab jacket hung up in my closet. Skirt exchanged for leggings. Blouse exchanged for a more relaxed top.

But first, Thai food.

I'd been craving Thai food all week. But not just any Thai food. No, it had to be my favorite dish from my favorite restaurant. The one I used to go to with Beckett. The one I'd avoided for months.

This baby wanted one particular dish. Nothing else. I had half a dozen frozen Thai options at home, and I would most likely toss them all. I'd even tried a restaurant closer to home. Eaten three bites straight out of the to-go container and tossed it in the trash.

Pregnancy cravings were all or nothing—some sort of tug-of-war between me and my unborn child. Whose will and wants were stronger? When it came to what I ate, the baby had already won. The other day, I'd gone into a grocery store with a specific list of items. For some still-unexplained reason, I'd added a jar of olives to my purchases. Then I'd sat in the car in the parking lot and eaten half of them.

And I hated olives.

Now I had a half-full jar of olives in my refrigerator because, apparently, this baby didn't want any more. But I didn't dare throw them away in case, weeks from now, the baby changed its mind in the middle of the night.

My only hope was that I'd be back in charge of what I ate once the baby was born.

Lisa, one of the teen girls managing the register, interrupted my thoughts. "I'm so sorry, but we mixed up your take-out order. One of the waitresses gave it to someone else. We're having to remake it."

I gripped the strap of my purse. How simple was it to keep orders straight? "Gave it to someone else . . ."

"It seems someone else ordered it for here and they overlooked the to-go order. They've already started remaking your order."

"Fine. I can't go home without what the baby wants." The statement popped out of my mouth before I realized it.

Lisa's eyes widened. "You're pregnant?"

There was no sense in denying it. "Yes, and right now the baby wants Thai food."

"I'm sorry we mixed up your order. We won't charge you."

"I appreciate it." As I settled on the cushioned bench near the cash register, an all-too-familiar laugh rose above the general din of conversation in the dining room—the laughter of someone who loved the pineapple curry as much as I did. I stood, peering over the half wall separating the foyer and the dining room. It took less than a minute to locate Beckett where he sat with a small group of men and women, gathered around a table laden with a variety of Thai dishes.

Beckett was probably eating my dinner.

I smothered a gasp, backing up against the wall, trying to make myself shorter. To disappear.

But my attempt to avoid attention did the exact opposite as I bumped into a group of businessmen waiting to be seated.

"Hey, honey. Want to join us?" Raucous laughter filled the crowded waiting area.

"I'm so sorry. Excuse me." There was nowhere to turn, to move. And of course, the loud burst of laughter attracted Beckett's attention—as well as most everyone else's in the restaurant.

This was like when I had to do one of those ridiculous team-building exercises and they asked, "If you could have a superpower, what would it be?" I could never pick one. I always went with the default of flying because, well, why not? Didn't all superheroes fly? But now, if I could choose, I'd pick invisibility. Instantly disappear.

But I couldn't.

And it wasn't like one of those ridiculous movie scenes where all the sound faded when the man and woman destined to fall in love saw each other across a crowded room. I could still hear the men's suggestive laughter. The conversations flowing around me. The phone ringing—probably another take-out order being called in.

If I couldn't disappear, I needed to look away.

No. If anyone blinked first, it would be Beckett.

Which meant I saw every single move he made as he pushed his chair back, rose, and crossed the room toward me. He might have blinked, but my eyes stung from my forcing them to remain open.

"I didn't expect to see you here tonight." Beckett sighed. "I'm sorry. That has to be the lamest way to start a conversation."

"We're not having a conversation." I blinked and focused on the cashier. Contest won.

"We can't even be civil with each other?"

"There's no reason to be civil. We haven't seen each other in months. I prefer we keep things like that. Not seeing each other. Not talking to each other."

"You're telling me you haven't thought about me once in all that time?"

"Oh, I bet your ego would love to think I have—to think I've missed you." I gave him the briefest of glances. "You think too highly of yourself, Beckett."

"I've missed you, Johanna."

"I haven't missed you." The words stiffened my resolve. I was fine. No, I was more than fine. I was better off without Beckett. "Why don't you go back to your friends and finish your dinner. I'm sure your girlfriend is waiting for you."

"Arlene is not my girlfriend—"

"I don't care."

I shouldn't have said anything about the dark-haired woman he'd been sitting next to—who'd been watching us ever since Beckett had come over to talk to me. She wasn't Iris—I remembered her face all too well. But Arlene had the air of someone who had every right to come over and interrupt our conversation. To introduce herself and ask, "And you are?"

My stomach churned. If I talked with Beckett much longer, I wouldn't be able to enjoy my Thai food.

Time to retreat before I cried.

"Miss Johanna, your order is ready now." Lisa appeared with a brown paper bag. "Again, we're sorry about the mix-up."

"Thank you."

"I added some spring rolls—just because." Lisa smiled. "And congratulations about the baby."

"Thank you." I grasped the bag, causing it to crinkle in my grip. Turned. Walked away without a word to Beckett. Maybe, with all the noise, he hadn't heard what Lisa said. He couldn't have.

I pushed open the glass door, lowered my head, and moved past a trio of teens about to enter the restaurant. Fast-walked to my car parked several spaces away from the door.

"Johanna."

I pretended not to hear Beckett call my name.

"Johanna!"

I was mere feet from my car when he grasped my arm,

turning me to face him. "What did she mean, congratulations about the baby?"

I yanked my arm free, but that only made things worse, revealing the baby bump.

"You're pregnant?"

"That's obvious, isn't it?" I unlocked my car door, positioning it between us.

"When were you going to tell me?" He ran his hand along his jaw.

"This doesn't concern you, Beckett."

"Are you saying I'm not the father of this baby?"

"I'm not the one who slept around when we were engaged—well, during our entire time together." His wince didn't affect me at all. "Of course you're the baby's father."

"Then this does concern me."

"No. It doesn't. We are not together anymore. I'm raising this baby myself."

"Johanna, you don't get to decide—"

"Yes. Yes, I do. You cheated on me. Our relationship is over. I gave you back the ring. I'm the one who's pregnant. Not you."

Beckett started to say something, but I slid into the driver's seat and slammed the door. Started the car, put it in reverse. Backed up. The man was wise enough to jump onto the sidewalk.

I was caught in yet another movie scene, thanks to Beckett. But this one had ended better. I had ended it better. I was stronger. He had the ring . . . and I had the baby. Not some sort of even trade, but now he also knew I had made my decision, without him. I didn't need him. I was going on with my life. My choices, as unexpected as they were.

The aroma of Thai food filled the car.

The baby better enjoy every single bite, because I was never eating it again.

And there was Beckett in my rearview mirror. Standing on the sidewalk. Watching me drive away.

Why didn't he go inside? Go back to his friends. His date.

I was going on with my life—and apparently so was he.

I focused on the road ahead. Tonight's unexpected meeting had been awkward, but it was also good to know I could see my ex-fiancé and not want him back. Not miss him that way anymore.

What an odd epilogue to our relationship. Maybe years from now, we'd see each other again. And it'd be easier because of tonight. Of course, I'd have to talk to my child about Beckett someday. But that was years and years from now.

I sniffed. Once. Twice.

There was no need for me to cry.

I wasn't sad.

Pregnancy hormones. What an inconvenience.

⌒

At least the baby was satisfied.

The craving was satiated by the time I'd finished half the pineapple curry. Now I sat on the couch, my plate beside me. I might not be sitting at the dining room table, but I certainly wasn't going to eat dinner out of the white to-go box. Or eat in my bed.

Beckett used to try to convince me to eat meals in bed, but I was not going to do that, no matter how much he wheedled and whined. Too messy. My bedroom was for . . . not eating meals in.

And so was my living room. But I'd blame this bit of slacking off on hormones, too. I never knew how often a woman could play the pregnancy card. Now I understood all the "I didn't want the (fill in the blank with some kind of indulgent food)—the baby wanted it" jokes that one of my pharmacy technicians had laughed about during her pregnancy.

I was all of twenty weeks pregnant and I was allowing myself to become a stereotype. Losing my grip on my personality. I'd always insisted I was a strong, independent woman. Someone who knew who she was and what she wanted.

But now I'd eaten less than half the Thai food—and I didn't want it.

The baby didn't want it.

Cravings were capricious.

And I'd fought against memories of all the times Beckett and I had eaten at the restaurant. The first time, we'd been dating for just over a year. I'd found the restaurant online and chosen it because it had a long list of rave reviews. It had been a good night.

"Yet another sign we're meant to be together." Beckett savored a bite of chicken pad Thai.

"What is?"

"We both like Thai food."

"A lot of people like Thai food."

"But we—" he motioned to the dishes on the table that included pineapple curry—"like the same thing."

"True."

"And we both like black-and-white photography." He took another bite of his meal, pausing to think. "We both like Fast and Furious movies."

"Correction. You like Fast and Furious movies. I'm getting used to them."

"Fine. But give me points for watching the Oscar contenders with you when the nominations came out—that was something new for me."

"Only because you happened to be in town."

"True—but it was fun." He leaned across the table and kissed me—one of his trademark lingering kisses, as if he didn't care that people were watching us. "Admit it, Johanna, we're good together."

For some reason, it had seemed important that I agree with him. That I make a verbal commitment taking us to some next level, there in the Thai restaurant.

And for a moment, I heard the echo of my voice agreeing with him. Saw the faint memory of Beckett's smile that almost seemed self-satisfied.

Had he won and I lost, even then?

There was no way to know if Beckett had been cheating on me that early in our relationship. But he probably had been.

I could sit on this couch all night—me and a plate of curry. But if I did that, I'd wake up cold sometime in the middle of the night. Stiff. And sorry.

I forced myself to go to the kitchen and toss the remnants

of Thai food in the trash. I wouldn't be going to that restaurant again. I could always find another favorite restaurant. There were plenty to choose from.

And when . . . *if* I decided I was ready for another relationship, there were other men who could be a father to my child. The choice was mine and mine alone.

I could choose what I told my baby about its father, too. When I told it anything about its father.

Now I could at least say he'd known about the baby, but that I'd made the decision to be a single mother because our relationship was over when I found out I was pregnant. It was better this way—just the two of us.

There. My child might not like it, but it was the truth. I'd start this Thatcher, boy or girl, off with the truth.

Something faint, tiny, fluttered inside me.

I froze in the middle of my kitchen.

Was that . . . ? No, I had to be mistaken. But if I wasn't, then that was my baby moving.

I needed to tell someone . . . call someone . . .

I couldn't call Mom. She didn't even know yet. It'd been easier to stay away from the family dinners on Sundays, but that would end the day after tomorrow.

Jill. I could call my sister . . .

I picked my phone up from the side table by the couch, ready to dial Jillian. Stopped. Would Jillian still celebrate this moment with me after what had happened between us? She'd always been there for me, even if it was hard for her. And I'd been there for her. I'd cut my hair for her, donating it to Locks of Love the first Christmas after she'd been diagnosed with cancer. Not that I was doing it for show. I did it because I loved her, not even thinking how much I loved my hair. Well, only a little.

Jillian loved me as much as I loved her—probably more, being Jillian.

She'd understand. She'd listen.

I autodialed her number. Waited. One ring. Two. Three. Then my call went to her voice mail message.

It wasn't like Jill was busy. She could have answered.

My sister had ignored my phone call.

The message had gone to blank air, waiting for me to say something. But this . . . this wasn't the kind of thing you told someone in a recorded message.

I disconnected.

Jillian might as well have answered my call, said hello, and then hung up on me.

I tossed my phone aside. Sat for a moment. And then I abandoned the couch again.

I wasn't going to sit around, waiting for something to happen. For my baby to move again—if it had moved at all. For Jillian to call me back.

I needed to do something.

And I knew just what to do. It was time to stop staring at the blank walls where Beckett's photos had been. To replace them with something else. Why I hadn't done so before now, I had no idea.

I didn't miss any of them. The one of the Washington Monument that he'd given me on our first anniversary to commemorate how we met in Washington, D.C.

Or the one of Big Ben, taken during one of Beckett's trips overseas.

Or the one of me relaxing in a gondola in Venice, a grinning gondolier behind me, from one of our more expensive vacations.

They were just black-and-white proof that I'd been made a fool of. Replacing them would be proof that I was fine without Beckett in my life.

Because I was.

//

MY PARENTS' HOUSE always smelled good on Sunday afternoons, with the aroma of the family meal filling the house. One week it might be steaks fresh off the grill, another week a favorite family soup like clam chowder or chili that we'd load down with cheese and onions and taco chips. Today, the scent of roasted chicken and potatoes made my mouth water. Most likely there was a salad to go with it, to satisfy Payton's dietary choice.

Even with the tempting smell of dinner, I wasn't sure how much I'd eat today, not with what I had planned. Of course, I could always eat first and confess later.

Confess. It was as if I'd committed some sort of crime.

I had nothing to be ashamed of. Nothing to be embarrassed about. I was thirty-six years old. I had a good-paying job. A mortgage. But showing up at Mom and Dad's and telling them that I was pregnant? It was as if I was all of eighteen years old, coming home from college, confessing I'd slept with my boyfriend.

Not that I'd ever told them that back then. And not that they'd ever asked. We didn't talk about the whole "Did we or didn't we?" kind of thing. I doubt my parents even knew when I'd had my first kiss. Confiding in my mother about anything ended once the twins were born.

I'd arrived later than usual today. My way of assuring everyone would be there, most likely engrossed in a board game or a movie, and that Mom wouldn't answer the door and see my *announcement* before I was ready. I'd worn a loose top and carried the biggest purse I owned for added camouflage, but Mom had been pregnant three times, including carrying twins. If anyone was going to notice that I was showing, she would.

Laughter floated upstairs from the family room. Voices blended in conversation. I tiptoed over to the top of the stairs, and there they were—Mom. Dad. Payton. Zach.

Wait. Jillian and Geoff were missing. No Winston yipping like a white furry early warning system.

Good thing.

I positioned my purse in front of my stomach. I could have giggled—*almost*—as I intruded on the family game of Codenames.

"Hello, everyone."

"Johanna!" Mom smiled over her shoulder. "I was beginning to wonder if you were still coming today."

"I decided to do my grocery shopping. Wanted to get that out of the way before the workweek started."

"Do you have groceries in your car?" Mom met me as I was halfway down the stairs, initiating an awkward hug with the purse between us.

"No. I took them home first." I slipped past her. "Who's winning?"

"It's guys versus girls. Mom and I just beat Dad and Zach." Payton raised her hand in victory—and then waved. "Again."

"Nice. Very nice." I positioned myself behind Dad's lounge chair. This was some sort of game of hide-and-go-seek—and I most definitely did not want to be found. Not yet. Not before I was ready.

Payton tilted her head in a silent *"Well?"* but I ignored her unspoken question.

All in good time, Sister. All in good time.

"Where are Jillian and Geoff? I thought they'd be here, too."

Mom sat next to Dad again. "This was the weekend of Geoff's conference, remember? The one where he was teaching a workshop."

"That explains why she didn't answer when I called her yesterday."

Payton's comment unfurled some of the tightness in my chest. At least Jillian wasn't ignoring me. She was enjoying some time away with her husband. "She must have turned off her phone or something. She didn't answer my call on Friday, either."

"Your dad's disappointed we didn't get to take care of Winston."

"But it makes sense to let their neighbor take care of him . . . I guess."

"Dad, you need to get a dog." Payton grinned at her suggestion.

"Absolutely not."

"You keep saying that, Mom, but you're going to cave one of these days."

It was time for me to speak up, before everyone started discussing what type of dog Dad should get.

I dropped my purse, which landed on the floor by my feet with a soft thud. All I needed to do was move out from behind the chair. If I was old enough to have a baby, I was old enough to tell my parents.

"Mom, Dad, I wanted to talk to you about something."

"Yes?" Mom barely glanced up from the table, where she was laying the playing pieces back out in a grid.

"I'm pregnant." As I spoke, I stepped forward, providing visual proof positive of my words.

For several heartbeats, no one spoke. No one moved.

"Pregnant?" Mom's one-word response was anticlimactic. What had I expected? Tears? A scream? A protest?

"Yes. I'm going to have a baby. My due date is August 30."

"Johanna!"

I tried to decipher Mom's reaction from just the statement of my name, but I couldn't. "Are you angry?"

"I'm . . . I'm . . . I don't know what I am."

"You're surprised." Payton spoke up. "Like I was. Right, Mom?"

"You already knew?"

"Yes. I—I noticed Johanna wasn't feeling well and I started asking questions, so she had to tell me."

"And Jillian? Does she know, too?"

"She overheard Johanna and me talking a few weeks ago, so yes, she knows."

Payton was doing a beautiful job of handling all of Mom's questions.

"But if you're due in August . . . that means . . . you're already in your second trimester." Mom's eyes were clouded as she pieced together information. "Why didn't you tell us sooner?"

"I wasn't certain I was going to keep the baby."

"Johanna!" Again Mom blurted my name. "You're not thinking of giving the baby up for adoption."

"No. No, I'm not. I'm keeping the baby."

And that was an honest answer. Now.

First hide-and-seek. Then I'd played dodgeball with Mom, letting Payton step up and block for me. But now I was in the direct line of fire. I hadn't played dodgeball in decades. Not since elementary school. I'd been good at it back then. I'd survive today, too.

Neither Zach nor Dad had said anything. I didn't care about Zach. But Dad's silence pulled my attention to him.

I'd just told him he was going to be a grandfather . . . and I'd disappointed him.

"Dad? Nothing to say?"

"Jo, I haven't told you what to do for years. You're a grown woman. I'm not about to tell you what to do now." Dad sat with his hands resting on the game table. "If you've decided you want to have a baby, then I support your decision."

"What your father means is, we're happy if you're happy."

That was not what Dad had said. Not that I'd expected my parents to be excited. I'd hoped for something . . . maybe at least happy. But I'd told myself that I didn't need them to be supportive of this—or anything else I did.

I'd stopped needing their support for anything I did years ago.

Flat. The conversation reminded me of when someone sang flat. How the sound hurt and made me want to pull away.

Now Dad reached out and held Mom's hand. Payton held Zach's hand. If Jill were here, she'd be holding Geoff's hand.

Fine. I'd get used to holding no one's hand in a room full of couples. Soon enough, I'd be holding a baby.

In the background, the front door opened and the next moment, Winston came running downstairs, straight for Dad.

"Jill? Jillian, where are you?" Geoff's footsteps pounded on the stairs. He stood on the bottom step, staring at all of us. "Where is she?"

Payton spoke first. "What do you mean, 'Where is she?'"

"Where's Jill? Is she upstairs taking a nap?" He half turned as if he was determined to check the bedrooms.

"She's not here, Geoff." Mom's reply was soft.

"Not here?"

"No. She was with you all weekend. Why would you think she's here?"

"She didn't go with me to the conference. We had a . . . She decided to stay home. You all know how tired she is." He pulled a piece of paper from his back pocket and held it up, his hand shaking. "But when I got home, I found this note saying she needed to get away for a while. I assumed she came here."

My sister had run away from home and Geoff thought she'd come to Mom and Dad's. That made sense. Jillian wasn't the rebellious type.

Dad had scooped Winston into his arms, holding him close and ruffling his ears. And now I was jealous of a stupid dog. Stupid hormones.

I turned my attention back to Geoff. "When was the last time you saw Jillian? Talked to her?"

"I left for the conference on Thursday morning around eight o'clock. She was home then. We haven't talked since."

"And you weren't concerned about that?"

"No. To be honest, we had an argument before I left." His face flushed. "I figured she . . . we needed time to cool down."

"Do you usually not talk for—" I counted on my fingers—"four days?"

"That is none of our business, Johanna." Payton stepped in. "It's more important to figure out where Jillian is. She's not answering anyone's phone calls. I've called her. Johanna's called her. Geoff, you said you tried?"

"Yes, the last time was before I came over."

"Why don't I try to call her?" Mom spoke up.

And now Mom was going to work her Mom magic. Wouldn't be the first time. It was working already because Geoff didn't look ready to shred Jillian's note into pieces.

Who knows? Maybe I would possess some of that maternal magic once I had a baby. Not that I believed in magic.

Mom retrieved her cell phone from upstairs and we all gathered around as she called Jillian. The faint ring sounded even as Mom held the phone to her ear. No sense in asking her to put the conversation on speakerphone. She wouldn't.

"Hello, Jillian. It's Mom."

Oh, we should have insisted Mom let us all listen in.

"Are you okay?" Mom pressed her fingertips against her forehead. "I'm glad to hear that. I wondered because, well, Geoff's here. He thought you might have come to spend the weekend with Dad and me."

Mom went silent again as Jillian said something.

"I'll tell him you're fine—unless you want to tell him yourself. . . . No? Do you want me to tell him you'll be home soon?"

Mom gasped, her eyes widening.

"What's going on?" Geoff stepped forward, reaching for the phone. "Let me talk to her."

Mom turned away. "You don't want to . . . Yes. Okay. I'll tell him. Love you."

Payton and Zach moved closer to Geoff and Mom disconnected the phone call.

"Jillian is fine." Her voice wobbled. "She's with Harper."

"In *North Carolina?*" Geoff made it sound like North Carolina was in another galaxy.

"Yes."

"That can't be right. Why would she go all the way across the country?"

Geoff moved away from the rest of the family. Payton reached for him. Stopped. Touched the cross she wore—the one Pepper had given her. Was she praying? Did she even notice what she was doing? Maybe she treated the necklace the same way some people carried a rabbit's foot for luck or a four-leaf clover or a penny.

"Did she say why she was there?" Geoff tucked Jillian's note back in his pocket.

"She said you had argued, just like you already told us. Nothing specific." Mom rushed to reassure him of that. "She said she needed time to think."

"She needs to *think*, so she goes to visit Harper? That doesn't make any sense."

"Jillian's missed Harper since she moved to North Carolina. You know that, Geoff."

"This is not about missing Harper. She left because she was mad at me. What am I supposed to do now?"

"Give her some time." Now Payton was playing the voice of reason. "Give her the space she needs."

"I don't know Jillian anymore. She keeps pressuring me about having kids. Then she decides she believes in God. Then she decides she wants to adopt . . ." Geoff faltered to a stop.

"I know you're upset, Geoff." I had to stop him from saying anything more. "But Jillian's been through a lot."

"I've been through a lot, too." Geoff retrieved Winston. "I'm sorry I came by."

Mom stopped him from leaving by putting a hand on his arm. "Stay and have something to eat."

"I'm not hungry. And I still have to unpack. To get ready for work tomorrow."

"Geoff." I spoke up, not even sure what I was going to say when Geoff paused at the foot of the stairs. "I'll let you know if I hear from Jillian, but I doubt that I will. She's made it clear she doesn't want to talk to me."

My throat tightened with tears. Geoff and Jillian's happily ever after was unraveling in front of all of us. I wanted to believe in them. Needed to believe in them.

A few moments after the front door opened and shut, I bent and picked up my purse. "It's been a day."

Mom took a step toward me. "Are you going to stay for dinner?"

My entire body seemed weighted down, the aroma of chicken unpleasant. "No, I don't think so."

"Yes, you are." Payton spoke up.

"Really? You're going to boss me around now?"

"I was going to say please if you hadn't interrupted me, Johanna. Please stay for dinner. I know Mom and Dad probably have questions about your pregnancy."

"I don't know what I'm having yet." And I didn't want to spend the rest of the evening dodging questions, although I'd invited them by making the "I'm pregnant" announcement.

"Let's wait to talk until we all sit down." Mom led the way

upstairs, Dad following close behind her. "We're all a little shaky still, finding out Jill's in North Carolina."

"At least we know she's with Harper."

"There is that." Mom seemed relieved to know Jillian was with her best friend.

"I'm surprised Harper didn't tell her to come home."

"Maybe Harper thinks she should stay for a while." Payton paused in the doorway leading into the kitchen.

"That's not her decision to make."

"No, it's Jillian's." Payton's words were deliberate. "And I'm not going to argue with you tonight, Johanna. We know where our sister is. That she's safe. That's the most important thing. We can't fix things between her and Geoff. We need to remember that, too."

"Fine."

I wasn't letting Payton win. I was just accepting her refusal to argue. There was a difference.

The soft flutter inside my body happened again, causing me to stop. To wait and see if it returned. Nothing. I resisted the urge to touch the lower part of my abdomen. Couldn't mention it. Couldn't ask Mom. Not now, when everyone was so concerned about Jillian.

I might as well be alone in my house.

12

THANKS TO MY APPOINTMENT earlier this morning, I'd now had two ultrasounds—and they couldn't have been more different.

Weeks ago, Dr. Gray had caught me unawares, at a time when I had no plans to keep my baby. I'd tried not to listen to what she was saying, turning my face away from the ultrasound screen.

But that brief interaction had changed my mind. Changed my life.

This morning, the ultrasound lasted a good half hour, and I'd focused on everything the technician told me, thanking her for the photo of my baby's profile that would be added to the folder where I kept the ones I'd received during my first visit.

Now all I needed was for Dr. Gray to arrive and talk me through the ultrasound. It seemed like every time I checked my schedule, it was time for another appointment with my obstetrician. For someone who'd made a lousy first impression, I was seeing her more often than I saw my family.

She entered the exam room with a cordial smile. "Hello again, Johanna. How are you feeling today?"

"Good."

"Still dealing with nausea?"

"Not morning sickness so much anymore. Just odd cravings and a lot of food aversions. All of a sudden, I love citrus fruits and soft pretzels from the mall. And I miss drinking my French press."

"It may get better by the end of the second trimester, or it may not change at all until after the baby is born. But then, if you decide to breastfeed, you might want to consider staying off caffeine."

Breastfeed? No. That particular inconvenience was not happening.

Dr. Gray scanned my chart. "For the most part, everything looks good here. Your weight gain is a bit low, but that's probably because you dealt with extended morning sickness. I'm not too concerned. The baby's growing well."

"You said for the most part everything looks good. Did the ultrasound this morning show some sort of a problem?"

"The baby is fine. No abnormalities. But there is a partial placenta previa, where the placenta is partially covering your cervix."

My brain scrambled to process the information. The baby

136

was fine. Good. Placenta previa. Not good. "And that's an issue because . . . ?"

"At this time, it's only a potential issue. It could resolve on its own before your due date."

"And if it doesn't?" I forced myself to be calm, trying to ignore how my heart rate had increased as Dr. Gray and I discussed the finding.

"If it doesn't, then there's a risk of bleeding. You might need a C-section." Dr. Gray's body language was relaxed, her hands clasped in her lap. "It's something we'll continue to watch."

Now the fact I couldn't drink my French press was a minor complaint. The word *bleeding* scared me more than the idea of a C-section. It was as if I'd built a Jenga tower of all these little presuppositions of how my life would go. Live in Colorado. Be promoted. Marry Beckett. And someone kept pulling out the wooden pieces, shaking the stability of my tower.

Dr. Gray sat across from me, wearing her white medical coat with the practice's logo embroidered on the chest pocket. I wanted to be wearing a lab coat. To be the professional, not the patient.

I'd never considered how being pregnant would scratch up my facade of professionalism. Of control.

"What do I do to handle this issue?"

"Nothing, at this point." Dr. Gray shut her laptop with a gentle click. "As I said, we monitor your pregnancy. We'll do another ultrasound at thirty-two weeks. If you experience any bleeding, I need to know immediately. Don't stop and ask yourself, 'Should I call Dr. Gray?' The answer is yes. Don't think, 'If it's only a little bit of blood, do I need to call Dr. Gray?' The answer is yes. You bleed, you call me. Understood?"

Dr. Gray's relaxed demeanor had disappeared.

"Yes. I bleed, I call you."

"I'm not trying to scare you. Well, maybe I am, but only enough to get your attention. I'm hoping and praying the placenta previa resolves. I'm not worried."

"If you're not worried, then I'm not worried."

This was like being told I was going white-water rafting without a life vest. But not to worry because right now, the water was calm. We might not run into any rapids. There was nothing to worry about. Yet.

During the ultrasound this morning, the technician had never hinted there was a problem. She'd done her job well.

I would mimic the technician. No one else needed to know about this potential problem because nothing might ever come of it. No need for anyone else to have to do the mental "I'm not going to worry" dance.

"Are you interested in knowing what you're having?" Dr. Gray shifted in the rolling chair. "It's noted here in the chart."

"It is?"

"Yes. I'm sure the technician talked you through some of the ultrasound, correct?"

"Yes. She showed me the baby's face. We saw the baby swallow. The spinal column. The baby was very active. The technician said baby Thatcher looked healthy."

"I prefer to look at the ultrasound, too, before sharing the baby's gender prediction. And of course, some parents prefer not to know. Ultrasounds are amazingly specific these days, but even so, there are occasional surprises in the delivery room."

"Okay."

"Okay . . . you do want to know whether you're having a boy or a girl?"

"Yes. Yes, I do."

And now I held my breath. What if Dr. Gray's announcement disappointed me? It wasn't as if I could return the baby for a refund or exchange it for a different gender.

"Then I'm happy to tell you the ultrasound indicates you're having a daughter."

A daughter.

Another Thatcher girl.

It was as if I'd gotten a sneak peek of my Christmas present. I couldn't keep it—had to wrap it up and put it back in its hiding place. But I could admit to myself that I'd wanted a little girl. I knew girls. I could do a girl.

Even so, it wasn't like I was going to do a fun little gender reveal with balloons or pink booties or a certain color of cake and then post it on Instagram.

This wasn't that type of pregnancy.

"Do you have any other questions for me?"

"No. I'm good. And like you said, you're not worried, so I'm not worried." Although mentioning not being worried again probably contradicted my statement.

"Then my receptionist will schedule your next appointment for four weeks from now. If you need anything—"

"I won't."

"I'm sure you won't. But you know you can call the office. Or the nurse on call after hours. Go ahead and continue your normal exercise routine. You're taking your prenatal vitamins?"

"Yes."

We continued talking as we exited the exam room, allowing me to treat this as a routine appointment. Other women like me—moms-to-be—sat in the waiting room. Were they having sons or daughters? Did they know?

I was a mom-to-be of a little girl.

And now I had something else to share with my family.

My thoughts crowded with me into the elevator.

I needed to decide who in my family I was telling first.

Not Beckett. Why I even thought of him, I didn't know. The man didn't qualify as family.

Not Jillian. My sister probably wouldn't answer the phone if I called her. She didn't want to think about my pregnancy, much less celebrate the news that I was having a little girl.

I could tell my parents first. Then Payton and Zach. Not necessarily together. And then tell Jillian and Geoff whenever my sister decided she was tired of being a runaway. I hadn't realized my pregnancy—deciding to keep my baby—would fracture my relationship with the sister I was closest to.

I should have, though. I had what Jillian wanted. And I wouldn't give it to her.

I couldn't give it to her.

It was good to get out of that overcrowded elevator. Let the doors close on all those thoughts that made my head ache and my heart hurt.

I'd made a decision. My decision. I didn't need anyone's approval.

But there was a part of me that wanted my family to at least be happy for me. To be there for me.

Not that I would ever tell them so.

13

JILLIAN MISSED WINSTON whenever she saw a dog. And since dogs were allowed on the beaches in Duck, North Carolina, she'd see several a day during her walks along the shore. Winston would have loved to take a walk by the ocean—not that he'd get the chance. He was a Colorado dog, and a visit to the East Coast wasn't going to happen anytime soon.

The dark sand squelched beneath her feet, and Jillian and Harper were close enough to the ocean to allow the waves to tease their feet with cold touches every once and again. The lowering sun was turning the sky multiple shades of orange.

"Did you have a good day?"

"Yes." Harper released her hair from her scrunchie, shaking it out about her shoulders.

"Do you enjoy your job?"

"Yes. I mean, it's retail, not the same as working in the bank, but I like it. And everyone tells me it gets busier during tourist season. I'm not saying I'll work there forever, but for now I'm good."

"What do you think you'll do in the long run? Go back to a bank position?"

"I don't know. The banking industry is in flux—we both know that. I'm thinking about a career change. And I have to decide if I'm staying in North Carolina."

"You mean you'd leave the lovely town of Duck?"

"I happen to love this town. It's quaint. And the beaches are beautiful."

"I'm not arguing with you. I'm still getting used to the name, that's all. Why don't you come back to Colorado Springs?"

"Not an option, unless Trent and his new happy family decide to move. I doubt that's going to happen—not that I'm following him on social media."

"You could relocate somewhere else in Colorado. At least we'd be in the same state." Jillian raised her hands. "Just a thought. So what kind of career change?"

"I'm mulling. I have to be careful what I decide. I'm not a wealthy divorcée, which I think is a misleading cliché."

"You'll meet a guy . . ."

Harper stopped walking, forcing Jillian to stop, too, and face her. "I am not waiting for some guy to come along and solve all my problems. We both know that is not how it works when you're married."

Harper's words were as good as a bucket of salt water tossed over Jillian's head.

A breeze brushed Jillian's face. She tasted salt on her lips, just like she had last night after she'd cried herself to sleep. But she wasn't going to cry now. She could at least wait until she was alone in her bedroom.

"What did you do today, Jilly?" Harper started walking again, stepping out of the way of an older couple engrossed in a conversation with each other.

"This is my third walk along the beach. I should confess I've had just as many naps as I've had walks."

"I'm not your mother. I wasn't checking up on you."

"I still feel bad showing up like I did."

"It's fine. I'm glad you're here. You hardly eat a thing, so don't worry about my grocery bill." Harper shrugged. "My mother is charging me minimal rent, and only because I insisted I was a big girl, not a charity case."

"I didn't think how relaxing walking along the beach would be—almost as good as a nap."

"I envy you, those three walks a day. I took quite a few walks myself when I first came here. They're probably just what you need."

"That and being here with you."

"I'm at work most of the time."

"I'll take any time I can get with you, Harper." They shared a smile. "A girl needs her best friend."

"And a girl needs her husband, too."

Harper's words were more of a gentle nudge than a reproof. Almost a suggestion, an echo of the brush of her shoulder against Jillian's as they continued to walk along the beach.

A girl did need her husband, but that didn't mean her husband was there for her.

"Did you call Geoff today?"

"No."

"Why not?"

Jillian stared straight ahead. "He was at work."

"I'm certain he would have answered your phone call, Jilly."

"I'm not certain he would have."

"Is it that bad?"

"We're in one of those loops you can't get out of—what are they called? An infinite loop? We keep talking about the same thing over and over again. We can't settle anything."

"At least you're talking to one another. When you stop talking, stop trying, that's when you should worry. And you and Geoff love each other."

Now it was Jillian's turn to stop walking. "Harper, what happens when you love each other but you want different things?"

"You always go back to the fact that you love each other."

"Why do you say that?"

"Because I still remember the day Trent told me he didn't love me anymore. I couldn't fight that. Couldn't fix that."

"I'm sorry . . ."

"Oh, Jilly." Harper closed her eyes, her mouth twisting into the semblance of a smile. "I try to treat all of that like a story that happened to someone else, although there are days it still hurts like it happened to me. I can't do anything about how Trent and I ended up. Not anymore. But you and Geoff still love each other."

Harper hadn't asked if she and Geoff still loved each other. She told her that they did. And Jillian did love Geoff. And every day since Geoff had found out she was at Harper's, he'd texted her "I love you" in the morning and "I miss you" in the evening. She responded with a red heart emoji each time, a symbolic *"Me, too."*

But her heart ached with the unspoken question.

"I don't know if I want to keep loving Geoff."

"You don't mean that!"

The waves lapped around her feet. "I haven't said it out loud before, but I've thought it. It hurts so much to love him right now. We're so different from when we started dating. He never told me that he didn't want children. That he had two brothers."

"And you didn't know you had breast cancer. Or that you'd decide to believe in God."

"Those aren't secrets I kept from him, Harper."

"Still, you're not the woman Geoff thought he was marrying, either."

"I gave him the choice to leave me . . ."

"No. You told him to leave. He wanted to stay. And when you demanded that he leave, he came back." Harper reached for her hands, forcing her to stand still. "Geoff probably worried what you would do when you found out about his secrets."

"It's not the same thing." Jillian's attempt to stamp her foot failed. All she did was slosh water up her legs.

"It is. And it isn't." Harper paused. "One thing is for sure: you're teaching Geoff that you're a runner."

With every word she spoke, it was as if Harper were backing her into the surf, her feet unstable in the shifting sand. Jillian dug her toes in as the waves swirled around her ankles.

She shouldn't have come.

"I thought you'd understand." She twisted out of Harper's hold, turned, walking away from her best friend.

"Where are you going, Jilly? You're kind of stuck with me." Harper's words were tinged with laughter as she caught up with her. "And I do understand how tough marriage can be—even more than you know. Only one of us is divorced . . . so far. I'd rather you call Geoff and fight it out than let this silence build between you. You're welcome to stay with me. I hope you do. But talk to your husband, even if it's to tell him that you don't know what to tell him."

"You think that will make a difference? Telling him that I don't know what to say?"

"Yes. Saying something—anything—is better than silence because silence can be misinterpreted to mean all sorts of wrong, horrible things. Call him. You don't have to talk forever. Tell him that you're hurt. That you're confused."

"I've told him that."

"Then tell him again—and keep telling him until he hears you. Suggest counseling—" Harper raised her hand, stalling Jillian's protest—"and keep suggesting it if Geoff resists the idea. Sometimes I wished I'd pushed harder with Trent, but that's old news. And tell Geoff you love him, even if it's hard. Loving someone is hard. Saying it is hard."

"Are you considering going back to school to be a marital counselor?"

"Ha-ha. Very funny."

"I'm not kidding."

"I'm not a counselor. I'm your friend with a bit more life experience when it comes to marital struggles than you." Harper increased her pace. "Come on, let's go back so you can make that phone call."

Jillian didn't feel any more prepared to call Geoff. Her emotions were as turbulent as a whirlpool, no matter how Harper tried to calm them with her "do this, do that" suggestions.

Maybe she should pray. But what was she supposed to say? The only word that came to mind was a feeble and ineffective *Help.*

It was as if she'd left both her husband and her fledgling faith back in Colorado. Both Geoff and God were letting her down. Right now, Harper was the most trustworthy person in her life.

Despite Harper's insistence that she call Geoff, Jillian had managed to stall for time, insisting that they make shrimp scampi for dinner.

They cooked, ate, laughed. Avoidance tactics, all of it.

When she'd needed to study for midterms in college, there were times she'd gone to the bookstore and spent too much time—and too much money—on all sorts of supplies to help her prepare. Index cards. Highlighters. Yellow legal pads. And junk food, of course—back then she never imagined not having an appetite. Never imagined not worrying about her weight. Or having short hair. Or only one breast.

Now she was alone in Harper's guest bedroom, sent there by Harper, who insisted she'd do the cleanup from dinner. With the door shut for even more privacy, Jillian sat on the floor, her back against the bed, her knees drawn up to her chest. She gripped her phone, one of their wedding celebration photos gracing her lock screen. Through all the "What did Geoff just say?" moments of the last few months, the photograph had remained.

No matter what, she loved Geoff. Didn't she?

She wouldn't think about that.

She needed to figure out what to talk about.

She wouldn't tell Geoff that she was calling him because Harper talked her into it. Admitting that would not get their conversation off to a good start.

Her refusal to talk to him when Mom called stood between them, unexplained. Jillian could only hope there would come a time when she'd want to talk to Geoff again.

Hope. The word held no meaning for her anymore.

They needed to stick to the basics. His work. Her . . . nothing. She could tell him about North Carolina, but what with her disappearing like she had, he wouldn't want to hear about it. Winston. She could ask about Winston.

All she had to do was call her husband and talk about anything but the reasons she wasn't in Colorado.

Call him.

Now.

Geoff answered before the first ring ended. "Hello?"

How could she have forgotten how much she loved Geoff's voice?

"Geoff . . . hi."

"Jillian."

"Do you . . . do you have time to talk?"

"Sure."

Geoff had gone all single-syllable on her.

"I wanted to let you know I'm okay."

Not that he was asking.

"Your mother told me that."

"I'm sorry . . . sorry I didn't talk with you on Sunday."

"That's what you're apologizing for? That you didn't talk to me on Sunday?"

"Yes . . ."

"How about an apology for not being here when I got home after the conference? For running off to Harper's without telling me?"

"Will you only talk to me if I apologize to you?"

"Don't you think I deserve an apology?"

Jillian disconnected the call.

What had happened to the man behind the twice-daily texts? Their conversation might as well have been tele-prompted. Or Geoff should have held up cue cards. *Say this. Now say this.* Jillian gripped her phone—it was better than throwing it across the room. She didn't like Geoff very much right now. But then again, he probably didn't like her very much, either.

Her phone buzzed in her hand.

Geoff.

She did not have to answer. Did not want to answer.

But she would.

Geoff needed to know he didn't get to dictate the conversation.

She couldn't even say hello before Geoff started talking, his words fast. Clipped. "You hung up on me. You realize that, right?"

"Yes."

"What was that about? Were you trying to make a point or something?"

Geoff was probably waiting for her to say she was sorry. She wouldn't apologize, but she would be honest. "I was angry."

"You're always angry."

"That's not . . ." She started to protest but swallowed the words that were fueled with heat. "You're right. I am."

"Why are you angry all the time? You weren't when I first met you."

"That's a fair question. I could say I'm not the same person, but it's more than that." The bed frame scraped against her shoulders. "I'm trying to figure out how to speak up for myself. Sometimes it feels like the only way I can get other people's attention—make other people hear what I have to say—is by stomping my foot and raising my voice."

"I'm not other people, Jillian. I'm your husband." Geoff's breathing was labored, raspy, as if he was holding himself back from saying more. Forcing himself to speak low and calm.

She wanted to tell him being her husband didn't exempt him from being one of the "other people" she was talking about. She couldn't do that.

And she couldn't hang up on him because there was no guarantee Geoff would call back. Or that she would.

"What happened to wanting to have hope?" Geoff had continued talking. "What happened to wanting to have fun together?"

"Focusing on one word is a lot harder than I thought it would be. You can't manufacture hope just because you decide it's your word for the year."

"Are you even trying?"

The question stung. What did he think she did all day?

"Yes. I'm trying. Did you hear me say it's hard? Do you think I don't want to have hope? It's a lot easier to go for fun than it is to keep having hope when people . . . when life keeps disappointing you."

"I'm not having much fun either, Jillian." He didn't seem to pick up on how people were disappointing her.

"That is not my fault, Geoff."

"I didn't say it was." His sigh tugged at her heart. "I missed you while I was in Denver. I wish you had come with me."

His words were an unexpected admission in the midst of their sparring, as if he'd stepped back, dropped his guard, giving her the freedom to throw a punch. His voice had softened, lost its edge.

Jillian leaned forward as if she could get closer to Geoff, reach across the distance separating them. "I missed you, too. I miss you every day . . ."

"Then come home."

She pressed her lips together, holding back a sigh. "I—I'm not ready yet."

"I don't understand." He hesitated for a moment. "You are coming back, right?"

"Yes . . . of course I'm coming back."

"When?"

She had to be honest, even when she knew her words would hurt him. "I don't know."

"Jillian . . ."

"I know this trip wasn't planned, but I'm glad I'm here. It's good to see Harper. To talk with her."

"Don't you think you and I should be the ones who are talking?"

"That's part of the problem. We're not doing such a good job at that, are we?"

Silence stretched between them. "We're having a hard time talking, but that doesn't mean we quit, does it? I mean, you and Harper aren't the ones who need to figure things out."

"She reminds me of that, too." Once again, they were talking and not solving anything. "I'm not avoiding you."

"You're not? Then what are you doing, flying across the country to North Carolina while I'm in Denver?"

"I'm regrouping."

"Fine." Geoff's exhale ended on a growl. "Regroup."

She'd have to accept Geoff's one-word agreement for what it was—halfhearted at best.

"Gianna's still okay helping with Winston, right? You can always take him to my parents' if you need to."

"Gianna's fine helping out if I need her to."

Silence settled between them again. There was nothing more to say—not tonight, at least. She needed to end this and hope . . . hope for a better outcome next time. "I'll call again soon."

"Fine."

"I love you, Geoff." She could say the words, no matter how she felt.

"I love you, too."

"Thank you for understanding."

"I don't understand. You never asked if I understood."

With those words, his guard was back up, and so was hers. Her stilted repeat of "I love you" was a failed attempt to step closer as Geoff disconnected the call. Had he even heard her?

Jillian sat in the bedroom, her phone on the floor beside her. Nothing had been accomplished. She shouldn't be surprised. Or disappointed.

Well, Harper would be happy to know she'd called.

And her best friend would understand, even if Geoff didn't.

14

How HARD WAS IT to ask for prayer?

Almost impossible, since Payton and Zach were several weeks into the couples' Wednesday night Bible study and she still hadn't spoken up and shared a request.

If she did, it would mean she had to pray out loud like everyone else in the group. And she was not going to do that. Not until she knew certain things.

Did she say "Dear God"? Or "Our Father"? Or just "Jesus"? Did she have to say "amen" when she was done or "in Jesus' name"? And was there a time limit for praying? A minimum time to pray?

But then Payton kept hearing how prayer made a difference. Changed things. And she needed to change her attitude. It wasn't that she didn't pray. She was fine praying by herself—silently. Short, easy prayers. She was fine praying with Zach—letting him pray out loud and saying, "Amen" after he did. But praying out loud in a group of people she barely knew made her want to find a paper bag and breathe into it until she didn't feel like passing out.

"Any more prayer requests?" Paul glanced around the group.

It was now or never.

"Yes." She cleared her throat. "Yes. I have one."

"Sure, Payton. How can we pray for you?"

She ignored how Zach froze next to her, which was hard to do when she was clinging to his hand. He was probably stunned she'd asked for prayer. Everyone in the room was staring at her.

"I coach a girls' volleyball team. I think I mentioned that, right?"

Paul nodded, his pen poised over the notebook where he recorded the prayer requests each week.

"One of the girls—she plays back row, um, defense—" No one else except Zach understood what she was talking about. "Anyway . . . she has a really poor attitude. Every single practice. She complains about the other girls. Doesn't let me coach her. I'm getting frustrated with her."

"How can we pray?" Paul's pen remained motionless.

Oh. She hadn't said that yet.

"I guess, if you could pray that I would have patience—"

She'd barely gotten the word *patience* out of her mouth when Sharon exhaled a loud gasp and a "No!" that cut her off.

What had she said?

"Payton!"

"What?"

"You never pray for that!" The woman's perfectly made-up eyes widened, and she covered her mouth with her hand. Then Sharon burst out laughing.

And everyone else joined her—Zach included.

The joke—whatever it was—was on Payton. All she could do was wait for everyone to tell her what was so funny.

Zach tugged on her hand, a "Come on, laugh with us" gesture. But what was she laughing at?

She was clueless, and if she didn't do something fast, she was going to look like a poor sport.

She'd treat the situation like an imposing, taller middle staring at her through the net. Not let on she was intimidated. All she had to do was not back down, so she'd take a step closer. She didn't have to do anything crazy, like the one player who barked like a dog to try to distract opponents. That was annoying, not intimidating.

"Um, what unspoken rule did I break?"

"Sorry, Payton." Sharon gained control of her laughter. Barely. "It's just something Christians say."

"I'm kind of new to this. What do we say?"

"Never pray for patience . . . unless you want to be tested."

"Ah. Got it. If I pray for patience . . ."

"God's going to put you in tough situations so you can learn to be patient." Sharon's husband offered her an apologetic smile. "That's not really how it works. People just say that."

She nodded. "This is when I withdraw my prayer request, then?"

"Of course not." Sara spoke up. "I'll pray for you."

And when everyone else had shared their approved requests, Sara did just that, in her soft, pleasant voice that took away the sting of laughter and didn't seem to invite impending disaster.

Zach held Payton's hand and no one seemed to expect her to pray. And she didn't, because her courage waned at the thought of praying out loud and getting it wrong.

She'd face that opponent next time.

Maybe.

Once the study was over, she hurried Zach through the chitchat and out to their car.

"What's the rush? Why do we have to leave so soon?"

"I've got stuff to do, Zach. You know that."

"What stuff?" Her husband rested his hands on the steering wheel. "I thought you said you were caught up on things."

"I'm . . . tired, okay? Can we just go?" She clicked her seat belt in place, facing forward.

"Sure." He started the engine.

"Do we have to go back to the study?" Payton's shoulders slumped. So much for bravado.

"What?" Zach slid the car back into park.

"I was wondering if you wanted to keep going to the study. I mean, we're both busy with work and classes and I'm finishing up club season . . ."

"I'm enjoying the study. Aren't you?"

BETH K. VOGT

"I wasn't really looking for more homework, Zach."

"Paul and Sara don't worry too much about that. I mean, it helps being part of the discussion if you work through the chapter—"

"Some of those people in there know all the answers without even cracking open their Bible."

"So?"

"And Greta . . . I've seen her workbook and she hasn't written a single word in it, but she talks more than anybody in the room."

Zach laughed, waving away her complaint. "She's a PK."

"A what?"

"A PK. Preacher's kid. Of course she knows all this stuff. She was raised in the church."

PK. Yet another term she didn't know.

"Then there's Ethan, who spouts off Scripture after Scripture. I try to write them down, but . . ."

"Oh, Paul calls him a 'walking concordance.'"

"A what?"

"A concordance. You know, a book that lists verses topically. Although they have online concordances now."

"Oh."

How had she missed the memo that there was so much lingo when it came to being a Christian? So many terms to learn? She needed to make a personal dictionary in the Notes app on her phone.

She'd expected competition on the volleyball court, not at a Bible study.

The echo of Zach's laughter still lingered in the car, but

Payton struggled to laugh. It shouldn't matter so much. But it did.

Zach reached over and took her hand. "Is this why you don't talk at Bible study?"

"Noticed that, did you?"

"Yes, I noticed. I think everybody has noticed."

"It's not going to help that I got shot down the first time I ever shared a prayer request." Payton's face burned at the memory. "I'm not too inclined to ever ask for prayer again."

"But you laughed!"

"While I was being laughed at."

"Everybody was laughing. You joked about it, Payton."

"What was I supposed to do, Zach? Cry?" She offered a weak smile in the darkened car. "I'm still getting used to praying out loud with you. So even asking for prayer is uncomfortable for me. I was afraid it meant I had to pray out loud, too."

"That's not how it works."

"I don't know that." She resisted pulling her hand away and pouting. "Didn't you notice that I stumbled around when I started talking about volleyball? I realized no one else would understand, so I stopped talking about it."

"But this is a Bible study. We're going to have things like lingo and praying and . . ."

"I know. I know . . ."

It was like being a rookie again, and she hadn't been a beginner in so long. She'd forgotten what it was like to not know what to do.

And now everyone else was coming out of the house and heading to their cars.

"Drive." She motioned toward the keys dangling from the steering column. "Now."

"What?"

"Everyone is coming out. They're going to see us still sitting here and think we're arguing or that something is wrong . . ."

"Maybe they'll think we were making out." Zach's laugh was just wicked enough to make her blush.

"Like that's better?"

"Hey, we're newlyweds. I don't mind if they think that."

"Come on, Zach. Drive, please."

"Are we going to finish talking?"

"Yes."

Zach maneuvered the car away from the curb. "Do you really want to stop going to the Bible study?"

At last, she had her out.

"I don't want to go back." And then Payton remembered that she and Pepper had never been quitters when it came to competition on the court. Why should she be a quitter now? "But I will if you help me."

"You want me to do the homework for us?"

"No! I'm not a slacker or a cheater, Zach Gaines."

"That was a joke."

"Here's what I want. What I need." She took his hand, his skin warm against hers. "Tell me there was a time you didn't know all this."

"'This' being . . . ?"

"All the right things to say. All the right things to do."

"Of course I didn't." Zach squeezed her fingers, his words warmed with a smile. "And being a Christian doesn't mean knowing all the right things and saying all the right things."

"It feels that way sometimes."

"Let's go back to basics."

"What does that mean?"

Zach pulled over to the side of the road before leaving the neighborhood. Turned the car off. Leaned across, until his hand found the diamond cross necklace that rested against her skin.

"Why are you wearing this? To make Pepper happy? To make me happy?"

"No. You know I wouldn't be wearing it if that's what it was about."

His eyes searched hers in the darkness. "Tell me."

"I wear this because God proved to me that He was real. That He loved me."

"There you go."

"There I go . . . what?"

His smile eased the tension that had surrounded her heart. "When you get frustrated with all the lingo and how much everybody else knows, you go back to that. God loves you. All that other stuff—praying out loud and the Christianese—it's stuff, Payton. I think God chuckles at us and all our catchwords sometimes."

Zach knew her. And he always knew how to draw her back to the truth. He'd helped Payton believe in God, giving her time and space to find God in her own way. He wasn't going to let her forget and lose her way because she got tripped up by code words and what she did or didn't know.

Zach's fingertips grazed the skin along her collarbone as he let the necklace drop, causing tingles to course up along her neck. Then the back of his hand caressed the curve of her jaw.

"Interested in making out with me, Mrs. Gaines?" He offered Payton a seductive half grin.

"You are a silly man, Mr. Gaines." She leaned closer, brushing a soft kiss across his lips.

"I am completely serious."

"If you're serious, then take me home, sir, and prove it."

"I'm more than happy to do so, love. More than happy to do so."

15

ONLY A FEW OTHER staff members occupied the hospital cafeteria, but Axton and I chose a table near the artificial waterfall, providing a pleasant view and additional privacy, thanks to the soft murmur of the water among the well-tended foliage.

"I have to admit I'm getting used to these weekly early morning meetings, Axton."

"I noticed you let me buy you tea this morning." Axton sat across from me, enjoying his usual muffin and coffee.

"True. I suppose one day I'll be able to drink my French press again." I raised the white ceramic mug with the logo of a columbine on it. "Until then, tea it is."

"Does your admission also mean you've bought into the monthly birthday celebrations?"

"Do you want an honest answer?"

"I've come to expect nothing less than an honest answer from you, Johanna."

"I'll always be more of a Lone Ranger than you." I held my hand up before he could interrupt me. "But I also admit the staff enjoys them. I see the smiles. Hear the positive comments. See how they read the messages from their coworkers inside the birthday cards. Who buys them, by the way?"

"I confess, my wife buys them."

"Ah, your cover is blown. You're not the perfect boss, browsing the card aisle and selecting just the right one for each employee."

"No. Dot enjoys it too much for me to take that responsibility from her. We have quite a stash of birthday, anniversary, get well, and new baby cards." Axton tore the wrapper off his bran muffin. "When I mentioned we were meeting this morning, Dot brought up the idea of planning a baby shower for you again."

"No." I sputtered on my sip of tea. "I do not want a baby shower."

"You do realize you need things for this baby—"

"Yes, of course I do. I'll handle that. And now that you mention it, there are some things I wanted to talk to you about—besides a baby shower." I stirred my tea—a useless action, since I didn't add sugar or cream to it. "I talked with Rose in HR, and Colorado law allows for up to twelve weeks of maternity leave—unpaid, it turns out. However, the hospital offers six weeks of paid maternity leave for employees—"

"Which you plan on using."

"I plan on using that—at least. Maybe an additional six." I consulted the calendar on my phone. "Six weeks takes us into October. An additional six takes us to Thanksgiving. I could ease back in after that. I do plan on coming back to work, but I also plan to give myself—and my baby—time to adjust to all of this."

"You'll be looking into day care then?"

"Yes. I'm not sure how to do that yet. But I've got time to figure it out."

"I can ask Dot if she knows anyone who can give you any recommendations."

"I'd appreciate that." I took another sip of my tea, the swallow convincing me yet again that I'd never prefer tea leaves over coffee beans. And also giving me time to get used to the idea of accepting help from Axton's wife. Maybe if she helped me with finding day care, she'd abandon the idea of a baby shower. "I want you to know this pregnancy isn't going to affect my job—other than needing the maternity leave, that is."

"You don't have to tell me that." Axton raised his mug in a silent salute. "You haven't missed a day so far."

"I know getting the chemo pharmacy up and running is a prime objective."

"Yes. We'll be fine."

Was anybody watching this? Videotaping it, maybe? Axton and I were talking. Relaxed. Agreeing on things. My pregnancy wasn't going to interfere with work. If I believed in miracles, this would count as one. But I wasn't one of those Thatcher sisters.

Axton and I weren't best friends, but we were finding a way to work together at last.

"Excuse me, Johanna, Axton. I'm sorry to interrupt." Dr. Lerner's voice sounded behind me. "I thought I'd find you here. Colonel Sager was looking for Dr. Thatcher."

I choked on my tea, grabbing a napkin and covering my mouth before I spewed liquid on my boss.

Axton took the mug from my hand, setting it on the table between us. Rose to his feet, reaching out to shake Beckett's hand. "Colonel Sager, I'm Dr. Axton Miller."

"Dr. Miller, please call me Beckett."

Axton angled his body as if he were protecting me. "Beckett. Absolutely. Call me Axton."

I stood, clearing my throat. "Dr. Lerner, I'm sorry you had to come find us—"

"It's no problem."

Beckett stepped forward. "I was hoping we could talk—"

I held myself rigid. "I'm at work, as you can see. In a meeting."

"If you want to talk to Beckett, we can finish talking later, Johanna."

If I wanted to talk to Beckett. No, I didn't want to talk to him. In all the years we'd dated, he'd never once come to my work. It seemed Beckett had forgotten the "plenty of space" part of our relationship motto—not that the term *relationship* applied to us anymore.

Beckett must have anticipated my no, because he reached for my hand. "I won't be here long. Please, Johanna."

I pulled away from his touch, tucking my hand in my lab coat pocket. "Fine."

This was no better than being forced to play with the school bully because some teachers said you had to be nice to your classmates. All of them.

His last name—S-A-G-E-R—was spelled out on the uniform name tag on the shirt that he filled out so well. It didn't take much to recall his muscular build. I once thought I'd be Dr. Johanna Thatcher-Sager.

Not anymore. I was happy—determined to be happy—with who I was. With my future, which now included being a single mom. There was no need to prolong this unnecessary conversation.

As Dr. Lerner and Axton excused themselves, I forced myself to focus on Beckett. "What do you want?"

"It's nice to see you, too, Johanna." Beckett slid into the seat Axton had vacated.

"Please." I was tempted to stay standing, but that would be childish. I would sit and have an adult conversation with my ex-fiancé. "This is not about 'good morning' and 'how are you,' Beckett. What do you want?"

"Fine. We can skip the pleasantries. I want to be part of my child's life."

"We've already had this discussion. Not an option."

"I have rights as the baby's father."

"Only if your name is on the birth certificate." That

wasn't true, but it didn't sound as if Beckett had done his homework. Yet. Time to bluff.

"You're not going to put my name on the birth certificate?"

"There's no need to if I don't want you to pay child support. And I don't need you to." A warm thrill coursed through my body as I spoke those words aloud.

"What about what I want?"

"Our relationship was always about what you wanted, Beckett. I just didn't realize it."

"You're going to throw that in my face every time you see me?" Beckett glanced around the room as if to make sure no one else had heard what I'd said.

"Does that bother you?" I leaned back, assuming a relaxed posture. "We can solve that pretty easily. Stop showing up in my life."

"I might have agreed to that—before I found out you were pregnant."

"Since when did you become so paternal? Being a playboy hardly goes with wanting to be a good dad."

The quick hiss of Beckett's breath told me that my comment had found an unexpected mark. I'd tossed the words carelessly, like someone would drop a used match to the ground, not aware there was still heat, still a spark lingering.

For a moment, victory flared inside me, but then the darkening of his eyes, the tightening of his jaw, caused me to brace myself.

Beckett slammed his hand down on the smooth tabletop, seemingly ignorant that several people glanced our way as he leaned toward me. "Don't talk to me about fathers, Johanna."

His eyes narrowed. "And stop acting like you know all about me. Because you don't."

We stared at one another until Beckett put space between us—and I could breathe again.

"You can fight me all you want on this, but you won't win. I am this baby's father just as much as you are his mother. And I am not going to have my kid show up on my doorstep when he's eighteen and ask me where I've been all his life."

I was talking with a stranger. I'd seen laid-back Beckett. Seductive Beckett. Intense Beckett—when it came to his work in the Air Force. But I'd never seen threatening Beckett. "It's just like you to show up, confront me . . . and then assume this baby is a boy."

I gripped my hands beneath the table. When I was researching maternity leave, I should have done a more detailed search on paternity laws. But I still had time. And I was a fast learner.

"This has all been very interesting. Quite an unexpected start to my day." I rose to my feet, surprised that my knees shook a bit. Beckett didn't need to know he'd reduced me to a nervous cliché. "And now I need to go to work."

"We're not done talking."

"Yes, we are. You're the one who chose to show up here, unannounced."

"Like you'd answer a phone call."

"You're correct. I wouldn't answer a call from you. But that doesn't give you the right to intrude in my professional life and start demanding that I do what you want."

"Johanna, you know I'm only asking for what's fair and legal."

Beckett was wrong. I didn't know what was legal. But I was going to find out.

"I know you want what you want—now. But you're only here at the Air Force Academy for a few more months. And then who knows where you'll be stationed."

"I'll request a follow-on assignment at the academy. Or Schriever. Or Peterson."

"There's no guarantee—"

"Then I'll retire and stay here."

I gripped the back of the wooden chair I'd just vacated to maintain my balance. If I wasn't careful, I'd ruin my French manicure.

"All those times I asked you to get stationed here for us, to consider retiring here . . . and you never would. Now . . . now that I'm pregnant, you expect me to believe you'll give up your oh-so-important career for a baby?"

"Not *a* baby—our baby. My baby."

Beckett might as well have told me he was willing to take a vow of celibacy.

I wanted to laugh. To cry.

To smack his handsome face.

But I wouldn't let him know how much he'd hurt me. Again.

The muted ring of his phone diverted Beckett's attention and he started to reach for it but stopped.

"Oh, go ahead and take the call, Beckett." I backed away from the table. "I don't care who you talk to anymore—even, what was her name? Iris. It's none of my business."

"We're not done here—"

"Oh yes, we are. We're done. You just need to realize that."

And as his phone rang again, I retreated.

⸻

When I'd left Beckett, I'd planned on going to my office, not to the atrium.

My overwhelming desire was to get out of the cafeteria. To get away from Beckett and how the ring of his phone threw me all the way back to the day in my bedroom when Iris called and I found out he was cheating on me. Away from his proclamations about changing his life for a baby.

Our baby.

My baby.

All our years together, he'd refused again and again to move to Colorado. And now he was ready to move to the Springs. To get assigned here. Or to retire.

How noble of him.

After calling him every offensive name I could think of under my breath—and repeating a few of them for good measure—I found myself sitting on the piano bench. I unclenched my fists but couldn't bring myself to touch the keys. The last time I'd been here, I'd recorded a song for Payton. For her wedding. I'd told myself the decision was a onetime break of my vow to never go near a piano.

And yet, here I was.

Just like the year in college when I decided to stop eating carbs. I did fine, so long as I avoided any and all carbs. Chips. Bread. Cake. Mashed potatoes—and I loved mashed potatoes. I survived fine with a strict no-carb policy until I came home for Christmas and Mom set her traditional smashed potatoes on the table. I couldn't say no—didn't want to say no—and decided to have a dollop. And another. And another. And my no-carb decision was derailed for good.

I positioned my hands so the smooth keys were beneath my fingertips. Then I moved my hands back and forth, finding the notes to the song I'd created for Payton. The melody seemed to travel up my arms, easing the tightness in my shoulders and neck.

I allowed my fingers to keep moving along the keys. To recall songs I hadn't played in years. I tried not to mind that my playing wasn't flawless, urging my hands to find the right position, the right sense of rhythm the first time, despite my lack of practice, the years and years away from music.

I knew this. I knew this still.

And then . . . then I stopped.

Someone was watching me.

I opened my eyes. A woman about my age stood nearby. She smiled, motioning to the piano. "Keep playing, please."

I flexed my fingers and tucked my hands into my lap. "I'm not that good."

"Not that good? That was beautiful. I recognized most everything you played, but not the first song. What was it?"

"You were here the entire time?"

"Well, yes. You were enjoying yourself—and I assure you, the people walking by enjoyed it, too."

People walking by . . . Oh, this was getting worse and worse.

"If you tell me what the first song was, I can look for sheet music. I'd love to play it the next time I'm here."

"The next time . . . Are you here to play the piano?"

"Yes. I volunteer when I can."

I pushed the bench away from the piano, the scrape of the feet against the tile floor echoing in the silence. "Don't let me stop you."

Here I was, some kind of impostor, when this woman played the piano. She carried a worn leather satchel filled with tattered music books. How long had she been playing if she still needed sheet music?

That was none of my business. Just because she used sheet music didn't mean she wasn't talented.

"You work at the hospital, then?" She scanned my white lab coat.

"Yes, I'm a pharmacist." She wore a flowing dress, short hair covered in a tribal print wrap. No lab coat or name tag to indicate what she did for a living. "You?"

"I work in billing. And like I said, sometimes I come in and play the piano."

"Why?"

"Why? You mean, why do I volunteer? You can hear the piano from the billing section of the hospital. Sometimes the patients comment on how nice it is to have music in the hospital. You don't always get the best interactions with patients when you're discussing their bills." The woman smiled and shrugged. "But people always smile back at me when they see me playing the piano, and I'm not even that good."

"I see your point. People can get frustrated about their prescriptions, too."

"I bet you're nice to them anyway."

No, I wasn't. But I didn't need to admit that to this stranger.

"I'm Robyn, by the way."

"Robyn—hi. I'm Dr. . . . I'm Johanna. It's nice to meet you."

We clasped hands. Casual conversation after my confrontation with Beckett. Making an acquaintance in the atrium. Quite a difference from half an hour ago.

As Robyn turned, a small brooch pinned to the scarf around her neck glinted in the morning sunlight. There was something familiar about the gold oval design with a small center sapphire and pearls on the north, south, east, and west points.

I'd seen that brooch before.

"That's a lovely pin you're wearing."

"Oh, thank you." Robyn traced the outline of the pin with her fingertips. "It originally belonged to a close family friend."

"Really?"

"Yes, she was my momma's best friend. She taught me to play piano, too. I like to wear it when I play."

There was no doubt I'd heard her correctly, but I couldn't stop myself from repeating, "Your piano teacher owned that pin?"

"Yes."

Now I knew where I'd seen that brooch. My piano teacher had the same one. She wore it pinned to various flowing silk shawls during my lessons.

"What was your piano teacher's name?"

"Mrs. Davenport." Robyn arranged music on the piano.

Mrs. Davenport. Not Miss Felicia. Not the same person. Just look-alike pins. Maybe piano teachers liked this pin for some reason.

I thought I was having some sort of moment—a connection with my piano teacher—but it was a near miss. Nothing. Today didn't mean anything more than meeting Robyn-who-worked-in-billing.

I'd almost been pulled into the past. Almost.

What I needed was to be grounded in the present. Not steeped in sentiment, tripped up by seeing a silly brooch that had no significance.

"What's the name of that first song you were playing?" Robyn's question interrupted my mental battle.

"Oh, that. I . . . I composed that for my youngest sister's wedding in February. I never gave it an official title."

"You wrote that for your sister? You must be very close to her."

I couldn't stop the quick burst of laughter. "No, we're not. We argue all the time."

Our conversation probably made no sense to the other woman, but there was no explaining the Thatcher sisters to an outsider. Payton and I didn't understand each other, yet we were trying, in a stop-start-stop-start way, to become friends. To learn to like each other.

Echoes of the music signaled one of the few times we'd connected. I'd found a way to be kind to her. She'd accepted it.

"The song was lovely. It made me think of walking in the

woods. If you ever want to share the sheet music, you know where to find me."

"No sheet music." I tapped my temple. "It's all up here."

"Wow. You must put in a lot of practice time." Robyn motioned to the music she'd positioned on the piano. "Would you please ignore all this?"

"I haven't played in years. Today was an anomaly."

"Today was lovely. You should play more. I'm sure somebody, sometime, told you that you played beautifully."

Yes. I'd heard that before. Plenty of times.

I knew it was true. That I could, as Robyn and so many other people had told me, play beautifully. It just didn't matter anymore. I didn't care . . . because no one was listening.

It was time to go to work.

I said good-bye to Robyn as she took the seat I'd vacated.

"You played beautifully" was an echo from my past. A half echo.

"You play beautifully, especially for someone your age."

"This is amazing for such a young child."

"She has a gift."

"Yes, three years old is early for lessons, but not for your daughter."

The echoes seemed to crescendo and then go silent—a silence that spanned decades.

16

"DID WE HAVE SOMETHING planned for today?" Johanna skipped the usual greeting as she stepped back and motioned Payton into her house.

"It's ten o'clock on Saturday morning—the time we usually meet for book club."

"But we're not meeting for book club." Johanna shut the front door. "Why would we do that when Jillian is in North Carolina?"

"I got to thinking about that this morning." Payton handed her a to-go cup of tea, pretty certain she still favored that drink over coffee. "Here you go. Anyway, I thought we could FaceTime with Jillian this morning. Or Skype or Zoom or something."

"You bought me tea?" Johanna held the insulated cup away from her as if Payton might have handed her Mountain Dew.

"You haven't been drinking coffee, so, yes, I brought you tea." Payton let her purse slip from her shoulder, balancing her own cup.

"Thank you for this." Johanna wrapped both hands around the cup. "What would you have done if I wasn't home?"

"I don't know. I guess I would have enjoyed the tea and then gone shopping or something. But you are home, so let's call Jillian."

"Can I get something to eat first?"

"Sure. How about if I text Jillian while you do that and see if she's around?"

"Fine. Do you want something to eat? I'm going to make avocado toast."

"I'm fine, thanks."

Being here with Johanna was a little bit like navigating rough waters without a guide—that would have been Jillian's role—but they were managing fine so far. Johanna's smile seemed genuine when she accepted the tea, not guarded. This morning was going much better than the last time she'd caught Johanna off guard.

Johanna disappeared into the kitchen and Payton found her phone to text Jillian.

Good morning. Well, I guess it's afternoon out there.

Yes. Harper and I are eating lunch.

That's funny. Johanna is making herself breakfast.

What?

I'm at Johanna's. She's making avocado toast.

Are you in an alternate universe or something?

No. I surprised her. Showed up with tea.

So what else do you have planned?

We wanted to see if we could Skype with you. Today would be our book club day. No book chat. Just say hi.

Now?

We can wait. Why don't you and Harper eat lunch. Text when you're done.

Sounds good.

The aroma of toasted bread led Payton into the kitchen, where Johanna plated her breakfast.

"Did you get in touch with Jill?"

"Yes. We're on for Skyping after you eat breakfast and she's done with lunch." She sipped her drink. "I told her it's casual. No book chat."

"We are probably the only book club that never discusses books."

"We're consistent if nothing else."

"True."

"For the sake of the book club, tell me what your favorite book was when you were in elementary school."

Johanna led them into her dining room area, taking the seat at the head of the table. "I loved Pippi Longstocking."

"Pippi Longstocking? That's not what I expected." Payton settled into the chair next to her sister.

"What did you expect me to say?"

"I don't know. Nancy Drew or something like that. Maybe *Black Beauty*?"

"Nancy Drew was fine, but Pippi Longstocking? Her best friends were a monkey and a horse. And she was a little girl who lived by herself in a house."

Johanna might as well have said she wanted red hair. Or that she wanted a monkey for a pet. Finding this out didn't fit the sister Payton knew. But she also didn't look like the sister Payton thought she knew. Her face was clean of any makeup and she looked younger, more approachable, than the usual carefully made-up version of Johanna Thatcher.

What else didn't she know about Johanna? What was the best way to find out?

"Have you ever thought of getting a pet?"

"Me? No."

"Why not? It doesn't have to be a monkey or a horse. Something basic like a cat or a dog."

"My life doesn't allow for a pet, unless it's a betta fish or something. And I don't like the idea of coming home and finding a dead fish floating in the bowl. Had that happen once and that was enough for me."

"When? I don't remember ever having fish."

"We had fish once before you and Pepper were born. Jillian and I won these goldfish at a school carnival. We got up one morning and there they were, floating on their sides . . . *eeew*. Yeah. That's when I decided no fish."

"A cat then."

"I'm having a baby, remember? This is no time to get a pet."

"Cats are very independent."

"And babies are not. I'm fine." Johanna sliced into her toast, her lips tight. "We had goldfish. And then Mom had twins. All good."

"I know that's not true."

"What?"

"I know it wasn't all good when Pepper and I came along."

"*Pffft.*" She waved her fork in the air as if dismissing the conversation. "Drink your coffee—at least one of us can."

"No, tell me. You weren't an only child before we were born. What was the big deal about me and Pepper?"

"It was just . . . an adjustment. Things were settled before you and Pepper were born."

"You mean just the two of you—you and Jillian?" Maybe if she kept asking questions, she could understand her sister a little better.

"Exactly."

"Mom having twins wrecked the status quo, is that what you're saying?"

"Yes."

"And then we just had the invisible line."

Johanna paused, her fork and knife suspended above her food. "What do you mean?"

If Johanna was being honest, Payton would be honest, too. "You know—on one side you and Jillian. On the other side, me and Pepper."

"Are you saying I drew that line?"

"No. I don't know how it got there. It was just there. No one had to draw it."

Their casual conversation had turned a bend in the road and crossed over into dangerous territory, littered with emotional land mines.

Johanna was cutting her avocado toast to pieces, not eating a bite.

And Jillian wasn't here to step in and provide a buffer. She hadn't been doing much of that lately—and she probably didn't miss the responsibility of having to defuse the tension between Johanna and Payton.

Not that it was her duty to always save the Thatcher sisters.

The ring of Payton's cell disrupted the conversation, Jillian unwittingly playing her assigned role.

"Hey, Jillian. Hold on a second." Payton positioned the phone on its side, motioning Johanna to move her chair closer. "Can you see both of us?"

Jillian's smile seemed forced, as if she was determined to prove to them that she was fine. Happy. "Yes. We finished lunch and Harper went to run some errands, although I think she really left to give me some privacy. So I thought I'd go ahead and call."

"Great. Johanna's still eating . . ." There was no need to mention that they'd been trying to unravel the mystery of the invisible boundary line.

"No problem. How are you both doing?"

Johanna made a small signal off camera for Payton to talk first.

"Good. Um . . . Mom and Dad are talking to a couple of different contractors about the back deck. Even a basic design can be pricey, or so they tell me."

"It'll be fun to see what they decide to do."

Payton nodded. "Dad's gone down and gotten Winston a couple of days and brought him back to their house, but you probably already know that."

"No, I didn't."

"Geoff hasn't mentioned it?"

Jillian glanced away. "Geoff and I aren't talking much right now. We're giving each other some space."

Johanna leaned forward. "What is going on with you two?"

"What do you mean?"

"Is this some kind of trial separation or something?"

"No. It's just a . . . a break."

"What does that even mean? *A break?* Is that like a marital time-out? You've got a timer going or something?"

With each question, Johanna was turning their first conversation with Jillian into an inquisition. If Harper had still been there, she'd probably step up and defend Jillian—play referee for the Thatcher sisters.

"It means . . . it means life got a bit overwhelming in Colorado. Between Geoff not wanting children and you having a baby . . . I needed a little time away from everything."

"My having a baby isn't going to change, Jilly."

"I know."

"Are we all supposed to wait until you decide you want to come home and be part of the family again?"

"Johanna!" Payton sat up, jostling the table and knocking the phone over.

"What?" Johanna set the phone upright again. "I thought you wanted to talk with Jillian this morning."

"I suggested we chat. Let her know how much we miss her."

"I do miss her. She needs to come home."

"Oh, right. She's going to want to come home right now."

"She's an adult. We're all adults. Adults don't run away from home."

"Hello?" Jillian tapped on her phone, causing the screen to shake. "I'm right here. And thanks for the phone call. I'm going to sign off now."

Jillian disappeared from view. It was as good as slamming a door in their faces. There'd been a bit of false bravado in her voice even as she'd ended the call.

"You call that a conversation?" Payton set her phone aside.

"We were all talking, so yes, I do."

"Jillian hung up on us, thanks to you, Johanna."

"She needs to grow up and come home."

"You know what? I'm surprised she stayed on your side of the line for as long as she did."

"What?"

"That line that separated Pepper and me from you and Jillian. The way you treat her, I'm surprised Jillian stayed on your side for all those years."

"I treat her fine—"

"No, you don't. Jillian treats you great. She's probably too nice to people. And you don't even see it." Payton's eyes filled with tears. "Sometimes I wonder what kind of mother you're going to be."

"What is that supposed to mean?"

"Think about it, Johanna. Do you think being a mother is going to be any easier than having a relationship with your sisters?"

"I think it's time for you to go." Johanna remained seated.

"You're right." Payton should apologize for what she'd said. Apologize for showing up unannounced.

But she wouldn't. It was too late for apologies.

⌒

"Do you want to sit inside or outside?" Harper stepped back from the counter at the coffee shop area in the bookstore after placing their drink orders.

"Let's snag some of those chairs on the front porch if we can."

"Why don't you go ahead outside? I'll bring the drinks."

"Sure." A few moments later, Jillian settled into one of the wooden Adirondack chairs on the bookstore's front porch. Closed her eyes. Leaned her head back. Relaxed.

Correction. Tried to relax.

With the echoes of the conversation with Johanna and Payton just a few hours ago still on replay in her mind, there was no opportunity to rest.

But then again, she hadn't rested in so long.

What was the verse in the Bible about being weary and needing rest?

Come to Me . . . Come to Me . . .

She hadn't picked up her Bible in so long. How could she when she'd left it back in Colorado—had it already been three weeks ago? It wasn't that she didn't think about God. She just didn't know what to say to Him anymore. What to believe about Him. *If* she could believe in Him.

"You asleep?" Harper's voice jerked Jillian upright.

"You know me. I'm not much for sleeping."

"I was hoping maybe being at the beach would help with that. The sound of the ocean lulls me to sleep at night, so I was hoping it would work its sand and surf magic on you, too."

"Not so much, but I'm enjoying my time here. I love being near the ocean, and some nights I sit on the balcony when I can't sleep. That's nice. But I didn't leave my problems back in Colorado."

"Problems have a way of traveling with us."

"You found that out, too?"

"Yes and no." Harper adjusted her position in the chair, careful not to slosh her coffee. "It's nice to not worry about seeing Trent and his new wife when I go to the grocery store. It's nice not to run into people who knew me as Trent's wife—losing that identity, at least a little bit. But I still have to live with the reality that I'm divorced, even if no one else knows it."

"Even though reality doesn't change with a location, you like being here?"

"I do. It was the right choice for me to move here—but it was my choice. I thought about it for a while."

"As opposed to running away, you mean?"

Jillian heard herself echoing Johanna's words from this morning. But unlike Johanna, Harper wouldn't attack her— she was trustworthy and would simply say what she meant. Even now, she sat quietly and waited for Jillian to process, savoring her coffee as if this were a casual chat between two friends, not the reality that one of them was questioning her marriage.

"Can I ask you a question, Jilly?"

"Sure."

"I don't believe in God—you know that. And I'm not trying to talk you out of what you've chosen to believe."

"Okay." That odd, out-of-sync sensation between them returned.

"You said you decided to believe in God because you wanted more hope in your life, right?"

"Yes."

"Has it helped? Do you have more hope?"

Harper asked a fair question.

"I wish I could say I did." Jillian seemed to choke on the unspoken words. "No, I don't. It seems every time I grasp even the smallest bit of hope, it gets taken away from me."

"Then what's the use of believing in God?"

"You're asking out loud the questions I've been asking myself . . . and I don't know." Even admitting this much caused her heart to ache. "I guess I took a step forward—a giant step—and I'm afraid to go backward. Stepping toward God seemed so right at the time. As if I was going to finally understand who I was. If I walk away from this, I'm scared I'll lose myself again."

"But you're not any happier."

"No, I'm not." Every admission scraped her raw. "Because everything I keep asking for . . . I keep hearing no. And then Johanna gets pregnant. The thing I want so badly? Johanna gets it. What's that about? How can that make any sense?"

"Then what are you going to do?"

"I was hoping you would help me, Harper." Jillian half

turned to face her friend. "It's funny. Geoff's disappointed me. God's disappointed me. But I knew you would help me out."

"That's an awful lot to put on my shoulders. You know that, right?"

"You haven't let me down yet."

Harper paused, looking away for a moment as if weighing her words. "I do have one thing I want to say, if you'll let me."

"Go ahead."

"You and Geoff? You need to find the common ground between the two of you."

"I want children. He doesn't. How is there any common ground?"

"You're looking at it wrong, Jilly."

"I don't think so—"

"You asked for my help, so hear me out, okay? It's not about what you did or didn't know was going to happen before you married Geoff. Or what he did or didn't know about you before he married you. It's not about breast cancer. Or unknown brothers. Or babies. Or anything else that might happen." Harper set aside her coffee, her voice earnest. "That's not the common ground you stand on. You love him. He loves you. That's your common ground. And nothing else—*nothing else*—should ever come between you. It's not *if* you love Geoff or *if* he loves you. It's *since* you love Geoff and *since* he loves you—what are you going to do now?"

Harper finished talking and they both sat in silence as people entered and exited the quaint bookshop.

"Nothing to say?" Harper broke the silence first.

"No, I think you said it all."

"Are you mad?"

"No. Have we ever been mad at each other?" Jillian sipped her now-tepid coffee. "You gave me a lot to think about."

"Well, here's something else to think about." Harper leaned forward. "So far you've taught Geoff that you run when you're hurting, Jillian."

Her words made Jillian wince. "I heard you the first time you said that."

"Maybe it's time to teach him that you'll stay and fight for your marriage. Show him that you love him enough to fight for him."

Jillian swallowed another gulp of coffee, wishing she'd tossed the remnants in the nearby trash can instead.

"Are you mad at me now?" Harper reached out and touched Jillian's arm.

"No. I've been mad at so many people. Geoff. Johanna. Myself. Even God. I don't want to add you to the list."

"It's okay if you are."

"I'm not. I'm just . . . tired. And disappointed. And trying to figure out what to do next." She shook her cup, the liquid sloshing against the sides. "I thought choosing faith would mean more, not less."

"I don't know anything about faith, but could it be a different kind of *more* than what you expected?"

"How so?"

"Maybe you were hoping for one thing, but you're going to get something else?"

"Maybe. It's worth considering, right?" Jillian offered

Harper a small smile. "Look at you, encouraging me to believe in God."

"Hey, I'm encouraging you to stay with your husband. And your faith is important to you, too. I don't understand it. But if there is a God out there somewhere, never let it be said I convinced you to give up on Him."

"Hedging your bets?"

"This is about you, not me, Jillian."

"Right. Keep telling yourself that." Maybe, just maybe, both she and Harper would think differently about God in the months to come.

17

I DIDN'T LIKE THE MALL. Ever. Online shopping was easier. No crowds. No searching for a parking space. No lurking salespeople determined to ply me with clothes I didn't want to try on.

And Park Meadows mall on a Friday night? I'd rather show up at work on a Monday morning and be told the hospital's computer system wasn't working. The brief drive from work had been slowed down by a fender bender, and then I'd cruised the parking lot for a good five minutes in search of a parking space.

But tonight's visit was an unavoidable compromise. This was the most neutral location I could think of for a meeting with Beckett. Weaving in and out of the constant flow of people would definitely cut down on personal interaction with him.

"This is not quite what I had in mind when I asked to get together." Beckett stood a respectful two steps behind me as we rode the escalator down to the bottom level.

"We didn't have to meet at all." I tossed the words over my shoulder.

"I realize that. I just thought maybe we could have dinner."

"I told you I was not doing dinner with you." I stepped off the escalator, turning my back on the entrance to Dillard's. "If you want to talk, you can talk while we walk around the mall."

There was no need to tell him I'd come early and indulged in a soft pretzel topped with yellow mustard. It should hold me until after we were done, and then I'd get the baby a nice slice of Chocolate Tuxedo Cream cheesecake. Maybe visit the tea shop in the mall first. If I was going to be drinking tea for weeks to come, I needed to splurge on some new flavors.

"How are you feeling?"

"I'm fine."

"Everything's good with the pregnancy?"

I almost started to say it was none of his business, but after agreeing to meet with Beckett, it was implied I'd be willing to talk with him.

"Yes, the pregnancy is fine, too." Talking to him didn't mean he had to know everything. Dr. Gray wasn't concerned about the placenta previa, which meant I wasn't concerned. And this was probably going to be the last time I talked to

Beckett during my pregnancy, so there was no need to concern him, either.

The mall was crowded with teens, families, and an overwhelming number of couples. Holding hands. Laughing. Walking with their arms draped over each other's shoulders or around each other's waists.

There was no denying Beckett and I looked like a couple—married or not. We looked like a couple expecting a baby together. And we were, but we weren't *together*. This wasn't a fun night out where we'd shop for baby clothes, all the while talking about possible names. Beckett didn't even know I was having a girl.

His daughter.

Yet another couple passed by, the husband pushing a stroller. I caught a glimpse of a tiny face with bright eyes and chubby cheeks. The mom held the hand of a toddler who wore a pair of black cowboy boots and seemed determined to hop on one foot all the way through the mall.

I suppose mall visits with my little girl were in my future, unless I could convince her that shopping online was more fun.

"I didn't plan on having this conversation dodging a crowd." Beckett's voice tugged my attention back to him.

"What kind of conversation are you planning?" I stopped. Faced him, not caring that people had to go around us. "Because if it's a 'Let's try again' one, I can save you the words and both of us the time. Not going to happen."

Beckett shoved his hands in the pockets of his jeans. "You've made that clear, Johanna."

"Then what do you want?"

"To tell you that I've asked my boss to help me get a follow-on assignment here in the Springs."

"Why?" I could only hope Beckett heard all the "I don't care what you do" that I infused into that one word as I moved away from him.

"I told you why the last time we talked. I want to be involved in our baby's life. And I meant it."

"And I meant what I said, Beckett. We are not in a relationship—which means I'm raising this baby by myself."

"But you don't have to—"

"But I'm going to. There are plenty of single moms who raise happy, well-adjusted children."

"Don't tell me about kids being fine with a single parent. We both know a child does better with both parents."

"It depends on who the parents are."

For every time Beckett pushed to be involved with our . . . with *my* baby, I'd push back. Harder.

We passed a group of teen girls, laughing, talking. Happy. If I could, I'd tell them to stay away from boys. They weren't worth the trouble. But I needed to be courteous with Beckett—courteous, but firm—and then go home.

"Can we stop walking for a minute?" Beckett placed his hand on my arm.

I put distance between us. Again. "Fine."

We'd managed to stop at the center of the mall, near the display of faux rocks and foliage and water. Not as nice as the one at Mount Columbia, but it was a pretty spot in the middle of the enclosed mall.

Beckett stood with his back to the small pool of water. "I don't think I ever talked about my family much when we were together. About my parents' relationship."

"You mentioned your mom on occasion."

"My dad was career military. Marine. We weren't a typical military family." His lips twisted. "The first time my dad went overseas, my mom moved back to California with her parents. And after that, she just stayed. Said it was better for us."

"Your dad moved with the military—"

"And Mom and I lived with her parents. Eventually Mom and I got our own place, but only a few blocks from them."

"Your parents never divorced?"

"No. Never divorced. Never separated. They just lived apart more than they lived together." Beckett stared at his feet for a moment before continuing. "They both seemed happy that way, and I got used to my dad coming and going."

"They lived together some of the time?"

"When my dad had leave. Sometimes. Other times my mom went to visit him. Sometimes she took me, sometimes she left me with my grandparents. When I got old enough, I stayed by myself."

"They must have loved each other a lot, despite—"

"Sure. Right. Every kid wants to believe that about their parents. It doesn't make any sense now, you know? But that was my family. My normal. When I grew up, I joined the military. I kind of thought it would connect me and my dad." Beckett gave a brief laugh. "He told me that I joined the country club branch of the armed services."

"What an awful thing to say."

"Yeah, well, that was my dad. He didn't pull any punches." Beckett fisted his hands by his sides.

"But your dad's dead—you don't have to deal with him anymore, right?"

"Now that's a fun story." Beckett stared straight ahead as if mesmerized by the display of women's summer clothes in the store window across from us. "He died overseas when I was twenty-three. Nothing heroic. Choked on a chicken wing watching the Super Bowl."

"I'm sorry . . ."

Beckett dismissed my sympathy with a quick shake of his head. "Want to know the ironic thing? I'm his beneficiary—not my mom. I don't know if he wanted to help me out or just stick it to Mom after all those years she refused to be a good military wife. I've never touched his money. I'm doing fine on my own. I've invested it, and I give the interest to my mom."

I hadn't felt any sort of kinder, gentler emotion toward this man, who stood half turned away from me, in months. But this brief glimpse into his life made me wish I'd known more about him while we'd dated. Maybe I would have understood him more. Recognized our "No pressure and plenty of space" motto meant something different to Beckett than I'd realized. That in a sense, he was modeling what he grew up with.

And unknowingly, Beckett had proved my point because he knew what it was like to be raised by a single mom. He knew it could be done.

"I haven't asked you for any money, Beckett."

"I'm not offering you any, although, like I said, I've got it." Beckett straightened his shoulders. "I want this baby to have both parents involved in his . . . or her . . . their life."

"Beckett—"

"Hear me out. I know you love living in Colorado. I can get assigned here. Or retire here if the assignment doesn't work out. I can be near my child while he's growing up. I can do better than my dad did for me."

Beckett's words created a bitter taste in my mouth, causing me to draw away from him. "That's what this is, then? Proving something to yourself?"

"This is about being a dad. A good one. I'm not saying that I don't have a lot to learn. But I'm willing to try."

I'd never seen Beckett so earnest, but then again, was it all for show? All those years I'd asked him to move to Colorado and he'd never been willing to do it for me. If I couldn't trust him with my heart—to be there for me—how could I trust him to be there for our daughter?

He brushed the back of my hand with his fingertips and I jerked away. The man needed to remember he had no right to touch me.

This was a greater risk than before.

"I—I don't know, Beckett. This could get messy. What if I get married . . . or what if you do?"

"We'll deal with it one step at a time."

"I'd have to discuss this with a lawyer. And you don't get to decide how things go."

"I am the baby's father. We probably both need to talk to a lawyer—"

"If I say you can be involved in any way, then you have to agree this is not a fifty-fifty relationship."

"That's hardly fair."

"Don't talk to me about life not being fair, Beckett. Not after what you did to me."

"Stop throwing that in my face like it's some unforgivable sin."

"Maybe to me it is. Did you ever think of that?"

"Then why are we even talking?"

"I didn't plan on ever talking to you again. I didn't plan on getting pregnant—"

"Are you blaming that on me, too?"

Our conversation would be laughable if it wasn't so sad.

"We were two consenting adults, Beckett. I am not blaming either of us for this pregnancy." What a conversation to be having in the middle of a mall, while small children ran up to the water display, wanting to toss pennies into it. "Are you asking if I can forgive you for being unfaithful with I don't know how many women? No. No, I can't. I loved you, Beckett. Yes, I know we had a long-distance, long-term relationship. But I didn't mess around behind your back—and believe me, I could have."

At last, I was having the conversation I'd rehearsed in my head for weeks after breaking up with Beckett. Saying the words, as true as they were, gave me a brief sense of victory.

And then a petite brunette walked by. Took a second glance at Beckett. I'd been blind before, but now my eyes were wide-open. I didn't want to be in a relationship where I always second-guessed what a man was doing when he wasn't with me . . . and who he was doing it with.

"I'm done here."

"What? We're still talking."

"No, we're not. You've had your say. I get it. You want to be involved." I was already putting distance between us. "Go ahead and talk to a lawyer because I'll be doing the same thing."

⁓

For once, Jillian had fallen asleep at a reasonable hour—before midnight—and stayed asleep.

But now something . . . something had woken her up. What was it?

There.

Her phone lit up on the bedside table and buzzed again, Geoff's face on the screen. Jillian sat up, shoving her pillow away. "Hello?"

"Jill, did I wake you up?" Geoff whispered.

"It's one o'clock in the morning." Jillian rubbed her hand across her face, stifling a yawn.

"I know, but you haven't slept well in months, so I thought you might still be up."

He had a point.

"It's fine. Is something wrong? Is Winston okay?"

Winston? Had she just asked about Winston?

"Brian's here."

The name didn't register in her foggy brain. "Who?"

"My older brother. He showed up."

Geoff wasn't making any sense. She grabbed the pillow she'd shoved aside and snugged it close against her body.

"Your brother showed up? Where?"

"At our house."

"How did he find out where we live?" She smothered another yawn behind her hand.

"I didn't ask."

"What does he want?"

"He wants a relationship with me again. That's a direct quote."

"Oh, Geoff, what are you thinking?"

"What am I supposed to think? He walks out . . . disappears for years . . . and then shows up and wants to be brothers again. I don't think so."

"Has he contacted your parents?"

"No." Geoff's reply was muffled, as if he'd covered his face with his hand. "He said he wanted to see me first."

"How do you think they'll react?"

"My parents wrote off Brian years ago."

Geoff's mother . . . yes, she was a "This never happened" kind of person. Jillian still remembered their tense conversation on Christmas morning, when Jillian had tried to talk to Lilith about her lost sons. The woman had shut her down and shut her out.

There would be no welcome for the prodigal from either the parents or the brother.

The air-conditioning chilled her skin with an unwelcome caress.

More complications for them with the appearance of Brian. Something else she couldn't fix.

Common ground.

Maybe this wasn't about fixing anything, but about showing Geoff that she loved him.

"I'll be home as soon as I can figure out a flight."

"You're coming home?"

"Yes." This was right. "I'm coming home."

Geoff's exhale sounded as if he'd been holding his breath ever since she'd left for North Carolina.

Jillian tried to figure out what she needed to do next. "I'll start looking at flights right now."

"You don't have to do that. Get some sleep and look when you get up."

As if she'd get back to sleep now.

"I'll let you know as soon as I have my flight figured out."

"I'll meet you at the airport."

"Okay." Some detail—an important one—rose up in her mind. "Wait. My car's parked there, remember?"

"Oh. Right."

"Try and get some sleep, Geoff. I'll be home tomorrow . . . I mean, tonight or the next day . . ."

"Thank you. Thank you for coming home."

"Of course."

"I love you, Jilly."

"I love you, too."

No matter that she was thousands of miles away from Geoff, sitting half-asleep in Harper's condo. Not sure how she and Geoff were going to repair their relationship. The words were true. They had to be true. They were her first steps onto the common ground Harper had mentioned earlier.

Her open suitcase sat off to the side on the floor. She'd never unpacked. She could have put her clothes in the dresser. Made herself comfortable. Acted like she was staying.

But she'd known all along she wasn't.

It was time to return to her real life. It was time to go home.

Instead of packing, Jillian found herself sitting on the balcony in the dark. Storing up the whisper of the ocean against the sand. The scent of salt carried on the breeze.

At least, for a few hours more, she didn't have to be anyone. Geoff's wife. Johanna's sister. Payton's sister. She didn't even have to be a cancer survivor.

She could be just Jillian.

And for once, those two words didn't lash out against her sense of worth.

She was choosing the label. Choosing to be Jillian without anyone's expectations on her. Something shifted inside her, allowing her to be herself in a way she hadn't been before that moment. To like herself.

Could she bring that acceptance back home with her?

18

IT WAS TIME to figure out what I was going to do with the spare bedroom in my house.

Of course, it wasn't truly a question of what I was going to do with the space—it was more adjusting to the unexpected change of theme. "Nursery" had never been even a slight option for this room when I'd ignored it and concentrated on decorating the rest of the house. Each area in my house was well-thought-out—from the paint and the light fixtures to the furniture and any embellishments. All of it had required time, attention to detail, and a decent investment of money, too, so I took it slow. One room at a time. My guest bedroom had been relegated to last on my list because, well, I didn't entertain overnight visitors often—except for Beckett.

And there was no need to think about him.

I stood in the empty space located as far from my bedroom as possible. Not very practical to have the baby here and me all the way over on the other side of the house, but moving the location wasn't an option. I wasn't disrupting my study by changing it into a baby's room. This was why parents invested in baby monitors.

The decent-size room was a blank canvas. Four walls, a wood floor, one window, and a basic closet. All I had to do was determine . . . everything else.

I retrieved my laptop from my office and settled on the couch. I wasn't one of those women who spent hours on Pinterest. Days went by when I didn't even pin anything to the few boards I had created. But the site was probably the best place to peruse a variety of potential ideas for a baby nursery.

Girl nursery ideas was easy enough to type into the search engine. And then a myriad of images appeared. So many different approaches for how to decorate a baby girl's room.

I was not doing pink, even if my own bedroom had subtle touches of the color. If my daughter wanted pink, she could choose it for herself. Her room could be feminine without being pink.

I scrolled through different pins, waiting for something to appeal to me and my sense of style. Jungle theme. No. Alphabet. No. Floral . . . *hmmmmm*. Maybe soft-gray walls with white furniture. A sleek upholstered rocking chair. And botanical prints.

I created a board, adding items, imagining the finished

room blending with the rest of my home. It was time to make a list of items to purchase—maybe even figure out the specific rocking chair, crib, and dresser I wanted to order. No need to wait if I found what I wanted, even though I had plenty of time before my due date.

I'd narrowed my choices down to two cribs when my cell phone rang. Once again, Beckett managed to disrupt my concentration.

"Yes?"

"Hello to you, too."

"I'm busy, Beckett."

"And being busy means you don't have time to be polite?"

I didn't have time for Beckett's supposed sense of humor. "Hello. What do you want?"

"I called to tell you something."

I waited for the "something," but Beckett had gone quiet on me.

"Are we playing twenty questions now?"

"No. No twenty questions. I've got some news—"

"That you called to tell me. Right. I'm listening."

"I had a long talk with the academy superintendent today and there's no assignment available for me in the Springs."

So much for Beckett's plans to be around for the baby.

"I'm sorry—"

"Don't worry. I'm going to fix this."

"There's nothing you can do if there's no assignment—"

"We figured out another option."

"Beckett, you're not going to retire. That would be ridiculous to walk away from your retirement benefits."

Not that I cared about Beckett or his future.

"I'm doing an early-out option. The military is trying to get higher-paid officers out to cut the budget. I'll still get a retirement, just not the same as what I'd have received if I'd stayed in for the full twenty years."

And now I was supposed to say something. *Congratulations*. Or *thank you*. But I knew what this was about. The baby. And Beckett's father.

Not me. It was never about me.

"You plan to be unemployed?"

"Very funny, Johanna." Beckett didn't sound amused. "I'll be looking for another job—a civilian job—here in the Springs. There are plenty of those."

"Right. And what if you can't find a job?"

"Have a little faith in me, will you?"

I chose not to reply.

"You still there?"

"Like I said, Beckett, I'm busy. Thanks for the update. And good luck with the job search."

I didn't say good-bye. It didn't seem to matter how many times I said good-bye to him, the man always showed back up in my life. And this baby . . . my baby . . . our baby . . . guaranteed he wasn't going to stop trying to be involved in my life now and in the future, for years to come.

19

JILLIAN WAS HOME.

Sort of.

Arriving at the airport terminal in Denver still meant she faced a good hour and a half drive, once she retrieved her luggage.

But she was back in Colorado. The land of no humidity and an expansive view of the mountain range she had to remind herself to look up and see on a daily basis, instead of becoming immune to its beauty. The never-the-same-twice sunsets she took photos of with the camera on her phone.

She'd caught an early flight Monday morning, the best she could do on short notice. Exhaustion caused her to lag behind the other passengers as they exited the plane. To sit at the back of the shuttle to the terminal. To cling to the side of the escalator, allowing others to stride past her, shoulders jostling her, luggage banging against her legs.

Let everyone else be in a hurry.

She was just another traveler who was home at last. Or rushing to make a connecting flight.

How ironic. Making a connection. That's why she'd gone to Harper's in the first place—because she and Geoff weren't connecting.

Jillian used her thumb to twist her engagement ring back into place above her wedding band. She wasn't thinking about any of that now. Couldn't think about all the reasons she'd gone to North Carolina. She'd returned to Colorado to support Geoff.

As she reached the top of the escalator, a small crowd waited for the arriving passengers. A young mom with a toddler asleep on her shoulder. A man with a bouquet of daisies wrapped in cellophane. An elderly couple who waved at the young family with a trio of children right in front of her.

"Jill! Jillian!"

Someone here knew her?

Wait. She knew that voice.

"Geoff?"

"Welcome home." He waited at the edge of the long metal barrier that separated people from arriving passengers, a baseball cap adorned with the Colorado flag pulled low over his face.

Should she hug him? Wait for him to hug her?

Step onto common ground.

"I'm so surprised to see you here." She pushed past the tiredness wending its way through her body and wrapped her arms around her husband, inhaling his familiar scent. "I'm so glad you came."

There was no hesitation as he pulled her close against his chest. "Thank you for coming home."

Home. Yes. She was home.

"I'm glad I'm here. Glad to be back."

Everything in North Carolina had been new. Different. Fun, yes, but not familiar. Except for Harper. Geoff was where she belonged—her broken, imperfect body fit against his and she didn't have to make excuses.

Neither of them seemed in a hurry to break the embrace. They were content to stand there, in the middle of DIA, and hold on to each other. And maybe that was the point after all—to hold on to each other.

She needed to remember this moment.

Hold on more.

Let go less.

"You're not supposed to be here." Her words were muffled against Geoff's chest.

Geoff jerked back. Stepped away.

"No, I didn't mean it like that. I'm way overtired and so happy to see you. But I have a car parked here, remember? And now you have a car here . . ."

"No, I don't. I took an airport shuttle up."

And with the profession of that modern-day act of chivalry, Jillian pulled Geoff close again and kissed him, not caring that other passengers might be watching.

He tasted familiar and seemed willing to keep kissing her, his arms tightening around to hold her against him. Despite all the tension, all the misunderstanding, she'd missed this.

At last she pulled away, standing on tiptoe and burying her face in the curve of his neck. "Geoff, that's the sweetest thing you've ever done for me."

"I don't know if it's the sweetest thing . . ." His laugh was warm and low.

"It absolutely is! I was dreading the drive all the way back to the Springs by myself."

"And I didn't want to sit around waiting for you to get home. If I could have figured out a way to bring Winston along with me, I would have. But then I figured I would have had to fight him for your attention."

"You're probably right." She leaned into him as he put his arm around her waist and led her toward the baggage claim area.

"No carry-on?"

"No. One checked bag and my purse. I traveled light."

The urge to apologize rose up, but she swallowed it. Now was not the time to discuss why she'd left. Where she'd been. To try to unravel all the reasons she'd run away from home.

Jillian wished there were some way she could see the future. Not far into the distance, more like skipping a few pages in a book. She just wanted to be able to read ahead and see that everything ended up okay. Then she could go back and get through the tense parts, where the imaginary characters made wrong choices. Said wrong things. And had to live with the consequences.

But that's not how real life worked. There was no skipping ahead and going back. She could only live life forward.

Geoff was wearing a shirt she'd given him when they were first married. Was it intentional? Some sort of attempt to look nice for her when she got home? And was he second-guessing her actions and thoughts as much as she was his?

Their conversation was minimal until they were in the car, heading south to the Springs.

"Are you hungry?"

"No, I'm fine. Thanks for the bottle of water, though. North Carolina's so humid I almost forgot how dry it is here. Almost."

"If you're tired, you can close your eyes and rest until we get home."

She was tired, but the last thing she wanted to do was doze. "Tell me about Brian. I still can't believe your brother showed up after all these years."

Geoff navigated traffic, easing into the far-left lane. Light and shadow moved across his face. "I'm finding it hard to believe myself."

"Have you talked to him again?"

"No. He's called me and I'm not certain how he got my phone number. Texted once. I ignored it."

"Are you going to talk to him?"

"I don't know . . ." Geoff's words trailed off as if he was unsure what to say next. "After all these years, what's the point?"

Jillian twisted halfway to face him. "Is that how you really feel? You aren't curious about Brian at all—who he is, what he's like?"

"If he wanted a relationship with me, where has he been all this time?"

"Maybe he's been getting his life together so he could reconnect with you? With your parents?"

Geoff tossed her a quick glance, the sunlight glinting off his glasses. "Are you siding with Brian?"

"No. Not at all. I'm on your side."

She needed to find her place on the game board quickly or she'd end up back where she was before she left for North Carolina.

She could just see the edge of Geoff's wedding band as his hand sat on top of the steering wheel.

This was about common ground. She was going to find it and stand as close to Geoff as she possibly could.

"What about your parents?"

"I called them last night. Told them we'd be there tonight—I hope that's okay. I didn't mention Brian. They didn't say anything, so I don't think he's contacted them yet."

"You are going to tell them Brian's here, right?"

"Yes. But I think it's best if they hear it from me face-to-face. It's going to be a shock."

"What do you think they'll say?"

"You know my parents, Jill." Geoff shook his head. "They don't discuss the past. And they chose to shut Brian out of our lives—out of our family—when he left. That's not going to change."

Jillian had to agree with Geoff. His mother lived in the moment, and his father followed her lead. "How did you explain my being gone to your parents?"

Geoff hesitated. "I . . . I didn't."

"You didn't?"

"We don't talk often—you know that. I kept busy at work while you were gone."

"Do my parents know I'm home?"

"I figured you'd tell them."

"Payton and Johanna mentioned Dad has been taking Winston over to his house. I didn't know if . . ."

"No. Winston was home today."

This wasn't a problem. It was normal to have to catch up with someone after a trip. To find out what had happened and what hadn't happened. This conversation just required more tiptoeing around the nontopics of the day.

Jillian slipped her hand over Geoff's. Waited. A few seconds later, he turned his hand over so their palms met, fingers intertwined.

They wouldn't figure everything out during the drive from DIA to the Springs.

But she was home again—and that was the needed thing.

⌒

Jillian had never admitted to Geoff that she was uncomfortable at his parents' house—and she couldn't confess the truth tonight. If she did, he'd ask why. And she'd never told him about her conversation with his mother Christmas morning. The "I suggest we keep this between the two of us" exchange, where Lilith had instructed her to let things get back to normal.

"Normal," meaning Geoff's mother forgot about Brian,

her oldest son who'd run away from home, as well as Kyler, her youngest son who'd died.

"You were quiet on the drive over." Geoff squeezed her hand. "You okay?"

"Yes. Just tired. Do you think your parents will mind that we brought Winston? And that we didn't bring his kennel?" She snuggled the dog closer to her body as they climbed from the car.

"It'll be fine. We couldn't leave him at home your first day back. And he would just make a racket if we tried to put him in the kennel."

The Hennesseys' front door opened, causing Winston to perk up and give a soft bark. "Settle, boy. Settle."

"Geoff. Jillian. It's good to see you. It's been too long." Lilith's navy pants and white top looked brand-new, her hair styled just so. "You brought the dog, too. How nice."

Jillian found herself trying to decipher any hidden meanings to Geoff's mother's words. "It's been too long" could be an implication they should call or come by more often. And the way she said, "How nice" when she looked at Winston made it sound as if Winston were a mongrel. They should have left *the dog* at home.

Visiting Geoff's parents was so different from going to her own parents' home. She didn't know the rules. Couldn't pick up on the cues. And it was like stepping into a model home. If she didn't know Geoff's parents lived here, she'd find it difficult to believe anyone occupied the house. Room after room, for five thousand square feet, there was nothing out of place. It always appeared just dusted. Just vacuumed. Display ready.

Lilith stayed on one side of Geoff, as far away from Winston as possible.

It was too late now to make another decision, to excuse herself and take Winston back home. They'd have to make the best of it.

"Why don't we put the dog—"

"Winston."

"Yes. Winston." Lilith's smile, if Jillian could call the slight curve of her lips that, was tight. "Why don't you put Winston in the backyard? We're having appetizers on the enclosed patio, so you can keep an eye on him."

"That's fine, isn't it, Jill?"

"Absolutely. Winston will enjoy running around."

"He doesn't dig, does he?"

Had Geoff's mother forgotten Winston had been there last Christmas? He hadn't dug up anything. Chewed anything. Climbed on anything.

"Jillian?"

"I'm sorry. Winston's not a digger." And if he made a mess, she'd make certain to clean it up before they left.

"Is Dad on the patio?"

"Yes. Go ahead and get the dog settled. Use the side gate off the garage. We'll see you in just a moment."

It was as if they were being shown to the rear entrance into the house.

"I can take him, Jill."

"I'll go with you." Jillian tightened her arms around Winston, lowering her voice as Geoff's mom disappeared. "I forgot your mother isn't much of a dog person."

"We'll be fine once we get Winston settled. Plus, we'll be able to focus while we tell them about Brian."

Winston was happy to romp in the yard, and they were ready to join Geoff's parents on the patio within a few moments, Geoff leading the way. But he stopped just inside the door, causing Jillian to collide against his back.

"Geoff? What's going—?"

"What is he doing here?" Geoff's shoulders tensed beneath her hands.

Jillian moved to the side. Who was Geoff talking about?

"We invited him to join us for dinner, Geoff." His mother's voice was smooth.

"You said you were going to talk to me first, Brian."

"I was. But you never returned my messages. I got tired of waiting." Across the room stood a man the same height as Geoff, with a similar build as their father. He wore a leather bomber jacket over a gray T-shirt and dark jeans.

"Geoff?" Jillian slipped her hand into his, coming to stand beside him.

"Jillian. This is our oldest son, Brian." Lilith made the introductions as if meeting her long-absent son was simple. Uncomplicated. "Brian, this is Geoff's wife, Jillian."

Geoff stood silent.

"Brian."

"It's nice to meet you, Jillian. Maybe the next time I come to Colorado, I'll bring my wife and kids."

What was the proper response in the midst of this charade? Should she be pleasant, like Lilith wanted? Keep the peace? "That would be nice."

"The next time you come?" Geoff released her hand, advancing into the room. "What is going on here?"

"Nothing's going on." Brian's relaxed demeanor was in direct contrast to the tension sparking off Geoff. "I thought it best not to bring my family with me this time, but I'd like you to meet Jenny and our kids."

"I don't think so."

"That's not your call, is it, little brother?" Brian's laid-back demeanor slipped. "Mom's already said she'd like to meet my family."

"What is it that you want, huh? Really?"

"Stop it. Both of you." Lilith's words were iced. "I am not going to tolerate some sort of childish brawl in my house. You are both adults and I expect you to behave like it."

The two men hadn't squared off like middle schoolers on the playground, ready to throw punches, but animosity simmered between them. Meanwhile, Geoff's father hadn't spoken a word, standing by the bar, seeming to prefer to watch over the array of appetizers, letting his wife referee.

Jillian could speak up. She'd had more involvement with the Hennessey family than Brian had in recent years. But before she could say anything, Geoff's mother gathered the reins in her hands again.

"Your brother contacted us, Geoff, and we invited him here." Lilith stood between the two brothers. "He says he's changed. Fine. He's changed."

"Just like that?" Geoff never took his gaze off Brian.

"No. Not just like that." Brian spoke up. "I know I'm the one who hurt the family by running away. I'm the one who refused the help that was offered me years ago—help that was offered more than once. It wasn't until I was twenty-five that I finally got my act together. I'd be happy to tell you my story—"

"That's not necessary." Lilith interrupted Brian's offer like an established student cutting in line on the new kid the first day of school. "We're glad to hear you've changed your life. Put your mistakes behind you."

"Yes. Welcome home." At last, their father spoke up. "Would you like a drink?"

Brian turned toward his father. "If you have club soda with lime, yes. I don't drink alcohol."

"I can manage that."

"Where do you live, Brian?" Jillian opted to ask an easy, neutral question.

"In Minnesota."

"And you're married?"

"Yes. Jenny and I met in our early twenties, but we didn't get married until I was twenty-eight. We have a son and a daughter. Mallory is four, and Jason is one."

Apparently Geoff was the only Hennessey brother who didn't want to have children because of the family's past.

But that wasn't the topic of discussion for tonight.

"What do you do?"

"Jenny does day care out of our home. I'm a mechanic. I hope to eventually open my own shop."

This was more awkward than the worst first date ever. Jillian fought to keep a conversation going—she'd ask a question, Brian would answer, and then there would be dead air. No one else seemed to care enough to engage, to join in, to find out anything about him.

Geoff stood beside her, stiff and silent. Felix remained in place by the bar, intent on pouring Brian's club soda. And through it all, Lilith reigned supreme, declaring everything fine and good, and that it would continue so until she decided otherwise.

Brian seemed unaffected by the family conflict swirling around them. He answered her questions, maintaining a relaxed posture.

By stepping into the middle of the Hennessey family's drama, Jillian was reprising her designated role—the role she knew best.

But if she didn't do it, who would?

As Lilith encouraged Brian to try some of the shrimp or the caprese skewers, Jillian focused on Geoff. "Do you want to stay?"

"Are you kidding me? No. I didn't come here to see him."

Now wasn't the time to ask Geoff why he wasn't willing to give his brother a chance. Why he couldn't at least try to be happy his brother wanted to be a part of the family again.

"Then let's leave."

"We can't—"

"Yes. We can. Go get Winston. I'll tell your parents we're leaving."

"I can't ask you to do that."

"I'm *offering* to do this, Geoff. We're family. We take care of each other. Your parents shouldn't have put you in this situation." Jillian gave him a quick kiss before nudging him toward the backyard. "Go. Get Winston. I'll meet you at the car."

But as Geoff disappeared, Jillian's bravado faded.

"Geoff and I are going to excuse ourselves from dinner." She pressed her hands together, cleared her throat, and chose to focus on Felix, the noncombatant, rather than face Lilith. Or Brian. "I know it's abrupt, but I think we can all agree this is a bit uncomfortable for everyone, especially since Geoff didn't realize Brian would be here. We need to figure out how Geoff . . . how we want to proceed."

Jillian escaped from the porch, allowing herself to exhale when Geoff's mother remained behind. She fast-walked to the front door, whirling around when someone touched her shoulder.

Brian caught her by the arm, stopping her from stumbling. "Whoa, there. Didn't mean to startle you."

"It's okay. I thought you might be Lilith."

"Just me." Brian chose to ignore any implications about his mother. "I wanted to apologize for upsetting Geoff. I realize I shouldn't have tried to force his hand. Shouldn't have tried to get him to talk to me if he wasn't ready."

"It wasn't the best move." She rubbed her hands up and down her arms. "He may be younger than you, but he's not a little kid anymore. You two are going to have to figure out who you are—as adults."

"You're right." Brian paused, then offered her a smile. "I'll let you go, but I hope this isn't the last time I see you."

"I—I don't know about that." She wanted to like Geoff's brother, but her loyalty was to her husband. "I should tell you that if I have to choose sides, I'm going to choose Geoff."

Brian took a step back. "Understood. Jenny would do the same thing for me."

Geoff occupied the front passenger seat, his face buried in the scruff of Winston's neck. Jillian slid into the car. Shut the door.

"I'm sorry." Geoff leaned back against the seat as she started the car.

"No apology needed. I didn't want to stay."

"Did anyone say anything?"

"Your mom and dad? No. Brian apologized for forcing your hand."

"Brian—!" Geoff muttered something under his breath.

"You don't believe him?"

"I don't *know* him. I don't know what to believe."

"Can you give him a chance?"

"So many years of our family without him . . . and now we're supposed to just welcome him back in? No questions asked?"

"That's your mother's way of doing things. You can decide differently. You can ask questions."

"I wouldn't know where to start." Geoff closed his eyes as Winston settled in his lap.

"Maybe you start with 'What have you been doing since I saw you last?'"

"Maybe." He glanced over, offering her a smile. "Thank you."

"For what?"

"For being the brave one tonight."

"Me? I didn't do anything so courageous."

"I know it's not easy with my parents. And then they added Brian into the equation like some unknown variable. But you didn't let it stop you from being you. Kind. Considerate." Geoff's tone softened. "That's one of the first things I noticed about you, Jill. One of the things I've always loved about you—how kind you are toward other people."

"Geoff—"

"No matter what else happens, no matter how you change, I can always trust your kindness will be there."

Jillian wanted to lean into Geoff's words, accept them for the encouragement they were. But they stung just a bit, intertwined with the rebuke that she'd changed.

But then, of course, she had changed. She'd wanted to change. Needed to change.

And Geoff had changed, too.

Jillian forced herself to keep smiling at Geoff. To reach for his hand for a quick moment of connection as she remembered the words *common ground*.

It was her. Geoff. And Winston. Going home.

And they were worth fighting for.

20

THANKS TO THE EPISODE with Brian, neither Jillian nor Geoff was sleeping well. Winston? Winston was happy. While she was at Harper's, Geoff had stopped putting him in his kennel at night. His new favorite place was beneath the blankets, his furry little body nestled right between the two of them.

When she woke up in the middle of the night on Tuesday, Geoff was already lying awake beside her, staring at the ceiling, arms tucked beneath his head. But when she asked him what he was thinking about, his answer was always the same.

"Nothing worth talking about."

Jillian knew what kept him awake, of course. But she wanted him to talk to her. To tell her what he was thinking.

She could only hope tonight wouldn't be a repeat of last night, but today—right now—she'd get outside and enjoy the clear blue skies and light breeze.

"Come on, Winnie. Let's go for a walk. And then we'll come back home and take a nap. How's that sound?" Of course, the dog had to stop dancing around so she could get the leash attached to his collar. "Settle down or I'll skip the walk and just go for the nap."

She'd walk. Think. Maybe talk to God. Even though she hadn't done that in weeks, He would listen to her. Maybe she could ask God to help her. Help Geoff.

Or maybe she'd just walk. Not think. Not pray. Just walk, one way and then the other, and celebrate that small accomplishment.

But when she opened the front door, all her maybes stalled out.

Geoff's brother stood on the other side.

His appearance couldn't be considered some bizarre answer to prayer because she hadn't had a chance to pray. He was just there—an unexpected guest. Not that she was inviting Brian Hennessey into her house. There would be no explaining that to Geoff this evening.

Brian didn't wear glasses or a baseball hat like Geoff, so it was easy to see he had the same color eyes as his brother.

She shouldn't be curious about Brian, but she was. He was someone she never thought she'd meet. One of her husband's long-lost brothers. And now he stood a few feet from her.

Brian broke the silence, offering her a smile that displayed slightly crooked top teeth. Only one of the Hennessey brothers had the benefit of orthodontia. "I'm sorry I didn't call, but I—"

Jillian held up her hand, interrupting his apology. "You don't have to explain. If you called Geoff, he wouldn't answer."

"No, what I meant was I didn't know your phone number."

Jillian shushed Winston, who'd started to bark the minute Brian started talking. "*My* phone number?"

"I was hoping to talk to you. Not Geoff." He shrugged as if he knew he should apologize but wasn't going to.

"I was taking my dog for a walk." Jillian motioned to where Winston sat by her feet. "This is Winston."

"Great." Brian took a step back. "I'd be up for a walk, if that's okay."

Yes. No. It was just a walk. It wouldn't hurt to listen to what he had to say.

"Sure. I don't see why not." She just had to ignore the image of Geoff shaking his head no.

"Lead the way."

Jillian tugged on Winston's leash, urging him outside so she could shut the door. "I should remind you that, whatever you have to say, I'm on my husband's side."

"I haven't forgotten whose side you're on." Brian fell into step beside her.

"I want to be honest with you, in case you're here to try and sway my opinion of you or the situation."

"Fair enough."

She'd drawn an invisible, but still vital, line in the sand. She and Geoff on one side. Brian on the other side.

Winston, the traitor, wanted to be friends with Brian.

He sniffed around his feet and then yipped, demanding attention.

And if she was going to be completely honest with Brian—which she wasn't—she'd have to tell him that Geoff wasn't talking to her. Ever since they'd come home from his parents', he'd pulled away, retreated into his own thoughts. Shut her out. Right now, Brian was the only Hennessey brother who cared enough to have a conversation with her.

"I'm surprised you're still in town."

"If Jenny were here, she'd tell you that I'm stubborn. That when I set my mind to something, I don't like to give up. But I'm not just a mechanic. I'm also part owner of the shop, so I have more flexibility when it comes to taking some time off." Brian offered her a smile. "And my wife knew how important this was to me."

"She knows it's not going well?"

"Yeah. I've reconnected with a few high school friends, so the time hasn't been a total waste. Seems I'm not the only one who's changed since then." Brian paused for a moment. "I guess you know the story about how I was the rebellious son."

"That's about all I know." She'd keep her explanation simple. "Geoff and I have only been married a couple of years. A lot happened during that time, including finding out about you and Kyler."

"Kyler. Yeah." Brian glanced away, rubbing the back of his neck. "Now he deserved so much more than he got out of life."

"You and Geoff agree about that." Jillian pulled Winston

out of a yard. "I'm sorry to say I don't know much about you, Brian. I'm still learning about my husband."

"Kyler was a good kid. Geoff? Good kid. Me? Not a good kid. If there was trouble, I was going to find it. If there wasn't trouble, I'd make it. I ran away from home because, well, it seemed like the next thing to do when it came to breaking the rules and throwing my actions in my parents' faces."

"I heard you tried to keep in touch with the family." The breeze lifted the soft fringe of bangs off her forehead.

"For a while, yeah. But that didn't go over well. It's easy enough to figure out my mother, Jillian. You do things her way, or you're uninvited to her life. Dad learned that early on in their marriage. I never learned." Brian's tone darkened. "My drug of choice? Alcohol. I didn't mess with anything else, believe it or not. But alcohol—beer, wine, whiskey, whatever—was enough to wreck my life for a lot of years. Some years I was a functioning alcoholic. Some years I wasn't."

"But now . . ."

"Now I'm a recovering alcoholic. Always will be. If I forget that part of my story, Jenny has promised to remind me. And I have a close group of friends who hold me accountable."

"Jenny sounds like she's good for you." Jillian ducked under a low-hanging tree branch while Brian stepped off the curb and into the street, keeping pace with her.

"She is. We're good together. She knew me at my worst and loved me in spite of it. Believed there was more to me than all of that even when I didn't. I would love to say I sobered up for her, but I didn't. I learned you can only sober up for yourself."

Jillian checked her phone, where she'd marked the house's location so she could always find her way back to where she wanted to be. To home. Brian didn't need to know she could get lost on a simple, short walk.

"Everything okay?"

"Yes, I'm fine." She tucked her phone back in her pocket. "I was just checking something. All good."

"To sum it up, mine is basically an 'I once was lost, but now I'm found' story."

"Interesting choice of words."

He nodded but didn't say anything more. "Look, you've been honest with me. I'll be honest with you. I came here today because I wanted to ask if you'd talk to Geoff about meeting with me for coffee or breakfast or lunch. Just to talk. I don't even know what my brother's favorite meal is."

"I can't convince Geoff to do anything he doesn't want to do." And Brian couldn't begin to guess all the hidden layers of that statement.

"I'm not asking you to convince him. I remember what you said earlier—you're on Geoff's side."

"Nice to know you were listening."

Brian rejoined her on the sidewalk. "All I'd like is for you to ask Geoff to meet with me so we can talk. That's it."

"Do you blame Geoff for not trusting you?"

"No. I don't. But he's not trusting who I was years ago. He doesn't know me now. I'd like another chance."

Jillian understood wanting another chance. Longing for something different. Longing to be someone different. Brian wanted a chance to be someone else. Wanted to prove to Geoff that he was someone other than who his family thought he was.

She understood because she'd wanted that, too.

There was no urgency in his voice. No defensiveness. He'd merely stated his request. And waited. He didn't hide his past. He was approachable and open about what he wanted.

Jillian stopped walking, Winston coming to a halt beside her and dropping to a sit. "Do you mind if we head back?"

"Your call. You know where we're going."

"Nice of you to trust me." A small laugh slipped out.

"Excuse me? Did I miss something?"

"No. Just a little humor. Joke's on me."

"Okay."

She glanced at her phone again. They'd been walking in an elongated circle. "We're headed in the right direction."

"I hope so—and yes, I'll admit there's a double meaning to that statement." After a few moments filled only with the barking of a dog in a nearby yard, Brian spoke up again. "Tell me about you, Jillian."

"What? Like how Geoff and I met?"

"Anything you feel like telling me. You're the woman my brother chose to marry, yes, but let's pretend we're getting to know each other just because. What would you like me to know about you?"

"Me?" There was nothing all that important to tell. "I have three sisters."

"No brothers?"

"No. All girls. The Thatcher sisters."

"I bet that was fun growing up."

"It was. Johanna—she's the oldest. She's, um, having a baby in a few months."

"Congratulations. You're going to be an aunt."

There was nothing more to say about that.

"And then there's Payton. She just got married in February. She's back in college, and she coaches volleyball."

"Johanna, Payton, and . . . ?"

"Pepper. She was Payton's identical twin. She died in a snowmobile accident when she was sixteen."

"I'm sorry." His response was brief, not requiring that Jillian share more of the story.

"It's been a long time. I don't think you ever stop missing someone, but in an odd way, you get used to it."

"I guess you do." Brian spoke almost to himself. "Even if you don't want to."

Jillian chose not to respond, unsure what to say. Unsure whether he was talking about her or Geoff.

"Are your other sisters in Colorado, too?"

"Yes. One's here in the Springs and the other in Denver— close enough that we can get together."

"Well, I'll be back in Minnesota by next Monday. I'd like to think I could leave here with at least the possibility of a better relationship with my brother."

"What about your parents?"

"My parents? I know what I'm getting from them. A relationship on my mother's terms. No other option. I'm hoping for something more from Geoff."

"You realize I haven't promised to help you."

"I know. But you listened. And I appreciate that." They

stopped in front of the house. "Would it be okay if I gave you my phone number?"

"Why?"

"That way you can let me know what you decide to do. Text or call. No pressure. I promise."

"Fine."

Brian stood in the middle of the sidewalk as he entered his number and then returned her phone.

Jillian tucked her phone back into her pocket. "I'll think about talking to Geoff."

"That's all I ask. I realize I might not hear from Geoff before I leave for Minnesota. But I'm available to talk whenever he's ready, even after that. I'm willing to wait."

They'd walked and talked without crossing the invisible line. Brian acknowledged it was there, but then he stayed on his side. No demands. Just a request. Winston obviously thought he was a nice guy, accepting a final pat and scratch behind the ears.

But Jillian couldn't promise him anything because she didn't want to be fooled. Didn't want her husband to be hurt any more than he already had been.

It wasn't like Jillian ever forgot she had battled cancer. The reminders stalked her every day.

The scar where her breast should be.

The fatigue.

The mental muddle.

The inability to get pregnant.

The last consequence reached past the insomnia that had pulled her out of bed tonight—again. Stalked her downstairs into the living room. Drained any hope out of her future.

Somehow, someway, someday, she needed to figure out how to not be so defeated by all of this. Find the hope she wanted.

Jillian shifted on the couch. She should have brought Winston downstairs with her, rather than sit here, wide-awake, by herself.

She opened the Notes app on her phone. Might as well update her to-do list. Cross off the few things she'd completed the last couple of days. Try to remember what new things she needed to add.

And there it was—the one thing she never expected to be on her list.

Talk to Geoff about Brian.

The echoes of her conversation with Geoff's brother lingered like the effects of her chemo and radiation. It hadn't been twenty-four hours since she and Brian had talked. Even if a week had passed, it wasn't like she'd forget going for a walk with Brian. Forget his request for help.

"I'm not asking you to convince him."

All she was supposed to do was ask Geoff to talk to Brian. She wasn't responsible to make it happen. But Brian was only in Colorado for a few more days. Would she find the courage to talk to Geoff before then?

"Jill?"

Jillian gasped, twisting to find Geoff standing at the foot of the couch. "I didn't hear you."

"I was awake upstairs. Thought I might as well join you down here, if that's okay."

Jillian shifted into a half-sitting position, pulling her legs closer to her body. "Did I wake you up?"

"No. I haven't been sleeping well . . ."

"Since Brian showed up."

It was as if his brother sat between them. Invisible but present.

"Yeah."

"Have you heard from him again?" Jillian stared ahead as she launched the question.

"No. He texted quite a bit at first. Called a few times. But he's gone silent now. And . . ."

"And now you wish he'd call?"

"No." Geoff's denial was swift. "I'm fine with the silence. I've done a lot of years without him around. This is normal."

"But sometimes normal . . ." Was she going to say this? "Sometimes normal needs to change."

Geoff glanced at her over his shoulder, his eyes for once not hidden behind his glasses. "What does that even mean?"

Jillian pushed herself to sit straight, turning to face Geoff, tugging the blanket into position. "Maybe we should table this conversation."

"I didn't start the conversation, Jillian, but you can't say something like that and not explain yourself."

Now she had a choice between a half-truth or the whole truth, so help her God. Why, why wasn't she asking God for help with this?

Because it was so hard to trust Him when she chose faith and still didn't get what she wanted.

Now that was the whole truth.

Geoff hadn't moved closer to her. Hadn't reached for her hand. He couldn't because she was twisting her engagement ring around and around her finger.

She could change this. Maybe if she reached for his hand . . .

But maybe not. Maybe he needed space.

"Brian came to see me." Her words were barely more than a whisper.

"What did you say?"

She cleared her throat. Raised her voice. "Your brother came to see me yesterday."

"What did he want?"

"He asked me to ask you to meet with him."

"Great. Now my brother is using my wife—"

Jillian rested her hand on Geoff's forearm. "It didn't feel like that, Geoff."

"How would you know? You don't know Brian—"

"And you do? The last time you saw him, Brian was seventeen and you were fifteen."

"He left home because he had problems."

"And he also said he's changed. That he's worked through those problems. You don't think your brother deserves a second chance?"

"This is not about a second chance."

"It's not?" Jillian kept her hand resting on Geoff's arm. "Then what is it about?"

"It's about . . . it's about the fact that I'm fine with how things are now."

"What does that mean?"

"I'm used to life without Brian . . . or Kyler." Geoff bent forward, his hands clenched together behind his neck. The action broke their connection. "Just let it be."

It was as if Geoff's feet were cemented together, holding him in place. The pain of his past—the losses—held him fast, so he couldn't move forward.

His shoulders were hunched as if he was protecting himself.

How could she convince him that he wasn't alone anymore?

She wouldn't push her husband. Couldn't force him to talk to his brother. "What am I supposed to tell Brian?"

"You don't tell him anything." Geoff's voice lashed out. "I'm your family, not Brian."

She said nothing.

"I didn't mean to sound so harsh."

"I know."

"This is why we're not getting involved with my brother. He always causes problems. He gets people riled up. My parents. Me. And then he walks away." Geoff pressed the palms of his hands against his eyes. "I'm not doing this again."

He stood, moving toward the stairs.

Was that it, then? Geoff's *no* ended the conversation?

"I—I think you should talk to Brian."

"What?" Geoff pivoted.

"Talk to him, Geoff. He leaves this weekend. We don't know when he'll be back. If it goes badly—"

"It will."

"—then you don't ever have to talk to him again. You'll know you're right. Suspicions confirmed. But maybe you and Brian can start over."

"That's a little too optimistic for me."

"Geoff, come on." Jillian rose, took a few steps toward Geoff. "Why won't you give him a chance?"

"Give him a chance? You don't know how many chances he's already had! Why should he get another one?"

"Because it's like Pepper said—sometimes you have to forget everything else and remember you're family."

A paraphrase of her sister's words, yes, but it was still true.

Geoff inhaled and exhaled as if he were struggling to breathe. "Fine."

Jillian froze, not daring to move. "Fine?"

"I'll talk to Brian." He rubbed his hand across his jaw. "But I don't think I can do this by myself. Will you go with me?"

"What? *No.* This is between you and your brother."

"Please, Jillian. We can meet for breakfast. Would you set it up? I assume you know how to contact him."

"Yes, but—"

"Can we just go to bed, Jilly? Try to get some sleep?"

"You go ahead. I'll turn out the lights and be right up."

The echo of his words rang in the silence.

"Please, Jillian."

She should have tried to convince him to talk to Brian by himself.

No. She needed to let him be. If she tried to talk to him now, they'd only argue. And then he'd change his mind about talking with his brother.

She'd send Brian a text and wait for him to respond—at a reasonable hour.

Her Bible and journal still sat on the table beside the couch, neglected for weeks after she'd forgotten them when she'd gone to North Carolina. She picked them up, the weight of them in her hands almost foreign.

She'd never imagined choosing faith . . . chasing hope . . . would be so hard.

She turned to her last journal entry, written all the way back in March, when she'd discovered the passage in James about being blessed if you persevered under trials.

I don't know anything about receiving a crown . . .
except it sounds like I only get it if I pass this test.
Okay. Fine.
But if You could make "passing the test" easier by
having Geoff decide he wants to adopt, that would be
great.

So much for God hearing that prayer. Life had only gotten harder, not easier.

But she didn't care about some far-off crown she might receive someday.

She wanted hope now. For today.

"Please, God. If I'm doing this wrong, just tell me." Jillian's whispered plea broke the silence in the room. "Show me what to do. How to handle things when we get together with Brian. And if You could do something so it goes well, please? And help me to keep believing in You."

Jillian paused as she remembered something Harper said to her right before she left.

"I don't know anything about faith, but could it be a different kind of more *than what you expected?"*

Maybe Harper was right. Maybe she was overloading her relationship with God with her expectations: If she did this—believed in God—then He'd give her what she wanted. He'd change Geoff. He'd give her a baby.

Was faith less about what she wanted and more about discovering who God was and what He wanted for her?

But what if God's idea of more ultimately meant less than everything she hoped for?

21

CRACKER BARREL was the restaurant from family road trips. Jillian liked the food, but the experience was the best part. Sitting in the wooden rocking chairs lined up along the porch outside. Playing checkers while they waited for their meals to be delivered—always debating about whether she and Johanna played first or whether Payton and Pepper played first. Browsing the store with its shelves filled with an ever-changing assortment of seasonal knickknacks, clothes, toys, and an eclectic assortment of sodas and candy. And they'd always left with old-fashioned candy sticks of their favorite flavors. Green apple for Johanna. Orange for Pepper. Blueberry for Payton. Lemon for her.

Jillian doubted candy sticks were an option for today.

"Since Brian wanted this meeting so badly, you'd think he could be here on time." Geoff shifted in his chair next to her.

"Come on—"

"What?"

She reapplied her ChapStick. "You agreed to do this. The least you can do is try to have a good attitude."

"I'm here, aren't I?"

"Yes. And you're acting like this is a trip to update all your vaccinations and have your wisdom teeth extracted."

"That's ridiculous."

"Did you come here planning to fight with Brian?"

"I'm not planning to fight—"

"Look at yourself." Jillian motioned at Geoff's rigid posture.

"What?"

"Body language speaks louder than words . . . or something like that. You want to unclench your fists?"

Geoff relaxed his hands, accompanied by a slow exhale. "I'm nervous. I'm not sure what to say."

"Brian's probably just as nervous as you are." Jillian scooted her chair closer, taking Geoff's hand and entwining their fingers. "We'll take this slow. Start with hello. Don't go looking for a fight—" Geoff's jaw tightened—"not that I'm saying you are. I'm on your side, no matter what."

"I know you are. And thank you for coming with me. It means a lot." Geoff rolled his shoulders, moving his head from side to side like a prizefighter prepping to enter the ring. "Let's just look at the menu while we wait for Brian."

A few moments later, Geoff's brother approached.

"I'm sorry for being late." Brian settled into the chair across from Jillian, offering them both a smile that, for just a moment, reminded her of Geoff. "It took me a little longer to pack than I'd expected."

"Pack?" Jillian opted not to wait for Geoff to respond, unsure if he would.

"Yeah. I'm heading back to Minnesota right after breakfast." He opened the menu. "Cracker Barrel. Haven't eaten here in ages."

"Me, either." Again Jillian spoke first. "Your family must be excited that you're coming home."

"We're all ready for me to be back home. It'll be a long drive—"

"You're driving?" If she kept talking, maybe Geoff would jump in sometime.

"Yes. It'll be a long day."

And Geoff finally joined the conversation. "You're going to do it in one day? That's crazy."

"I did it in one day coming to Colorado. I can do it going back. But thanks for your concern." For all the changes in his life, an air of rebelliousness still clung to Brian. The leather jacket. Longer hair, same color as Geoff's.

The arrival of the waitress to take their order interrupted the two brothers, who seemed all too ready to argue about anything and everything.

Jillian knew her position well. She was the buffer between two opposing forces. Only this time it wasn't the familiar struggle between Johanna and Payton. She was stuck between her husband and his prodigal-returned brother.

She had to be vigilant this morning, no matter how tired she was. It didn't matter that she'd had her typical night of interrupted sleep, using the shower to wash away the lingering effects of exhaustion. Jillian couldn't quit on this meeting. She had to track the conversation, try to defuse the tension. She could collapse later.

"Are you waiting for me to start this conversation?" Geoff pulled the plastic pieces out of the triangular peg game that sat on every table at Cracker Barrel. Orange, yellow, blue, and white pieces piled in front of him.

"Geoff!"

"It's okay, Jillian. You don't have to try and smooth things over."

Brian didn't understand how things worked—what her role was when it came to complicated family dynamics.

"Geoff." Brian leaned forward, resting his elbows on the table, waiting until Geoff made eye contact with him. "I want to apologize for how I handled everything."

"Everything?" Geoff placed a single white peg into the center of the triangle.

"Okay—I can't apologize for everything. Or maybe you think I should. Can I start with saying I'm sorry for showing up here without any warning? Bad move on my part. I talked with Jenny about it and realized I should have avoided Mom and Dad altogether. I should have just contacted you."

Geoff added another peg to the board. "What do you mean, you should have avoided Mom and Dad?"

"The odds of them changing after all this time? Not

gonna happen. But you and me? We're adults now. We're our own people. We don't have to do what they tell us to do."

"Figures."

"What does that mean?"

"You're still playing the rebellious son."

A sigh shifted Brian's shoulders. "That is not what this is about."

"Really? Sounds like it to me."

"I haven't had the chance to tell you everything—haven't gotten past apologizing for one thing. And I'm not too sure you even heard that."

The conversation was like a car stalling out. A few noises, sounding like it was going to start, and then it sputters and the engine dies.

Geoff wasn't even looking at Brian. Instead, he jammed game pieces into the small holes drilled in the wooden triangle. If he wasn't careful, he was going to have to pay for a bunch of broken plastic pegs.

And Jillian wasn't going to be able to defuse this situation. She could only sit there and let it run its course. Hope the waitress delivered their breakfasts soon to give everyone a little bit of a breather.

"Look, Geoff. I left home because I was a troubled kid. Wanted my own way. I mean, to be honest, I wasn't just getting into trouble—I was looking for it every chance I got."

Geoff crossed his arms over his chest with a "Tell me something I don't know" look on his face.

"But once I got sober, I stayed away because I wanted to

stay healthy. And I knew I couldn't do that if I reconnected with Mom and Dad."

"What's that supposed to mean?"

"You know how they are. You're a Hennessey. Everything has to be done their way—Mom's way—and that's true whether you're thirteen or thirty. What kind of parents don't talk about their son when he dies?"

"It was better that way—"

"For who?" Brian's words were tossed out just as the waitress arrived with the tray of food. She wouldn't get a tip based on her timing. Silence reigned as she arranged plates on the table, asking if they needed anything else. Refilled their white coffee mugs. As she left, Brian spoke up. "And don't say it was good for us. Mom and Dad decided that."

"That's what parents are for. You certainly never had a problem showing your anger—"

"Fine. I was an angry kid. But Mom and Dad never wanted to talk about why I was angry. I think they were glad when I ran away from home for good. Life was easier without me. At least then, their problems weren't staring them in the face, yelling at them."

"You were the biggest problem."

Jillian forced herself to not interrupt. To not apologize for what Geoff had just said. And it would be a waste of time to mention that everyone's food was getting cold.

"Mom and Dad had problems long before I started acting out, Geoff. But like everything else, they didn't talk about any of it. They invoked the 'Hennessey vow of silence' and moved on."

"Things were good once you left."

"Geoff!" Jillian's fork clattered against her plate.

"Don't worry about it, Jillian." Brian shook his head, his smile twisted. "That's the way the vow of silence works, little brother. They cover up the hurt and guilt and grief until you can't hear it screaming at you. I used alcohol. Mom and Dad turned their backs on whatever they didn't want to deal with. A dead son. A rebellious teen. You? You were the good Hennessey son because you didn't have the gall to die or drink. You behaved."

It was as if she were ringside at a boxing match where the opponents were mismatched. One was a pro. One had never been in the ring before. Geoff tried to stand his ground with Brian but couldn't.

Geoff sat back, his breakfast ignored, the game pieces scattered.

"I gave up wanting to have a relationship with Mom and Dad a long time ago because it meant sacrificing too much. Sacrificing myself." Brian's words were rough. "But I always had this dream that maybe . . . somehow . . . you and I could be brothers again. I knew it would take time. We'd have to be willing to get to know each other again. I never forgot about you . . . or Kyler. I wasn't running away from you back then."

"You left the family." Geoff swiped his hand across his eyes, knocking his glasses askew. "You left *me*."

"I'm sorry, Geoff. Really sorry. I may have left, but I never forgot you." Brian shifted in his chair, pulling his wallet from his back pocket, opening it as he talked. "I didn't take much with me when I left. A few clothes. But I made sure I took this."

He slid a laminated photograph across the table. Geoff traced the edge with his thumb and forefinger. Jillian had only seen the three Hennessey brothers together in the photos Geoff had shared with her last Christmas, but she recognized them easily enough.

"I couldn't be the son Mom and Dad wanted me to be— or the brother you needed. It hurt too much to ignore everything. To pretend Kyler didn't die. To wake up every morning and realize I wasn't going to be enough for them. *Again.* At least once I left home, I would only fail myself. And I got really good at failing—until I couldn't fail anymore." Brian's eyes filled with tears. "I had to face all the bad things in my life. Deal with them. I'm far from perfect, but I've got an honest life. A good life. And if you can figure out a way to forgive me, I'd like to get to know each other again. No—get to know each other for the first time. That's it. That's why I'm here. Because I never forgot you."

Maybe Geoff wasn't hearing any of this, but Jillian was. She knew what it was like to wake up every morning and feel like a failure. But she was trying, again and again, to understand, to believe, that her life was good, even if it wasn't perfect. Maybe that's where faith came in. Maybe faith bridged the gap between perfection and failure.

Geoff's chin quivered as he struggled to respond.

She couldn't answer for him. This was his brother. His choice.

"I don't know . . ."

The silence stretched between the two brothers as Jillian held her breath, willing Geoff to say something more. To say yes.

"Well, that's not a no." Brian retrieved the photograph and then removed some bills from his wallet, tossing the money on the table. "I'll take it. Breakfast's on me."

"What?" Jillian clutched Geoff's arm. "Tell him to sit down and finish his breakfast. Talk to him."

"It's okay, Jillian. Like I said, it's not a no—and that's more than I had when I came in here." Brian picked up his plate. "I'll ask them to box this up for me on my way out."

"Geoff—"

"It's your call, Geoff. You've got my number." Brian nodded. "I won't bother you again. I promise. And I do keep my word now."

"You're going to let him leave?" Jillian twisted to face her husband.

"Until I figure out what I want . . . yes."

22

Today had come so much sooner than I had expected.

Sooner and out of order.

There'd been no lavish Broadmoor wedding. No, I'd been denied that dream and, instead, had fast-forwarded past a honeymoon and being a newlywed to pregnancy and morning sickness to . . . today, when I would share that I was having a little girl with my family.

Yay.

First everyone had to arrive so they could hear the news. Until then, small talk, which was a waste of time—like trying to train the most recent pharmacy technician who proved to be untrainable. She'd just never caught on to the routines, no matter how many times they were explained to her by another more experienced technician or by me.

But the last thing I wanted to do was share the gender-reveal news with people one by one. It was better to chitchat with Mom while she prepped the new vegan recipe she'd found. You couldn't say Mom didn't try to support Payton's dietary choices.

"What did you and Dad decide about putting a deck on the house?"

"Zach talked with us and we decided to do a ground-level deck with a fire pit. His friend who's doing the design also offered to help build the deck." Mom finished chopping asparagus. "The two of them say it'll take a couple of weekends. Dad wants to lend a hand, but I think it'll be mostly Zach and his friend Brandon."

"Only a couple of weekends? That's it?"

"According to Zach, yes. We're using composite so we don't have to worry about upkeep. I want a storage bench on one end. And some kind of shaded area. But other than that, it's not complicated. I think Zach will have a sketch today."

"Sounds like it'll be fun." I stole a bite of asparagus, avoiding Mom's playful smack of my hand. "What do you think about—?"

"I always love your ideas, Johanna, but we're happy with what Brandon's designed. He's a professional, after all. Maybe when we decide on the new patio furniture, I'll see what you think, although Payton's shown me a few things already."

I pressed my lips together. If Mom didn't want my opinion, I wasn't going to insist. Let Payton and Zach be the patio experts. "Everyone is coming today, right?"

"As far as I know, yes. I talked to Jillian earlier and she said she'd see us later."

All right then. Today would be the day the Thatcher sisters would be back together again.

We couldn't avoid each other forever. We didn't always get along, but we were like the lost socks or gloves that somehow found their way back to each other. Jillian, Payton, and me. We belonged together, whether we liked it or not.

I ran my hand across my stomach, surprised at how often I found myself replicating the motion during the day. I couldn't hide the fact I was pregnant anymore. I shouldn't have to. But with Jillian and Geoff arriving sometime soon, I fought the desire to go to the coat closet and find the biggest, roomiest coat to wrap myself up in.

Ridiculous. I had nothing to hide—except my pregnancy. And even if I did, Jillian already knew I was having a baby. It wasn't as if they'd forget.

The front door opened and I froze as if someone had tapped me in one of those once-upon-a-time childhood games of freeze tag. But at the sound of Payton's and Zach's hellos, I could shake off the moment of being caught.

"Are you okay?" Mom paused from her dinner prep.

"Yes. Of course." I didn't need to draw Mom into the sister drama. I raised my voice so Payton and Zach would hear. "We're in the kitchen."

"We brought a quinoa salad." Payton entered, holding up a large ceramic bowl, Zach close behind her.

"Perfect. Dad is going to grill portobello mushrooms as well as some steaks, and I'm trying an asparagus frittata that uses chickpea flour, of all things. I always worry there's not enough for you, Payton, and it wasn't difficult at all."

"I'll eat Payton's steak." Zach wrapped his arms around Payton's waist as she set the salad on the counter.

"She hasn't convinced you to go vegan?"

"No." Payton leaned into Zach's embrace. "I'm not even trying."

"I brought the plans for the deck, so whenever you want to look over them, Mom T. I left them in the car."

"Let's wait until after dinner. That way Geoff will be here, too."

"Sounds good."

"How are you feeling, Johanna?" Payton found the pitcher of tea in the fridge and poured herself a glass.

"Still not drinking coffee, but my doctor says my taste for it may not come back until after . . . after the baby's born."

"What was that? You paused there for a moment." Payton lowered her voice, setting down her tea and pulling me aside. "Do you know what you're having?"

I raised my eyebrows. "I'm having a baby."

"You do! You know!" Payton's quick hug caught me off guard.

Mom stopped mixing the sauce into the potato salad. "Johanna knows what?"

"Johanna knows if she's having a boy or a girl."

Winston's sharp bark and the arrival of Jillian silenced all of us. It was as if someone had set the timer for an explosive.

Tick. Tick. Tick.

Payton made eye contact with me, but neither of us said anything, for fear we'd detonate the bomb. I didn't want Jillian to walk in on this moment, which was why I'd waited for the entire family to be together. And I wanted her to be happy for me. To be happy *with* me, if that was even possible.

"Jillian! I'm so glad you're here." Mom hugged Jillian.

"I'm glad I'm here, too, Mom." Jillian watched Payton and me. "What are you two whispering about?"

The words stuck in my throat, but Payton came to my rescue. "Johanna knows whether she's having a boy or a girl."

Mom wiped her hands on a towel. "Well, I should get your dad."

Jillian didn't come running into the kitchen with a "Really? Tell us!" The smile on her face was forced, and she carried Winston close to her body like a shield, with Geoff following close behind. "Is it true, Jo?"

The use of my childhood nickname had no warmth in it.

"Yes, um, I had an ultrasound a few weeks ago . . ." There was no sense in making this any sort of dramatic, drawn-out announcement, but I did have to wait for Mom and Dad. "And everything looks good."

"We're here!" Mom returned, Dad right behind her. "What did you say?"

"I said the baby looked healthy on the ultrasound I had a few weeks ago." Everyone watched me. Waiting. Wondering. "The doctor also said it looks like I'm having a girl."

Within moments, Mom had wrapped me in a hug, but

all I could see was Jillian. The absence of a smile on her face. How she blinked back tears.

"*I'm sorry.*" I mouthed the words.

I was caught in the middle of celebrating and hurting my sister at the same time. Knowing Mom's excitement at my announcement snuffed out Jillian's dream yet again. I hadn't planned any of this. I hadn't wanted to be pregnant.

Regret stained the moment gray, dimming my anticipation.

"Another Thatcher girl." Payton spoke first.

"Yes. Another Thatcher girl." Mom seemed unable to let go of me, her words woven through with the music of laughter and tears. "Isn't it wonderful? Have you thought of names?"

"Yes." I couldn't give more than a one-syllable answer.

"And?"

"I'm . . . I'm still thinking about it."

"You're not going to tell us?"

"Maybe once I decide . . ."

"We could help—"

"If I can't decide, I'll let you know."

"You know what we do need to talk about?" Payton stood in the center of the group. "A baby shower!"

"Yes!" Mom seemed ready to hug me again.

"No!" My response was a crack of thunder. "No baby shower."

Jillian had whispered something to Geoff and then disappeared.

"Johanna, you have to have a baby shower. You need everything. A crib. A car seat. A high chair . . ." The way she named items so easily, Mom had been making a list.

"Clothes!" Now it was Payton's turn to jump in. "Think of all the adorable clothes for a baby girl."

"Speaking of clothes, you don't have any maternity clothes." Mom's tone implied this was a grievous mistake.

"I'm managing fine with leggings and loose tops."

"How many weeks are you?"

"Twenty-six."

"It's a good thing you were so slender before you got pregnant. That's the only reason you've managed this long. And you lost weight, too." Payton continued to take charge. "We're going shopping."

"No, we are not."

"Yes, we are. We're all here. We'll eat, and then we'll shop."

This conversation had gone from bad to worse to what was Payton thinking? Going shopping was going to be excruciating compared to telling my family that I was having a little girl.

And I was saying no—and being ignored. This did not happen. But at least we weren't talking about baby names anymore. "Weren't you going to tell everyone about your plans for the deck?"

"That, big sister, is an evasive maneuver." Payton hadn't noticed Jillian's absence.

"Do we have time to look at the deck plans before dinner?" I would ignore Payton, even if she was right.

Payton skated right past my question with her answer. "Why don't we look at them while we eat and then we can let the guys talk about them while they clean up? Thatcher tradition, right? And we'll go shopping."

"No."

"Yes." Jillian stepped back into the kitchen, her eyes bright and rimmed with red—a telltale sign she'd been crying. "I think it's a . . . a great idea. Payton's right. You need to get some real maternity clothes."

I couldn't fight with Jill. Payton, yes. Jillian . . . once in a while, maybe. But not today. The brief touch of her hand was almost as good as a hug, the way it reconnected us for just a moment. We'd get through my pregnancy and beyond . . . one painful choice at a time.

⌒

This was the mall Mom had taken us to when we'd needed school clothes. She'd also taken us here for our haircuts. When we'd needed to shop for homecoming and prom dresses. At least, this was where Jillian and I had come. I had no idea where she'd taken Payton and Pepper.

"What do you want to try on first?" Payton had designated herself the leader of this little shopping expedition.

"I don't want to try on anything. This wasn't my idea, remember?"

"Stop arguing, Johanna." Payton lightened her reprimand with a smile. "You know you need some basics."

I could enter the store kicking and screaming—not my style at all—or at least appear willing. Buy a few items. And be done with this ordeal in under an hour.

"I don't even know what they sell in a maternity store."

"The same types of things you find in other stores, but with more room . . . and access."

"Access?"

"Nursing bras and tops? Do you want to look at those now or wait until later?"

"I won't be looking at those at all. I plan on bottle feeding."

"Bottle feeding?" Mom's attention turned from a rack of tops to me.

"Yes." I should have known better than to mention my decision. "And this topic is not open for discussion. I'm going to be a working mother . . ."

I was going to be *a mother*.

It didn't matter if I was going to be a working mother or not. I was having a baby. *A baby.* And all these changes to my body—watching my waistline and flat stomach disappear—just hinted at all the other ways my life was going to change. My job would be affected. I might be single—a single mom—*forever*. What man would want to marry a woman like me? A career-minded, settled-in-Colorado, mother-of-a-daughter kind of woman?

Who knew that walking into a maternity store would bring my future into such sharp focus?

Mom clapped her hands together once. "Let's just look at maternity clothes. Things like tops and pants first."

"Those kinds of things *only*."

I had to make this quick or I was going to have some sort of out-of-pregnant-body experience. Graphic images of smiling, contented, perfect mothers-to-be were everywhere.

I was no such thing. The perfect life I'd planned for myself eluded me. It had started crumbling the day Dr. Lerner had introduced Axton Miller to me, but I would maintain control of today.

"Why don't we each pick out a few things?" Mom was trying to make it a fun shopping trip, and Jill still hung back, standing just inside the store.

"No. I'll grab a few things. This. And this. And this . . ."

"Wait. Slow down." Payton removed the hangers from my hands. "You don't even know if you've got the right size."

"If it's not—"

"If we need another size, I'll ask the saleswoman for help." Mom spoke up, nodding to one of the trio of women at the counter who smiled and moved our way. "For now, I'll ask her to set up a dressing room."

Payton held up a bright-yellow top. "How about this?"

"I am not wearing anything with words on it. No supposed-to-be-funny pregnancy slogans." I shook my head. "And I think the last time I wore yellow, I was in middle school. I want things I can wear to work."

"Fine." Payton returned the T-shirt to the rack. "Are you open to a peplum top?"

"Yes."

Mom returned, taking my hand and leading me toward the back of the store. "Go ahead to the dressing room and we'll see what we can find."

My mom and sisters had pulled a page from one of Axton Miller's books and turned shopping into a team event. But Jillian still stood rooted at the same spot—she might have even inched closer to the exit. Neither of us wanted to be here. I should release her from this obligation and tell her to leave.

A couple pieces of clothing hung in the dressing room. Gray leggings. A basic black V-neck T-shirt with short sleeves.

"Here." Mom peeked through the curtain and offered me a hanger with a top on it just as I started to peel off my regular leggings. "Payton said you wanted to try this on."

"Right." My sister hadn't mentioned the peplum top was a floral print. I didn't wear floral prints.

"I'm going to look for a few more things."

"Mom, I don't need much."

"Johanna, this is probably the only time we're going to get you to try on maternity clothes. I have every intention of taking advantage of it." Mom had the nerve to grin as if she knew she was victorious, standing there with her clothes on while I got undressed. "And you have a few more months left before you deliver. You'll get tired of wearing the same things over and over again."

"You're taking advantage of a pregnant woman."

"A mom does what a mom has to do." Mom disappeared with a laugh.

I was being treated like a child. Everyone was having fun at my expense.

That wasn't true. For all I knew, Jillian was walking the mall, putting as much distance between us as possible.

I paused, my hands still on the waistband of my leggings. I could call a halt to all of this. Walk out and then buy some clothes online and return them if they didn't fit.

Instead, I tugged off my leggings. They only worked because I snugged them below my protruding belly. Then I pulled my top up over my head, hanging it on one of the hooks on the wall. And then there I was. Pregnant. From three different angles. Pregnant.

I turned my back on the mirror.

Too much reality at one time.

The whisper of my name was so faint, I ignored it the first time. And then the sound came again.

"Joey."

I flung one arm across my stomach, pulling the curtain aside just an inch, holding the material against my body. "Jill?"

"Yeah. Here. Try this on." She held out a sundress in a pale blue. No logo or words.

"Thank you."

"Of course."

"Jill." I grabbed her hand before she could move away.

We held hands, me in a bra and panties behind a dressing room curtain, Jillian with tears in her eyes. And I couldn't find the words to say.

"I know . . ." She squeezed my hand. "We'll figure it out."

"We will."

Back inside the dressing room, I hugged the sundress against my skin. It was a peace offering from my sister who knew how to move past misunderstandings better than I did. I chose to ignore them. She chose to mend them.

It didn't matter what I looked like in this dress. I was buying it.

23

As much as I'd resisted going shopping with Mom, Payton, and Jillian, I had to admit—to myself, not to them—it was nice to wear a pair of leggings that covered my stomach, instead of rolling the waistband down below my belly button. I'd even purchased two of the peplum tops Payton had found, but in solid neutral colors, not floral, because they worked well beneath my lab coat. Paired with my flats, I looked professional and was no longer wearing an outfit that was merely okay and mostly uncomfortable.

"You look nice today, Dr. Thatcher." Libby, one of my most reliable pharmacy technicians, complimented me as she left for the day. "Is that a new outfit?"

"Yes. Thanks." Libby didn't need to know I'd been forced to go shopping. I'd accept the comment and leave it at that.

"When's your baby due?"

I'd never announced my pregnancy, but the news had made the rounds of the hospital grapevine, not unlike the news of Axton Miller getting my promotion months ago. Dr. Lerner sending an official e-mail back then had been unnecessary. Protocol, yes, but unnecessary.

"The end of August. My doctor says August 30."

"Do you know what you're having?"

"The ultrasound showed I'm having a girl."

"How fun. I have two little girls—ages five and seven. Have you picked out a name?"

"Still thinking about it."

I was chitchatting with a coworker as if it were something I did every day. But I'd never done this. Ever.

Libby wore a sterling silver necklace with two tiny initials dangling from it. Were those for her daughters? Maybe next time I'd ask.

I'd gained entrance into a private club—the moms' club. But I didn't know the rules. Or if I could learn them well enough to fit in. I'd never really worried about fitting in before.

Was motherhood about fitting in so my child would have a place, have a chance? What would having a child cost me?

Five minutes after Libby left, Axton Miller showed up as I shut down my computer.

"How are you feeling?" Axton leaned a shoulder against the doorjamb.

"I'm fine." I should probably have stood but chose to

remain seated. Some days, the pregnancy got the best of me, not that I would admit it to my boss. "No reason to slow down here."

"About that . . ."

"What? I haven't slowed down, Axton." I really should have stood.

"I didn't say you had, Johanna. Calm down." He stepped into my office, pulled up a chair, and straddled it. "I wanted to remind you not to push yourself too hard. It's the beginning of June and you're still all about coming in early and staying late—every single day. You can ease up a little. I should have said this weeks ago."

"I'm pregnant, not an invalid."

"I know the difference. But don't wear yourself out to prove a point. I'm happy with your work. We're on schedule with everything."

"But I haven't heard anything about the off-site chemo program."

Axton broke eye contact for the briefest of seconds. "Dr. Lerner and I decided I'll handle the project. You'll focus on more of the day-to-day events."

"But I've been involved with this up until now—"

"You're pregnant, Johanna. Depending on how quickly we move things along, we can't have you exposed to particular chemicals."

"I can be involved until then—"

"If we're going to pull you off the project, it makes sense to do it sooner rather than later."

"You know this is discriminatory."

"No. This is about health and safety." Despite my accusatory tone, Axton's posture remained relaxed. "Your health. Your baby's health."

And here I was, in yet another tug-of-war with Axton. But he had all the power on his side because he was my boss.

I sat there, my hands fisted in my lab coat pockets, shaking. My entire body was shaking. But I couldn't speak, for fear my voice would shake, too. I was not going to come across as some emotional, hormonal female.

"Johanna, can we forget about titles for a minute? Forget I'm your boss. I'd like to think we're friends, too. Aren't we? I'm concerned for you as a friend. I want you to take care of yourself."

I had nothing to say to his unexpected request. I had just experienced chitchatting with Libby for the first time. And now Axton was talking about being friends.

"I don't have many friends, Axton."

The moment I admitted that, I wished I could take the words back. Then again, the man wouldn't be surprised to hear I had no friends.

"I know some people warn against being both business colleagues and friends. But I've found that it can work, when there's mutual respect." Axton held out his hand. "Friends, Johanna?"

"Yes." Axton's grip was sure. "Friends."

Axton didn't linger after my concession. And I was no longer surprised to find myself at the hospital atrium. I was just thankful no one else was there.

I sat on the bench in front of the piano, allowing my

fingertips to brush the tops of the ivory keys. No sound. But then I adjusted my shoulders. Settled my fingers into position. Within moments, a melody from years ago flowed through me. Around me. The notes anchored in a yesterday I'd left behind.

Back then, it had been all moving past focusing on practicing and being perfect . . . and then being left alone . . .

"That's lovely." The young woman—Robyn?—who'd played the piano several weeks ago stood a few feet away. I'd walked by the atrium several times since our first meeting but had never seen her.

My fingers stilled.

"Oh." I settled my hands into my lap. "I haven't played that in years. I'm surprised I even remember it."

"How long ago did you play it?"

"More than twenty years ago, for a piano recital."

"And you still remember it. That's amazing."

"Not so amazing, really. You practice something enough times and it gets embedded in your brain. It was automatic."

"If that was automatic, I would love to hear you play when you put emotion into it."

It was time to change the topic.

"You're wearing your pin again. Are you here to play for a while?"

"Yes."

"I didn't mention it last time—the first time we met—but my piano teacher wore the same pin." The admission slipped past my normal reserve. I could only thank my interactions with first Libby and then Axton.

"She did?" Robyn touched the edge of the gold brooch.

"Yes. At first, I thought maybe we had the same teacher, but they don't have the same name."

"Who taught you piano?"

"Miss Felicia—Felicia Hill."

"Miss Felicia!" Robyn's eyes widened. "She was my mother's best friend."

"But you said your piano teacher was—"

"Mrs. Davenport. She got remarried in her forties."

"Miss Felicia is remarried?" The idea shifted my memory of the tall, slender woman who'd lived alone in a small house filled with an assortment of antiques and a stately grand piano. "How wonderful. I always thought she was so lovely. And her house. I loved the hutch in her dining room—how it contained all these beautiful teacups and saucers. We used to drink tea after my lessons. And she'd tell me stories about traveling overseas . . ."

As I talked, a curtain seemed to pull back for just a moment so I could glimpse a time in my past I rarely thought about. What else could Robyn tell me about Miss Felicia? Did she have children now? Did she still teach piano?

"Does Miss Felicia still live here in the Springs? Or did she move after she got married? I'd love to contact her."

Robyn glanced away. "I'm sorry . . . there's no easy way to say this. She died. It's been about eight years now."

"She . . . died?"

"Yes. In a car accident. Her husband let my mom and me choose some of her jewelry since they didn't have any children. I chose the pin." Robyn reached out as if to touch my hand, but I slipped my hands into my lab coat pockets. "I'm so sorry to tell you like this."

"It's fine . . . I mean, I hadn't seen her in years."

"How long did you take lessons with her?"

"I started when I was three."

"Three? That's so young for piano lessons. And my mom said Mrs. Davenport was very particular about who she took on as a student."

"Yes. Well, I was advanced for my age—or so people said. I took lessons until I was ten."

"And then?"

"My mother had twins when I was eight . . . and life got hectic. After a while, my piano lessons didn't fit anymore."

"I'm sorry."

"It's not important—certainly not all these years later."

It was as if I'd been given a gift, only to open the box, dig through the tissue, and find it empty. I'd almost reconnected with a brief time of joy from my childhood—only to discover Miss Felicia had died. I had no chance to return to her as an adult and thank her for who she'd been in my life.

I pressed the palm of my hand against the sudden tightness in my chest. I hadn't realized how much I'd lost all those years ago, when I'd chosen to stop taking piano lessons, despite Miss Felicia's protests.

"Johanna, this makes no sense. You are my best student—and I do not give praise lightly." Miss Felicia sat beside me on the piano bench.

Her nearness surprised me. It couldn't matter all that much to her if I played the piano or not. It didn't matter to my own parents.

"*Nothing to say? To explain why you're stopping lessons? Your mother told me it's your decision.*"

"*I don't like playing the piano anymore.*"

And that was the truth. I didn't.

It was better that I'd decided to stop lessons before my parents told me I had to. Why play when no one cared? When no one listened? And it wasn't as if my parents had tried to talk me out of quitting. They'd probably been relieved to have more time for the twins.

I pushed away from the piano, stumbling a bit as I stood so that I braced myself against the keyboard with a small clash of sound. "I should let you have the piano."

Robyn pulled sheet music from her satchel, arranging it on the piano. "Do you ever think of taking lessons again?"

"No. Never." I slipped my purse onto my shoulder. "I'm a pharmacist, not a pianist."

We all had to grow up sometime.

ANOTHER WEDNESDAY NIGHT. Another Bible study get-together where Payton sat beside Zach and listened to him and everyone else in the room discuss the how-did-they-know-all-these-details of Galatians.

Payton was perfecting the art of listening. Bringing a fruit salad and listening.

She still struggled to remember if Galatians was spelled with an *-ians* or an *-ions*, but every week she brought a bowl of fresh mixed fruit to share with the group. And so far, no one even knew she was a vegan. No need to stand out for any other reason besides the fact that she was so new at all of this that she didn't know what to do. Didn't know what to pray for. There was no need to be labeled as the newbie believer who didn't eat meat. Or dairy. No, thanks. She'd let everyone think she just had a thing for fruit.

"So how was everyone's week? Any updates?"

Paul's question signaled the end of casual chitchat. This was the most relaxed part of the study for Payton—when Paul and Sara had everyone go around the room and share a brief update about their week. She'd learned to let Zach take the lead and then she'd chime in with some version of "Pretty much the same for me. Volleyball. Classes."

But this time, as the conversation veered in her direction, warmth invaded her body, causing her to shift in her seat.

No. She was not sharing. She didn't have anything to say.

"Zach? How are you this week?"

See? Even Paul was sticking to the routine, expecting Zach to talk, not Payton.

Zach was unaware of her inner struggle. "It's been a pretty normal week—"

"I, um, had an interesting experience." Payton raised her voice, rushing over him, heat flushing her face and neck. "Related to the study. My prayer request for patience, actually, if you can believe that."

And now she had the group's attention, as if she'd stood up in the middle of the room, prepared to give an impromptu speech. But now everyone was staring at her and she realized she hadn't prepared. She should have written something down on index cards to get through this.

Zach, bless him, grabbed her hand and squeezed so that her wedding rings pressed into her fingers. Was he telling her to stop? Go ahead? That she was crazy to have said anything?

That he was praying for her? Well, Paul had asked how everyone's week had gone. And she was a legit member of the group, no matter how inexperienced she was.

Besides, it was too late now.

"I know you're not supposed to pray for patience, but I only learned that after I asked everyone to pray for me about coaching one of my volleyball players. And I figure someone here has been praying because, well, she's continued to be a challenge."

Payton ended her words with a laugh, but no one joined her. Well then. She'd just keep talking. "Um, you all know I'm probably the youngest believer in the group. I've been reading and rereading Galatians, trying to keep up with the rest of you. Not that it's a competition—there's just a lot I don't know."

"That's a great idea, Payton." Sara nodded, offering her an encouraging smile.

"I was reading Galatians 5 a few weeks ago—where it talks about 'faith expressing itself through love.' And that phrase stayed with me all week. I wondered if I was trying to love this girl, or was I trying to boss her around? Get her to do what I wanted her to do?"

All the while she was talking, Payton wondered why she hadn't let Zach talk. Stayed with the routine. But she couldn't stop now—like an awful first date where a guy sat silently across from you and you had to keep the conversation going until you could end the date, go home, and eat a bowl of cereal while you commiserated with your best friend about whether your date topped her worst first date.

Paul scribbled something in his notebook with his old-fashioned blue Bic pen. Probably a note to skip the Gaineses next week. After tonight, she'd bring lots and lots of fruit salad and never say another word in Bible study—ever, ever again.

"I noticed the word *love* came up a few more times in the chapter." She needed to keep this short. "I remember hearing the pastor saying in one of his recent sermons that 'love is patient'—"

"That's in 1 Corinthians."

Paul's comment, offered with a quick smile, didn't bother her. "It stayed with me because of, well, you know, the prayer request I never should have prayed."

"Did something change with your relationship with the girl?" Sara asked.

"Honestly? She hasn't changed how she's acting. But I'm trying to change how I react to her. I'm trying to love her more."

"How?"

Payton hadn't anticipated the questions. "I pray for her before practices. Then I try to encourage her during practices. Turns out, she responds really well to one-on-one coaching, so I've asked her to come early a few times so I can give her some focused attention. It's helped a lot. Our team was working well—and I thought this one girl was hindering us. But then I realized it was my attitude toward her that was tripping us up. I needed to change how I interacted with her."

"What's the girl's name?" Deanna asked. "We can pray for you and her better if we know her first name."

"Laney." Payton was going to hug her—hard—for asking such a simple question. "And thanks. I appreciate that."

The truth was, everyone in the group was listening to her. No one yawned. No one stared at their plates of food.

For the first time, Payton was part of the group. She was seen. Heard—at least by Paul and Sara. And Deanna. And Zach. Always Zach.

She'd been waiting for the others to include her, but maybe she needed to try to be more involved, rather than relying on Zach all the time. And maybe she needed to stop being so hard on herself. Remove the label of "newbie," which translated as "less than" in her head. Remember that relationships took time.

"I think Payton gave us our lesson for the week." Paul stuck his pen into his notebook, closing it.

"I don't think so." Payton shook her head.

Now laughter went around the group.

Paul stood. "Why don't we refresh our drinks and food, and then we'll start the study."

Sara stopped Payton as she headed toward the dining room. "Thanks for sharing."

"I hope I didn't talk too long."

"Not at all. It's good to have a new believer in the study."

"Kind of like comic relief, right?" She infused humor into her voice. "'What is Payton not going to know this week?'"

"That's not what I mean at all. Sometimes we forget . . . I forget how precious my faith is. Take it for granted because, well, I've believed for so long. It becomes a habit. You remind me of when I was first a believer. I'm not laughing. I'm thankful."

That was an unexpected perspective. Like an optical illusion, where you look at a black-and-white picture and first see one image, then stare long enough so that another image comes into focus.

Conversation floated from the other room.

Payton needed to stop being so concerned about how uncomfortable she was and discover who everyone else was.

"Payton! There you are. I've wanted to ask you a question." Molly approached her, and Payton scrambled to remember her husband's name. "I have a stepdaughter who's going to be starting middle school next year and we want her to try a sport. Is this a good age for her to try volleyball?"

"That's a perfect time to try it." Payton's shoulders relaxed. Volleyball questions she could handle. "A lot of schools and volleyball clubs offer summer camps where kids can come and see what it's like."

"Could you recommend any?"

"Besides mine?" When she laughed this time, Molly joined in. "Absolutely. I can give you my e-mail and send you some information."

"That would be great. I have some friends who are interested, too. Do you mind if I share it with them?"

"Go right ahead." Across the room, Payton noticed Zach watching her, probably wondering if she needed him to come over and rescue her from an uncomfortable situation. She offered him a quick smile to let him know she was okay, that tonight she could manage on her own.

I WAS SO READY to go home and start the weekend—even after I'd come to work two hours later than usual. I'd pushed back the guilt, reminding myself that Axton was the one who'd encouraged me to adjust my schedule. To work less, if I needed to.

And it seemed that, as my pregnancy progressed, I needed to.

"Johanna, do you have a minute to talk?"

I twisted around in my chair to face my boss. "I guess so. I mean, yes. Absolutely."

"Are you busy?"

"No. Just finishing up for the day."

"This won't take long." Axton continued to stand in my office doorway.

"Do you want to come in?" I motioned to one of the chairs in my office. "You're welcome to sit down."

"Actually, I could use a cup of coffee. Want to walk with me?" Axton took a step back. "We can go get a cup at the staff cafeteria . . ."

"But that's closed right now while they clean between the day and evening shifts."

"Don't tell anyone, but sometimes they let me slip in to grab a cup."

Exhaustion warred with my desire to accommodate my boss. I swiveled my chair a half turn away. "Why don't you go and come back . . ."

"But we can walk and talk and—" Axton seemed to be searching for words—"and you said you were getting ready to leave, right? *Right.* Grab your purse and whatever else you need. If we walk and talk, the sooner we'll be done and you can go home from there."

Axton was in one of his not-taking-no-for-an-answer moods. "Fine. I'll go with you—if they even let us in the cafeteria. Which I doubt."

This was the first time in a long time that Axton was irritating me. The old Axton Miller had shown up in my office. And now he was glancing at his watch as if he was the one who had someplace to be, not me.

This had better be important.

Axton almost fast-walked down the hallway.

"What's the rush?"

"Huh?"

"The rush? I'm having a hard time keeping up with you, to be honest. One of us is pregnant here, Axton."

"Oh. Sorry." He slowed his pace. "I just don't want to be late."

"Late? You said they'd let you in."

"Right. They will."

"What are we talking about?"

"Talking about?"

My steps slowed even more. "Are you okay?"

"Sure. I'm fine. Why do you ask?"

"Because you asked to talk to me, but you don't seem to remember that."

Our arrival at the cafeteria prevented Axton from having to reply. The area was empty of staff. Workers were cleaning. Wiping down the wooden tables. Running several vacuums. Setting out small glass vases with white daisies and sprigs of baby's breath. Axton bypassed the coffee area, heading toward the physicians' private lounge area in the back.

I stopped. "Where are you going?"

"Back here. Come on."

"Why would we go there? The coffee's over that way."

"Come on."

"Axton—" I waved my hand toward the coffee station— "the coffee is right here, where it's always been."

He grabbed my hand, tugging me forward. "We're going this way, Johanna."

My boss was confusing me, not scaring me, but I had the

strongest desire to dig my heels into the floor and demand he explain why he was behaving so oddly.

And then I heard the sound of muffled laughter.

I knew Jillian's laugh—even if it was out of place. And I was not going to fall for this.

"Who else is here?"

"I'm not at liberty to say." Axton lowered his voice. "All friends. No foes."

Hadn't I just explained to Axton a few weeks ago that I didn't have any friends? "I'll be the judge of that. And I'm looking at a foe."

"It'll be fun, Johanna."

"Once again, I'll be the judge of that."

Axton stepped aside and ushered me into the area. A jubilant shout of "Surprise!" overwhelmed me.

It seemed all my protests, all my insistence that I didn't want a baby shower, didn't matter. I was surrounded by a crowd of people—it would take me a moment to figure out just who was there—all intent on celebrating my pregnancy.

Mom was the first person to hug me. "Do you love it? Payton planned it."

"Payton?" I still hadn't seen either of my sisters.

"Of course. She contacted her former business partner at Festivities and they worked their party-planning magic." Mom motioned Jillian and Payton forward.

My sisters hugged me in rapid succession, and Jill spoke first. "Payton knew you didn't want a baby shower, so she opted for a French market soiree theme. She set a two-hour time limit."

Payton's smile held just the smallest bit of self-satisfaction. "We know you kept saying, 'No shower, no shower,' but you didn't expect us to listen, did you?"

"Yes. I did."

"Sorry. That was unrealistic." Jillian laughed. "But you'll forgive us, right? It's only two hours—we promise. And technically it's a soiree, not a baby shower. Try to relax and enjoy yourself."

Two hours. I could survive two hours. "Promise me there are no games."

"Not a one." Payton raised her hand. "It's conversation, food, and presents."

"I could have skipped the conversation . . ."

"Don't be ridiculous." Mom gave me another side hug. "You're the mom-to-be. Everyone wants to talk to you."

Perfect.

But Jillian was right when she said this didn't look like a typical baby shower. Payton had chosen a black-and-white theme—considering how I'd decorated my home, perhaps? A mix of white silk hydrangeas and faux white poppies spilled out of tall pewter containers beside a food table covered in white linen and laden with croissant sandwiches wrapped in white paper. Mixed veggies and olives on skewers were assembled in white plastic cups, and an elegant cheese, meat, and crusty bread selection was arranged on several long white porcelain trays. Short stacks of small plastic boxes wrapped in delicate black cloth ribbon contained macaroons and were arranged on another table—delectable party favors for each guest. And a two-tiered cake was understated elegance, decorated with the faux poppies and the same black ribbon that adorned the favors.

"Wait a minute . . ." I stopped in front of the table piled high with gifts for my baby, each one wrapped in a different type of white paper, but all with the same black ribbon. "How did you manage to coordinate my gifts?"

"Payton told the guests to select any type of white wrapping paper they wanted—keeping it simple." Mom stood beside me. "And then we supplied the ribbon when they arrived."

My sisters . . . everyone . . . had put a lot of thought into this soiree.

⁓

One hour down. One hour to go.

I'd survived the "conversation" part of my one and only baby shower. It didn't matter that they were calling it a soiree. We all knew what it was. I'd mingled until my lower back ached and my smile strained my lips. I knew everyone. They were all the people I saw throughout the day. The people Axton had taught me to value as more than expendable employees who could be replaced by someone else with a decent résumé. Of course, Mom and Payton and Jillian were a hit. And even Axton's wife was there, playing hostess and plying everyone with more food, more drink, and plenty of nonstop conversation.

But now I had to open gifts.

"Where are you going?" Payton stepped forward, blocking my escape.

"To the bathroom."

"You just went to the bathroom."

"I'm pregnant. I have to go again."

"Even if you were pregnant with twins—and you're not—you wouldn't have to go to the bathroom every two minutes." She looped her arm through mine, attempting to turn me around. "It's time to open your presents."

"Can't I just take them home? Open them there? I promise to write a thank-you note to every single person here."

"No, you can't do that. What is wrong with you?"

"This is going to be so awkward, sitting around, unwrapping gifts while everyone's watching me. Telling me to just tear the paper! I do not tear wrapping paper, Payton. You know that."

"Then don't tear it. I even have a small pair of scissors so you can cut through the tape." Payton produced a pair of craft scissors, accompanied with a conspiratorial wink.

I could have hugged my sister. "What do I do if I don't like something?"

"Johanna, I can't believe we're even having this conversation. Mom raised us right. Jillian will be sitting next to you, writing down who gave you what. Just say something like, 'Oh, look at this, Jill,' and hand it to her."

"'Oh, look at this' is code for I don't like it?"

"Yes. But no one else needs to know that, not even Jill." She tugged me forward. "Let's go, momma-to-be. Everyone's waiting on you."

"You had to say that, didn't you?"

I would not tell my sister how I felt like a fish in a

fishbowl—a very pregnant, introverted fish in a fishbowl. But the crowd wasn't standing outside, looking in. No, the crowd had climbed into the glass bowl with me and was getting closer and closer.

And now I did have to go to the bathroom again. But Payton would never believe me.

Before I knew it, I was down to one last gift—and I hadn't once needed to use the "Oh, look at this, Jill," code. My daughter had a delightful ensemble of dresses and sleepers, as well as a car seat, high chair, and an assortment of books, plush animals, and bibs.

"Here. This is from Mom. And me. And Payton . . . and Pepper, too." Jillian whispered the last name so only I could hear it.

"Pepper?"

"Open it. You'll understand."

As I had with every other gift, I took my time. Slipped the black cloth ribbon off the rectangular package, handing it to Jillian. Cut through the tape and removed the wrapping paper, folding it so it could be used again.

"This is a . . ."

"Turn it over." Mom's voice trembled.

I did as she asked, running my fingers over the smooth glass covering a series of black-and-white photographs.

Mom's baby picture.

My baby picture.

Jillian's baby picture.

Payton and Pepper—so identical, even as newborns.

One blank opening in the mat. A small neon-pink Post-it

note was stuck on the glass. I peeled it off to read the words printed on it.

We're all waiting to meet the one who starts the next generation of Thatcher women.

Those words, written in Jillian's script, welcomed my daughter into our family as a blessing, not a mistake.

The photos were glimpses of our individual beginnings.

Which was more important? The beginning or where we were now?

26

IT WOULD BE FAIR to say Payton had avoided celebrating her birthday for years, when it was too tangled up with loss and guilt. Her birthday had always been *their* birthday, the day she and Pepper were born. It seemed wrong to open presents and sing and eat cake when her sister was dead.

But Zach had overruled Payton's insistence about not making a big deal of the day, telling her to leave it to him, that he'd plan everything. That her twin sister would want her to have fun on their birthday. And this year, she could accept his offer.

"I have to admit this was quite an unusual way to celebrate my birthday." Payton pulled her hair out from the high ponytail she'd styled it in earlier, shaking the strands loose around her shoulders.

"What? An escape room doesn't say, 'Happy birthday' to you?" Zach laughed as he closed the car door behind her.

"Locked in a room with family and having to solve puzzles to defuse a bomb? Um, it's different . . ."

"It wasn't a real bomb—"

"I was very thankful they made that clear at the beginning of all the fun." Payton laughed.

"—and we all sang to you once we beat the clock."

"There was that." Payton wrapped her arms around her husband. "It was great. A complete surprise."

"And we won." Zach gave her a quick kiss.

"Yes, we won, and that made everyone very happy. You can't say we're not a competitive bunch of people. And you did tell me we were going to dinner after." She scanned the restaurant's parking lot. "Are we the first ones here?"

"I think so. No, wait. I see Geoff and Jillian waiting by the front door."

"Great."

Zach and Geoff exchanged high fives with cheers of "Bomb defused!" as Payton and Jillian shared a hug.

"I think the guys took the whole 'There's a bomb' scenario more seriously than we did." Payton whispered the words loud enough for Zach and Geoff to hear.

"Geoff talked through an entire replay of everything we did—right and wrong—on the drive over." Jillian shook her head.

"We need to go again." Geoff's grin mirrored Zach's.

"Maybe you and Zach and Dad should go. Pick out a different scenario."

"That's a great idea." Zach pulled out his phone. "What other room themes were there?"

Payton covered the phone with her hand. "Before you do that, would you go check on our reservation?"

"Sure thing."

"I'll go with you." Geoff followed Zach into the restaurant.

Jillian shook her head. "We can only hope they remember your request to check on our dinner reservation."

"It seems like my birthday surprise was a hit with everyone."

"I have to say I'm surprised Mom and Johanna joined in."

"I was, too, at first. But Mom and Dad enjoy board games, so why not this?" Payton motioned to a bench positioned outside the restaurant. "And Johanna, well, she's the most competitive Thatcher there is, so I couldn't see her sitting out in the lobby while we all tried to beat the clock."

"She was a big help, too." Jillian sat beside Payton.

"You know what? I think she even had fun." Payton smiled. "Pepper would have loved it."

"I wondered if you were thinking of her."

"I think of her every day, but especially on our birthday. All she's missing out on. I wonder if she'd be married now. If she'd still be involved with volleyball. If she'd still be living in Colorado like the rest of us."

"I'd like to think all the Thatcher sisters would still be living here."

"Me, too." Payton settled back on the bench. "How are you doing, Jill?"

"Me?"

"Are you and Geoff doing better?" Jillian and Geoff came to some of the Sunday dinners and they seemed fine. Not back to normal, but then their life had been anything but normal for months.

"You don't want to be talking about this on your birthday—"

"I asked, didn't I?"

"Yes."

"Well, then . . ."

"Nothing's changed." Jillian leaned forward, resting her arms on her knees. "Geoff and I still want different things. But I'm trying to remember that, despite our differences, we still love each other. I'm hoping that's enough."

She should have talked to Jillian about this sooner. They were both facing challenges. Both new at living life as believers. That changed how they acted and reacted to things.

"Have you been praying about it?"

"No." Jillian flushed, her voice small.

"Jillian, why—?"

"It's hard, Payton. I thought believing in God would make things easier. That I'd have hope. And nothing's changed. I wake up to the same hard things every day."

"I should have asked you sooner. I'm so sorry." Payton pulled her sister into a hug. "Here I've been worrying about whether I'm saying and doing the right thing in Bible study—"

"What?"

"Believe me, we'll laugh about it later." Payton kept Jillian close. "You're more important. We're both new at this and we should be encouraging each other."

"Oh, Payton, I'd love the chance to talk to you about all this. And to pray, too."

"Here come Mom and Dad and Johanna, so we'll have to talk more later." Payton offered Jillian another smile before standing. "But we need to remember we're not on our own in this—we've got each other."

"Now hearing you say that gives me hope." Jillian whispered the words just as their parents and Johanna came up.

It was funny how admitting she was struggling too encouraged her sister. How being less than perfect brought them closer together.

"Happy birthday to me—imperfections and all." Payton waited while Jillian went and greeted their parents. "And happy birthday to you, too, Pepper. Miss you."

27

I'D COME TO APPRECIATE the Fourth of July more while I'd dated Beckett.

He didn't just wear his uniform—he believed in the military. Was proud to serve his country. If we went to an event and the national anthem played, he stood at attention. Being with Beckett for eight years had instilled a sense of patriotism in me. Even though our relationship had ended badly, an appreciation for men and women who served in our country's military remained.

For my family, the summer holiday was all about a cookout, sometimes with friends, sometimes not. Mom's potato salad and baked beans. Dad's burgers. Watermelon. And now that Payton was a vegan, there were always more untraditional side dishes. She'd arrived today with two recipes she promised the entire family would enjoy.

Mom came to stand beside me, just inside the sliding-glass doors off the family room. The rest of the family was outside, with Dad prepping the grill while Zach and Payton paired off against Geoff and Jillian in a game of cornhole. "What do you think of the new deck?"

"You and Dad made a wonderful decision. You'll never regret the composite. It's going to be so easy to take care of."

"That's what your dad keeps saying every time we sit out there in the evening after dinner." Mom sighed, her shoulders relaxing. "We're both happy. Zach and Brandon did a beautiful job."

"We're all going to enjoy it today, although I might sit inside some, too, if that's okay."

"Whatever you want to do, honey."

"What I want to do is enjoy air-conditioning as much as possible. I'm so glad you and Dad opted to install that on the house years ago."

"Are you sleeping well?"

"Not great, but I manage. I miss sleeping on my back. Dr. Gray suggested I invest in one of those body pillows, so I may do that and see if it helps."

"We can run out later today and pick one up if you want to."

"Maybe. Or I can stop at the store in the next couple of days. Let's see how the day goes."

I didn't want to be one of those women who talked about her pregnancy all the time, cataloging every little ache or pain. How tired I was. How often I had to empty my bladder.

Like now. My bladder never let me forget I was pregnant.

It might be easier to move my office to one of the ladies' restrooms at work. But that would make things awkward when Axton came looking for me.

"I'll be right back, Mom. I need to use the bathroom. Again."

Mom offered a knowing smile. "I remember those days, especially when I was pregnant with the twins."

"I can't even imagine being pregnant with two." I waved away the thought. "We can finish prepping the burgers—"

"I'll do that. Go to the bathroom, and after that sit and relax. Do you want some iced tea?"

"Sounds perfect."

As Mom disappeared upstairs, I opted for the convenience of the half bathroom right off the family room. Lowered myself to the toilet . . . then gasped and clutched the side of the vanity at the sight of bright-red blood spotting my underwear.

I was bleeding. Why . . . *why* was I bleeding?

My fingers gathered the pale-blue material of my sundress. The dress Jillian had selected for me when we'd gone shopping.

Her peace offering.

This made no sense. Today was supposed to be a fun family day. Traditional backyard barbecue. Time to relax. Maybe watch fireworks. Not this. It was as if someone had come and scraped the length of my parents' beautiful new deck with a rototiller. Scarred it.

My heart pounded.

I couldn't just sit here asking myself, "Why?" I needed to call someone. Get help.

Not for me.

For my baby.

I drew a shaky breath, swallowing the rising urge to scream. What I needed to do was stay calm. It wasn't that much blood.

I forced myself to relax my grip on the vanity. Pushed myself to my feet, refusing to look in the mirror over the bathroom sink as I readjusted my clothing.

The first thing to do was call Dr. Gray's office.

I took the stairs, a slow step up and stop, step up and stop procedure, retrieving my phone from my purse in the foyer. Easy enough to slip into the living room with Mom in the kitchen and everyone else outside admiring the new deck.

"This is the answering service for Dr. Gray's office. How can I help you?"

It was a holiday. Of course the office was closed.

"This is Johanna Thatcher. I'm one of Dr. Gray's patients. How do I reach her?"

"Is there a problem, Miss Thatcher?"

"I wouldn't call unless there was a problem." I chewed my bottom lip. Modulated my tone. "I'm sorry. Yes, I'm thirty-two weeks pregnant. I have placenta previa and I'm spotting."

"Are you bleeding heavily? Are you light-headed? Short of breath? Do we need to call 911 for you?"

"No. So far, it's only spotting. I'm not certain when it started."

"We can contact Dr. Gray for you, but she's going to tell you to go immediately to labor and delivery. Are you in the Springs?"

"Yes. I'm supposed to deliver at St. Francis."

"Then go ahead and go there—and have someone drive you. Immediately. If no one is available, call 911."

"I'm with family."

"We'll contact Dr. Gray. She may call you back or she may just phone in orders for you to go to St. Francis and then meet you at the hospital."

Talking to the unknown woman on the phone was a lifeline. She was calm. Emotionless. That meant I could be calm and emotionless, too.

I'd turned away from the downstairs, from the sliding-glass doors that led outside to where most of my family was having fun. I only wished they could talk to the woman on the phone, too. After ending the call, I stood for a moment, debating what to do. Mom was in the kitchen. Everyone else was outside.

Maybe, just maybe, Payton had her cell phone with her.

My call went to voice mail. I'd have to walk downstairs, get my sister, and walk back up again. It couldn't be avoided. Despite the air-conditioning, sweat dampened the material of my dress.

Once I stood just inside the sliding-glass doors, I waited until Payton glanced my way, motioning her over.

"Do you need something, Johanna?"

"Be calm. Don't react." I gripped her arm, pulling her close. "I need you to drive me to the hospital. Now."

"What?" When Payton tried to jerk away, I held her steady.

"*Don't react.* Please." I kept my voice low. "Just drive me to the hospital."

My sister still refused to move. "Johanna, what is going on? Are you in labor?"

"No. I'm bleeding." Saying the words out loud caused my heart rate to ratchet up again. "Spotting, really. I called my doctor's office and the answering service told me to go to labor and delivery at St. Francis right away. They're contacting Dr. Gray."

"We have to tell the family—"

My fingers tightened around my sister's arm. "Please, Payton. I don't have time to deal with everyone's reactions. We have to leave. *Now.* You can call them while we're on the way. I don't care. I can't drive myself." I shoved my car keys into her hands. "I need your help."

How did I get caught in such a role reversal? I took care of others. I was the in-charge Thatcher sister. I preferred it that way. If Payton didn't say yes and start walking upstairs toward the front door, I would snatch the keys back from her and ignore what the woman had said about having someone drive me to the hospital. It wasn't that far of a drive.

Don't make me ask you twice.

"I'll drive you." As if she'd heard my unspoken declaration, Payton stepped up beside me, grabbing her purse from where it sat next to the family room couch. "Let's go."

With one quick motion, I closed the sliding-glass door, muffling the sound of everyone's laughter.

Now we just needed to get out of the house without Mom seeing us.

Tears brimmed when I realized no one had blocked my car in the driveway. I was not quite as calm as I thought I was.

Payton slid in behind the steering wheel, locking her seat belt into place. "You said St. Francis, right?"

"Yes. You need to head north—"

"I've got this, Johanna." She started the engine, backing the car into the street. "You said you're bleeding. When did it start?"

"I don't know. I went to the bathroom and that's when I realized something was wrong. Everything's been fine up until now. We were going to do another ultrasound next week . . ."

"Do you want to call the family while I drive?"

"No." I closed my eyes, leaning back against the headrest. "Just call Mom, I guess. Tell her what's going on and that we'll let them know when everything's fine."

"Everything will be fine." My sister gripped my hand. "I'm praying."

"Go right ahead and keep doing that." If it made Payton feel better to pray, fine. It wouldn't change anything, but it wouldn't hurt. I only wished I could find some comfort in her offer, but I never had before, and I wouldn't let emotions rule my choices now.

"Listen, if you dial Mom, I'll do the talking, okay? Just put it on speaker." Payton never took her eyes off the road.

"Okay."

"And you know no one's going to wait at home, right?"

"There's no reason for everybody to come to the hospital—"

"You're the reason, Johanna. You and the baby."

Again, tears blurred my vision.

I'd called on Payton in a crisis because I didn't have a choice. Jillian and I were still finding our way back to each other. Who knew? Maybe it would be easier for her if I miscarried.

The thought came from out of nowhere, causing me to catch my breath.

"Are you okay?" Payton still hadn't let go of my hand.

"Yes. Yes, I'm fine."

I pleated the soft material of the sundress. Again. And again. And again.

I was not going to lose my daughter.

~

I'd missed the Fourth of July.

Everyone in the family had, but at least they'd been able to go home and sleep in their own beds. And none of them were hooked up to monitors, with IVs stuck in their arms. None of them had to drag an IV pole along with them whenever they had to use the bathroom.

And they most definitely were not afraid to pee.

I might not ever feel comfortable going to the bathroom again until after this baby was born.

Now, here I sat in a hospital-issued gown, my hair finger-brushed into place, having a different kind of "morning-after" discussion with my doctor.

"I'm sorry I ruined the holiday for everyone—especially for you, Dr. Gray."

"I'm thankful you did what I asked you to do." She stood at the foot of the bed, the stereotypical stethoscope around her neck. "Calling the office and then following the on-call nurse's instructions to come to the hospital was the right thing to do."

"But it was a false alarm. The baby is fine."

"We wouldn't know that unless you had called and come in."

"I still don't understand why I can't go home. I haven't had any more bleeding."

"It's routine to keep you here for observation—" Dr. Gray raised her hand, forestalling my protest. "Yes, even though everything looks good—blood work, ultrasound. Even though you're not contracting. And you still need to make arrangements to stay within twenty minutes of the hospital for the duration of your pregnancy—with someone with you twenty-four hours a day."

I continued to balk at the last two requirements. "I'm an adult. I can take care of myself."

"Not if you're home alone and you start hemorrhaging."

With those words, Dr. Gray won. There was no way I could find an argument that conquered the word *hemorrhage*. I gripped the edge of the bed the same way I'd gripped the vanity in the bathroom.

Nothing had happened. There'd been no real crisis, just the possibility of one. But there could be one in the future— as much as I wanted to insist there wouldn't be.

"You're coming home with me, Johanna." Mom spoke up from where she sat in a corner of the room. I'd forgotten she was there, even though she'd stayed all night, having enough foresight to bring a blanket and pillow from home, but still getting no more sleep than I had. "We already agreed to that."

"I know. And I appreciate it. I do. But now I have to call my boss and deal with my job. And then I have to get stuff from my house . . ."

"I can do that for you." Beckett strode into the room that was already too crowded.

"What are you doing here?" I tried to sit up straighter, but the two monitor bands around my stomach restricted my movement.

"Your parents called me last night. They thought I should know—"

"Mom, why would you call him?"

"Don't get upset." Mom rushed to stand beside my bed. "We all talked about it. We know you and Beckett aren't together anymore, but he is the baby's father . . ."

"Beckett and I are discussing how that's going to play out." And now Dr. Gray was an uninvited witness to the consequences of my failed engagement.

"We understand that. We weren't sure what was the best thing to do, but we thought, just in case something went wrong—"

"Your family did the right thing, calling me." Beckett held his position beside Dr. Gray.

"Nothing happened. I'm fine. The baby's fine."

"And what if something had happened? Do you think I would want to get a phone call after the fact?"

"To be honest, Beckett, I wasn't thinking about you at all during any of this."

My words brought silence to the room. Beckett and I were like patients who chose to mix their medications with alcohol—a dangerous combination.

He was as handsome as ever. The father of my child.

But what we had—what we'd meant to each other—couldn't matter anymore. It didn't matter.

Dr. Gray stepped into the silence. "Excuse me, I'd like for things to settle down. I'm trying to care for my patients—both mother and unborn child. I'd prefer not to have to escort anyone out of this room or this hospital. But I will."

Beckett pulled himself up to his full height, shoulders back. "I apologize. I'm Lt. Colonel Sager, the baby's father—"

"And I'm Dr. Hayden Gray, and in this hospital, I outrank you. I don't mean to be rude, but my concern right now is Johanna. If you'd step into the hallway, please."

"I was offering to help."

"I believe there are family members in the waiting area you can talk to about that."

She waited, her gaze unwavering, until Beckett exited the room, then shut the door on him. "I hope you don't mind, Johanna, but I thought it best to not let—Beckett, is it?—get out of control."

"No." I had to hold back a laugh. "That was perfect."

"He's not the first temperamental boyfriend I've had to deal with."

"Ex. Ex-fiancé."

"It's not the topic of the day, but you can decide who is with you when the baby is born and who can visit you now and when you deliver."

"Thank you. Beckett's not abusive. He's just assertive."

I must be more tired than I realized. I'd let another woman do battle for me.

Voices murmured outside the door. My family—and now Beckett—were not staying within the confines of the waiting area.

A couple of civil interactions, including Beckett telling me about his father, didn't mean I owed him anything—even the chance to help me. He needed to respect my boundaries, but instead, he was skewing them.

"I'll be back tomorrow to discharge you, Johanna. Until then, rest. And yes, I know that's hard to do in the hospital, hooked up to these monitors. But try. It's only another twenty-four hours."

"When you put it that way, how can I complain?" I could only hope Dr. Gray took note of my muted sarcasm.

"Remember my instructions, which I'll repeat tomorrow before you leave and also print on your discharge papers. Bed rest. No exercise. No going to work. If you have bleeding of any kind, you call me, and then you come right to labor and delivery. Understood?"

"Yes."

"We'll talk more tomorrow." Dr. Gray faced Mom. "It was nice to meet you, Mrs. Thatcher. I hope the next time I see you for an extended period of time, it's for your grand-daughter's birth day."

"I hope so, too, Dr. Gray."

And then it was just Mom and me.

"I like your doctor."

"I do, too." I was surprised to hear myself say the words—and to realize I meant them. "Mom, I'll go back to your house tomorrow, like we agreed. If I make out a list, would you ask either Jillian or Payton to get what I need from my house?"

"What do you want me to say to Beckett?"

Beckett.

"I'd forgotten about him."

"Do you want me to talk to him for you?" Mom stepped toward the door.

"No. I can talk to him. It's not as if I have anything else to do except sit here."

"Then I'll go talk to your sisters and have Beckett come in."

A few moments later, Beckett and I faced off again, the silence stretching between us until Beckett shifted his feet and cleared his throat. "Your mother said one of your sisters is going to get your stuff for you."

"Yes."

"I wasn't trying to irritate you, you know."

"You were trying to help."

"Yes."

"I know, Beckett." I ran my fingers through my unwashed hair again. It was bad enough that my natural color was showing at the roots, letting everyone know I wasn't a true platinum blonde. One of the first appointments after I had my baby would be with my hairstylist. If only I'd had the chance to put on some makeup, but it wasn't as if Beckett had never seen me without it. "You want to help, but you're not that person in my life anymore."

"I just . . . I just got scared when I heard. For the baby. And for you." Beckett shrugged. "There's not much I can do, so I thought—"

"Thanks. I appreciate the offer." I tugged the blanket higher on my body. "We've agreed we'll figure this out for the baby. But it's going to take time."

"Right."

"I'm going to be staying at my parents' now until the baby is born."

"Would it . . . would it be okay if I check in with you?"

"Sure. I don't mind a text now and then."

"And you'll let me know if anything happens—"

"We're counting on everything being quiet from here on out."

"Yes."

"Would you ask my mom to come back in?"

"Will do." Beckett paused. "Thanks, Johanna."

"We'll figure it out." I offered him my most self-assured smile.

"We will."

And then I was alone again—at least for a moment.

I shifted in the hospital bed, careful not to move the belts around my body. It would take me a while to get used to having to be on my side all the time. The ever-present beeping of the monitors both irritated and soothed me, letting me know my daughter was okay.

It was true I hadn't wanted to be pregnant. Hadn't wanted this baby at first. But now . . . now I didn't want to lose her.

I'd been given an assignment to rest. Take care of myself. Take care of my baby. But I wasn't in charge. Not really.

A door separated me from the normal world. But when I walked through it tomorrow, it wouldn't be the same world that I'd known.

It seemed scarier. Unfamiliar.

Tomorrow I'd be back home. Not in my house, but what had been home a long time ago. The room where Jillian and I stayed up late and talked about school and boys. The house where Mom and Dad had surprised Jillian and me with not one, but two little sisters.

The house where everything changed.

The house I left behind when I went to college, ready to be independent.

And now Mom was going to take care of me again.

"Johanna?" Mom stood beside my bed, where Beckett had been just moments before.

"I'm sorry. I didn't hear you come in."

"I could tell. Are you okay?"

"Just thinking. All of this has been a lot to absorb."

"I understand. We've all been scared. But Dr. Gray talked to all of us just now and we like her a lot."

"I do, too. It's funny because I didn't at first."

"You're too much alike."

"What?"

"You and she are both medical professionals, and I believe she holds her views strongly like you do."

Sometimes I didn't give Mom enough credit. "Yes, we do."

"Payton said she'd pack your suitcase for my house."

"I haven't had a chance to make a list because I was talking to Beckett."

"We're going to get some breakfast, so why don't we make a preliminary list and then we can talk it out when we get back?"

"Sounds perfect." I motioned for my purse. "And if you'll hand me my phone, please, I'll call Axton and fill him in. At least it's a long weekend. I think they went out of town, but I'm not sure."

But Axton didn't answer—his wife did.

"Hello, this is Dr. Miller's phone."

"Mrs. Miller—um, Dot? This is Johanna Thatcher."

"Johanna? Is everything okay?"

"I'm fine." That was true—now. "I'm sorry to bother you on the holiday weekend, but may I speak to Axton, please?"

"Absolutely. Let me get him out of the pool."

Perfect. Of course, I was continuing to disrupt everyone's weekend.

"Johanna, is everything okay?"

"Yes and no." Now it sounded like I was hedging. "I'm in the hospital . . ."

"Working? Johanna, I thought we'd agreed you'd take the weekend off."

"Not Mount Columbia. St. Francis. I had a minor pregnancy complication, but I'm fine. The baby's fine."

"What exactly is going on?"

"I have placenta previa, which has become more problematic than we originally thought. I experienced some bleeding yesterday and I'll be spending another night here at the hospital. But like I said, the baby is fine."

"I'm thankful to hear that." Axton paused for a moment as Dot spoke in the background. "Hold on for a moment, please. Let me just update Dot."

"Sure." I allowed myself to sink back against the pillows and count the rhythm of my daughter's heartbeat.

"Sorry about that. What does this mean for you long-term?"

"I'm on modified bed rest at my parents' house until I deliver. And that means I can't go back to work."

"Whew. That's quite a change for you."

"I know. And I'm sorry because this also inconveniences you. I can try and work from home—well, from my parents' home. It turns out I can't be by myself, and I have to be within twenty minutes of the hospital."

"That's quite a lot of changes for you."

"I'm thirty-two weeks, so it's not forever."

"Why don't we talk after the weekend? Nothing's so important that it can't wait until Monday."

"You're right. I'm sorry I interrupted your vacation—"

"Johanna, I'm glad you called. Even more, I'm very glad you and the baby are okay."

"Thank you, Axton."

After I ended the phone call, I sat there holding my phone. I'd checked a necessary box and contacted my boss. But it was more than that. Axton Miller was proving to be a friend—when I let him.

The door to my hospital room was closed. I was safe, but I also didn't feel so alone. My family was helping me. Beckett had tried to help, even if that came with some complications. Axton's concern was another layer of support.

But the reality was, everyone else had their own lives. Payton had Zach. Jillian had Geoff. Mom had Dad. I didn't know if Dr. Gray had anyone, but she was my obstetrician, not my friend, even if she had defended me from Beckett. Beckett's involvement in the baby's life would be restricted by legalese and my own emotional limitations.

In the future, when this crisis was long past, it would be me and my daughter.

We'd do life on our own.

And we'd be enough for each other.

28

I WANTED TO GO HOME.

It wasn't that my parents weren't supportive. Attentive. Going out of their way to make certain I was comfortable. That I liked my meals. Dad continued working full-time, but Mom had taken a leave of absence from her part-time job since I couldn't be left alone. And she didn't complain once about the adjustment.

Me? I wanted my life back. All of it.

My morning get-ready-for-work routine.

My busy workday.

My too-many-things-to-think-about-at-night struggle, not to mention the freedom to sleep in my own bed. On my back. Not that I'd been doing that before the spotting episode on July 4, but if I was making a list of everything I wanted, it was going to be complete.

I didn't want Mom asking me how I was every time I went to the bathroom. Sometimes I delayed going until I was afraid I'd have an embarrassing accident on my way there. And sometimes I went every five minutes just to ensure I wasn't spotting. That my unborn daughter was fine. I avoided the bathroom off the family room—and not just because I was limiting walking up and down stairs. After what happened there, I might not use that bathroom ever again.

There were so many hours in the day demanding to be filled—and so much not to be done. I could only hide in my old bedroom, resting or watching the TV my parents had put in the room, for so many hours a day. Mom had left a pile of her favorite books, but I'd never read a Regency romance in my life, and I wasn't about to start now.

But tonight . . . tonight I was so bored, I was almost tempted to pick one up.

The Toll-Gate. Regency Buck. Faro's Daughter. Bath Tangle.

None of the titles made any sense. The last thing I needed was more confusion in my life.

I used a few of my limited steps and wandered into the kitchen and found the leftover carrot cake in the fridge. Standing beside the counter, I took slow bites, savoring the taste of cream cheese, nutmeg, cinnamon, and golden raisins. Might as well let the diversion last for as long as possible.

"Hungry?" Mom spoke from the doorway.

"No. Bored. And it was either this or read one of your romance novels."

"They're not so bad, Johanna. The authors I like weave quite a bit of history into the story."

"I can't remember the last time I read a novel." I plunged the fork into the carrot cake again.

"Tell me some of your favorite authors and I'll be glad to pick up some books for you to read."

"I can't remember having any favorite authors since I went to college and was loaded down with mandatory reading."

"Genres, then. You've been in a book club with your sisters for months now."

If I asked Mom to pick me up a set of Pippi Longstocking books, she'd do it.

"Your dad likes a good mystery." As she talked, Mom poured a glass of milk and set it beside the cake. "Here, you probably need this. Do you want to sit down?"

"Subtle, Mom, very subtle."

I should appreciate her concern, but she was smothering what little independence I had left. I couldn't even sneak into the kitchen and snitch a late-night snack. Her encouragement to sit was like someone insisting you carry an umbrella because the weatherman said there was the slightest chance of rain. Next week.

I forced myself to swallow my bite of cake without touching the glass of milk. I needed to regain control of this situation somehow. All of these limitations. This avoidance. This wasn't me.

"Mom, you don't have to stay up with me. I'm almost done."

"I don't mind." She settled at the table in the breakfast

nook, carrying the glass of milk with her, any attempt at being subtle gone.

"Fine, Mom. I'll sit."

Mom had the graciousness not to smile. "I know this is difficult for you, Johanna. You went from working—having a very busy life—to moving back in with your dad and me. You weren't even given a choice. You're an independent person. Always have been, more than any of your sisters."

"If that's a nice way of saying I like to do things my way, I'll admit it. But except for the relationship fiasco with Beckett, I'm usually right. He was a major mistake on my part."

And now I was doing true, late-night kitchen confessions with Mom.

"Have you talked to him since you've been here?"

"A text or two letting him know that I'm fine. We still need to figure out how we're going to handle things once the baby's born."

"Does he want joint custody?"

"He's never used those words. He says he wants to be involved. I need to figure out what I'm comfortable with."

"Do you have a lawyer?"

"Not yet, although I know I need one. I got a little side-tracked, what with the bleeding episode." I used my fork to separate the icing from the cake. "It was simpler when Beckett didn't know I was pregnant."

"He would have found out about the baby sometime."

"Yes. But I wanted to control when and how he found out, not run into him at a Thai restaurant."

Every day I got closer and closer to having a baby, and

every day I seemed to lose a little more control of my life. Was that what motherhood was, then? Have a baby, give up control of my life?

As Mom sat across from me, I couldn't help but notice all the ways she'd changed through the years. Gray hairs and wrinkles. Those changes were surface. Then there was the loss of one daughter, which led to changes I couldn't begin to fathom.

But I also couldn't imagine labor and childbirth. Holding a newborn. I couldn't imagine dealing with a sick child—and being the mom. Couldn't imagine being the one who was supposed to have all the answers. I couldn't imagine so far ahead, when my daughter would be an adult, dealing with grown-up problems.

Mom settled back in her chair. "I was thinking about things yesterday . . . and I found myself wishing we hadn't gotten rid of the piano."

"The piano?" Mom's words scattered my thoughts. "Why?"

"I'm just sorry we don't have it anymore." Mom hesitated as if unsure how I would respond. "If we did, you could play a little bit each day."

"Why would I want to do that?" I gripped the fork tighter, smashing icing into what was left of my cake, while trying to comprehend why Mom would even mention the piano—my playing—after all these years.

"I thought, when you wrote the song for Payton's wedding, I thought maybe you missed—"

"I don't. The song for Payton? That was an anomaly. I

hadn't even been near a piano in years, much less played one. Not since . . . not since my last recital." Unspoken words burned in my throat.

"You were so gifted, Johanna." Mom smiled at the remembrance, as if the memory of my piano playing meant something to her. "I never understood why you stopped your lessons."

"Life just got so busy after the twins were born . . ." The mention of Payton and Pepper slipped out, and I took a quick gulp of milk before I said anything more, the liquid slicking my throat.

"That's true. But the twins being born was no reason for you to stop playing piano."

"It's not much fun when your parents don't come to your recitals." I stood, crossing the room to scrape the destroyed cake into the trash before dropping my plate and fork in the sink with a clatter of china and metal against stainless steel.

"What?"

"You don't remember?" But then again, why should she when the recital wasn't important to her? The incident that convinced me how unimportant my "special talent" was. "My last recital—you didn't even come to hear me perform. You had to stay home with the twins—"

Mom's brows drew together as she seemed to try to remember that night so many years ago. "The night of your last performance? The twins were sick, Johanna. They both had fevers."

"It was always something with Payton and Pepper. Some reason you had to be with them. Pay attention to them." A rogue wave of emotions threatened to pull me under. "You used to sit in on my lessons sometimes. Or stop what you were doing—making dinner—and listen to me practice. And then you had the twins. After that, you never even had the time to say, 'That was lovely, Jo,' when I practiced."

"Johanna—"

"Don't say it's not true, Mom." I wanted nothing more than to leave the kitchen. "There was no time for me or Jillian after you had the twins."

I was dragging Mom and me back—decades backward— jumping up and down like a small child and demanding, "Look! Look at me!"

Mom's eyes were wide, unblinking. After all these years, I had her unwavering attention. What was the point of saying any of this? It wouldn't change anything.

But if I didn't say it now, I'd never say it. And maybe I shouldn't have.

"Honey, after the twins were born, there were days I didn't shower." Mom shook her head. "But that's no excuse."

"The night of the performance, I kept waiting backstage, looking around the curtain, hoping you'd show up. I wasn't counting on Dad because you told me that his flight back from his business trip was delayed. But you said you'd be there. Miss Felicia finally told me to come away from the curtain . . . I even told her I wasn't going to perform. But she told me I had to play."

"I can't play tonight. I don't feel well." I tried to make my voice sound raspy, like I had a sore throat.

"Suddenly you're sick? I don't think so, Johanna." Miss Felicia

scanned me from head to toe. "Are you nervous? You're never nervous."

"Yes. Yes, I'm too nervous. Please, don't make me."

"I don't believe this. Tsk. And even if you are, this is no reason to not perform. We ignore our nerves and we play." *She cupped my chin in her hand, bending down so that I had to look at her, the silk material of her shawl skimming my face.* "I saved your piece for last, Johanna. It is the best one. You are so talented. You will astound everyone with your gift. You always do."

But I didn't care about anyone else. I wanted Mom to hear me play.

And she wouldn't. Because of the twins.

It was an unwelcome memory, like the ache of a bone I'd broken years ago. I'd convinced myself that I was fine. Healed. And then the pain would flare up and remind me that some injuries never quite heal.

This ache was lodged in my heart.

Why was I mentioning this now, all these years later? Mom and I would never agree about this because we'd never agree on Payton and Pepper.

"Johanna, I was there that night."

I couldn't have heard Mom right. "What?"

"I came to your recital."

"No, you didn't."

"Honey, listen to me." Mom crossed the room and gathered my hands in hers. "The twins were sick. I couldn't leave them. But I also couldn't miss your performance because that was important to me, too. *You* were important. At the last minute, I asked our next-door neighbor to come sit with

Payton and Pepper, and I drove over just long enough to hear you play your song."

"But . . . but I never saw you." My voice cracked and pitched high, like that of a little girl trying to not cry.

"I stood in the back—just inside the auditorium doors—and I left as soon as you were done. I saw the audience give you a standing ovation." Mom's whispered words were earnest. Truthful. "I know I told you that you did a beautiful job when you came home."

"I thought . . . I thought you were just saying that."

"You mean you quit playing piano . . . ?"

"Because I was angry. I didn't think it mattered to anyone—to you or Dad—if I played or not."

Mom released my hands, but only so she could wrap her arms around me. "Jo . . . Jo . . . I always loved when you played. Your music was like the soundtrack for our family."

Mom's words were like an author rewriting the ending to a book, telling me that somehow what I did, what I offered the family, mattered.

I leaned into Mom's embrace. Her tears wet the soft cloth of my robe. But I couldn't cry as I faced an unwelcome question.

What else had I been mistaken about?

⌒

Two hours after Mom and I had talked, I was still awake. I shifted on my side, drawing my legs up to my body . . . well, as close to my body as my baby bump would allow, the top sheet cool against my skin.

The quietness of the house surrounded me. If I could, I would reach out and push it back, like the power of light against the darkness.

But I wasn't that strong.

Mom was probably asleep, content that all was well between us. After a few moments more of reassurance and another hug, she'd dried her tears—not questioning why I wasn't crying—and sent me off to bed with a motherly "You need your rest."

But the discovery that I'd been so wrong all those years ago kept me awake.

I'd walked away from something I'd loved because I believed Mom had chosen the twins over me.

I'd shoved music out of my life. I'd shoved my family away, too. And I'd replaced them with . . .

Nothing.

Oh, some people might assume I replaced my music with my career, but I didn't have that when I was ten years old. I didn't even dream of being a pharmacist back then. And becoming a pharmacist hadn't been a dream so much as a good career choice.

Only now could I grasp how alone I'd been all these years because I'd chosen to separate myself from what I loved. From anyone who might love me . . . or anyone I might love.

"Johanna, how are you coming with packing for college?" Mom stood in the doorway of the bedroom I shared with Jillian.

"Just about done."

"You'll be ready to head out early, then?"

"Yes. No problem."

"I wanted to ask you something . . ."

"Okay." I tossed an old tube of mascara into the trash can beside my bed. "But I'm pretty certain I've got everything. I'm just cleaning out my makeup bag."

"It's about your piano."

I froze for just a moment, then continued sorting through old eye shadow. Keep. Toss. Keep. Keep. Toss. "The piano?"

"Yes. You haven't played it in years, and no one else seems interested." Mom remained standing in the entrance to my room. "Payton and Pepper seem to be more interested in athletics. They liked the introductory volleyball clinic they tried this summer."

Hard to miss that, the way they passed balls back and forth around the house, ignoring the fact that there was a perfectly good backyard for that, no matter how many times I told them.

"Anyway, would it be okay if we sold the piano?"

Sold the piano. How long had my parents been planning to do this?

"You don't have to ask me, Mom."

"We bought the piano for you—"

"Like you said, I haven't played in years." I turned my makeup bag over, gave it a quick shake, and dumped the contents into the trash can. "Whatever you and Dad want to do is fine."

I'd meant it when I told Mom that and then finished packing for college. Believed it. Returned home for Christmas months later to find blank wall space where my . . . where the piano used to sit.

No one said anything about what was missing. Maybe everyone was used to the piano being gone after all those months. Mom had mentioned a family with several young children had bought the piano. And I'd gone up to my room after dinner and an impromptu game night, crawled into bed, and refused to cry over something I didn't care about.

I'd allowed music into my life through the years, indulging in the occasional symphony. But just like the people in my life, it was allowed only so close. No closer.

I'd deprived myself of so much because I'd looked . . . and seen the wrong thing.

29

THIS WAS JUST BREAKFAST with Jillian.

Breakfast and the chance to talk. To catch up with each other.

Of course, Payton and Jillian had both brought their Bibles, setting them in the center of the round Formica table, not too close to their yellow mugs of coffee.

In years past, Payton had been at restaurants or coffee shops and seen two friends, or even a small group of people, talking as they paged through their Bibles. She'd always thought chatting about the Bible in public was, well, odd.

And now, here she was, one of those peculiar people sitting in a local breakfast place in Colorado Springs, planning on talking about just that with one of her sisters.

Jillian gestured above the circular booth at the oversize orange light fixture that complemented the restaurant's muted yellow, green, and brown colors. "This is my first time at Snooze. The decor is fun."

"I've been to the one in Denver. I like their breakfast burrito with tofu."

"It's a great menu." Jillian had flipped through the pages of the menu several times before selecting the brioche French toast. "Lots of options."

"I'm glad we found time to get together."

"Me, too." Jillian clasped her hands around her coffee mug. "Can I admit I'm nervous?"

"Nervous? Why? It's just you and me."

Jillian tapped the cover of her Bible. "There's so much I don't know."

Payton couldn't hold back a laugh. "We're both new at this. That's why we're here—because we both have more questions than answers about God. Our faith. How to do all of this."

Maybe her words would begin to break down any lingering sense of a wall between them. Bring them closer together. They both had questions. They both were unsure of themselves. They could stand together—be strong together—in their uncertainty.

"I was surprised you were having a tough time with your faith." Jillian wore no makeup. Her short hair was casual, accentuating the bit of curl left over from her chemo.

Jillian was being honest.

Payton would be, too, when her turn came. She took a sip of her coffee, savoring the warm sweetness. "Why?"

"Because Zach is a believer, too. I would think it would make your being a Christian easier. At least he supports what you believe."

"Unlike Geoff."

"Right."

"Do you and Geoff argue? Does he not want you to go to church?"

"No, it's nothing as blatant or bad as that." Jillian paused as the waitress brought out their food. "We're too busy arguing about other things. The one other thing."

"I'm sorry, Jill."

"Me, too. But I'm also realizing Geoff is sorry." Jillian poured syrup onto her French toast. "At first, I was so mad and hurt and . . . well, self-centered, I couldn't see it. He doesn't want to hurt me, but he can't change the way he feels to make me feel better. At least, not yet. And I can't force him."

"So that leaves you . . . where?"

"I've been stuck. For months, I wanted Geoff to agree with me. But I realize now that's not the right thing to do. Not if I want to protect our marriage."

"That's . . ." Payton hesitated. "I was going to say that's very wise, but it's actually very loving."

"Harper was the one who helped me realize all of this, and she doesn't even believe in God."

Jillian's words were such a good reminder of what it was like to be a new believer—how they learned from others who had been believers longer. And sometimes God worked in unexpected ways, like using Harper, who still had questions about God but knew Jillian better than her own sisters did. And that was okay. It made sense. Now.

The aroma of a variety of breakfast dishes filled the air in the restaurant. Eggs. Breakfast meats. Coffee. Hash browns. Toast. Payton had no right to go back in the kitchen and make breakfast for herself or any of the customers. She'd leave that to the cooks, who were trained. She wouldn't even try to deliver the food to the tables, because she'd drop plates and glasses, making a huge mess. She could have learned, if that was important to her, from someone who would take the time to teach her.

She and Jillian could help each other.

"What are you struggling with the most, Jill?"

"Finding hope. Holding on to hope. I'm not doing enough to be a good Christian, either. So it's probably my fault—"

"No."

"No?" Jillian tilted her head to one side.

"*No.* We're not going to think like that. We're not going to blame ourselves for getting things wrong. For not knowing things." Payton took a quick bite of her burrito. Chewed. Swallowed. "We can learn, right? Thatchers are smart."

"Yes."

"That's why we're here—to help each other. I know we both want to learn more about prayer—not that I'm going to suggest we pray right here. But I do have a funny story about that."

"Really?"

A good time to be honest. She shared the prayer-for-patience fiasco, joining in with Jillian's laughter.

"Not my best moment at the study, but it's getting better." The laughter had helped them both relax. "One day at a time, I'm learning more about prayer. What would you like to learn more about?"

"I'd like to know what the Bible says about hope. That's my word for the year, but how do I have hope when it feels like nothing is going my way?"

"Maybe we could look up Bible verses on hope."

Jillian's eyebrows furrowed. "How do we do that?"

Payton shoved aside her plate and opened her Bible to the back pages. "There's a concordance in the back—it's like a verse dictionary. It lists verses alphabetically by topic. Like hope or mercy or grace . . ."

This was kind of like coaching, showing her sister something she already knew. But she didn't want it to be all one-sided.

The waitress paused just short of their table, holding a carafe of coffee, her gaze pinging back and forth between them and their open Bibles.

Yes, they were those people.

But Payton couldn't worry about what the waitress, or anyone else, might be thinking.

Jillian, unaware of the young girl's scrutiny before she began refilling their mugs, turned to the back of her Bible until she found the word *hope*. "Now what?"

"What's the first verse?"

"It says . . . Job 13:15."

"Turn there. That book is in the Old Testament. I've heard Zach talk about Job. He lost everything—his possessions, his family—when God allowed Satan to test his faith."

"O-kay."

"Obviously you have other questions, but let's focus on the verse about hope for now." Payton started searching for the chapter in her Bible. "What's the verse say?"

"'Though he slay me, yet will I hope in him'?" Jillian sat back. "Whoa. Did we have to start with that one?"

"What do you mean?"

"Isn't that like saying, 'Even though everything is wrong, I'm still going to trust God'?"

"Ye-es."

"Just because I understand the verse, Payton, doesn't mean I know how to do it." Jillian slumped against the low back of the booth.

"You're not the first person to struggle with this. And look—Job says that in the middle of the book. Maybe he struggled to say it at first." Payton shrugged. "I don't know."

"Good point."

"Maybe—" she couldn't believe she was saying this— "maybe we could do a Bible study on hope."

Payton sipped her coffee, hot once again, thanks to the waitress refreshing it. They'd both be asking for take-home boxes since they'd talked so much and ignored their food. She didn't have a lot of spare time, with college and volleyball and driving back and forth to the cabin on weekends. This was a crazy suggestion. But it might help her sister, and her, too, while giving them a reason to meet on a regular basis.

"Really?"

"Sure." Payton schooled her features to hide her doubts.

"Do you know one?"

No. "I'll ask Sara. She and her husband lead the couples' study Zach and I go to each week. I'll tell her we don't want anything too intense. How does that sound?"

"Perfect. Something basic, introductory, to help me understand what hoping in God looks like."

"Sounds good to me, too. Do we want to plan to meet every other week? What's a good time? Weeknights? Weekends?"

"Are weekdays an option at all?"

"I hadn't thought about that. That just might work around my college schedule, once I get it finalized. And weekends aren't the best, since Zach and I go back to the cabin."

"How long are you going to keep that up?"

"Funny you should ask." Payton didn't back up her words with a laugh. "Zach and I have been talking about that. We think it's time to make a change. This whole 'Winter Park on the weekends, living at my place during the week' routine is beginning to wear on us."

"Do you have a plan?"

"Nothing firm yet. But we're thinking we might sell my house and look for something closer to the Springs." Payton paused, unsure of how much to share. "And I'm thinking about becoming a college dropout."

"What?" Jill's eyes widened.

"I'm not so sure I want to be a teacher." The admission lifted an invisible weight off her shoulders. "I thought it was the best thing for me to do if I wanted to coach. But Sydney asked me if I'd be interested in becoming more involved with Club Brio. More full-time, becoming a partner eventually. And that excited me."

"Oh, Payton! I love that idea." Jill grinned.

"The more I think about it, the more I do, too. And Zach supports it. There may be changes up ahead, but that can be a good thing, right?"

"Right. Changes for you, me, and Johanna. We need to be praying for all of us."

"Especially that the rest of Jo's pregnancy goes well."

"I'm already praying for that." Jill's words rang true, no hesitation, despite the fact that, weeks ago, Johanna's pregnancy had almost separated her from Johanna.

"Me, too, Jill. Me, too."

30

THERE WAS NO SENSE in asking Mom if I could help with the dinner dishes. I'd asked every night in the two weeks I'd been here, and every evening, her answer was the same.

"Don't worry about these, Johanna. I can manage loading the dishwasher."

And no matter how many times I'd told Mom I wasn't an invalid, she'd laughed and shooed me out of the kitchen, telling me to rest.

I hated the word *rest* almost as much as I hated the words *relax* and *sit* and *nap*.

"You know what you should do—"

"Please, Mom. Don't tell me to read a book."

"You girls can always have your book club here, you know. I don't mind."

"I'll mention it, but I think we've put the book club on hold until after my baby is born."

"What I was going to say originally is that you should look at ideas for the baby's nursery." Mom paused from rinsing the dinner dishes. "Or have you already decided how you're going to decorate the room?"

"I'll be using that empty spare bedroom. I don't like the fact that it's across the house from me, but she'll be sleeping through the night soon enough—"

"Said every first-time mom there ever was." Mom had the grace not to laugh. "Here's hoping your daughter is kinder to you than you and your sisters were to me."

"And on that note, I'm going to leave you to the dishes."

"Fine. I'll join your dad outside when I'm done here."

"I know if I can't find you two, you're outside on that new deck."

"We should have done it sooner."

"Saying that means you know you did the right thing."

"You can join us, you know. I don't think Dr. Gray actually limited you to a specific number of stairs per day, did she?"

"No." And since our talk, I'd been trying to spend a bit more time with Mom—and Dad, too. Not that I could regain all the years lost. "But I'm good. I could check the status of the items I ordered for the nursery. The rocking chair arrived a few weeks ago, but I'm still waiting on the crib. And I never got the walls painted or the prints hung."

"You can always let her sleep in a bassinet by your bed for the first month or so. It will be easier for both of you and give you time to finish her room."

"I hadn't thought about that."

And I wouldn't confess to Mom that I wasn't sure I wanted to share my room with my newborn daughter. Did wanting a little bit of privacy make me a bad mother?

I hadn't even pulled up the information about the crib order when the front door opened.

"Knock, knock? Johanna?"

I closed my laptop. That sounded like—"Beckett? What are you doing here?"

"I stopped by to check on you." He stepped into the entrance of the living room. "Are you going stir-crazy yet?"

I was just bored enough to be glad to see him. "You know me too well."

"Having to move back home with your parents—I figured you wouldn't last forty-eight hours."

"I managed seventy-two before I thought about climbing out a window and running away from home. I stayed because I was exhausted. And because I promised Dr. Gray I'd be on my best behavior. Doctors are pretty influential."

"Yes, I met Dr. Gray, if you recall."

"I do. She put you in your place."

"Don't remind me. Was she ever in the military?"

"I never asked her."

"How's it going on house arrest?"

I refused to laugh. "Not funny, Beckett."

"Sorry. You think you can do this until you deliver?"

"Well, I've stuck it out for just over two weeks so far. Besides, I have no choice. I have to take care of this baby."

"And yourself."

"Well, yes."

"I have no doubt you can do this." Beckett offered me a smile. "If anyone can see this through, you can."

"Thank you."

Part of me wanted to lean into the compliment. Instead, I held myself still, kind of like an awkward half hug with an acquaintance.

Beckett carried a large brown paper bag in one hand. He didn't advance, possibly waiting for me to indicate what would happen next.

I couldn't leave him standing there.

"What can I do for you, Beckett?"

"The question is, what can I do for you?" Beckett held up the bag, offering me a glimpse of the grin I used to love. "Where can I unpack this?"

"I'm pretty much restricting myself to the main floor or my bedroom. Avoiding the stairs as much as possible. Which is too bad, since my parents put a deck out back off the family room . . ."

"A deck? Well, we have to see that, don't we?"

"My parents are going to be out there. And I'm not going down those stairs . . ."

Beckett crossed the room in two quick strides, dropping the bag on the floor. In one fluid motion, he bent down and swept me up in his arms. "You okay if I carry you?"

"Beckett—"

"Purely in the interest of seeing this new deck. And giving you a chance to get outside." He shifted me so that I landed against his chest. "You have to admit you're more than ready for a change of scenery."

I crossed my arms, avoiding the need to loop them around his neck. "True."

I hadn't been this close to Beckett in months. I shouldn't be this close to Beckett now, so that by merely leaning forward, my lips could brush his scruffy jaw. So that I caught the hint of his aftershave, reminding me of how my bed pillows used to carry the same scent.

I should have somehow resisted—kicked and screamed—when Beckett picked me up. But that would have been a bit melodramatic and over-the-top for me. And probably not good for the baby.

I just needed to tolerate the whole "he-man" moment Beckett was having. Act like it didn't faze me. Besides, it would be nice to go outside again.

Of course, Mom came through the kitchen door as Beckett carried me out of the living room. "Oh. I didn't realize Beckett was here."

"Good evening, Mrs. Thatcher. I stopped by to check on Johanna." Beckett's grin was in full force, but it would not disarm me. "I thought she might like to sit out on the new deck she just told me about."

"That sounds nice. I've been wishing she could see it. Johanna, would you tell your dad to come up here, please?"

"I thought you were going to sit outside—"

"No. Not tonight. I want to, um, talk to him about

something." She smiled at Beckett. "There are drinks in the small fridge in the family room if you two want anything."

"Right."

Beckett's shoulders shook as he carried me downstairs.

"Stop." I would not laugh. "Although I admit Mom was a bit too obvious."

Dad greeted Beckett with the same surprise but didn't argue about going inside as Beckett settled me in a chair by the table.

"I'll go grab the bag and something to drink. Do you want anything?"

For you to leave. "There's ginger ale in the fridge. Grab whatever you want, too."

"Be right back."

"No rush."

Really. No rush.

I refused to watch Beckett leave. I'd use this time to concentrate on settling my heartbeat back to normal. I was surprised Beckett had picked me up, nothing more.

Mom's wildflowers were blooming, butterflies darting back and forth among the vivid blooms. I hadn't been outside in days, and I tried to forget how Beckett's presence unsettled me and just enjoy the breeze against my skin. The sense of openness.

When Beckett returned, I was able to offer him a nothing-but-friends smile as he set our drinks on the table and positioned the bag between us.

"Are you ready to see what I brought you?"

"You didn't have to bring me anything."

"I know. But you'll be glad I did."

"Fine." I twisted the lid off my bottle of ginger ale, releasing a soft hiss of carbonation. "I'm ready."

"First, we have a puzzle." He held up his hand to forestall my protest. "Now before you say, 'I don't do puzzles,' take a look at this one."

"Colorado columbines." The purple and white wildflowers were spread across a mountain vista.

"I thought you might want to assemble it—maybe when you're too bored to do anything else—and then frame it and put it in the baby's room."

"I'm not sure I've ever done a puzzle."

"There's always a first time." Beckett winked.

I chose to ignore him. "And this could be a little touch of color in the nursery. The baby's going to be a Colorado native, after all."

"I'm glad you like it." He set the puzzle box aside. "Next item is . . . some nail polish."

"You bought me nail polish?"

"I didn't know if you could leave the house for your monthly pedicure or not. I thought maybe you could do your own nails. Or maybe ask your mom?"

I sorted through the four bottles of colors. Beckett might as well have offered to do a pedicure for me. "You selected these yourself?"

"Technically, yes. But I asked a saleswoman for help and she pointed me to a display of new colors. Is that cheating?"

"No. That was smart."

My comment earned me another smile as he began

stacking magazines on the table. It seemed my immunity to Beckett's smiles was weakening. I'd blame it on lack of sleep. And boredom.

"I went for an even dozen here. Just something to flip through. Women's magazines, cooking magazines. And last but not least—"

"There's more?"

"Of course. I couldn't forget snacks. And I should confess I enlisted help here, too."

"Help? Who helped you?"

"Payton and Jillian. They insisted on Warheads. And peanut M&M'S. They stressed it had to be peanut. But I remembered you like sour cream potato chips and chocolate-covered caramels from Rocky Mountain Chocolate Factory."

Spread out on the table before me was an extravagant act of kindness from the man who'd wrecked my heart.

"If you're being nice to try and get on my good side, then you can just put it all back in the bag and go home."

My words snuffed the light out of his eyes. His smile disappeared, and I could breathe again. "That's not it, Johanna. I know being confined to your parents' house is hard for you."

"The fact that my life is hard is not—"

"Stop. Stop saying things like 'this is not your concern.' Just because we broke up doesn't mean I stopped caring about you." Beckett sat in a chair across from me. "And just because I admitted that, you're going to have to believe me when I say there are no hidden strings attached to any of this."

"You're not being nice to get me to give you what you want?"

"I don't even know what I want, even though I know what

I lost." Beckett blew out a raspy exhale, scraping his fingers through his short hair. "I lost you. I lost *us*. We should be married—or at least planning our wedding at the Broadmoor. Celebrating the fact that we're having a baby. I lost all of that. I want to be a part of this baby's life—and I'd like to figure out how to talk it out before the baby is born, if possible, so my name can be on the birth certificate."

"Because then you'll have leverage."

"No, because it's the truth. Legally, I don't need leverage." Beckett sighed. "I had a dad who didn't care. I don't want my child thinking I'm that kind of father—even though I know it'll grow up knowing I messed things up with its mother. Please, Johanna, I'm asking for a chance to be the kind of dad my father wasn't."

Jillian had given me a maternity dress as a peace offering. Now Beckett had shown up with a brown bag filled with an array of peace offerings.

"Beckett." Could I do this? "I'll try."

"What?"

"I'll try. Not for us. We're done. But for our daughter."

He half rose as if to hug me. "Wait . . . what? Our daughter? You're having a girl?"

All these weeks into my pregnancy, and I'd withheld this information from Beckett. "Yes. According to the ultrasound, I'm having a girl. I hope you're okay with that."

"A girl. I hadn't really thought about it. I mean, so long as she's healthy . . ." He fell back in his chair, arms limp at his sides.

That was a good thing. There didn't need to be any hugging between Beckett and me. We needed to limit our physical interaction. No sense in confusing our daughter—giving her any false hope that we'd be getting back together.

"You said you'd talked with a lawyer?"

"Yes. I wanted to get a basic idea of my rights." Beckett shifted in the chair. "Fathers have equal rights in Colorado, Johanna. But I don't want to throw that at you—force you to let me see the baby. I hope we can come to a reasonable agreement that's fair for both of us."

"I found out the same thing when I contacted a lawyer." I might as well admit that, rather than try to stall him with some sort of bogus information—not that it would have worked in the long run. "It might be best to let our lawyers talk to each other and draw up a preliminary agreement— maybe even before the baby is born."

"Okay. Sounds good. I won't be unreasonable."

"Thank you." I could be reasonable, too. "There's something else we need to do."

"What?"

"You need to help me get started on this puzzle, but we should take it inside."

"I'd be glad to. I'll take you back first—"

I held my hands up, shaking my head. "I can walk, Beckett. You grab the bag and I'll meet you upstairs in the living room. Maybe Mom and Dad will want to help, too."

Beckett's smile was back. Not his wicked, self-assured grin, but a more relaxed smile. The hardness in my heart seemed to soften. Maybe we could be friends again someday, if I could find a way to let go of everything I'd hoped for with Beckett and embrace what my life looked like now.

31

I'D MADE A BAD DECISION last night. A very bad decision.

But I'd never imagined ignoring a sneeze could go so horribly wrong.

Of course, it wasn't only the sneeze I'd ignored. I'd gone to the bathroom right before bed and seen a dime-size spot of blood on the stupid pad I had to wear all the time. Doctor's orders.

Then I'd ignored doctor's orders and decided not to call the hospital because that tiny spot of blood was nothing to worry about.

It couldn't be.

And that decision was my mistake.

But I didn't know then that I'd wake up this morning—

now—and find the same pad soaked through with bright-red blood. And that some of the same blood would be staining Mom's yellow fitted sheet.

There was no ignoring any of this.

"Mom!" I shoved the blanket off my legs. If I tried to stand, I'd collapse beside the bed. *"Mom!"*

Nothing.

She had to be here. She couldn't leave me alone. Mom had followed Dr. Gray's orders without fail every single day since I'd come home with her three weeks ago.

"Mom!" Her name ended on a shriek that startled me, my hands shaking as I cradled my stomach.

Footsteps pounded on the stairs and down the hallway leading to my bedroom. The door was flung open so that it crashed against the wall before Mom stumbled inside. "Johanna—what? Why are you yelling?"

"I'm . . . I'm bleeding."

Mom's eyes widened as she reached out for me. "What?"

"I'm *bleeding*."

"How badly?"

"A lot worse than last time. A lot . . ." I couldn't tell her about last night's episode of spotting. It didn't matter now. "We need to go to the hospital. I need to get dressed."

Mom's gaze scanned the room. "Do we have time?"

"I can't go to the hospital in my nightgown." I shifted my legs over the edge of the bed as if I were moving in slow motion. "Give me the blue sundress. Please. I can slip into it sitting down. And a fresh pad and underwear."

"I'll go get my purse and put my shoes on."

"Perfect. Five minutes—no more. That's all I need."

I'd woken up in a nightmare. A medical nightmare.

As I smoothed the dress over my stomach, the baby kicked. I pressed my hand against the area as tears filled my eyes. "Stay with me, baby. I don't want to lose you. I can't lose you. Stay with me."

When Mom insisted on helping me to the car, sliding her arm around my waist, I didn't resist. My legs seemed unable to hold my weight.

"Did you call Dr. Gray?"

"Not yet. I'm calling the clinic—" I spoke as I speed-dialed the number I'd stored in my cell. "Hello? This is Johanna Thatcher. I'm on my way to the hospital because I'm . . . I'm bleeding. . . . No, I wouldn't say spotting. I woke up less than ten minutes ago and I'd soaked through my pad."

"What are they saying?"

I held up a hand to stop Mom from distracting me, then covered my ear with it. "I'm only fifteen minutes away. My mom is driving me. . . . Fine. Thank you."

When the phone call was finished, I hung up and spoke to Mom. "Sorry. I didn't mean to be rude."

"It's okay. I'm just worried."

"They're calling Dr. Gray. It's Friday. She's in the clinic."

"She'll still come to the hospital, right?"

"I think so."

I hoped so.

"Are we going to the ER?"

"No. Her MA said to go straight to labor and delivery. They're expecting us—no pun intended."

Neither Mom nor I laughed at my weak attempt at humor.

"How are you feeling?" Mom clasped my hand.

"Fine." Not that the word meant anything. "I don't think I'm contracting, but that's why we're going to the hospital, to let the experts tell us what's going on. She's moving around, so that's good, right?"

"Yes. Yes, that's good."

I was reassuring myself. Reassuring Mom. Lying. Telling her I was fine, when I couldn't get the sight of bright-red blood staining my clothes . . . staining the bed . . . out of my mind. All the while, my hand rested on my stomach waiting . . . waiting . . . for each movement. Each kick. They were like oxygen to my lungs, allowing me to breathe again.

I was doing all I could.

But I should have done something more last night, instead of assuming everything was fine and going to sleep.

For all the rush to get me admitted, I couldn't understand why I was lying on my left side in a hospital bed, waiting.

"Don't you think Dr. Gray should be here by now?" Mom had paced the confines of the room over and over again since the nurse had left, after encouraging her to sit.

"Of course I'd like her to be here, Mom. But I'm not her only patient. The nurse said she's on her way."

Mom stared at the fetal heart monitor. "Her heartbeat sounds strong."

"It does." Right now, that steady beat was my favorite sound. "Do you want to call the family?"

"I don't want to leave you alone."

"Please, Mom, make some phone calls." I motioned to the door. "People need to know what's going on. At least Dad and Payton and Jillian."

"We still don't really know what's happening."

"We know enough. Call people. And go get some coffee." Maybe getting out of the room for a while would help Mom relax. "We don't know when Dr. Gray will get here."

At last Mom agreed, and within five minutes of her departure, Dr. Gray arrived. She stood at the end of the hospital bed, her air of calm assurance wrapping around me, allowing me to take an easy breath again. "Tell me what happened."

"I woke up this morning about eight o'clock. Everything seemed fine. No cramps. Nothing. And then I realized I felt . . . damp. I checked and I'd soaked through my pad. So much that there was blood on the sheet. I called my mom— yelled, actually—and then I called the hospital."

Dr. Gray shrugged. "Two strikes and you're in—the hospital, that is."

And now it was time to be completely honest. "Technically . . . this morning was three strikes."

Dr. Gray stiffened. "What do you mean?"

"I—I didn't think it was important at first." I forced myself to maintain eye contact. "Last night, about an hour before I went to bed, I sneezed. Just this little sneeze. A little while later, well, I noticed the tiniest bit of blood. About the size of a dime. It wasn't like the first time. Or like this morning—"

"What part of 'If you bleed again, come to the hospital immediately' do you not understand?" Dr. Gray's voice cut through my explanation with the precision of a scalpel. "Was there blood last night? Is that called bleeding?"

I didn't respond.

"You're smart, Johanna, but that was anything but a smart decision. At all. You could have woken up in a pool of blood in your bed this morning. Would you want your mother dealing with that? We could be fighting for your baby's life right now—and yours, too."

"I just thought—"

"How many cases of placenta previa have you dealt with in your career?" She paced in front of me, giving me no time to answer. "I'm your physician. I expect you to take my advice regarding something you have no experience in. And I have more experience than you'll ever know."

And on those words, Dr. Gray walked out.

The interaction had been like watching your best friend from middle school toss her matching "BFF" bracelet in the trash and then turn her back on you, linking arms with some other girl before walking away. Not that Hayden Gray was my friend. Or that I had friends. But my calm, kind physician had turned on me—lashed out—and then walked away. She might as well have slammed the door, the way the swish of the closing door reverberated in my heart. And she had every right to say what she'd said.

I needed to go after her to explain, but I couldn't.

And there was nothing to explain because she was right.

I closed my eyes, resting my head against the pillow. Swallowed against the tightness in my throat, the bitter taste of salt and unshed tears. My hands clenched the blanket as I tried to fend off the accusations assaulting me. Not the ones Dr. Gray had thrown, but my own.

Why had I risked my baby's life, not to mention my own, last night? Was control so important to me that I was blind? Foolish?

This had to stop.

The sound of my baby's heartbeat pulled me from my regret. When I'd played piano, a metronome had produced a steady pulse, a beat, helping me keep the rhythm of a song when I practiced until it was effortless.

I'd rarely used a metronome except for the most complicated pieces. Miss Felicia said I had an internal metronome. An innate sense of rhythm.

But somehow, I'd lost the rhythm of this pregnancy. Forgotten there were two hearts beating inside my body now.

The door swished open, and I raised my head, hoping for a chance to apologize to Dr. Gray. Seeing Mom, I slumped back against the pillows.

"Has Dr. Gray been here?"

"Yes, she's come and gone."

"I should have waited to call everyone. What did she say?"

"Nothing I care to repeat."

"What?"

I shook my head, unable to meet my mom's eyes. "I'm as good as grounded—complete with a stern lecture."

"Well, I called your dad and your sisters and let them know what's going on." Mom smoothed the blanket covering my legs. "Why don't I call Jillian back and ask her to go pack your suitcase?"

"If I make a list first, it will be easier for her."

"How long are you here for?"

"The duration. I don't know Dr. Gray's plans exactly—she got a little sidetracked. But you've lost your houseguest."

My doctor had as good as put me in solitary in this hospital room—four walls, a whiteboard with my name and the nurse's name scrawled on it, a basic clock, a chair, and a monitor that let me know my daughter was fine, just fine.

For now.

I needed to remember this wasn't punishment. This was safety for both me and my baby.

Dr. Gray returned less than a half hour later, her demeanor all business. "I wanted to let you know I finished up your admittance paperwork, so everything's official."

"Thank you."

"And I also wanted to apologize for what happened earlier."

"I understand. You had every right—"

"Let me explain. I'm sorry for how I said things—not for what I said." Dr. Gray pulled the chair up beside the bed and sat. "A few years back, I lost an OB patient who bucked me the entire time during her pregnancy. She either didn't understand or didn't believe how serious placenta previa was. We evaluated her after she had an episode of bleeding, but she refused to stay in the hospital. She . . . she went home and hemorrhaged. We lost both the mom and the baby."

I pressed my hand to my lips, overcome with a sudden wave of nausea. That could have been me. Me and my baby.

"Admittedly, Johanna, that's a rare occurrence. But it did

happen to one of my patients—and therefore to me, too. You can understand my desire to keep you and your daughter safe."

"I do." I cleared my throat. "I'm sorry I didn't listen to you."

"Thank you." She rose, pausing to touch my hand before stepping away from my hospital bed. "A nurse will be checking your pad every twelve hours. Standard protocol, I assure you. You still need to report anything—"

"Of course."

"You're thirty-five weeks. The goal is to get you to thirty-seven, if at all possible. The longer baby girl can incubate, the better."

"I can still get out of bed and use the bathroom, right?"

"Yes. Limited activity—even more than when you were at your parents'. You won't be roaming the hospital hallways. And you also won't be going to full term."

"Does this mean we're looking at a C-section?"

"Yes. No induction."

"This is quite a change of expectations."

"I know. But if you keep all of this information in the context of safety—yours and the baby's—it will be easier to accept."

"No arguments. You're looking at your most compliant patient."

"Nice to know." Dr. Gray smiled at me.

With that, it was as if low-level static had been turned off. I'd won back my doctor's approval—and I hadn't even realized how important it was until I'd lost it.

32

I WASN'T GOING TO ADMIT I'd looked forward to Beckett's visit tonight. His arrival was just a break from the hospital monotony of eating meals, having my vitals checked, tolerating the nurse checking my pad twice a day.

He hadn't come by every day since I'd been admitted, but when he did, he'd made me laugh—and he'd never once mentioned lawyers or how we were going to settle things between us about our daughter.

Tonight, though, something was wrong.

Ever since he'd arrived—a mere ten minutes ago—he'd been on edge. Refusing to sit. Glancing at the clock. Pacing.

"What is going on, Beckett? And don't say, 'Nothing,' because I'm not stupid."

Beckett shifted from one foot to the other. Glanced away. "I came to tell you something."

"Then tell me, already. But sit down, please." I motioned to the hard, plastic chair in the corner. "Pull up a seat. I've got all the time in the world."

Beckett remained standing. "Well . . . I don't."

"What's that supposed to mean?"

"I have to catch a plane out of DIA."

"What? Where are you going?"

"California. I've got a job interview."

"That doesn't make any sense. You said you were getting a job here. In Colorado."

His announcement carried echoes of that day in my bedroom—the one that ended our relationship. The phone call from Iris. The first time he betrayed me.

No. Beckett had betrayed me before that. I just hadn't realized it.

My hands gripped the smooth metal of the hospital bed railing.

Stupid. Stupid. Stupid.

"I *am* applying for a job in Colorado. A good job. And right now, I'm one of the top candidates. But the headquarters is located in California, so I have to go do this interview. For the baby."

"Right. For the baby." There was no way I could believe Beckett. After all his talk about wanting to be part of his daughter's life, he could be lining up a cushy job on the West Coast, deciding not to be involved at all.

Which was fine with me.

"What, Johanna? You want me to say for *you*? We don't have a chance—you've told me that over and over again."

"And you've lost your chance with your daughter, too, Beckett."

"I said I'm coming back." He banged his fist against the railing, jostling the bed and causing me to pull away. "I'm not deserting you or the baby. You don't believe me? Here's proof. I've deposited twenty thousand dollars into an account for the baby—"

"Twenty thousand dollars? Since when did you start playing the lottery?"

"It's the money my father left me. Until now, I haven't touched it. I never wanted it."

"What am I supposed to do with the money?"

"It's for the baby—not you. Use it to start a college fund. Get a nanny to help you. I don't care. There are no stipulations on how it's used."

This was the oddest offer of help I'd ever received—his words laced through and through with anger and frustration. My heart pounded, and if I unclenched my fists from the blankets, I might be tempted to slap Beckett.

He needed to stop throwing money at me and leave.

A nurse entered the room. "Excuse me—is there a problem?"

"We're fine." Beckett never once looked away from me.

"Yes. Yes, there is a problem." My body was rigid beneath the blankets. "I'd like Colonel Sager to leave. Now."

The nurse lasered in on Beckett. "Colonel Sager, I need you to leave."

"But I'm—"

"I don't care who you are, nor do I care why you're here. Johanna is my patient and I'm here to take care of her." She opened the door and stepped aside. "So again, I need you to leave."

"Johanna—"

I couldn't turn off my side, so instead, I turned my face into my pillow.

I didn't know myself anymore. It seemed I was always having to let someone else fight my battles for me. I swallowed against the lump in my throat, but I couldn't stop the tears that trickled down my face, over my chin, and onto my neck.

When Jillian arrived fifteen minutes later, I'd reminded myself that Beckett wasn't worth crying about. Convinced myself that I wasn't depending on him to raise our . . . *my* daughter. And I certainly wasn't going to touch a single cent of the money in that bank account.

Ever.

"Johanna, I saw Beckett leaving the hospital. He seemed upset."

"I'm not concerned about Beckett right now, Jill."

"I'm sorry."

"No, I'm sorry." I held out my hand, thankful they'd put the IV access site in my forearm, not in either hand, and covered it with a wrap of protective gauze. "I shouldn't have barked at you like that. I'm stressed."

"It's okay." She squeezed my fingers. "But at the risk of stressing you out more, I'm going to mention Beckett again. He asked me to give you this."

I tried to ignore the slim legal-size envelope she offered me, but Jillian held it between us until I accepted it. "What is it?"

"He said it was information you'd need. And he said he'd see you in three days." She waited while I examined the contents. "So?"

"It's a bank statement."

"Why would Beckett give you his bank statement?"

"It's not his bank statement." At Jillian's confused look, I pressed my fingertips against my temple. "I mean, yes, it's his bank statement. But it's for an account he opened for the baby." I shifted in the bed, careful not to jostle the monitors. "He was here earlier to tell me that he deposited twenty thousand dollars—"

"What?" The look on Jillian's face was almost comical. Almost.

"You heard me. He put the money into an account for me to use for the baby."

"That's nice of him—"

"It is not nice of him. It's presumptuous. And manipulative. Anything but nice." I swallowed hard. "I'm sorry I ever met Beckett Sager."

My words broke on a sob.

"Johanna!"

I pulled one of my pillows in front of me, cradling it against my body as best I could. "I'm not crying . . . I'm not . . ."

"Okay, okay . . . you're not crying." Jillian sat on the side of my bed, pulling me close and wrapping her arms around me.

The dam had burst. The last straw had been loaded onto my camel's back. My last nerve had been stepped on. The control-freak Thatcher sister had freaked out.

I wanted to cry and never stop.

But I couldn't keep crying. I couldn't be upset. I had to stop thinking of myself, what I wanted, and think of the baby.

"Joey . . . Joey, you're going to be okay. Shhh . . . shhh. . . . You're going to be okay." Jillian patted my back as if she were a mom comforting her child—and that thought made my heart hurt all the more.

My sister would be a better mom than I would.

"You don't know that." My words were muffled against the pillow between us. "Everything's wrong . . . everything. . . . No matter how much I try to control it, I can't . . ."

"Tough lesson to learn, huh?"

"Beckett hurt me . . . I hurt you . . ."

"You didn't mean to."

"No. I didn't." I spoke the words through my tears, hoping Jillian could hear the truth. "I really didn't, Jilly. I'm sorry."

"I understand." Jillian inhaled a shuddering breath. "I should never have . . . never have asked to adopt your baby. I'm sorry."

"At first, I didn't even want her." I pushed away from my sister, swiping at the tears on my face. "Isn't it horrible? Now I'm so afraid I'm going to lose her."

"You won't."

"You don't know that."

"I do. She's a Thatcher girl. We're all strong. Stronger than we all realize. And we'll make sure she knows that sooner than we did."

"I've missed you, Jill." I leaned my head on her shoulder. "You're not just my sister. You're my best friend."

Jill hugged me close, as if she would never let go. "I've missed you, too."

I could only hope my sister would keep holding on to me. I didn't have any strength left. I wanted—needed—to lean into hers. Like a transfusion, Jillian's strength was infusing my weakness. With her help, I wouldn't quit.

33

STAYING IN THE HOSPITAL involved so much waiting.

Waiting for someone to come check my vitals. Waiting for my meals. Waiting to talk to Dr. Gray. Waiting for visits from my family. Waiting for the baby to move, which she did quite often. Waiting to fall asleep . . . or to fall back asleep after waking to find a more comfortable position in the hospital bed, which was becoming more and more difficult when I had to lie on one side. Waiting for a chance to use the bathroom—a highlight of my day because it meant getting up out of bed.

Sometimes, like now, I found myself waiting for multiple things at one time. For the transition of nurses from one shift to the next so the night shift nurse could check my pad and for the arrival of someone—anyone—to help me get through the evening without resorting to TV.

But not Beckett. He'd been gone twenty-four hours and that was fine with me.

The door to my room opened and a tall nurse walked in. Payton would have asked her if she'd played volleyball in school.

"Hello, Miss Thatcher. I'm Cara." She took the marker and wrote her name on the whiteboard on the wall facing my bed. "I need to do your vitals and then I'll check your pad."

"I've felt fine all day. There was nothing earlier today."

"I'm glad to hear that. And I know you know the drill." After taking my blood pressure, temp, and pulse, she put on a pair of blue disposable gloves.

I slid the blanket back. I did know the drill. I was tired of the drill.

"You were last checked at seven this morning. You say you haven't felt anything all day—no cramping?"

"No."

Cara's expression never changed. "Well, you are bleeding. You haven't soaked the pad, but you have a quarter-size spot of blood and a dime-size blood clot."

I needed to move my legs. To pull the blanket back over my body. But my limbs were frozen in place.

Cara positioned the blanket for me. "I'm going to call Dr. Gray and let the in-house OB know what's going on. I'll be right back."

Breathe. Breathe. I needed to breathe. And all I could do was wait.

Cara came back in, pushing the familiar fetal heart rate monitor, followed by another nurse pushing another machine.

"What are we doing?"

"This is to monitor the baby's heart—"

"I know that. Why are we getting an ultrasound?"

"Dr. Gray's going to want to take a look when she gets here."

"When will that be?"

"As soon as possible. She's on the way." All the while she talked, Cara arranged the fetal heart monitor around my abdomen.

The door to my room opened, allowing a swift glimpse of the hallway, as a young woman with a long black braid down her back entered the room. Both nurses nodded a greeting but focused on what they were doing.

"Miss Thatcher, I'm Dr. Chambers." She shook my hand, unaware that I wanted to ask when she'd graduated from medical school. "I'll be covering until Dr. Gray arrives. I understand you have placenta previa. This is your fourth episode of bleeding. You're thirty-six weeks."

"Yes."

"We're going to check your blood count. We're also going to monitor your oxygen and pulse, and you'll be on continuous fetal monitoring now." Dr. Chambers turned her attention to Cara. "I'm going to want a second IV site. And I'm going to do a brief exam."

I seemed to be the center ring in a circus—surrounded by a lab technician doing a blood draw, the second nurse returning to start a second IV, Cara setting up the ultrasound, and Dr. Chambers stepping up beside my bed to do an exam.

"Is your abdomen tender?" She pressed my stomach. "Are you feeling any contractions?"

"No. I don't think so."

"I haven't seen a previous ultrasound, but I'm going to go ahead and look at the placental condition and see if there's any concern."

"Fine."

Her mannerisms were efficient. Sure. "You have a placenta previa, so there's no change there. I think you have some blood in the vaginal vault. You definitely have some in the cervix. The blood the nurse saw is likely part of a bigger bleed."

A bigger bleed. There was no way those words could be good for the baby.

Dr. Chambers turned to Cara. "Start some IV fluids in the first IV to ensure it still works. And how's the second IV coming?"

I had to say something, to feel like I was more than just an observer. "You seem to be doing a lot. Dr. Gray's not even here yet."

"These are all standard precautions. Dr. Gray would be doing the same thing." With those words, Dr. Chambers turned back to Cara. "Does she have blood typed and crossed?"

"She did when she first came in last week."

"She needs two more units typed and crossed now. Call me when Dr. Gray is here."

As the obstetrician left, the electronic rhythm of my daughter's heartbeat came into focus. For a moment, I allowed myself to center on the reassuring sound, letting it lull me into a sense of peace. But only for a moment.

"Excuse me, can I call anyone?"

"Yes." Cara nodded. "Now would be a good time to do that."

Mom answered on the third ring. "Johanna? I was going to head over in about an hour. Did you want me to bring you something?"

"No. I needed to let you know . . . I'm spotting again."

"What?"

"It's okay, Mom. I'm in the hospital, remember?" I tried to keep my voice light, to not let her know how scared I was.

"What do you want me to do?"

"It's pretty busy in my room right now. I'm getting hooked up to monitors again. Dr. Gray is on her way here. I'm not sure what's going to happen. Would you call everyone and then come on over?"

"I'll call your dad and ask him to call your sisters. That way I can come right over."

"Okay. Thanks."

"I love you, Johanna."

"I love you, too, Mom."

Dr. Gray arrived before Mom, her familiar presence calming me as she pulled up the chair and sat beside my bed. "Dr. Chambers talked to me as I was coming to see you. You've had a significant bleed this time."

"I only had a little bit of spotting on my pad." As if my words would convince Dr. Gray of anything.

"The ultrasound showed evidence of hidden bleeding—and that's our concern."

"Why don't you do an ultrasound and check for yourself?"

"I trust Dr. Chambers."

"Even though she looks like she just graduated from medical school?"

"Now there's the Johanna Thatcher I know." Dr. Gray chuckled. "Yes. Dr. Chambers is very competent. And I've looked at the ultrasound findings. It's a moot point, Johanna. All of this declares the need to get your baby delivered."

"You're talking about tomorrow morning, then?"

"No. As soon as possible. But you ate dinner at five. It's now going on eight, so we're going to try and wait until nine or so to give your body time to get the food out of your stomach."

For all my complaining about having to wait, things were happening too fast. "That soon?"

"You're the case of the day, Johanna. The OR is going to be a little crowded. The neonatal ICU team will be in the room, including a neonatal NP for the baby." Despite the concern about delivering my baby, Dr. Gray seemed relaxed. "One of the complications can be excessive bleeding. We talked about this when you were admitted, remember? Sometimes we can't stop the bleeding without taking out the uterus. This, of course, means you can't have any more children—and you may not be able to give your consent then, which is why I'm talking to you now."

I hadn't expected my ability to have any more children to be a topic of conversation tonight. "Let's talk about something else—like how I expect you to make sure I have as minimal a scar as possible, okay?"

"The incision will be big enough to get the baby out safely and promptly—no bigger."

"It was a joke." I offered her a smile. "I trust you."

"Thank you, Johanna." Dr. Gray returned my smile. "You're my one case tonight. We'll get you and your baby through this."

The trip to the operating room was not rushed, but they pushed my bed down the hall with intention. For a moment, I expected to hear some sort of ominous background music playing, like in a TV medical drama or movie, but the only sounds were normal hospital noises. Elevator pings. Phones ringing. Muted conversations.

Then came my awkward contortions as I moved over to the operating table, trying not to disturb the IVs and fetal monitoring lines. For a week, I'd been bored because nothing much was happening, and now I wanted everything to slow down.

"Do you want someone with you in the OR?" Cara covered my hair with a protective cap.

I'd always envisioned myself alone when my baby was born. Well, me and the doctor, of course. "Can I have someone here?"

"Yes."

"My mom. Please. She's in the waiting room. I'm pretty sure she'll come in."

"I'm certain she will. Most women are thrilled to be present when their grandchild is born."

By the time Mom arrived, the anesthesiologist had finished the spinal and settled me on my back with my head slightly elevated. He was seated above my head, watching a quietly beeping set of monitors. A pad of some kind was placed beneath my right hip to elevate it. My arms were spread-eagle—an uncomfortable position, but I had no real say in the matter.

"Johanna." Mom came and stood next to my outstretched left arm, wearing scrubs, booties, a cap, and a mask.

"Well, aren't we both stylish?"

"Thank you." Mom clasped my left hand. "Thank you for letting me be with you."

"Thank you for being here, Mom."

Before I could say anything else, an OR nurse spoke up. "We're doing a primary C-section on Johanna Thatcher."

As the nurse checked my hospital wristband, I agreed. "Yes, that's me."

Dr. Gray stood on the right side of the operating table, a cloth erected at my chest level so I couldn't see my stomach— or Dr. Gray. "Just so we're on the same page—Miss Thatcher has a complete previa. She's bled several times. She's thirty-six weeks, which is why NICU staff is here. Miss Thatcher is also a higher risk for postpartum hemorrhage, but we've taken all the precautions and we have two units of blood typed and crossed for her in the blood bank."

Murmurs of agreement sounded throughout the OR.

Dr. Chambers entered the room. "Dr. Gray, I'm here to assist."

"All right then. Johanna, let's meet your daughter."

And once again, I waited. The anesthesia had numbed me to Dr. Gray's actions. All I could feel was pressure against my stomach.

Mom squeezed my hand, her gaze focused over the curtain, intent on the arrival of her first granddaughter. I knew the moment she was born because of the tears that brimmed in Mom's eyes and spilled down her face.

"Johanna, your daughter is beautiful. Ten fingers. Ten toes." Dr. Gray's voice sounded from the other side of the curtain.

"Her name is Ellison Pepper."

"What?" Mom gasped.

"Surprise—I decided to use your maiden name for her first name."

"Thank you . . ." Mom's gaze never wavered from Ellison.

"Wait . . ." I wished I could remove the barrier between me and my daughter. "Why don't I hear anything?"

"She's a little stunned by an early and abrupt arrival." Dr. Gray's usual calm tone reassured me once again.

A member of the NICU team strode by carrying a large sterile drape, offering me only a brief glimpse of Ellison's foot. "We'll bring her back when she's warmed up."

"Johanna, she's so precious." Mom's gaze followed the person carrying my daughter.

"Go with her, Mom." I pulled my hand away. "I'm fine. Go be with Ellison."

Dr. Gray's voice still came from the right side of her table. "You did bleed some, Johanna. I'm glad we did this now. Dr. Wilson, is the Pitocin running?"

"Yes."

"Johanna, we're getting you taken care of, but the placenta seems to be more adherent to your uterus, which complicates things. I'm dealing with it, but you may feel some pressure on your abdomen."

"Okay." If Dr. Gray wasn't worried, then I wasn't worried. Besides, my daughter was born—and that was the most important thing.

A soft cry reached my ears—the best music I'd ever heard. A few seconds later, the nurse practitioner returned with Ellison, cradling her so I could see her swaddled in a white blanket, her eyes closed, her head covered with a light-pink cap. My daughter. "She's needing a little bit of oxygen. Not much, but we're going to take her to the NICU and get her stabilized. Ellison will meet you back in your room."

The nurse held her cheek against mine—so soft and warm—and her tiny hand popped out of the swaddling blanket and touched my ear. I longed to hold my daughter close, to insist that she remain with me. "Stay with Ellison, Mom. I'm fine."

"Are you sure?"

"Yes. Please. I don't want her to be alone."

"All right then."

"Hayden, how much blood do you think she lost?" The anesthesiologist's question pulled my attention away from the ache of wanting to hold my daughter.

"Why?"

"Pulse is 120 and BP is 90 over 60."

"Let me take a look." Dr. Gray muttered under her breath. "Johanna, you're still bleeding excessively. You're on Pitocin and we've given you prostaglandins preventatively. . . . We're going to have to give you a transfusion—"

"Dr. Gray, she just passed another blood clot." The OR nurse's voice overrode Dr. Gray's.

"Ask Dr. Chambers to get back in here. Get the blood up here now and open up both IVs. And type and cross four more units after these two."

I hated to interrupt everyone, but I wasn't sure what was going on. "I . . . I don't know if this is normal or not, but I'm nauseated . . ." I licked my dry lips. "And you all sound like you're talking in a tunnel . . ."

"I only have a couple of minutes to let the medicines do their work before I'm going to have to do some surgical options." Dr. Gray peered over the sheet, her gaze connecting with mine. "I'm going to get you through this."

I fought against the darkness obscuring the edges of my vision. "I told you . . . I trust you."

⌒

"I wish I was back there with Johanna and Mom." Jillian gripped her phone between both hands so hard her knuckles whitened. Why hadn't Mom texted them an update?

"Not sure I'd be up to seeing a C-section—especially when Johanna is the victim." Payton sat beside her, twisting the pages of an unopened magazine.

"Don't call Jo a victim." Jillian shook her head. "She's a patient. And I don't want to see a C-section, either, but I do want to know she and the baby are okay."

"Just because Mom hasn't texted doesn't mean anything's wrong." Payton set the magazine aside and it unfurled into a loose pile of curved pages. "We don't even know if she was able to take her phone back with her."

"Dad told her to, but that doesn't mean the nurse let her keep it."

"Are you okay, Jill?" Payton lowered her voice and leaned closer. "Being here isn't too hard for you?"

"I'm fine. I won't lie and say this isn't difficult, but there's no way I wouldn't be here. I'm trying to remember today isn't about me and what I can't have."

"I'm sorry—"

"This isn't your fault. It isn't Johanna's fault. The truth is, there are going to be a lot of hard days ahead. I'm not certain how I'm going to feel the first time I see Jo holding her baby—her daughter. Or how I'll feel the first time I hold her. If I'm even going to be brave enough to hold her."

"I read somewhere that being brave is feeling scared and doing it anyway."

"I think for me, being brave might be saying, 'I'll let Mom hold her granddaughter today and take my turn tomorrow.' Or maybe the next day."

"And that's okay, too."

"Can we talk about something else besides me? Did the doctor give us a time frame for how long the C-section would take?"

Before Payton could reply, a female voice sounded over the hospital intercom.

"Code white to labor and delivery operating room. Code white to labor and delivery operating room."

It was as if all the activity in the waiting room slowed, the conversations muted. "That can't be good. 'Code' anything is never good."

"We don't know that it concerns Johanna." Payton's words were calm. Assured.

"I didn't say that. They have more than one operating room in labor and delivery, right?"

"I know nothing about hospitals, except what I see on television. But I do know how to find out what a 'code white' is. You can google anything these days."

Jillian stood and paced. "Well?"

"For this hospital . . . code white means someone on the OB ward is hemorrhaging." Payton rose to her feet, turning her back on where their dad sat across the room with Zach and Geoff. "But they said operating room."

"Johanna's in an operating room, right?"

"Yes." Payton pressed her lips together. "But we don't know anything for sure."

A nurse wearing scrubs, her hair covered by a light-blue tight-fitting surgical cap, entered the waiting room. She scanned the area before crossing over to Payton and Jillian. "You're with Johanna Thatcher, right?"

"Yes, we're her sisters." Jillian motioned to Geoff and the others. "Hey, everybody. Come on over here."

The nurse waited until their small group had gathered

around. "Johanna is still in the OR. Dr. Gray had to open her back up—"

"Open her back up?" Payton interrupted. "What does that even mean?"

"After the C-section was finished, there was some excessive bleeding. Dr. Gray's addressing that right now. She'll come talk with all of you once Johanna is stable."

"What about her baby?"

"She had a little girl. Your mother is in the NICU with her."

"Is there . . . is there something wrong with the baby?" Jillian leaned into Geoff, his arm encircling her waist.

"She's a preemie and a C-section baby born at altitude. She needs some extra attention."

"Can we go see her?" Payton spoke again.

"No. I'm sorry. Only one person in the NICU until she's stabilized." The nurse took a step away. "As I said, Dr. Gray will come and talk with you as soon as she can. If it's taking too long, I'll try to check back with you."

And with that limited amount of reassurance, she slipped behind the operating room doors.

The nurse had appeared and disappeared as quickly as one of Colorado's unexpected hailstorms. The day could be sunny, and then the sky would dump ice the size of golf balls on you. Here they were, waiting to celebrate the news of Johanna and her daughter . . . good news of a safe, albeit early, delivery.

And now this.

Wasn't this when they should pray?

Jillian had no words. No strength to move from the safety of Geoff's embrace.

Dad pressed his hands together, one hand rubbing the back of the other again and again. "What do we do now?"

Payton exhaled a soft sigh. "What we've been doing. We wait."

"We're going to pray." Zach spoke up, his words including everyone.

Thank God someone had the strength to pray.

Payton came to stand beside her husband, reaching her hand out to Jillian and drawing her close. Geoff came alongside her, never releasing his hold on her, while Dad chose to close the circle by coming around to Zach's other side, clasping his hands in front of him like he did when he was waiting in a long line at the grocery store. Jillian closed her eyes. If she was going to pray, she couldn't watch how Geoff and Dad handled Zach's prayer.

"God, please take care of Johanna." Zach kept his voice low, so as not to disturb anyone else in the room. "Help Dr. Gray figure out why she's bleeding and how to stop it. And help the baby to be okay, too. Whatever she needs . . . we don't know, but You do. Amen."

"That's it?" Geoff spoke as soon as Zach finished.

"Yes." Zach raised an eyebrow. "You want to add anything?"

"No. It was just shorter than I expected."

Payton still clung to both Zach's and Jillian's hands. "Jillian, why don't you and Dad go over to the NICU? I'm not certain where it is, but someone will help you find it.

Maybe they'll let you take turns being with the baby. It's worth a try, right? And I know Mom would be glad to see you."

Jillian froze. "What? No . . . Maybe you and Zach should go . . ."

Payton clasped Jillian's hand, pulling her aside, away from the warmth of Geoff's embrace. "You should go. It's all about being brave even when you're scared."

"Did you forget I was going to be brave tomorrow?" Even though she tried to make a joke, Jillian's voice trembled. "I don't know if I'm ready. . . ."

"You also said you didn't want to make today about you, right?" Payton gave her a swift hug. "Johanna needs us. Our niece needs us. And besides, I can't go because I have something else I need to do."

"And what is that?"

"I'm going to call Beckett." Payton retrieved her cell phone from her purse.

Jillian gasped. "I'm not sure Johanna would want you to do that, based on their last interaction."

"We can't ask her right now, can we? And Beckett is the baby's father. I know he and Johanna are still figuring out all the details, but Beckett has the right to know his daughter has been born. And he would also want to know about . . . about Johanna, too. She's going to be fine." Payton closed her eyes and pressed her lips together. "Beckett can decide what he wants to do—but I am going to talk to him."

"Johanna is going to be upset."

"Won't be the first time, will it?" Payton gave a short laugh. "I'll handle it."

Despite the seriousness of the situation—the words *excessive bleeding*—they were all taking their assigned places, which meant Payton was going to irritate Johanna.

And Jillian . . . she was going to meet her niece.

Jillian took a deep breath and squared her shoulders. She didn't know where the NICU was. Didn't know if the nurses would let them see Johanna's baby once they found the NICU. She could only hope no one would guess how scared she was. "Are you ready, Dad?"

"We're ready." Dad nodded as Geoff took her hand, lacing their fingers together.

"I wasn't expecting you to come, too."

"Jill." Geoff pulled her to a stop as Dad exited the waiting room. "I know this—all of this—is breaking your heart. That you weren't sure how you'd feel once Johanna had her baby. Now you're worrying about Johanna and the baby—"

"Don't say it, Geoff." Tears choked her. "Please . . . don't say it."

"I love you. You're not facing this by yourself."

"Oh, Geoff!" Jillian wrapped her arms around his neck, collapsing into his strength. "I'm so scared . . ."

"I know . . . I know." Geoff brushed the hair away from her face, leaning his forehead against hers. "I'm glad Zach prayed. I'm not even sure why . . . but it seemed to help. Let's not give up hope, okay?"

"You're right. We can't give up hope."

Payton sought out a secluded corner in the waiting room, Zach standing nearby. During the time Zach had prayed, Payton realized she needed to call Beckett, despite how uncertain things were between him and Johanna.

She'd do what she thought was right and face the consequences later.

But even so, she hesitated. "You understand why I'm calling Beckett?"

"Yes—but even if I didn't, if you're certain, you need to do it."

"Thank you for saying that." Payton gave Zach a quick kiss. "Will you watch for the nurse, in case she comes back?"

"Yes. You focus on the phone call. I'll be praying, too."

Payton turned her back on Zach and everyone else in the room. Whatever Beckett was doing, he was about to be interrupted in the worst possible way.

"Hello?" Beckett answered on the first ring.

"Beckett, this is Payton, Johanna's sister—"

"Is everything okay?" Beckett's words were rapid-fire. "Johanna? The baby?"

Tricky question. "We're at the hospital. Johanna started bleeding again a few hours ago and her doctor decided to do a C-section."

"And . . ."

"Your daughter is in the NICU, but the nurse who came out to tell us seemed pretty calm about her condition. She talked about the baby being born a little early and at high altitude. My mom is with her." Payton needed to just say things straight up. "Johanna . . . Johanna is having problems with bleeding. The nurse said she's bleeding a lot . . ."

"What are they doing?"

"I don't know." Payton swallowed, searching for what the nurse had said. "Dr. Gray is still with her. She's supposed to come talk with us as soon as she can—or the nurse said she'd come back. I thought you should know about the baby and Johanna, too."

"Thanks, Payton." Beckett cleared his throat. "I just finished a round of interviews here. I'm supposed to meet with the CEO tomorrow."

"I understand. I'll keep you posted. Put my number in your phone and you can text me, too. Anytime."

"I want to be there, you know that, right?"

"You don't have to explain anything to me, Beckett."

"Thanks. Tell Johanna . . . tell her . . ."

"I'll let her know we talked when I see her. And I'll send you a photo of the baby as soon as I can."

There was silence on the other end of the phone for a few seconds. "Thanks. . . . I'll be waiting for that."

Hanging up on Beckett was like seeing someone struggling in the deep end of the pool and leaving him there. She had nothing to offer him. Beckett had nothing to hold himself up with, either, except for his own strength. And Payton knew how that could fail him.

Her eyes glazed with tears as she added Beckett's number to her Favorites list, making it easier to retrieve later.

Should she have offered to pray? But she also knew better

than to push God on someone just because they were emotional or hurting.

A few moments after she returned to the waiting room, the same nurse came in again.

"Where's the doctor?" Payton asked the question under her breath. "This can't be good."

Zach took her hand. "Let's go hear what she has to say."

"I'm scared . . ."

"I know." He slipped his arm around her waist. "Come on. We'll do this together."

The nurse looked around. "Where's the rest of the family?"

"They went to the NICU to check on the baby—and my mother. How's Johanna?"

"Dr. Gray won't be out for a while. She had to go back in through the C-section site to try and slow down Johanna's bleeding using surgical procedures."

A shock of cold coursed through Payton's body, leaving her so weak she had to lean against Zach. "Are you saying . . . are you saying Johanna had a hysterectomy?"

"No. There are other things they can do. I wanted to give you an update. Let you know why it's taking so long." The nurse disappeared before Payton could even say thank you.

This was the part of a movie where things go from bad to worse, and then the scene ended as the nurse vanished, once again, behind the OR doors. Payton wanted to know specific details about what was going in the operating room, but then again, she didn't. As long as she didn't know the final outcome, she still had hope that Johanna would be okay.

I WAS WARM.

That was different. The last thing I remembered . . . *how long ago was that?* . . . I had been cold. And I'd been falling . . . falling into darkness, trying to find my way out. To open my eyes . . .

Something was beeping.

Now *that* I recognized. But . . . but . . .

The beeping accelerated.

That wasn't my baby's heartbeat.

It had to be my heartbeat. Why weren't there two hearts beating together?

I needed to wake up. Figure out where I was. Where Ellison was.

I forced my eyes open, squinting at the small bit of sunlight coming through the partially open curtains. "This isn't my room . . ."

"Good morning, Johanna." A young woman wearing scrubs, her dark hair pulled away from her face, entered the room. "I'm Penny, your nurse. You're no longer on labor and delivery. You were transferred to ICU after your surgery last night."

"After my . . . surgery?" As I spoke again, something brushed against my upper lip and the sides of my face. I swiped at it with the palm of my right hand, tugging at an IV line.

"You have a nasal cannula for oxygen right now—" the nurse eased my hand away from my face—"as well as several IVs. The doctor may decide you don't need to be on oxygen once she sees you."

"Dr. Gray?"

"You're under the care of Dr. Prisha Anand, the ICU attending, as well as Dr. Gray. They'll both be in to see you."

It was as if I'd planned a trip to New England and dozed off on the flight only to find out that the plane had landed in Chicago—and I had no hope of booking a flight to my original destination.

The lone sound of my heart beating continued in the background, a slower pace than my baby's.

Hours ago, I'd given birth to my daughter. And I'd caught the briefest glimpse of her. Never held her.

Right now, this nurse was my only connection to life outside this room.

"Where's my baby?"

"She spent the night in the NICU—"

"What's wrong with her?" My attempt to sit up straighter had me gasping at the sharp pain caused by my too-quick movement.

"Your daughter's fine—and I need you to take it easy. Remember, you had a C-section a few hours ago." Penny eased me back against the pillows. "She's a few weeks premature, so it took a bit to get her temperature regulated. And you, unfortunately, had quite a go of it after your C-section, which is why you spent the night here, instead of with your daughter."

"Quite a go of it—care to translate that?"

"I'll let your doctors discuss everything in detail with you, but suffice it to say, you required a blood transfusion. Several, actually." The nurse checked my IVs. "You're on IV fluids and antibiotics and you have a catheter."

"This is not quite how I imagined my first day of motherhood would go."

"I admit, this is a tough way to start. Dr. Gray and Dr. Anand will be by to discuss how soon you can move to a room with your daughter. But I can have the NICU nurse bring her down to see you, if you'd like."

"Now?"

"Let me get you settled first—take your vitals, get you up and moving around a little bit, and then I'll notify them that you're awake."

I was never one for fairy tales, and yet I'd pulled some kind of Sleeping Beauty act during my daughter's first hours of life. Granted, I'd had a medical emergency, but still, retelling her birth story and having to say, "I don't remember this part because I was asleep" wasn't going to impress Ellison in years to come.

Part of me wouldn't mind closing my eyes and going back to sleep again, but I couldn't do that. I had to choose whether I was going to be a new mother or an invalid. If I wanted to see Ellison, I had to ignore the temptation of sleep.

I would do everything the nurse demanded of me because I was not going to wait any longer than necessary to see my daughter. Some strange person was holding her. Feeding her.

That was my job.

"Why don't we try you sitting up?"

Fine. If the nurse wanted me to sit up, then I'd sit up. Slowly. There was no need to rush things.

"Good. Now let's get your legs over the side."

"Who knew putting my legs over the side of the bed would be such a monumental task?" I caught my breath as pain seared my abdomen. "I guess I won't be going back to my Pilates class right away."

"Not right away, no." Penny stood beside me. "And now we'll stand . . ."

"You're already standing."

"True. Why don't you join me and we'll take a few baby steps?"

"Baby steps. How appropriate."

By the time I completed my three-phase morning exercise, I wanted to cheer and collapse in my bed—opting for just collapsing.

Penny arranged the blankets and multiple lines attached to my aching body. "The NICU nurse is on the way with your daughter, so let's get you comfortable before she gets here."

"Sounds like a good idea."

"You're not going to be able to lift her right away—and then nothing heavier than your baby for the first few weeks. Again, Dr. Gray will discuss all this with you."

"Then how am I supposed to manage taking care of her?"

"You're going to need some help. While you're in the hospital, someone will give you the baby and take her from you to put her back in the bassinet."

After a soft knock, the glass door slid open and yet another nurse asked, "Is Ms. Thatcher ready for her daughter?"

"Yes. I am." No one needed to answer that question for me.

Penny held the curtain back, and the next minute the nurse stepped in, and then a clear bassinet appeared, being pushed by Jillian . . . *Jillian*, who offered me a huge smile. "Here she is, Jo."

"Jill? I didn't know you were here."

"Mom and I talked about it. I offered to stay with Ellison last night so Mom could go home and get some sleep."

"You . . . you were with Ellison all night?"

"Yes. We all thought you wouldn't want her to be alone." Jillian eased the bassinet toward my bed. "She's so sweet, Jo. She has long fingers. And I think she may have your hair color . . . your natural hair color. Of course, it's too early to know what color her eyes will be."

For a moment, this conversation seemed wrong, Jillian's

words blending together as she told me things I should be telling her. I struggled with the idea that I'd slept while my sister had rocked Ellison. Fed her. Mothered her.

But who better to be with my daughter than Jillian? Her aunt. The sister who'd seen me at my worst and loved me— forgiven me.

"Are you ready to hold your daughter?" The nurse brought the bassinet closer.

"Yes."

Penny exited the room as the other nurse stepped forward. "Let's raise the bed up and then I'll position a pillow over your stomach to protect your incision site so it won't hurt you when you hold her."

"Fine."

"Why don't I go call Mom and Payton and let them know you're awake?" Jillian backed toward the door, her smile warm. "They were going to go shopping for some preemie outfits for Ellison this morning."

"Thank you for being with her." I blinked away tears. "I'm so glad you were with her."

"I was thankful I could do it for you." She eased the door open. "Now you spend time with your daughter."

Once the nurse had positioned the pillow, she lifted my baby—*my baby*—and placed her in my arms.

And for the first time in months, I was no longer waiting for something.

"She's tinier than I expected." I found myself whispering, afraid to startle Ellison as she slept in my embrace.

"She weighs five pounds, two ounces, and she's nineteen

inches long." The nurse handed me a tiny bottle. "She's sleeping now, but in case she wakes up, she might be hungry. Your mother and sister told us you didn't plan on breastfeeding."

"No. I'm going back to work full-time."

"Some women still choose that option—"

"I'm not one of those women."

"And some moms choose to breastfeed for the first six to eight weeks because it's proven beneficial for the baby. If you'd like to talk with a lactation specialist—"

"I'm just going to hold my daughter now. I've got some catching up to do."

"I understand."

I didn't want my first meeting with Ellison interrupted with a public service announcement. I knew the nurse meant well, but right now, I wanted to get to know my daughter. Even though we had years and years ahead of us, I wanted these first moments—this delayed meeting—to ourselves.

Ellison's little face was perfect—unmarred by any sense of worry or pain or sorrow. Soon enough she'd cry. Fuss. Get angry—even if it was only about a messy diaper or because she was hungry.

I should know her, but I didn't.

But oh, how I wanted to.

"Hello, Ellison Pepper Thatcher. What a surprise you are." I pulled back the edge of the blanket that was snugged so tightly around her tiny body. Touched her delicate fingers that were long, just like Jillian had said. "I can honestly say you are the most unexpected thing I've ever experienced. And I'm so happy you're here."

Ellison's perfect mouth parted in a silent yawn.

"I'm sorry if I'm boring you." I dared to press my lips to one tiny hand. "It's you and me, Ellison. Life's going to be interesting, I can tell you that. And I'll be the first to tell you that I'm not always the easiest person to get along with—but choosing you, holding you, has done something to my heart."

Tears blurred my vision again and I blinked them away. I didn't want anything to interfere with my view of my daughter.

"I think . . . I think you're going to be very, very good for me. And I'm going to try and be a good mother to you. I know I have a lot to learn. Let's just start with today, okay?"

I had to be different. I had to be better for Ellison. Life wasn't just about me anymore. My choices affected her.

And I needed to start by admitting I was wrong. It wasn't just me and her. She hadn't been alone while I faced a medical crisis. We both had a family who loved us.

"Welcome to the world, Ellison. You're a Thatcher, baby girl. You're named for your grandmother, who you met right after you were born, and your aunt Pepper." Tears again? Childbirth made me weepy. "I'm sorry you won't get to meet her, but we'll tell you stories about her. And your grandmother and Aunt Payton are out shopping for you right now. And your aunt Jillian . . . your aunt Jillian is my best friend, so it's only right she stayed with you last night when I couldn't be with you."

Ellison would learn soon enough that being a Thatcher was a good thing. Complicated, yes, but a good thing.

35

My life was good.

Not perfect, but good.

My neck, shoulders, back, and arms ached from holding Ellison. No one ever told me that holding something—someone—who weighed less than six pounds could make me so tense I hurt. And that the thought of coughing or sneezing could scare me. Yet there was an altogether different sort of ache when she wasn't in my arms.

My C-section site hurt on the surface where the staples were visible, but also inside where they'd had to sew off two of the uterine arteries to stanch the flow of blood. Even though I'd been given a medicine pump to mitigate the pain, I tried to avoid using it. No sense in depending on it too much since it wasn't coming home with me.

"I can't say Dr. Gray and Dr. Anand were totally convinced about moving me back up to the postpartum ward."

Mom adjusted the pillow behind my back. "They both realized you were going to fight them about staying in the ICU. And they recognized how stubborn you are."

"Like I told them, the hospital is the hospital. They both admitted I'm doing well overall—better than they expected—and that being together is better for both Ellison and me."

"Everyone agrees on that. A baby should be with her mom."

"It also helps that you agreed to stay with me tonight."

"We're all here to help you, Johanna."

"I know." I hesitated. "I was jealous of Jillian . . ."

"Jealous? Why?"

"Just for a moment I was jealous because she was with Ellison that first night after she was born, instead of me." Even now the thought caused my throat to tighten. "But then I realized it was an irrational response. I was thankful Jillian stayed with her. There's room in Ellison's life for Jillian and you and Payton . . . and we'll all make certain she knows about Pepper."

"Her namesake."

"One of her namesakes."

"Thank you, Johanna."

"Thank you, Mom. I didn't realize that you'd always been there for me."

It was as if I was stepping closer to Mom, even as I sat in a hospital lounger holding Ellison. How odd, to be with Mom, holding my daughter. Her first granddaughter.

Ellison's eyes opened for a brief moment as she turned her head, and she moved one tiny fist up against her face. I rested my hand on her body and savored the sense of her inhaling and exhaling. Her breathing was my new favorite sound. Earlier in the day, we'd both fallen asleep, Ellison in her bassinet, and me in the hospital bed, on my side, one hand draped over, resting on her little body, feeling the rise and fall of her breath.

My daughter's breathing was a precious distraction.

"Where's Dad? I thought you said he was coming over tonight to see his granddaughter."

Mom paused from folding some of the clothes she and Payton had purchased for Ellison earlier that day. So many tiny outfits that they'd taken home and washed and dried and presented to me with huge grins of satisfaction.

"Um, he should be here anytime now." She glanced at the clock on the wall facing my bed. "How are you feeling? Are you good? In pain? Is it time for your medication?"

"I'm fine, Mom. I'm tired, but that's my new normal. And I've got the pump—but I don't want to get attached to that."

"Right. Right. I forgot. Do you want me to get you some more water? Remember, they told you to keep up on your fluids so you don't get—"

"Yes. I remember. We are not discussing that, even if you are my mother." I shifted my position just a bit. "What is going on?"

"Nothing. Everything's fine."

"Mom. You are a terrible liar. What aren't you telling me?"

And then the door to my room swung wide and Beckett strode in.

"Traffic was a bit of a mess coming from the airport—" Dad came in right behind him, smiling as if showing up with Beckett was a wonderful, welcome surprise—"but we're finally here!"

"You're supposed to be in California." I tightened my grip on Ellison, as if Beckett might take her from me.

Beckett stopped a foot from where I sat, his gaze ricocheting between my face and the tiny form in my arms. "I'm supposed to be here."

I didn't know how to process his words. The room seemed hazy, reminiscent of when I was in the operating room, losing too much blood. Only then I'd told Dr. Gray that I trusted her. And I didn't trust Beckett Sager. I didn't want to trust him.

Ellison—innocent, hours-old baby that she was—was oblivious to everything. Peaceful. Asleep. Her breathing quiet and steady beneath my hand.

Beckett had said the right thing. But he was no longer the right person.

"Who told you?"

"Payton . . . Payton called me after Ellison was born and told me you were having serious complications." Beckett swallowed hard. "And no, Johanna, no one asked you if she should call me. But it was the right thing to do."

"You had a job interview—"

Beckett raked his hand through his hair. Muttered something under his breath. I was half-tempted to say, "Watch your language in front of the baby," but my sense of humor failed me.

"I told you I was coming back, Johanna. I only went to the interview because I'm trying to get the job here in the Springs."

"And you've probably lost it now . . ."

"Not necessarily." Beckett's eyes held a wicked gleam even as his face flushed. "I explained that my . . . my daughter was being born earlier than anticipated . . . an emergency C-section. The interview team insisted I get back to my wife right away."

"Beckett Sager!" I had to whisper the rebuke to keep from disturbing Ellison. "Did you set them straight?"

"I didn't have time—I had to make arrangements to get back here."

"I hope your ticket cost you *triple* what you'd normally pay."

"I couldn't find a regular flight."

He wasn't making any sense, or maybe I was too tired to follow him. "Then how did you get here?"

"I have a buddy with a private pilot's license. Let's just say he owed me for something . . . and I said I'd pay for the gas and putting him up in the Springs for a couple of days if he'd get me back here."

"That's quite a story."

"I was worried sick about you and Ellison." Beckett took a step forward. "I flew into the Springs and your dad picked me up. My car's in Denver."

Beckett hadn't come to my rescue—Dr. Gray had done that last night. But he had come back like he said he would. And he'd risked losing the job he wanted to get here.

Even road-weary, Beckett still had the charisma that had always appealed to me. He was being nice. Concerned. But he was still Beckett, the man who had betrayed me.

Wait.

I had changed.

Maybe Beckett could change, too.

Not that we'd resume our romance, but enough to establish a relationship for Ellison.

"Do you want to see her . . . our daughter?" Saying the words caused my throat to ache.

I wanted her to be *my* daughter. Only mine. But that wasn't the truth. Ellison was here because of me and Beckett . . . because of something we once had.

"That's why I'm here." Beckett dropped to one knee beside my chair.

I shifted, stifling a hiss of pain as I moved my arms to angle Ellison so he could see her. "Ellison Thatcher, this is your dad."

"She's so tiny." Beckett's voice was the softest whisper. "Can I touch her?"

"She won't break."

"I don't want to wake her up."

"I'm learning you can't wake this little girl up when she wants to sleep."

"She's beautiful, Johanna."

"I know."

"How are you feeling?"

"I hurt all over, to be honest." That wasn't the entire truth—the best truth. "But I've never been happier. Isn't that crazy?"

"You look like a natural. I came into this room and saw you holding her . . ." Beckett stopped. Cleared his throat. "I'm so glad you're both okay."

For the first time in months, I didn't want to be angry with Beckett. It was as if Ellison was a tiny little buffer . . . a reason to gentle my response, my reaction to him. When he touched the side of her face, I was tempted to rest my hand on top of his. To complete the connection between the three of us.

But I couldn't do that.

Beckett and I were here for our daughter. Not for each other.

The nurse returning to the room broke the connection. I wasn't even certain Beckett was aware of the moment.

"Johanna, are you ready to get back in bed?" She stopped when she saw Beckett kneeling beside the chair. "I didn't realize you had a visitor."

"Yes. . . . I'm not sure where my parents are."

"They said something about going to get something to eat."

Ah. I hadn't heard that.

"This is . . . Ellison's father." I appreciated the nurse's nonreaction. "And yes, I'd like to get back in bed."

"Maybe Ellison's father would like to hold her while you get settled?"

Beckett rose to his feet. "Would that be okay with you, Jo?"

"Absolutely." Even as I agreed, I almost wanted to change my answer. But Beckett had to hold Ellison sometime.

"Then let me take this little sweetheart—" the nurse lifted the slight weight of my daughter from my arms—"and give her to her daddy."

For a moment, I couldn't see Ellison as the nurse instructed Beckett on how to hold her. Support her head. Hold her close to his chest.

"She's moving . . ."

"Yes. Newborns do that. She's fine. Why don't you step over here with her? I'm going to pull the curtain around the bed while I get Johanna settled. You just hold your daughter."

"But what if she cries?"

"If she cries, we'll all hear her. It's a curtain, not a brick wall. Here's a bottle. You can always try to feed her." And with those words, the nurse pulled the curtain around us, blocking Beckett and Ellison on the other side.

"You okay over there?" I couldn't keep the laughter from my voice.

"We're fine . . . so long as she stays asleep." Beckett's words were spoken in a stage whisper. "Is it okay if I walk with her?"

"Yes. Just don't drop her."

"Don't even say that. I've never been more afraid in my life."

"Take little steps . . ."

It was quiet for a few seconds . . . until Beckett started counting.

"Are you counting your steps, Beckett?"

"Yes." A soft laugh followed his admission. "I don't know why. Counting seems to help. I've never held a baby before."

"And now you're holding your daughter."

"Our daughter." The sound of Beckett counting came from the other side of the curtain again. "Ellison is your mom's maiden name?"

"Yes. And I assume Payton told you that I chose Pepper as her middle name."

"Ellison Pepper Thatcher. It's a beautiful name. She's beautiful."

The nurse drew the curtain back, exiting the room and leaving the three of us alone.

"Is it okay if I hold her a bit longer?"

"You flew all this way . . ." I smiled. "Yes."

Beckett eased into the chair I'd just vacated. "Thank you."

"I wanted to let you know that I haven't had a chance to fill out her birth certificate yet. . . . Things have been a bit hectic."

"That's an understatement."

"But I'm listing you as Ellison's father."

Beckett didn't respond at first—seemed to struggle to respond, his chin quivering as his eyes filled with tears. "Thank . . . thank you, Johanna."

"It's the right thing to do, Beckett."

Until I said the words out loud, I'd believed I was doing the right thing for Ellison. But now I knew I was doing the right thing for all of us. For me. For Beckett. And for our daughter. I was stepping away from anger.

I started to reach for Beckett's hand . . . and stopped.

This was not the time. It might never be the time for that again. Ever.

I had to choose what was best for Ellison . . . and that meant being more kind to Beckett. And probably more kind to myself, too.

36

I HADN'T EXPECTED the trio of pink balloons decorating my front door. The hand-painted *Welcome Home, Ellison* sign draped across the garage door, complete with streamers.

"And who is responsible for all of this?" I cradled Ellison in my arms as Mom and Dad ushered me into the foyer, the air-conditioning a welcome relief from the August heat.

"Two very excited aunts." Mom offered to take Ellison, but I declined. "Jillian and Payton wanted their niece to have a proper welcome home."

"Make sure Dad texts them the photos you took."

"Already done." Dad held up his phone.

"At least I know the house is clean, thanks to the service coming in earlier this week." I inhaled the fresh scent of citrus that still lingered in the air. "I'm sorry I never finished the nursery. But Ellison will be sleeping in my room for a while anyway, just like you suggested, Mom."

I hadn't been here in over a month, but the weeks away seemed longer. I stopped in the living room, almost unable to comprehend that I stood in my house, holding my newborn daughter. "We're home at last, baby girl."

"It must feel good." Mom came and stood beside me as Dad carried my suitcase to my bedroom.

"To be honest, I'm a little scared. But don't tell anyone I admitted that. It feels odd not to be surrounded by nurses and doctors and machines. I'll get used to all this space and all this quiet—and also to having to think about Ellison all the time."

"You're not by yourself completely. Don't forget I'm here for a few days." Mom gave me a gentle half hug. "Why don't we show Ellison her room?"

"But it's not finished."

"Still, she needs to see all of her new home."

"She's wide-awake now, anyway. Want to see your room, Ellison?" It was funny how easy it was to talk to my days-old daughter as if she understood me. "I'll get it fixed up nice for you soon."

Mom moved ahead of me down the hallway, opening the door to Ellison's unfinished room and turning on the light as she stepped inside. I tamped down my disappointment. It couldn't be helped that the room contained a crib in a box and pictures leaning against the wall—

"Welcome home!"

Payton and Jillian stood in the center of the room—the

completed nursery that looked exactly as I'd envisioned it, with the addition of the framed puzzle that I'd managed to finish with Beckett's and my parents' help. Walls painted a soft gray with a trio of botanical prints hanging above the white dresser. Ellison's crib centered against the opposite wall, with the rocking chair positioned by the window, the curtains pulled back to allow in the afternoon sunlight. An area rug arranged on the wood floor.

I stumbled back, startling Ellison so that she began to cry.

"Oh no, we scared our niece." Jillian's voice dropped to a stage whisper. "What were we thinking?"

Payton covered her mouth. "Sorry, Johanna. We got a little excited."

"It's okay." I repositioned Ellison to my shoulder, rocking back and forth. "Shhh. Shhh. Look at your beautiful room."

"Do you like it?" Mom turned a half circle. "Is it done the way you wanted?"

"It's perfect." I blinked back tears. "How did you all manage this?"

"Everyone pitched in. We took a couple of days." Jillian stood by the crib. "Zach and Geoff tackled the crib. I have video of that. Payton and I painted the walls. Mom and Dad hung the pictures and organized her clothes—"

"We had so much fun!" Payton interrupted, going to the closet and opening the door. "Look at all these adorable outfits on the tiny hangers."

"Of course, the bassinet is still in your room." Mom motioned to the rocking chair. "Do you want to sit for a minute?"

Ellison's cries quieted as I eased into the chair and rocked gently back and forth, the sunlight warm on my skin. "This is the perfect location to sit and hold her."

"Mom suggested we put the chair there." Dad put his arm around Mom's shoulders.

"We can always move it—"

"No. Everything is just right. How did you—?" And then I noticed the towering stuffed giraffe positioned by Ellison's crib. "Wait. Who do I have to thank for *that*?"

"I was wondering when you were going to notice the giraffe." Jillian was most definitely enjoying my surprise. "Elle's daddy left that for her. We didn't know what your plans were for the room, but Beckett knew the password for your laptop."

"Beckett gave you my password?" Even with the shock of that revelation, and of the stuffed giraffe in my daughter's nursery, I still savored the nickname given her by her aunts. *Elle*.

"How else were we supposed to know what color to paint the walls?" Jillian straightened the big white bow tied around the giraffe's long neck. "Thanks to Beckett, we got access to your laptop and got all the intel we needed to finish Elle's room. He wanted to help with the room but was finishing up his job interviews in California."

"I don't recall having a giraffe anywhere on my list."

"No, I don't think you did. That was all Beckett's idea." Payton closed the closet door. "Other than that surprise, you like the room?"

"I love the room—even the giraffe. It's perfect. Thank you."

"That's what family is for—to take care of their niece . . . and granddaughter."

I'd underestimated how much Ellison was going to change things. At first, I'd resisted how she'd change my life—never realizing how she would affect Jillian and Payton and Mom and Dad.

What we would have missed without her.

Everything her life opened up for all of us.

Such a huge responsibility for such a tiny baby. She didn't know she was a new beginning for so many people.

"You're awfully quiet, Joey." Jillian's voice drew me back to the present.

"I was just thinking . . . how Ellison changes so much for our family . . . in a good way. And I almost said no to her."

"But you didn't. Sometimes the best part of life is saying yes to the unexpected."

"I'm learning that."

"I think we all are." Jillian knelt beside me. "You know how they say good things come in small packages? Elle is our good thing."

Payton stood in the doorway. "Do you need anything?"

"No. We're all good." I smiled at my sisters. "The best we've been in a long time."

37

THE CHILL OF THE LATE-AUGUST MORNING made Jillian thankful she'd added a Windbreaker to her outfit at the last moment.

"You warm enough?" Geoff took her hand and pulled her close as they walked toward Memorial Park.

"Yes. I always forget how cold it can be when we decide to go early and watch the balloon launch."

"It'll warm up by the time it's over."

"True." She stopped walking, causing Geoff to stumble. "Today's the thirty-first, isn't it?"

"Ye-es."

"Yesterday was Johanna's original due date—and Ellison is already over three weeks old. Isn't that amazing?"

Geoff resumed walking toward the park, joining the other people wanting to see the hot-air balloons take to the sky. "Things are finally quieting down . . . just a little."

"For us, maybe. Not for Johanna. Not for quite a while."

"Ellison Pepper Thatcher—she's something, isn't she?" Geoff seemed to get a kick out of the baby's name.

"I don't know what meant more to Mom—that Johanna used her maiden name or that she also used Pepper's name."

"For all her toughness, Johanna gives some of the most thoughtful gifts of anyone I know."

"What do you mean?"

"The Christmas you were first diagnosed with cancer? She donated her hair to Locks of Love."

"Right."

"When Payton and Zach got married, she wrote—and recorded—a song for their ceremony. I remember how surprising that was because I didn't even know your sister played the piano."

"She surprised all of us that day."

"And then she names your mom's first granddaughter after her—and Pepper."

Why was it that Geoff was the one who saw Johanna as a gift giver—and recognized how her sister gave a piece of her heart with each of those actions?

"You, Husband, are very observant. Johanna doesn't just give things. You can't put a price tag on any of those things you mentioned."

"She's a lot different than I originally thought." They stopped at an intersection, waiting for a chance to cross the street.

"And motherhood is going to change her even more." Jillian ruffled her short hair with her fingers. Maybe now was a good time to move the conversation in a different direction. They were relaxed and they had plenty of time to walk and talk while they waited for the launch. "I've been thinking about us."

"Okay."

"And I don't want to talk about us anymore."

Geoff huffed a laugh. "That . . . wasn't what I was expecting you to say."

"I'm not saying I'm giving up on us, Geoff. I know it may sound like it, so I need you to hear me out."

"I'm listening." As if to prove his point, Geoff joined their hands together, swinging their arms back and forth.

"We've been through a lot since we met—more than the average couple, I would dare say. The way things have gone in our lives, we really shouldn't have been surprised that Brian showed up again."

"When you put it in the context of the entirety of our relationship, you're right." Geoff raised his hand. "And forgive me for interrupting you here for a moment, but I— I want to say I've been thinking about the breakfast with Brian. A lot."

She almost tripped over Geoff's unexpected admission, as if his words were the unwieldy river rocks used by landscapers that she hated walking across. "I didn't expect you to say anything about him. I mean, you haven't for weeks."

"Just because I haven't said anything doesn't mean I'm not thinking about him. I keep hearing him say how he wasn't running away from me back then—and yet, that's what it felt like. I knew how hard it was between him and Mom and Dad. But for weeks—months, really—I hoped I would be enough of a reason for him to come back home. But I never was."

"Oh, Geoff . . ." An ache centered near her heart, thinking of a much-younger Geoff, missing his older brother. Wishing he'd come back home.

"And then I decided if he didn't care enough about me, well then, I didn't need him, either. I didn't miss him." Geoff kept walking, eyes straight ahead. "It wasn't true. But Mom's way was easier. Not to talk about it. Not to talk about Brian. Or Kyler."

She eased closer to her husband, their arms touching. "Are you thinking anything else?"

"How Brian said we're adults now." Geoff shrugged. "You'd figure I'd know that. But it's more than that. He said we don't have to do things the way my parents always did. I can't shake that thought. It's like I've been sitting in this closed-off, stuffy room and somebody walked by and cracked a window open just enough to let some fresh air in."

"Have you contacted Brian at all?"

"No. I'm still trying to untangle my thoughts from what I'm feeling. I'm not sure what to say."

Jillian hesitated a few seconds before wading into the silence between them. "Maybe just call him and say hello. Tell him you've been thinking about him."

Geoff nodded, quickening his pace just a bit. "Maybe it's that easy. I don't know. For now, I just wanted to let you know what I was thinking."

"Thanks for telling me."

"Okay, so my brother is a topic for another day."

"Yes. Tabling this topic for another day." A weight lifted from her heart. "But I have to say I'm so glad to hear you say this."

"Thanks. Now, back to you."

"Me. Right." She took a deep breath. "I want to call a time-out."

"A time-out." Geoff stopped walking, turning to face her, his eyes widening behind his glasses. "Like . . . a separation?"

"No—no, not at all like that. I wouldn't say something like that *here*. And besides, I would never want that." Jillian slowed their steps so that they lagged behind the crowd, keeping them at the edge of the park. Reached for Geoff's hand to create a connection again. "I'm sorry I broke off our engagement months ago. And I'm sorry I ran away to Harper's—both times my actions taught you that I would run away when things are hard for us. No more. I'm staying. I promise."

Her words seemed to echo the scene in the romantic comedy where Julia Roberts handed Richard Gere her running shoes and promised him she wasn't running anymore. But all the people around them—like extras brought in to move around in the background—didn't realize how pivotal the scene was.

She'd found her common ground with Geoff. They loved each other. And that was enough. She just needed to remember that.

Jillian motioned to a park bench. "Can we sit down?"

"Sure."

"Last winter, we talked about wanting hope." She sat so that their knees touched. "Wanting more fun. But we . . . I got tripped up by the question of whether we were going to have children or not."

"That wasn't all your fault—"

"It was just another huge issue we were dealing with. Fine. I mean, I could list everything, but you've been living them all with me. I want a time-out from all of that."

"What? You want to run away to a deserted island together?"

"If it was in the budget, yes, but we depleted that with the kitchen renovation, remember?" It was good to share a smile with her husband. "But you said the word *together*. That's the most important thing. I want to focus on us."

"We're both in a time-out?" Geoff's grin widened, accented with a wink.

"Yes. It won't be as much fun if you're not with me."

"What does this time-out look like exactly? Because the ones I've heard about never sounded fun."

"I'd like to table the topic of kids for two years. I won't bring it up if you agree to discuss it again with me in two years—with a counselor."

"A counselor?" Geoff's eyebrows furrowed together behind his glasses.

"Yes. A neutral person who can guide us as we make our decision about children. Not your decision. Not my decision. *Our* decision."

"And our decision can be yes or no?"

She'd thought about this for weeks. Knew what she was about to agree to was the right answer. But it was still difficult to say out loud. "So long as we agree together—*our* decision can be a yes or a no."

Jillian wasn't waving a white flag. She wasn't giving up. She was choosing to stand on common ground. To tell Geoff that she loved him. That she chose him.

She refused to look away. Refused to blink. This wasn't a game. This was real life—and sometimes life cost you something—something you wanted with your whole heart.

But saving her marriage was worth the sacrifice.

"What if . . . what if we can't agree?"

"We won't be the same people in two years. Right now, we can't agree. But I think that's because, right now, I can't get past what I want so I can understand what you're feeling. And I think . . . maybe that's true for you, too." Jillian could only hope she was explaining herself in a way Geoff could understand. "We're still operating like single people—not like a married couple. I don't know how else to explain it. All the things we've dealt with? They've gotten between us. Rather than push us together, circumstances and challenges have pushed us apart. We started off loving each other. Let's go back there. Plant our feet there. That's our common ground."

"I do love you, Jill."

Jillian stole a quick kiss from her husband. "I love you. And I want to love you better, Geoff, so that you don't wonder if I'm going to run."

Geoff covered her hand with both of his. "We go back to square one, then?"

"No. We can't do that. Too much has happened. But we've changed together, even if the change has been uncomfortable. From now on, we could promise not to let the circumstances separate us."

Pikes Peak loomed right in front of them.

It was always the same mountain, day in, day out, even though it looked different depending on the time of day. The weather. But you couldn't move that mountain.

Jillian wanted her marriage to be that solid.

"During this time-out, we can still have fun, right?"

"Of course. And I still want more hope. And I'm realizing that Harper was right."

"Right about what?"

"She said that maybe the *more* I'm looking for in my faith isn't about getting what I want. That maybe it's about trying to trust God more. Learning about who He says He is."

No response.

"I'm all in about our marriage, Geoff, but I'm still going to be focusing on my faith, too."

"I know. I know. I'm just not . . ."

"Not interested in God."

"No."

"I'm not asking you to be. But I'll still be going to church on Sundays."

She wouldn't mention getting together with Payton—not today.

"I know that's important to you."

"It is. I haven't grown as much as I'd like, but my faith is still there. Weak. But still there." It was probably best to change the topic. "So to sum up, we're not making any major decision about children for two years."

"Right. It's not a topic up for discussion."

"Hope is still on the agenda."

"Fun is still on the agenda."

"Faith, for me, is still on the agenda."

"Anything else?"

"When all else fails, one of us has to remind the other that we love each other no matter what."

It was like they were taking turns driving invisible stakes into the ground.

Geoff drew her close, and she rested her head against his chest so that she could hear his heart beating. Two becoming one wasn't easy. Unity wasn't easy when they were both so different. Wanted different things. Their perspectives were at odds and their futures unknown.

They needed to remember why they started—and everything they loved about each other. But for now, they'd enjoy today. Watch the balloon launch. Just be together. Let that be enough.

38

WE WERE AT CHEYENNE MOUNTAIN ZOO. In December. At night. And it was decorated with Christmas lights.

No one had told me this was a thing parents did with their children.

"What's this event called again?" I took the diaper bag from Beckett as he closed the door to my car.

"The Electric Safari. I read about it when I bought the zoo membership. It sounded fun." He adjusted Ellison's carrier against his chest. "There we go, Little Bit."

Little Bit. The nickname he'd given Ellison still tugged at my heart.

"I don't think she's going to remember anything from tonight." We joined the other families—parents and kids of all ages—heading from the parking lot to the zoo entrance.

"Which is why we take pictures." Beckett stopped, rested his arm over my shoulder, and snapped a quick photo. "The annual trip to see the Christmas zoo lights starts tonight. We have photo proof."

I chose to ignore the warmth of Beckett's momentary closeness, the scent of his aftershave mingling with the night air. "And now I know why you insisted on bringing your camera."

"I always bring my camera, Johanna." Beckett grinned. "You also know that. But I promise not to be all about the photo ops tonight."

"Right. You've done nothing but take pictures of Ellison for the last four months."

"Do you blame me? Besides, photographing a baby is both challenging and captivating."

"You have a new favorite model."

"Guilty as charged."

"You'll hear no complaints from me. You've taken some of my parents' favorite photos of Ellison." And some of mine, but I didn't need to tell him that and inflate his ego. "I don't know that I've ever come to the zoo at night. To be honest, I can't remember the last time I came to the zoo—maybe when Payton and Pepper were little."

"Me either." Beckett paused at the window to gain admittance. "But someone at work mentioned how they have an annual membership because their kids enjoy it so much, so I thought we should do it for Ellison."

"Are their kids under a year old?"

"No, they're all in school. But I figured we didn't have to wait to let her start having fun."

I wasn't going to ruin Beckett's fun by telling him Ellison was going to sleep through most of tonight. "How's she doing?"

"She's fine. Happy to be with her daddy, aren't you, Little Bit?" Beckett patted Ellison's bottom. "I'm glad it's not too cold tonight. You think she's warm enough?"

"She's fine, so long as we keep her hat on." I retrieved gloves from my coat pocket and tugged them on. "She's got her body heat and yours, too."

"She's wide-awake, so why don't we go feed the giraffes? Or should we take her to see Santa?"

"Ellison won't know the difference between the two." I ignored Beckett's frown. "Seriously, Beckett, let's relax. Enjoy the lights. Not worry about doing it all tonight, especially since Ellison could decide to snooze through it all. Is it important to you that she see Santa?"

"I just want to make good memories for her—"

"The only memories she'll have are the ones we tell her about when she looks at the pictures you take."

A soft coo sounded from the snuggly. Beckett's eyes widened and then he chuckled. "Well, I guess you two have told me. I'll relax."

"Let's start at the giraffes."

I almost regretted my suggestion when the pungent smell of the giraffe house assaulted my nose. But Beckett insisted I take photos of him and Ellison feeding lettuce leaves to the giraffes, their long purple tongues coming much too close to my daughter's face, before we could escape into the cool, fresh night air.

Multicolored lights decorated the trees and bushes, and some lit displays formed various animals in motion. Kangaroos. Bears. Butterflies. A peacock. Live animals roamed some of the exhibits, while some slept, oblivious to the nighttime zoo visitors.

"Do you want to ride the carousel?" Beckett paused in front of the ride that was doing a slow twirl around and around. Some parents stood next to their young children as they perched atop a carousel horse. Others waved to them outside the enclosure as they spun past.

"Not this time." I nodded toward Ellison. "She's asleep. No sense in risking waking her up."

"True."

"Plus, I've always found carousels kind of sad."

I regretted the admission as soon as I'd told Beckett.

"Sad? With that kind of music?"

"It's not the music. It's how the carousel keeps spinning . . . and you lose sight of someone. You can't stop it from happening. Whenever I rode a carousel when I was a kid, it always made me afraid. I wondered if my parents would be there when I came around again. It's silly, I know."

"No. Not silly." For a moment, it seemed as if Beckett was going to reach out. Take my hand. And then he moved away.

I shouldn't have said anything. Beckett and I were doing well, managing this co-parenting relationship, so long as we kept things on the surface. Respected one another's space. Concentrated on Ellison. What she needed.

"Your job . . . you're still enjoying it?" Not the smoothest transition, but it moved us back to neutral territory.

"Yes." Beckett rubbed Ellison's back, his hand moving in slow circles. "I am. And I've gotten good feedback, too. All's good there."

"I'm glad."

"I did want to tell you a couple of things."

"I'm listening." I tried not to tense up. *Telling me a couple of things* didn't have to mean something bad. Even so, I found myself stuffing my hands in my coat pockets.

"I've been looking at cars."

"Cars?"

"You've got to admit my sports car doesn't work too well for Ellison. I've been shopping around for something more practical."

Practical. Beckett was going to buy a *practical* car?

"You're not selling the Z, are you?"

"I'm not quite ready to do that yet. I mean, I love you, Little Bit—" Beckett's grin was directed at our daughter—"but Daddy still likes his sports car."

He wasn't asking my permission to buy a car. Didn't need it. But this was quite a change for Beckett—buying a family car. Not that we were a family, despite outward appearances.

There was no way to miss how other people smiled at him. At us. Women looked at him differently now. He wasn't just a handsome guy. He was a handsome guy with a baby. A dad. And people saw all three of us, not just Beckett.

"Did you say there was something else you needed to tell me?"

"Yeah." But he continued to walk for a few moments

without saying anything. "I wanted to give you my new phone number."

Now that . . . that made no sense at all.

"Did you lose your phone? Break it?"

"No." Beckett took my hand, drawing me off the pathway, toward one of the areas where a welcoming fire burned in a fifty-five-gallon steel drum so visitors could warm their hands. "Look . . . I know we're not together anymore. But I want you to trust me. I—I can't tell you how much. And I thought if I changed my phone number . . ."

He pulled his phone from his coat pocket. Held it up. On the screen was a photo of me cradling a sleeping Ellison in my arms. "My lock screen. And my home screen is Little Bit. I'm always showing people at work photos of her. So far, they're putting up with me."

The sound of Beckett's phone crashing against my bedroom wall echoed in my mind. The image of Iris's face behind his cracked screen.

A new phone number? Was this Beckett's way of trying to say I didn't have to worry about Iris—or any other woman from his past—calling him anymore? Of course, he could always give them his new number. Or I could choose to trust him.

"Thank you, Beckett."

I handed him my phone. Stayed silent as he deleted his old number. As he typed in his new number.

People passed by us, talking. Laughing. Drinking hot chocolate and eating popcorn. Bundled up against the cold night air.

Never again had shifted to *maybe*. I couldn't voice anything out loud, but for the first time, I dared to hope our future could be better. That it could include the three of us, together. Not just for Ellison. But for Beckett and me, too.

Tonight, though, I accepted my phone without jerking my hand away when his fingers brushed against mine.

Progress.

"Ellison's asleep." Beckett's voice was pitched low. "Should we head back to the car?"

"I'm okay with staying longer. You?"

"I'd like that, too."

We fell into step alongside one another. There was no need to rush. We could take our time tonight and tomorrow and in the days to come. For us and for our daughter.

⌒

We had a schedule to keep—and I knew that better than anyone else. Even so, my sisters almost had to force me to release Ellison so I could put on my coat, pick up my purse, and leave.

"Do you think Ellison's going to be okay?" I stopped on the sidewalk outside Jillian's house, half-turning toward the front door that was adorned with an evergreen wreath decorated with a bright-red bow.

"What you're asking—*again*—is whether Dad, Geoff, Zach, and Beckett are going to be able to take care of her." Jillian linked her arm through mine, easing me a step forward. "You just spent forty-five minutes telling them how to take care of Elle—*after* you'd handed out multiple copies of a very detailed list of instructions that included each of our cell phone numbers."

Payton came alongside me. "There's enough formula to feed Elle for a week. Enough diapers for a month. And enough toys—"

"I get it. They're more than adequately prepared." I slowed my steps again. "But it's a bunch of guys taking care of my daughter."

"They're family, not random strangers we picked up off the street. And you arranged this afternoon for us, Johanna, including the babysitting." Mom spoke up as we approached my car, her smile softening her words. "Ellison will be fine for the time we'll be gone."

"Of course, we have no idea where we're going. Or how long we're going to be gone." Jillian clicked the remote, unlocking the doors. "If you want to tell me what you've got planned, I'd be happy to drive."

"No." I took the keys and, with one last glance at the house, rounded the front of the car to the driver's seat. No one appeared holding my wailing daughter in their arms. "This is my Christmas gift to each of you. I'm driving."

"I'm only getting in this car if you promise me that you're not going to be worrying about Elle the entire time you're driving." Payton stood with her arms crossed.

"I'm fine." Payton didn't move, despite my assurance. "*Let's go*. We don't want to be late."

"Aha! We're on a schedule. Dinner reservations at the Broadmoor, maybe?" Jillian motioned Mom into the front seat.

"Keep guessing, but I'm not telling you."

"It's one o'clock in the afternoon, Jill. A little early for dinner." Payton settled in the backseat behind me. "And we just ate lunch, remember?"

Let them keep guessing. It would distract them while I drove—and also keep me distracted, too. That way I wouldn't think about Ellison and all the men who'd promised they wouldn't watch a single second of football while we were gone.

I'd forgotten how close Jillian's house was to the Pikes Peak Center. In less than ten minutes, my surprise was revealed.

"The Christmas Symphony? We're going to the symphony?" Mom craned her neck as I drove past the front of the center.

"Good guess, Mom. I have tickets in my purse for the afternoon performance."

"Jo! This is fantastic." Jillian leaned forward, her voice loud in my ear.

"I'm glad you like the idea—hey! Are you wearing your seat belt?"

"Yes . . . well, I was, but I thought you were parking the car."

"I'm going around back to the parking garage. Buckle up, little sister."

There was a festive air to the center that was decorated for the holidays. And our decision to dress up added more fun to the day. Even ever-athletic Payton had found a dress, and we'd all chosen the boots and coats we'd worn for her outdoor wedding ten months ago.

I led the way down to the center section at the back of

the orchestra area, stepping aside so Payton and Jillian could take their seats. "I hope you like this location."

"This looks perfect." Mom settled next to me, with Jillian next to her and then Payton.

Without even glancing at her program, Payton nodded to the seat next to her. "Did you see this? There's a single rose left in this seat. Do you think someone had that put there for his date tonight? We'll have to watch—"

"Um, no . . ." I paused for a moment, glancing from Mom to my sisters. "The rose is there in honor of Pepper."

Mom's program slipped from her hands to the floor with a soft flutter of pages. "P-Pepper?"

Now that it came time to explain the gesture, I hesitated, thankful that no one else was entering our row. "Yes. This is something we're doing as sisters . . . with you, Mom. And I wanted to somehow include Pepper, too."

"You bought a ticket for Pepper?" Payton picked up the orange rosebud.

"I think she would have enjoyed tonight, too, don't you?"

"Yes." Mom took my hand. "Yes, I do. Thank you, Johanna, for tonight. And for including Pepper."

"I'm curious, Jo. Why did you pick an orange rose?" Jillian took the delicate bud from Payton and handed it to Mom.

"I researched the significance of the different colors of roses. Yellow ones symbolize joy and caring. And peach ones can symbolize gratitude." I could only hope everyone agreed with my choice. "Orange roses stand for enthusiasm and energy and can also mean admiration. All of that reminded me the most of Pepper."

Mom's eyes glistened with tears and her smile trembled. "I think Pepper would have loved your choice, Johanna." She handed the stem back to Jillian. "Go ahead and put it back in the seat. It'll seem like Pepper's sitting there, enjoying the music with us."

Behind the curtain, the musicians were tuning their instruments before the performance. I closed my eyes, enjoying the interrupted notes, signifying the performance to come. Soon, the orchestra's preparation would blend into something beautiful—not unlike how all the unexpected circumstances of the past months had formed something precious. At first, none of it made sense. The discordance of my unplanned pregnancy had been the one thing I'd never wanted. But now Ellison was the one thing I'd never let go. And while the relationships with my sisters were certain to falter because we were distinctive individuals, there was an underlying stability to it that had never been there before.

We were the Thatcher sisters—in spite of our differences.

When the symphony began, there would be a give-and-take of melody and harmony, creating something magical. Maybe . . . maybe we could become better at being sisters *because* of our differences. We had to allow room for each of us to be who we were without demanding that we be the same because at one time we'd shared the same last name.

"Are you okay, Johanna?" Mom leaned close, her words a whisper.

"Yes . . . yes, I am." I clasped her hand. "I'm the best I've ever been."

Be sure to read the rest of the Thatcher Sisters novels

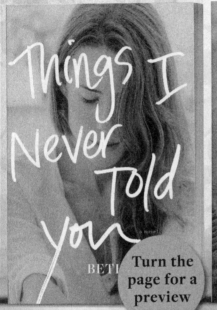

Turn the page for a preview

THE WHAT-IFS TAUNTED ME every time I visited my parents, but any hope of beginning again had vanished years ago—if there'd ever been one.

What would have happened if my parents had gone through with selling the house in Colorado Springs my sisters and I had grown up in? If they'd labeled and taped up all the boxes—the clothes, the books, the dishes, the photographs, the awards, and the trophies—and unpacked them in a different house?

A change of location. A chance to start over.

But unexpected loss held my parents captive.

For the most part, our family seemed unchanged. The kitchen clock—a porcelain plate decorated with bright red-and-yellow flowers but lacking any numerals to designate the passing of time—hung in the same place it had since a dozen Mother's Days ago. The same white wooden shutters hid the bay windows in the breakfast nook. The same worn round table in the middle, surrounded by four chairs adorned with nondescript blue cushions our mother changed out every few years—whenever Johanna reminded her to do so.

I pushed the Start button on the once-new dishwasher. My parents had installed it at the Realtor's recommendation when they'd planned to move into the larger house that offered a coveted view of Pikes Peak.

Time to focus on the cheesecakes—the engagement party dessert finale. The hum of the dishwasher blended with garbled conversation as the door between the kitchen and dining room opened, the sound of Jillian's fiancé's booming laughter sneaking in. Geoff and his corny jokes.

"Just getting the dessert, Kim—"

"I'm not your timekeeper, little sister." Johanna's no-nonsense voice interrupted my concentration.

I stiffened, gripping the handles of the fridge. Why hadn't I posted a Do Not Enter sign on the door? Maybe I should have caved to Nash's insistence to attend the party, even though tonight was more work than play for me. Why not have my boyfriend act as bouncer outside the kitchen? Flex his muscles and run interference?

I had no time for my oldest sister. Any minute now, Kimberlee would return from setting up the silver carafes of coffee and hot water for tea, along with cream, sugar, spoons, and other necessities. She'd expect the trio of cheesecakes to be arranged on their individual stands—my job tonight, since we'd only had the caterers deliver the food for such a small gathering.

"Do you need something, Johanna?" I pulled the first cheesecake from the fridge, my mouth watering at the thought of key lime and dollops of whipped cream. Being the party planner for tonight meant I'd had no chance to indulge in the hors d'oeuvres or cocktails, despite this being my other sister's engagement party. And vegan or not, I could appreciate a decadent dessert—and postpone interacting with Johanna.

"You and Kimberlee are pretty good at this event-planning business." Johanna leaned against the kitchen counter.

"Mom and Jillian seem happy. That's the important thing." I settled the cheesecake on its stand, the plastic wrap clinging to my fingers as I uncovered it. "It's all about finding out what people want and then making it happen."

"Festivities is making enough to pay the bills, apparently."

"Yes."

Not that I was going to produce an Excel spreadsheet of our accounts payable and receivable for my oldest sister.

"You two didn't charge Mom and Dad full price—"

"Really, Johanna?" Not sparing my sister a glance, I shoved the fridge door closed with my hip, a turtle cheesecake balanced in my hands.

"Oh, don't get in a huff, Payton. Honestly, how do you manage your customers if you're so touchy?"

And this . . . this was yet another reason why I didn't

come home unless absolutely necessary. I concentrated on transporting the second cheesecake from the fridge to the island, refusing to square off with my sister. Best to change the subject and prep the desserts.

"Jillian and Geoff seem perfect for one another, don't they?"

Johanna took the bait. "Of course they do. They enjoy the same foods. The same movies. He makes her laugh. They're content with a typical version of happily ever after."

And now my question had set Johanna's sights on Jillian. Should I ignore the unspoken criticism or not? "You don't approve of Geoff?"

"I wouldn't marry him. They remind me of that old nursery rhyme. 'Jack Sprat could eat no fat, his wife could eat no lean . . .'"

"And I suppose one of the reasons you're marrying Beckett is because you make such a good-looking couple?"

"You've got to admit he's easy on the eyes."

Easy on the eyes? Who said stuff like that anymore? "Not that he's around very often for anyone to get a look at him."

"If I don't mind being in a long-distance relationship, I don't see why you should be so critical." Johanna's stilettos tapped a sharp staccato on the wood floor, her platinum-blonde hair caught up in a tight ponytail that swished down between her shoulder blades.

"I'm not criticizing. Just mentioning that Beckett plays the role of the Invisible Man quite well."

"You're almost as funny as Geoff." Ice frosted Johanna's words.

Time to change the subject again unless I wanted a full-blown argument with one sister during my other sister's party. Not that I could think of a topic Johanna and I agreed on. "Isn't it odd? You and Beckett have been engaged for over two years now. Shouldn't we be planning your wedding so Jillian and Geoff don't beat you two down the aisle?"

"It's not a race. Beckett's stationed in Wyoming and I don't want to give up my job to move there—"

"Did I know Beckett was in Wyoming?"

"Honestly, Payton, he's been there for a year." Johanna sniffed. "But then, it's not like we chat every other day, is it? You and Pepper were the close ones—"

Heat flushed my neck. My face. "There's no need to bring Pepper into the conversation, is there?"

"Why, after all this time, are you still so sensitive about talking about her?"

"I'm not sensitive. I just don't see why you had to mention Pepper when we were talking about you and Beckett—"

The sound of voices rose once again as the kitchen door opened. Poor Kimberlee. She didn't know she'd have to assume Jillian's usual position as the neutral zone between Johanna and me.

"Have you seen Jillian?"

Not Kimberlee. Mom, who was also an expert human buffer.

"Isn't she with Geoff?" I removed the cling wrap from the cheesecake.

"She was a few moments ago, but now I can't find her." Mom circled the island as if she expected to find her middle daughter crouching down hiding from her. "Isn't it almost time for dessert? And aren't we supposed to open gifts after that? They certainly received a lot of presents, didn't they?"

"Yes. It's a great turnout." If only the kitchen didn't feel like a revolving three-ring circus. How would Johanna like it if our family showed up at the hospital pharmacy where she was in charge?

Before I could say anything else, Kimberlee, the one person I'd been waiting for, joined the crowd. "Are we all set in here, Payton?"

"Just about." I swallowed back the words *if people would stay out of my kitchen.* This wasn't my kitchen. And family or not, Mom was a client, at least for tonight, and needed to be treated like one. And I'd been dealing with Johanna for years. If I wanted tonight to be a success, the less said, the better.

"Mom, why don't you and Johanna join the guests?" I removed the classic cheesecake from the fridge. "I'll find Jillian while Kimberlee makes the announcement about dessert and Jillian and Geoff opening their gifts."

As Johanna and Mom left, I faced my business partner, shook my head, and sighed. "Family. And before that, a longtime family friend wandered in, asking for the crab dip recipe."

"It comes with working for relatives." Kimberlee took the cheesecake from me, the eclectic assortment of rings on her fingers sparkling under the kitchen lights. "But honestly, everything has gone beautifully. There's hardly any food left."

"That's because I know how to plan portions."

"It's because we know how to throw a good party."

"Well, let's keep things going and get this dessert set up."

Once the trio of cheesecakes was arranged on the table in my parents' dining room, I nodded to Kimberlee. "I've got to go find our bride-to-be."

"No problem. I can handle this." Kimberlee smoothed a wrinkle from the white tablecloth and repositioned the vase filled with bright-red poppies, my mother's favorite flowers. "It's not like she wandered far. She's probably in the bathroom touching up her makeup."

Not that Jillian was a "refresh her makeup" kind of gal. Mascara and a little bit of basic eyeliner was her usual routine. Lipstick was reserved for fancier affairs. She'd probably be cajoled by the photographer into wearing some on her wedding day.

The upstairs bathroom was empty, lit only by the flickering flame of a cinnamon-scented candle. Where could Jillian be? A thin band of light shone out from beneath the door of Johanna and Jillian's former bedroom at the far end of the darkened hallway. Why would my sister be in there? As I moved past my old bedroom, my fingertips brushed the doorknob for a second. I pulled my hand away, balling my fingers into a fist.

I paused outside the bedroom and then rapped my knuckles against the door. "Jillian?"

Nothing . . . and then, "Payton? Do you need me for something?"

Just for her party. I eased the door open, stepping inside. "What are you doing up here? It's time to open your gifts."

What had once been Johanna and Jillian's room was now

a generic guest room. At the moment, the only light came from the slender glass lamp on the bedside table. My sisters' beds had been replaced by a single larger bed covered in a gray-and-white paisley comforter. An idyllic outdoor scene adorned the wall across from the dark oak dresser.

Jillian, who'd been hunched over on the corner of the bed, straightened her shoulders. "I, um, got a phone call and decided to take it in here away from all the noise."

"Is everything okay?"

"Yes. Absolutely." Jillian's smile seemed to wobble for the briefest second. "Did you need me for something?"

"Your engagement party? It's time to dismantle that Jenga tower of gifts in the family room." I shook my head. "*Tsk*. And after all the hard work I put in arranging it."

"Right." Jillian smoothed her yellow empire-waist sundress down over her hips. "It's been a wonderful party, Payton."

"Thank you for saying so, but it's not over yet." I touched Jillian's shoulder. "You're really okay?"

She nodded so that the ends of her hair brushed against the back of my hand. "Yes. Nothing that won't wait until Monday."

I didn't know why I'd asked. It wasn't like Jillian would confide in me. We weren't the "Will you keep a secret?" kind of sisters. "All right then. Why don't you go find Geoff and I'll bring you both some dessert? Do you want key lime, classic, or turtle cheesecake?"

Now it was my sister's turn to shake her head. "I should skip it altogether. We're going wedding dress shopping soon enough, and I know I'm going to look awful—"

"Oh, stop! Don't become a weight-conscious bridezilla."

My comment earned the ghost of a laugh from my sister. "What's wrong?"

"You know Mrs. Kenton?"

"Of course—the family friend who can get away with saying, 'Oh, Payton, I knew you when . . .' and does. Every time she sees me. She pull that on you tonight?"

Red stained my sister's face. "No. She just said—in the nicest way possible, of course—that she hoped I'd lose a few pounds before the wedding."

"And what did you say?"

"Nothing."

Of course she didn't. "Jillian—"

She waved away my words. "Forget I said anything."

"It was rude." And Mrs. Kenton, family friend or not, could forget about ever seeing the recipe she'd requested. "How about I bring you a small slice of each cheesecake? Calories don't count at engagement parties, you know."

"Really small slices?"

"I promise. This is a celebration. Your one and only engagement party."

"You're right." Jillian stood, brushing her straight hair away from her face. "Tonight, we celebrate. Tomorrow . . . well, we're not thinking about that, are we?"

"No, because tomorrow means playing catch-up for me. And prepping for next week."

And Saturday morning breakfast with my family.

Something else I wasn't thinking about.

ACKNOWLEDGMENTS

*"Not to us, Lord, not to us but to your name be the glory,
because of your love and faithfulness."*

PSALM 115:1

THERE'S A STORY BEHIND every story, and that's true for *The Best We've Been*. When Tyndale House Publishers accepted the Thatcher Sisters series, I knew a lot about Payton, the main character in book one, some about middle sister Jillian, and only a little bit about the controlling oldest sister, Johanna, who wouldn't step front and center until book three. And now, here we are, wrapping up this series with Johanna's story. Along the way, there have been so many changes in my real life, and there have been changes to my initial ideas for each one of these books, too. But there's been one constant along the way: I've been encouraged and supported by so many different people. This is why writing the acknowledgments is one of my favorite parts of every book.

My family never fails me. Their love and support are constant, even as we go through our own life changes, including my husband, Rob, and I launching our youngest daughter,

Christa, into college (and volleyball); our son, Josh, getting married and then he and his wife, Meagan, welcoming a newborn into their family of three children; our daughter Katie Beth and son-in-love Nate juggling full-time ministry with their two children; our daughter Amy and son-in-love David moving back to Colorado and taking up residence in our basement apartment; and my mother-in-law turning 101 years old. Whew! Family is the best.

My Tyndale House team: Jan Stob (acquisitions director) and Sarah Rische (editor): Thank you for ensuring *The Best We've Been* ended the Thatcher Sisters series better than what I originally imagined. At times, Sarah, you seemed to know the series better than I did.

No book is complete without the efforts of the marketing and publicity team, Colleen Gregorio (author relations), Andrea Garcia (marketing manager), Mariah León (publicist), and Elizabeth Jackson (acquisitions editor), who stepped in to help as needed.

Julie Chen (senior designer): I am so thankful you designed all the covers for this series. Once again, you created the perfect image for this book.

The daily text group/prayer group: Lisa Jordan, Melissa Tagg, Alena Tauriainen, Tari Faris, Susie May Warren, Rachel Hauck: Our morning texts start my days off right. Knowing we can turn to each other for encouragement and wisdom makes so much difference in my writing journey.

Gianna Nelson, my virtual assistant: You are gold, my dear. Absolute gold. You lighten my daily load and bring organization to my life—and beauty, too.

Rachelle Gardner: I'm honored to call you my agent and thankful we are friends, too. To know that you believe in me keeps me going on the days I forget "writing is not brain surgery."

Advance readers: Jeanne Takenaka, Casey Herringshaw, Angie Arndt: Thank you for reading the first draft of this story, back when it was called "book three." I know it was a sacrifice of your time, but I value your insights to help me improve Johanna's story.

I'm grateful for a community of writing friends across the country whose support and creativity enrich my life and inspire me: Edie Melson, Carla Laureano, Cathy West, Cara Putman, Kristy Cambron, Amy Sorrells, Lindsay Harrel, Deborah Raney, Robin Lee Hatcher, Becky Wade, Denise Hunter, Cheryl Hodde, Colleen Coble, Katherine Reay, Tammy Alexander, Julie Lessman, Courtney Walsh, and Wendy Schoff.

ABOUT THE AUTHOR

BETH K. VOGT is a nonfiction author and editor who said she'd never write fiction. She's the wife of an Air Force family physician (now in solo practice) who said she'd never marry a doctor—or anyone in the military. She's a mom of four who said she'd never have kids. Now Beth believes God's best often waits behind doors marked *Never*. *The Best We've Been* is the final book in Beth's Thatcher Sisters series with Tyndale House Publishers, following *Things I Never Told You*, which won the 2019 AWSA Award for Contemporary Novel of the Year, and *Moments We Forget*.

Beth is a 2016 Christy Award winner, a 2016 ACFW Carol Award winner, and a 2015 RITA finalist. Her 2014 novel, *Somebody Like You*, was one of *Publishers Weekly*'s Best Books of 2014. *A November Bride* was part of the Year of Weddings series published by Zondervan. Having authored ten contemporary romance novels or novellas, Beth believes there's more to happily ever after than the fairy tales tell us.

An established magazine writer and former editor of the leadership magazine for MOPS International, Beth blogs for

Novel Academy and also enjoys speaking to writers' groups and mentoring other writers. She lives in Colorado with her husband, Rob, who has adjusted to discussing the lives of imaginary people. Connect with Beth at bethvogt.com.

DISCUSSION QUESTIONS

1. *The Best We've Been* begins with Johanna facing an unwanted pregnancy, which opens up a myriad of issues: the sanctity of life, women's choice, abortion, adoption, and the emotional tug-of-war between personal beliefs. What was your reaction to Johanna's dilemma? How did you feel about her doctor's approach to their first appointment? Have you ever clashed with someone else over deeply held beliefs? What was the result?

2. This story explores the question *How can you choose what is right for you when your decision will break the heart of someone you love?* How did this play out between Johanna and Jillian? If you've had to make a choice like this, how did you handle it?

3. Jillian struggles with her newfound faith because it doesn't seem like God is answering her prayers. How do you react when your prayers aren't answered

the way you'd hoped? What would you say to a new believer who is struggling to trust God? Or to someone who is bitter toward God because of how things have gone in their life?

4. Family roles often define us as we're growing up: we're the middle child or the athletic one or the quiet one. Several characters in this story comment on what it means to be adults and how sometimes family members don't let us grow up—don't recognize that we've changed from who we were as children. What has helped your family recognize that you are no longer a child? If they haven't, how do you think you can help them see that you're different?

5. There are some interesting—and humorous—scenes that show Payton struggling to fit in to the couples' Bible study she and Zach attend. Have you ever been a newcomer to a group and found it hard to learn the "rules" and lingo? Or maybe you found yourself as the one using the insider language. What can we learn from both perspectives?

6. Johanna misinterpreted past events because she didn't know all the details. As a result, she cut herself off from her family relationships and from playing the piano, a pursuit she loved. When have you looked back at an event or time and realized you had misjudged a situation or a person? What did you do about it?

7. In the Thatcher family, Johanna has always been in charge, Jillian has always been the mediator, and Payton has always believed that there was an invisible line separating her from Johanna and Jillian—that their relationship is stronger than one she could have with them. How do the sisters' relationships change from the beginning of this book to the end?

8. The title *The Best We've Been* implies that things are good for Johanna, Jillian, and Payton—that their circumstances, possibly their relationships, have improved. But did their stories end the way you expected them to?

9. Jillian tells Geoff she wants to take a "time-out" from conversations about their future. Do you think this was a wise choice? How do you think the time-out could benefit them? Or what do you think they should've done instead?

10. As the story ends, Johanna and Beckett have found a friendly dynamic, but their relationship has no clear resolution. What do you think will happen for them in the future?